Our Little Secret

Rosie Goodwin

Our Little Secret

headline

First published in Great Britain in 2007
by HEADLINE PUBLISHING GROUP

1

Cataloguing in Publication Data is available from the British Library

ISBN 978 0 7553 3491 9

Typeset in Bembo by Palimpsest Book Production Limited,
Grangemouth, Stirlingshire

Printed and bound in Great Britain by
Mackays of Chatham plc, Chatham, Kent

Headline's policy is to use papers that are natural, renewable and
recyclable products and made from wood grown in sustainable
forests. The logging and manufacturing processes are expected
to conform to the environmental regulations of the country of origin.

HEADLINE PUBLISHING GROUP
An Hachette Livre UK Company
338 Euston Road
London NW1 3BH

www.headline.co.uk
www.hodderheadline.com

Dedication

This book is for Donna, Christian, Aaron and Sarah,
my wonderful children. I love you all millions!

Acknowledgements

I would like to say a special thank you to the people named below:

As always, the team at Headline, especially my editor Flora Rees, and Jane Morpeth, who believed in me. Thank you both!

Not forgetting my family, my biggest fans.

And last but never least, Trevor, my husband and soul mate, who had faith in me when I was ready to give up . . .

Prologue

Gatley Common, Warwickshire, Summer 1982

The glow from the street-lamp shone through the bedroom curtains, casting a pool of light onto the bare wooden floorboards. Beyond the circle of light, ten-year-old Claire McMullen lay on her bed listening intently to the noises that reached her through the thin adjoining wall. Pulling her knees up into her chest, she screwed herself into a tight little ball, her heart thumping painfully. She had no way of knowing how long she had lain there, straining her ears into the darkness, but to her it seemed an eternity.

The noises ceased abruptly and her eyes stretched wide with terror. Then, just as she had feared, she heard footsteps on the landing. They stopped outside her bedroom door and within seconds it slowly creaked open. Unable to control her trembling any longer, the girl opened her eyes and stared up into a man's face. Fearful as she was, she uttered not a sound, for she was afraid of waking Tracey, her six-year-old sister who was fast asleep in her own room further along the landing.

The tall man was her mother's latest boyfriend; he was bare-chested and smiled at her menacingly. 'Now then.' His tongue flicked out to moisten his thick lips. 'Are yer goin' to be nice to me tonight, then?'

Claire shook her head, too terrified to answer, and shrank back in the bed until her spine touched the cold wall. She watched him undo his jeans and slide unsteadily out of them, leaving them to fall in an untidy heap on the floor.

'Now, Claire,' his voice was as cold as the floorboards he stood on, 'would yer rather I went and woke Tracey?'

Defeated, the girl shook her head, and tears stung the back of her eyes as he grinned with satisfaction at her response.

'That's better.' Lifting the thin blanket, he slipped in beside her as she gazed at him with hatred blazing from her eyes. She cast one imploring glance at her mother, who had come to stand in the doorway, but saw at once that there was no help to be found there; her mother's eyes were glazed and she was smiling encouragingly at her.

His hand quickly found its way beneath her nightshirt and his warm breath, reeking of beer, fanned her face. Biting down hard on her lip, the young girl lay unresisting as he rolled heavily on top of her; she had learned that if she kept still it would be over all the sooner.

'That's better, that's a good girl now,' he muttered as his foul breath began to come in quick gasping sighs. 'You just lie still, and tomorrow I'll get yer a nice little present, eh? You'd like that, wouldn't yer? But remember . . . it's our little secret. You must never tell a soul what a bad, bad girl you've been – an' what you've made me do.'

For some time after he had finally left the room she lay hardly daring to move, until eventually the noises from her mother's bedroom resumed. Then she climbed out of bed and crept along the landing, pausing only once to listen outside her sister's bedroom door. When Tracey's gentle snores reached her, she let out a soft sigh of relief and tiptoed on. Once in the bathroom, she locked the door securely behind her and after clicking on the bare lightbulb, she stared at herself for some minutes in the cracked mirror that hung above the sink. Dull eyes stared blankly back at her, the huge dark circles beneath them seeming to reach halfway down her cheeks. Her long fair hair was matted and dishevelled, and as pain and shame washed over her she grabbed a sponge and began to fiercely scrub every inch of herself. By the time she was done her skin was tender and sore, but still she felt dirty.

Finally, exhausted, she crept back to her room, and there as the comforting darkness enfolded her, she cried herself to sleep.

Chapter One

Nuneaton, November 1982

'Are you quite sure that there's nothing troubling you, Claire? You look very tired.' The kindly Headmistress's eyes were concerned.

'No, miss. There's nothin'.' Claire shook her head and shuffled sullenly from foot to foot as the teacher regarded her solemnly. An awkward silence stretched between them as Mrs Jenkins's heart went out to the child standing before her. She looked so desperately unhappy and pale, and yet there was a determined jut to her chin that told the woman that her concern was unwelcome. She could have almost imagined that she was addressing an adult instead of a young girl who had recently turned eleven, for Claire seemed to be far more mature than her age warranted. And yet for all that there was a fragility about her that put her teacher in mind of a china doll. She was dressed in a cardigan that was two sizes too big for her, and it covered a dress that looked as if it hadn't been washed for weeks. Her shoes were down-at-heel and her long blond hair was scraped back into a severe ponytail at the nape of her neck.

As Claire stared back at her, her eyes guarded, Mrs Jenkins found herself trying to imagine the girl smiling and relaxed. Almost as if Claire could read her thoughts, she flushed and dragged her eyes away from the woman's face to stare at the floor, her face resentful.

The Headmistress sighed with frustration. Every instinct she possessed warned her that something was dreadfully wrong, but she realised that whatever it was, Claire was not going to share it with her. So not wishing to prolong the little girl's discomfort she smiled at her kindly.

'All right, Claire, I won't keep you from your lesson any longer, but remember . . . if there *is* anything wrong, anything at all, you can always come and talk to me about it. Do you understand?'

'Yes, miss . . . thank you, miss.' The child's head nodded as she backed towards the door, then relieved, she turned and fled, slamming it firmly behind her.

Mrs Jenkins rose from her chair and crossed to the window where she stood gazing out across the deserted playground. Lately, members of staff had reported that Claire had come to school sporting bruises. But whenever they questioned her about them she always had an excuse: she had tripped over something, or fallen down the stairs. Her schoolwork was suffering too, and only last week she had actually fallen asleep in the middle of a lesson. It was all very disturbing, but without Claire confiding in her, Mrs Jenkins was at a loss as to how she could help her.

She was pondering on this when a knock sounded on the door, and pulling her thoughts back to the present, she called sharply, 'Come in.'

A school prefect staggered into the room balancing an armful of class registers, which she deposited on the Headmistress's desk.

'Thank you, Jenny,' Mrs Jenkins smiled, and soon she was engrossed in them, and for now her concerns for Claire were pushed to the back of her mind.

Once in the safety of the empty corridor, Claire rolled her eyes to the ceiling. 'Nosy old bitch,' she muttered beneath her breath. 'Why can't she just leave me alone and mind her own business!'

Hoisting her school bag higher onto her shoulder she sped through the corridors. When she reached her classroom, she peeped through the glass in the door and frowned; the rest of her classmates were already seated. Her late entrance caused a ripple of giggles and she scowled as she slid behind her desk.

Mrs Rogers, her class teacher, rapped on the blackboard with a chalk. 'All right then, children, that's quite enough, let's settle down now,' she ordered, and then after flashing Claire a sympathetic smile, she continued with the lesson.

Claire was so tired that she found it hard to concentrate and when the bell sounded for break she sighed with relief. Following the stream of chattering children into the playground, she immediately looked for Tracey, and after finding her, took her hand firmly and led her to a far corner. Heedless of the cold concrete beneath them, they sat down and Tracey stared up at her, her eyes alight.

'Guess what, Claire?' she bubbled excitedly. 'Miss Taylor said it might snow soon. Do you think it will?' Her knees were tucked tight up beneath her chin.

Claire smiled at her fondly. Miss Taylor was Tracey's teacher and Tracey adored her almost as much as she did Claire.

'Well, I suppose if Miss Taylor thinks it might, then it might.'

The little girl's grin broadened. 'Miss Taylor said it's only six weeks till Christmas – wouldn't it be lovely if it snowed fer then?'

Before Claire could answer she spotted a group of girls sauntering towards them. She and Tracey were soon surrounded, and Melanie Wilson, the ringleader, stared down at them with contempt. As usual she was immaculately dressed in a warm coat, with thick gloves on her hands and a woolly hat pulled low down over her ears. Tracey leaned against her sister nervously as Claire's arm moved protectively about her shoulders.

'What do *you* want?' Claire glared up at Melanie as the girl's lip curled in a sneer.

'Well, not you, that's a fact.'

Her followers giggled.

'Just go away and leave us alone,' Claire spat, and Melanie laughed, her breath hanging like smoke from a kettle on the frosty air.

'Don't worry – I wasn't planning on getting any closer. I don't want to catch nits.'

Claire began to tremble with rage but luckily, before Melanie could say any more, Miss Taylor, who was on playground duty, summed up the situation at a glance and bore down on them like an avenging angel.

'*Melanie Wilson*, all of you – get away now, this instant! I will *not* have bullying – do you hear me? Now *go*!'

Melanie swaggered away, a smirk on her plain face, closely followed by her band of hangers-on. When they were at a safe distance, Miss Taylor turned to Claire and Tracey and said gently, 'Take no notice of them.' Her heart twisted as the two pinched faces stared up at her. 'I'll tell you what – why don't you go and spend the rest of the break in the cloakroom, eh?' she suggested. 'It's nice and warm in there, and if anyone questions you, tell them I told you it was all right for you to be there.'

Tracey stared up at her gratefully as Claire unceremoniously dragged her to her feet, and without a word the two sisters scuttled away.

The warmth of the cloakroom wrapped itself around them as they wove their way through the long lines of metal coat-hooks until they reached a long narrow bench, which stood next to a huge metal radiator. Here they dropped down and huddled together.

'Why does Melanie always pick on us?' Tracey asked her sister. 'Is it because we don't have nice clothes and hats and gloves an' things?'

'It's because Melanie is a bully and a snob, and she thinks she's It, just 'cos her dad has a good job and she lives in a posh house,' Claire declared sulkily.

Tracey pondered on Claire's words for some seconds, but then her face brightened. 'Well, one day when our dad comes home he'll buy *us* nice things, won't he? Then we'll be posh too.'

As Claire stared down into the blue eyes that were almost identical to her own, a large lump formed in her throat. Lately, the hope she had always had of her dad returning to them had begun to fade. But she couldn't tell Tracey that, so she just smiled reassuringly, and satisfied, Tracey leaned against her. Tracey could barely remember their father. She had been just a baby when Robbie McMullen had left them. But even so, in her mind he was a very real person brought to life by the lovely stories that Claire would tell her about him.

As Claire thought of him now, her heart ached. If only he would come home, things would be better again, she felt sure of it. Before he had left them, the bad things hadn't happened. She shuddered involuntarily and Tracey glanced up at her curiously, but ignoring the questions in the little girl's eyes, Claire blinked back the tears and stroked Tracey's dark curls gently, and there they sat in companionable silence until it was time for them to return to their lessons, the dark head and the fair one bent close together.

The day had lost its brightness when eventually the school bell sounded for home time. As Claire stepped wearily from the building, her eyes swept the throng of children and mothers milling about the playground. Almost immediately she saw Tracey waiting for her at the tall metal gates at the entrance to the school. She looked as dejected as the great black clouds that hung in the sky above, and suddenly Claire found herself remembering happier times. In her mind she could see her mother standing there, watching for her with a warm, welcoming smile on her face. But that had been a long, long time ago now, and the remembering only added to her feelings of loneliness and despair. She knew deep down that if it wasn't for Tracey, she would have run away, or at least told someone of the deep dark secrets that she was forced to keep. Secrets that sometimes caused vomit to rise in her throat as she recalled the terrors of the night. But she knew that while Tracey relied on her she could never tell, ever. If she did, she had been warned that they might be separated and never see each other again, and that was unthinkable. Straightening her shoulders, she fixed a bright smile on her face and picked her way across the playground to stand in front of her sister, whose excited mood of earlier in the day had been spoiled by the bullies.

'Had a good day, then?' she enquired. Tracey nodded, her eyes downcast, and Claire tried to think of a way to cheer her up. Suddenly it came to her.

'I'll tell yer what, how about we go the long way home, through the woods and past the Blue Lagoon, eh?'

Tracey perked up immediately. 'Ooh, yes – but won't our mam be mad at us if we're late?' she asked.

'No, I'm sure she won't.' Claire doubted that their mother would even notice if they didn't go home, but didn't say so, and with Tracey in a slightly more light-hearted mood now, the two sisters set off.

The little village of Gatley Common in Warwickshire where they lived was a close-knit community. It consisted of a council estate and a newly built private estate nicknamed 'Nob's End' where Melanie Wilson lived. There were also a number of the original pit houses where the miners had lived. It had been some years now since the mines had been the sole source of income for the village men, but even so, many of the men and their families still lived in their original homes, and it was these that Claire and Tracey were passing now. They stood in straight terraced rows, their doors and windows opening directly onto the pavement. Tracey couldn't resist peeking in as they passed. In one particular house she spotted her schoolfriend, Jane, who raised her hand in a cheery greeting. She could see Jane's mother laying the table ready for tea, her plump figure outlined by the light from a roaring fire, and the sight made Tracey's stomach rumble noisily.

'I wonder what Mam will have ready for our tea?' she mused, more to herself than to Claire, but Claire merely shrugged. Their mam probably wouldn't have anything ready at all – if she was even in, that was.

Soon they reached the end of Plough Road and began to climb the steep hill that would take them out of the valley. Their breath hung on the air and Tracey giggled as her feet slipped on the frosty grass. More than once she would have fallen had it not been for Claire's hand guiding her. Eventually they fell silent with the exertion of climbing until at last they reached the crest of the hill where they stood breathless, admiring the view. Even though the late afternoon was dull and overcast, they could see for miles and miles, and as Tracey stared off into the distance, there was a look of awe on her face.

'Are we on top o' the world here, Claire?'

The innocence of the question made her older sister smile. 'Not quite,' she answered softly. 'It just feels that way.'

Tracey fell silent; she never doubted anything that Claire told her, and stood content at her side. From up here, they could see people scurrying up and down the streets of the village, appearing scarcely larger than ants. Street-lamps began to light up in sequence, like fairy-lights on a Christmas tree, making the frost on the pavements glisten like fairy dust. In the distance on their right, they could see the town of Nuneaton, huge in comparison to their village. And on their left, around the perimeter of the valley, the now redundant pithead stretched its sooty chimneys up towards the sky, scarring the landscape. They could hear the faint rumble of a Midland Red bus as it trundled past far below them, and slowly the dull ache that had throbbed behind Claire's eyes all day began to heal as she started to relax.

The girl prided herself on knowing every inch of the surrounding countryside, and this view never failed to please her. She could vividly remember standing in this very same spot with her father, and could still recall the lovely stories he would tell her of his home in Scotland, before he came to work in the mine in the village, where he had met and married her mother. Robbie McMullen had been orphaned at an early age and adopted by an elderly aunt whom he adored. It was after she had died, that he had made his way down to the Midlands seeking work.

A smile played about her lips as she stared out across the fields. In her head she could hear him pointing out the different landmarks, likening the ever-changing colours of the fields to a giant patchwork quilt. From here she could also see what had once been her grandma's house. Claire had only a very vague recollection of her now, for she had died when

Claire was five years old, but the memories she did have were happy ones. Her grandad had died in an accident when Claire's mother Karen was just a child, and her grandma had brought Karen and her older sister Jean, up single-handedly. Jean had emigrated to Canada before Claire was born, and the girl found the idea of having an auntie on the other side of the world quite exciting, although part of her wished that Auntie Jean was still here, because sometimes she felt that she had no one apart from her mother and Tracey.

'Come on, Claire,' Tracey said, getting restless, and yanked at her hand, the lure of the Blue Lagoon too strong to resist any longer. Melanie Wilson and her cruel taunting were forgotten for now, and she was impatient to continue with their adventure.

They turned away towards the woods, the tall leafless trees forming a protective canopy above them. Eventually they emerged to find the Blue Lagoon coated with a treacherously thin layer of ice, the last of the daylight reflecting on its surface.

'Don't go standing on there,' Claire warned her sister. 'It's only thin – you'll go straight through it.'

Tracey nodded obediently and scampered away to return with a handful of pebbles. The girls spent the next half-hour skimming stones across the lake's surface, seeing whose would go the furthest without sinking. They played hide and seek and tig amongst the trees, their laughter hanging on the air as they gave themselves up to playing as only children can. For a brief, wonderful interlude Claire pushed the nightmares to the back of her mind, and her pale cheeks grew rosy in the chilly air.

But at last she called Tracey to her side. 'Come on,' she said regretfully, 'we'd better be making tracks. We don't want to get stuck up here in the dark, do we?'

Hand in hand, happier now, their good mood continued as they slipped and slithered down the hillside, and Tracey waved cheerfully to friends and neighbours as they made their way through the village. As they neared their house, the darkened windows told their own tale.

Claire cursed beneath her breath. 'Damn, I hope the fire's still in,' she muttered.

They passed the rows of council houses, all built exactly the same, until they came to their own. Claire fumbled beneath an upturned plant pot by the back door until she found the key. Inside, she immediately spotted a hastily scribbled note propped up against an empty milk bottle on the kitchen table.

Dear Girls,

Have gone out with Don, expect me when you see me. Make yourselves some tea and don't be late to bed.

Mam

'Right then.' Crumpling the note, Claire threw it into the fire which, although low, was still burning. 'We'll get this goin' then we'll have a look in the cupboard and see what we can find for tea, eh?'

'Mam *is* coming home soon, ain't she?' There was a tremor in Tracey's voice and Claire quickly reassured her. 'Of course she is. Now you get yer coat off an' watch the telly till yer tea's ready. Go on, off yer go.'

Obediently, Tracey shrugged out of her coat as Claire threw some lumps of coal onto the dying embers. Within minutes, a few welcome flames licked around them and the room began to warm as Claire prepared their meal. They dined on beans on toast; the toast was a little burned and Claire had to scrape the beans out of the saucepan, but Tracey was so hungry that she didn't complain and cleared her plate in minutes. After a cup of tea and some stale biscuits, Claire collected up all the dirty pots that were scattered about the room and washed and dried them. Then she set about emptying the overflowing ashtrays and tidied the sparsely furnished room as best she could. At seven-thirty when their mother had still not returned, she drew the curtains against the dark night and ushered Tracey upstairs for a wash.

'Oh Claire, can't I just have another half an hour, *please*?' The little girl's face was imploring but Claire shook her head.

'No, you can't. Now come on, get into that bathroom.'

By the time Tracey was washed and Claire had helped her into her old faded nightdress, her teeth were chattering with cold. Claire hurried her along the landing to her bedroom. There she brushed the child's hair until it shone and gazed down into her clean, scrubbed face.

'That's better,' she grinned. 'Now come on, hop into bed like a good girl before yer catch a chill.'

Tracey obediently scrambled into bed and Claire stared down at her. She looked angelic with her dark curls spread across the pillow, and all the love Claire felt for her shone in her eyes as she told her softly, 'I'll tell yer what, if yer hotch over, I'll get in with yer and tell yer a story. Would yer like that?'

Tracey nodded vigorously as she squirmed across the bed, making room for Claire to climb in beside her. For long seconds they lay together, enjoying each other's warmth until Claire whispered into the darkness, 'So what would yer like a story about?'

Without hesitation, Tracey replied, 'Tell me about our dad, and how happy we'll all be when he comes home.'

'Well,' Claire began, 'one day our dad will come home and we'll have lovely clothes to wear . . . so lovely that even Melanie Wilson will be jealous of us.'

'Will we have a scarf, and a hat, and some gloves too?' Tracey interrupted.

Claire nodded. 'Oh yes. In fact, we'll have lots, all in different colours, and we'll go out on day trips to the zoo and on picnics. Even on holidays to the seaside.'

Tracey sighed at the wonderful pictures Claire was conjuring up in her mind.

'An' will we have a bucket and spade, and play on the beach?' she asked drowsily. The nearest Tracey had ever been to a beach was the sandpit in a far corner of the school playground, so the idea of a whole beach full of sand was almost more than she could imagine.

'We'll play on the beach all day long,' Claire promised. 'And then we'll go and stay in a posh hotel and they'll serve us lovely meals so big that we'll feel like we're going to burst when we've eaten 'em.' She felt Tracey nestle further down into the bed and whispered, 'We'll go to live in a lovely house over at the Nob's End of the village, not too near Melanie Wilson though. An' when it snows, our dad will build us a big snowman in the back garden and play with us on the sledge. On Christmas morning we'll have a great big turkey for dinner and then we'll have a Christmas pudding with thick creamy custard all over it.' She was so lost in the dream that for a time a silence settled on the room.

'What do yer think of that then?' she eventually asked, but when there was no reply, she peeped down at her sister.

Tracey was fast asleep, her long dark lashes curled on her cheeks and a look of contentment on her face. Satisfied, Claire slipped quietly from the bed.

'Don't worry,' she whispered to the slumbering child. 'I'll keep yer safe always. No one will ever hurt yer if I can help it.' Then, gently kissing her sister's cheek, she tiptoed away.

By the time she had washed herself in the chilly bathroom and changed into her own nightclothes, Claire was shivering with cold again and glad to hurry back to the warmth of the living room. Feeling peckish, she dug out the half-empty packet of custard creams. They had gone soft around the edges, but even so Claire mashed herself another steaming mug of tea and dunked them greedily. Before she knew it, she had eaten every one and she now snuggled down into the old settee, drowsy and warm, her belly comfortably full. The wind outside howled and the television droned, making her feel that she wasn't alone. As she nestled further down into the cushions, her eyes grew heavy.

'I'll just have five more minutes and then I'll get meself off to bed,' she mumbled. But in a trice she had fallen fast asleep right where she was.

Chapter Two

An icy blast of air and the slam of the back door heralded Karen McMullen's return. A high-pitched giggle echoed around the living room and Claire started awake. Bleary-eyed and disorientated, she knuckled the sleep from her eyes and gazed up to find her mother and Don grinning down at her. The stale smell of alcohol, which Claire had come to associate with unpleasant things, hung about them. Glancing at the clock that stood on the tiled mantelpiece she saw that it was well past midnight, and fearful now, she glanced guiltily at her mother.

'I'm sorry, Mam,' she apologised. 'I didn't mean to stay up this late, honest I didn't. I must have fallen asleep. I'll get up to bed now, shall I?' She was inching her way across the settee, but before she could make her escape, Don laughed loudly, and dropping down beside her, he scooped her onto his lap.

'Now then, there's no need to rush away, is there? I think it's nice that you waited up fer us, I do. In fact, I think it deserves a little kiss.'

A knot of fear was forming in Claire's stomach as she turned her face away from his stinky breath and slobbering lips. She felt his grip on her tighten.

'Now then, there's no need to be rude,' he slurred. 'I was only bein' kind to yer. Anyway, if yer didn't want to see me, yer wouldn't have waited up fer me, now would yer? So stop teasing and be nice to me, eh?'

As his large hand clamped down on the skin of her inner thigh, a feeling of such absolute terror and hopelessness washed over her that the cry that rose from deep in her stomach stuck in her throat.

Her mother swept past them, stumbling drunkenly as her high heels clip-clopped on the linoleum. She gave an encouraging smile as she disappeared through the doorway that led to the stairs, and Claire knew then that the nightmare was about to begin again. Don laid her, surprisingly gently, onto the settee, and stood over her as he clumsily undid the belt that stretched around his ample waist. Paralysed with fear, she lay as if hypnotised, longing to tear her eyes away yet unable to do so. She watched him unzip his fly and let his trousers drop to his ankles, and all the time she was screaming, although not a single sound escaped her dry lips. In other circumstances she could have found the sight of him almost amusing as he stood there in his shirt and brightly coloured socks. But Claire knew that there would be nothing amusing about what he intended to do to her, and although she had promised herself that she would be brave, she began to tremble uncontrollably.

Above, she could hear her mother lurching about the bedroom as she tried to undress and her heart cried out to her, *Mam, Mam, help me, please!* But her mother didn't help her, nor did anybody else as tears ran from her eyes and soaked into the cushions. Don leaned over her, and slowly his hands raked up her nightshirt until her shivering body was revealed. Shame brought a flush to her face as he slowly pulled his pants down over his hairy legs and guided her head towards his groin. Her heart was thumping so hard that she felt sure he must hear it, but he was oblivious to her torment, intent only on his own release. Waves of nausea rose within her and to her horror Claire suddenly tasted again the tea and biscuits that she had eaten earlier. She gulped deep in her throat, and Don, taking the sound for one of pleasure, moaned with delight.

'That's it,' he gasped. 'Just let yerself go an' enjoy it, eh?'

It was then that Claire felt a hate so powerful that it frightened her; because she knew in that moment that, had she had a knife in her hand, she would have used it on him. As if he could read her mind, he suddenly stopped to stare down at her, and for one moment she dared to believe that the nightmare was over. But then he swung her off the settee and yanked her nightshirt over her head. As she stood, naked and cowering in front of him, humiliation washed over her in waves, and then the tears that she had tried so hard to hold back suddenly erupted in harsh wracking sobs.

Heedless of her distress, he pulled her across his body, pausing to smile at her mother as Karen tottered back into the room. It was then that it happened. Claire felt a rush of warmth on her inner legs as her bladder suddenly emptied itself all over him. She watched fascinated as yellow

14

urine slowly ran in little rivers through the dark hairs on his legs. But worse was still to come, because as he stared down, the tea and biscuits that had been threatening to reappear suddenly spurted from her throat and deposited itself all over his shirt-front. They all stared in disbelief at the glutinous dripping mess – and then all hell broke loose. With a scream of disgust, Don flung her from him so hard that she bounced across the floor to land with a sickening thud against the sideboard.

'Ugh, ugh!' He stared down with horror at his shirt-front and in the same instant Claire's mother seemed to fly across the room. Yanking the girl to her feet, she pulled back her hand and swung it with full force into Claire's petrified face.

'*Why, you little devil!*' she screamed. Grabbing Claire by the hair, she began to drag her towards the stairs. The child could feel something hot and sticky pouring from her nose, and a knife seemed to be stabbing into her ankle, but terror made her numb. Her mother was shaking her so hard that her teeth were chattering as she threw her on to the stairs.

'Get out of me sight *now*! I'll deal with you in the mornin',' her mother ground out.

On hands and knees, sobbing, Claire crawled up to her ice-cold bedroom.

It was that night, as she lay in the darkness in her lonely bed, soaked with urine and blood, that Claire made her pledge. '*One day they'll pay,*' she whispered into the gloom. '*One day I'll get away from all this and no one will ever hurt me again, ever.*'

Her oath hung on the air as darkness wrapped itself around her, the only silent witness to her total misery. She knew that, even if she took a million baths, she would never feel clean or fresh again. She also knew that she would never forget this night, for it was branded into her memory. And in that moment, Claire McMullen felt her childhood dissolve away from her like mist in the morning sun.

Chapter Three

September 1983

Tracey clung to Claire's arm. 'I don't want to go in without you,' she sobbed.

The older girl hugged her briefly as she blinked back her own tears. 'You'll have to,' she told her bluntly. 'You know it's my first day at me new school, an' I'm goin' to be late as it is. So go on, get yerself inside an' let me get off.' Disentangling Tracey's fingers from her sleeve, she then pushed her gently inside the school gates. 'Go on,' she said. 'You'll be all right, I promise.'

Turning about, she began to stride away, and as Tracey watched her go, her tears turned to soft, hiccuping sobs.

Claire was feeling so many different emotions that she barely knew if she was even walking in the right direction. She was nervous at the prospect of beginning at the High School. The new school uniform her mother had promised her had never materialised, although in truth she hadn't really expected it to. The shapeless jumper and scruffy shoes that she had been forced to wear made her feel ashamed of her appearance, but worse than this was the anger and resentment she felt towards her mother; and this emotion frightened her far more than any of the others. Karen had promised her faithfully that today *she* would walk Tracey to school. But where was she? Lying in bed with a hangover, as usual.

Frowning, the girl thrust her hands deep into her coat pockets as she blinked back tears of self-pity. Why does nothing ever go right for me? she wondered. In her mind's eye, all she could see was Tracey's tear-stained face when she had left her, and that added guilt to her already troubled mind.

There was no secondary school in the village, so Claire had to attend the one on the outskirts of Nuneaton, which meant a considerably long walk. Normally she wouldn't have minded but the day had gotten off to such a bad start that now the journey seemed endless.

The day continued as it had started. She was late, and worse still, she then discovered that she and Melanie Wilson were to be in the same form. Melanie, who was dressed in a smart new uniform, wasted no time at all, during the breaks and the lunch-hour, in singling Claire out.

'Well, well,' she sneered, looking Claire up and down. 'Off to a tramps' ball, are we?'

'Piss off!' Claire snarled, feeling her cheeks redden. Then turning away, she pushed through Melanie's admiring gang, elbowing them roughly aside.

On top of all this, Claire soon found out that the High School was huge compared to the little village one that she had attended with Tracey, and twice during the first morning she got hopelessly lost as she tried to find her way to the different classrooms. There were no bunches of wild flowers standing in jars on the windowsills here; no pictures to brighten the walls as there had been at the village school. Every single corridor was cold and impersonal and looked exactly the same as the next. The older children eyed her scruffy appearance curiously, and the teachers seemed to be much stricter here.

By the time she arrived home later that afternoon her mood had not improved, and it became even blacker when she found her mother draped across the settee still in her dressing-gown. Claire managed a smile for Tracey, who had walked home on her own, but then glaring at her mother she asked, 'Ain't you even bothered to get dressed all day?'

The woman narrowed her eyes as she stared back at her, wagging a cigarette in her direction. 'No, I ain't. Not that's it's any o' your bloody business. An' watch yer lip, me gel, else you'll feel the back o' me hand, I'm warnin' yer.'

Claire turned away in disgust and after stamping into the kitchen began to rummage about in the cupboards for something to eat.

'We're about out of groceries, Mam,' she called through the open door, and her mother, rousing herself from the settee, lurched unsteadily into the room.

For a brief second, Claire felt a pang of pity for her. Her mother's eyes were swollen from crying, and the eye make-up she had worn the night before was streaked down her cheeks. Thankfully, she and Don had parted some months ago, but there had been others to take his place since then, and no doubt now she had been crying over the latest bloke who had dumped her the week before. Karen picked up her purse and drew out her last note as she ran a hand through her tangled, bleached hair.

'Here.' She thrust it at Claire. 'Go down the shop an' get us a bottle of milk an' a loaf. Nothin' else, mind! I need the rest o' that money for bingo tonight. You'll have to make yerselves some toast an' make do with that.'

Tracey's face fell at the prospect of toast yet again, but Claire shot her a warning glance before taking the money and hurrying away.

When she returned, her mother was sitting at the kitchen table with the free local newspaper spread out in front of her. 'Huh, just look at this.' She stabbed a painted fingernail at the page. 'Bloody unemployment figures up again. So much for Maggie Thatcher, eh! I thought once we got a woman Prime Minister the state o' the country would improve. But things seem to be goin' from bad to worse, like this bloody village. Never been the same, it ain't, not since they closed the pit.'

Claire nodded, not really understanding why her mother should care one way or the other. As far as she knew, Karen had never done a day's work in her whole life. But even so she knew better than to voice the thought, so instead she turned on the grill and busied herself making Tracey and herself some tea.

While they were eating it, Tracey asked, 'How was yer new school, Claire?'

Karen dragged her eyes away from the newspaper, briefly feigning interest. 'Oh yeah, yeah, o' course – how did it go? I forgot to ask.'

'It was all right,' Claire muttered, and quickly losing interest, Karen turned her attention back to the newspaper.

Claire began to collect up the dirty pots and carry them to the sink. She washed and Tracey dried. Shortly afterwards, their mother made her way upstairs to prepare for her night out. Two hours later, bathed and made up to the nines, Karen again stood in the lounge, expertly applying scarlet lipstick. Then, screwing the top back on, she tossed it into her open handbag and gave her hair a final pat.

'There then, that's me all ready for the off.' Shrugging her arms into a smart navy coat she glanced at the two girls as she buttoned it against the chilly September evening.

'Right then, you two, be sure an' get yerselves washed an' into bed early. I don't want yer late fer school in the mornin'. Do yer hear me?'

Claire merely nodded as without a final glance her mother left, banging the door to behind her.

The girls settled comfortably onto the settee and were soon engrossed in *Coronation Street* until Tracey suddenly broke the silence.

'You hadn't forgotten it's yer birthday soon, had you?'

'No, of course I hadn't. I'm the oldest in our class,' Claire told her sister.

'Well, I've made yer somethin' really nice,' Tracey told her excitedly. 'I did it at school an' me new teacher Miss Murgatroyd helped but she said I'm not to tell you what it is 'cos it's a surprise.'

Claire smiled at her fondly. 'Well, I'll look forward to that then – but come on, it's time we were getting ready for bed now.'

Tracey hopped off the settee and skipped up the stairs ahead of her sister. 'What would yer like most in the whole world for yer birthday?' she asked. 'If yer could have anythin' yer wanted, I mean.'

Claire shrugged. 'I'm not sure really. I haven't thought about it. Now come on – let's get into our nighties. It's dead parky on this lino.'

Much later that night as Claire lay in bed she found herself thinking back to Tracey's question. And looking up into the darkness, the answer came to her. *What I'd like most in the whole world is for me dad to come home and for me mum to really love me and keep me safe.*

Screwing her eyes up tight, she tried to imagine how wonderful it would be. But all the time, deep down, she knew that her birthday would be just like any other day. Her mother probably wouldn't even remember to buy her a card. The thought made her feel sad, but then she cheered up a bit as she thought of her little sister. At least she had Tracey, and Tracey loved her. On that comforting thought, she fell asleep.

Claire's twelfth birthday dawned on a bright October morning in 1983. Tracey ran into her room and kissed her, and before Claire was even properly awake, pressed a card into her hand. She had made it herself and painstakingly coloured in every inch of it. She also presented her with a nightdress case that she had sewn for her out of scraps of material at school.

Claire hugged her, touched at all the trouble her sister had gone to. 'They're really lovely,' she assured her, and Tracey flushed, proud of her handiwork. Soon afterwards, they were sitting at the kitchen table having cornflakes when their mother joined them.

Claire glanced up in surprise. 'You're an early bird,' she quipped.

Her mother grinned, obviously in a rare good mood. 'Less o' yer lip, me gel,' she laughed, and then as she caught sight of the birthday card standing on the edge of the table, her smile slipped and she glanced at Claire guiltily. 'Look, I ain't got yer anything for yer birthday yet but I'll get yer somethin' nice at the weekend,' she told her. 'Will that be all right?'

Claire nodded; there was no disappointment because she hadn't expected anything anyway, and besides, it was nice to see her mother in such a good mood.

'You seem happy today,' she commented, as she pushed the teapot across the table.

Her mother winked at her as she poured tea into a large mug. 'I am happy. I met a really nice chap last night – a long-distance lorry driver, he is. You'll meet him tonight when he comes to pick me up. He's takin' me to the pictures. His name's Ian an' he's tall, dark an' handsome.'

A little worm of fear began to wriggle its way through Claire's stomach, but then she tried to look on the bright side of things. He might not be so bad. Some of her mother's boyfriends had even been quite nice. *And some of them haven't,* a little voice whispered in her head. Claire quickly pushed the bad thoughts to the back of her mind, determined to give Ian a chance. Then, catching sight of the clock, she took a last gulp of her tea and snatched up her school bag.

'I've got to go, else I'll be late again,' she said, and after planting a hasty kiss on Tracey's dark head she hurried away.

The day passed slowly, one lesson running into another, and Claire found it hard to concentrate. During her break she went to a quiet corner of the playground, as usual keeping herself to herself. It was easy to do as she seemed to have very little in common with the other girls of her own age. All she overheard them talking about was boys, music and make-up. Once or twice a couple of them had tried to befriend her, but Claire's standoffish attitude soon made them leave her to her own devices, and today was no different. No one knew it was her birthday and as usual she walked home alone.

Tracey was swinging on the front gate waiting for her. 'Mam's getting all dressed up,' she giggled. 'She's goin' out with her new boyfriend tonight.'

'I know that,' Claire replied shortly, and taking Tracey by the hand she led her into the house.

Their mother was wearing a new dress that she had bought especially for the occasion. 'Do you like it?' She twirled around girlishly, waiting for their approval and, just for an instant Claire felt resentment so strong that it threatened to choke her. She glanced from her mother's dress down to Tracey's shoes, which were almost falling apart on her feet. Once again, their mother had put her own needs before theirs.

It was something that Claire was noticing more and more lately, but she knew the repercussions that would result if she voiced her opinions so she remained silent. However, her mother's cheerful mood was infectious and soon Claire's resentment faded. Her mother *did* look nice, and she told her so.

Almost an hour later, as Claire sat at the kitchen table struggling with her homework, there was a sharp rap on the kitchen door.

'That'll be him,' her mother said, and hurrying to the door, she flung it open and ushered him in.

'Claire, this is Ian,' she gushed, formally introducing them, and as Claire stared up at him, she found herself wondering what her mother saw in him. He was tall and dark, admittedly, but to Claire's mind he was far from handsome – and when he smiled at her, Claire subconsciously registered the fact that his smile didn't quite reach his eyes. Even so, she took his extended hand and shook it politely.

'It's very nice to meet you, Claire,' he said. 'I've heard all about you from my friend, Don. He told me your mother had two good-looking daughters, and now I can see that he wasn't lying. I think you and me are going to get along *just* fine.'

Claire disentangled her fingers from the grip that seemed to be holding on just a fraction longer than was necessary, and her stomach lurched. So Ian knew Don. Her mother had been out with lots of men since him, but Don stuck in Claire's mind as one of the most detested. She wondered what Don had told him about her, and Ian grinned at her obvious discomfort. At that moment, Tracey, who had been watching television, skipped into the kitchen and looked up at him. Kneeling to her level, Ian ruffled her hair and after reaching into his pocket, he pressed a large packet of sweets into her hand.

'Ooh, thank you.' The little girl was instantly won over and flashed him a brilliant smile.

Ian put his arm around Tracey's waist as he pulled her to him. 'Now then . . . *you* must be Tracey,' he said caressingly. 'My, my, you're a pretty little girl, and I'll tell yer what – if you're good, you're gonna get lots of nice treats off your Uncle Ian.'

Claire felt the urge to run over and snatch Tracey away from him. But controlling it, she screwed her hands into tight fists and glared at him instead. Her look was not lost on her mother as she crossed to him and took his elbow.

'Come on, you,' she chirped. 'If we don't get off now, we'll miss the beginnin' of the film.' She led him towards the door and with a last wink at Claire, he disappeared into the darkening evening.

Her mother paused with her hand on the door-handle to stare back at Claire. 'I think I'm goin' to have to teach you some manners, miss,' she hissed. 'You were all but rude to Ian then. You ain't even given him a bloody chance. I'm tellin' yer, you ain't heard the last o' this yet. Ian's a nice bloke.'

'If you say so,' Claire muttered insolently, and her mother bristled. Had it not been for the fact that Ian was waiting for her outside, she would have smacked her daughter there and then. But he was, so instead she lowered her voice ominously. 'You just make sure you alter yer attitude, me gel, or you're goin' to be sorry, I promise yer.' And with that she left, slamming the door behind her so hard that it danced on its hinges.

Claire found herself trembling uncontrollably and angrily she swiped her homework from the table. Tracey hovered in the background, her eyes huge.

'Don't look so worried,' Claire sighed. 'You know what me an' Mam are like. We're always rubbin' each other up the wrong way. She didn't mean what she said. I'll tell you what – I'll say I'm sorry when she gets back, eh?'

'Don't you like Ian?' Tracey whispered.

Claire shrugged. 'Well, I can't really say, can I, seeing as I've only just met him. But I suppose I was a bit rude. I just get fed up of all the different blokes she brings home an' this homework is getting me down, that's all, so stop frettin'.'

Tracey visibly relaxed, and then she remembered the sweets. 'Well, I think Uncle Ian's lovely,' she said, beginning to open them. Ignoring her comment, Claire bent to retrieve her homework from the floor.

It was much later, when Tracey was safely tucked into bed, that Claire gave herself up to the terrible sense of foreboding that had settled on her. Seated in the corner of the settee, she prayed as she had never prayed before.

'Please, God, if You're there and You can hear me, *please* don't let the bad things happen again.' She sat there, listening intently for a sign that He had heard her. But the only sound was the ticking of the clock on the mantelpiece and so eventually she dragged herself off to bed.

Chapter Four

On a murky late afternoon in November, Claire entered the kitchen and threw her bag onto a chair. It had been a particularly long day at school and she was glad to be home. But almost immediately she heard Tracey softly crying and her mother's voice raised in anger.

'For God's sake, I won't be gone fer long. What's *wrong* with yer? Anyone would think I was leavin' yer fer good, from all the fuss yer makin'.'

Crossing quickly to stand in the doorway to the living room, Claire saw her mother putting the finishing touches to her make-up in the mirror over the mantelpiece. She was wearing what looked like a new coat that showed off her slim figure, her blond hair had been teased into curls on top of her head, and the blue eye-shadow she wore exactly matched the colour of her eyes. Tracey was curled up on the settee, miserably sucking her thumb, and Claire immediately noticed the small suitcase standing by the door. Catching sight of Claire in the mirror, her mother swung around to face her.

'Now don't *you* start,' she shouted. 'I've got enough with this one here tryin' to lay the law down an' tell me what I can and can't do.' Snatching up a pair of warm gloves, she began to pull them on. 'I'm goin' on a run with Ian,' she informed Claire shortly. 'I'll probably be back tomorrow night. If not, it'll be Sunday.'

'Where are yer goin'?' Claire was trying to keep the panic out of her voice, and sighing deeply now, her mother picked up her case and swept past her into the kitchen, leaving a waft of cheap perfume in her wake.

'If yer *must* know, Ian's got a run to Yarmouth an' I thought the break would do me good. I spend half me life panderin' to you two, and now that you're old enough to look after yerselves, why *shouldn't* I have a bit o' pleasure?'

24

Claire bit back the retort that had sprung to her lips. From where she was standing it appeared that Karen did very little pandering to them. Tracey had come to stand at Claire's side and both girls stared at their mother with large, frightened eyes.

'Here . . . have this.' Fumbling about in her purse, the woman withdrew some coins and flung them onto the kitchen table. 'There's some money for food. Get yerselves whatever yer need – but don't go wastin' it, mind. There's plenty o' coal in the coalhouse, enough to last yer a week if need be. But I'll be back long before then.'

Claire stared at the money, unable to speak for the large lump that had formed in her throat, and it was as she was standing there that they heard Ian's lorry rumble to a halt outside. He blasted his horn impatiently and instantly, an excited smile sprang to Karen's face. Suitcase in hand, she hurried to the door. It was just as if she had already forgotten the two children that she was about to leave behind. But then her footsteps slowed and just for a second she glanced back at the two accusing faces. She felt a faint flicker of guilt but then Ian's horn sounded again and it was gone. After all, she told herself, she was entitled to a life, wasn't she?

'Right then, I'll see yer both when I get back. Just make sure that yer behave yerselves. Oh, an' another thing, don't yer *dare* tell anyone – and I mean *anyone*, mind – that I've gone. Do yer hear me? An' that includes *her*.' As she stabbed a finger towards the neighbouring wall, she scowled at them. 'I especially don't want that nosy old cow Tolly knowin' all me business. Right?'

Claire nodded numbly, too miserable to argue – and then their mother was gone. They heard the cab door of the lorry slam as she climbed in, and listened to it rumble away down the road until there was only silence. Tracey had begun to cry again and Claire pulled her close into her side.

'Come on now, don't be a crybaby, you've still got me,' she soothed. 'We'll be fine. In fact, we'll have a lovely time, you'll see. We'll make it into an adventure and pretend that we're grown-ups, eh?' Her words sounded far braver than she felt but they had the desired effect, for Tracey's sobs slowly subsided.

'That's better.' Claire knelt to bring her face on a level with Tracey's then tenderly she wiped the tears from her sister's cheeks and smiled at her.

'What shall we have for tea then?' she asked brightly. Without waiting for an answer, she crossed to the cupboard and swiftly scanned the almost-empty shelves. 'Mm, not much in there. I'll slip down the shop an' get us one of those steak an' kidney pies that yer like, shall I? An' we'll have some bread and marge with it. Would you like that, eh?'

Tracey nodded, instantly feeling a little better, so crossing to the table Claire pocketed the loose change that her mother had left for them.

'While I'm there, I'll get us a packet of Sugar Puffs for breakfast an' all, an' if you put a bit o' coal on the fire while I'm gone I might even treat yer to a chocolate bar.' Claire noted with relief that Tracey's tears had been replaced with a smile of anticipation. 'That's better,' she grinned. 'Now you put the kettle on an' I'll be back before yer know it. But just be careful you don't burn yerself, all right? An' don't go answering the door to anybody neither.'

'Yes, Claire.' Tracey skipped across the kitchen in the direction of the sink, and satisfied that the little girl was feeling happier, Claire hurried out into the chilly evening.

'I'm tellin' yer, Sid, there's somethin' not right wi' young Claire next door. Skinny as a rake she is!' Mary Tolly exclaimed. 'The poor little sod looks as if she's got the weight o' the world on her shoulders half the time, an' the little 'un ain't much better. Though the same can't be said for their mother. I saw her goin' off again, not half an hour since wi' her latest fancy man – all dolled up like a dog's dinner as usual. I don't know why she don't just put a red light in the window an' be done wi' it.'

The snow-white net curtain twitched as she peeped from behind it, following Claire's progress down the street, and behind her at the kitchen table, Sid, her long-suffering husband, dragged his eyes away from the job ads to glare at her over the top of his glasses.

'For God's sake, woman, come away from the window an' mind yer own bloody business, can't you?' he said irritably. 'We've got enough troubles of us own wi'out takin' on anybody else's.'

Offended, she dropped the net and turned to face him, and instantly contrite he smiled at her. 'I'm sorry, love, I didn't mean to snap at yer. I reckon this job-huntin' must be getting' me down more than I thought.'

She plodded to his side in her comfy old slippers and patted the hairy arm that poked from his rolled-up sleeve. 'No, love, it's me as should be sorry. You're right, me mouth tends to run away wi' me. It's a wonder as it ain't got me hung before now. But yer know I don't mean no harm, it's just that I'm worried about them two little girls. Karen don't seem to give 'em the time o' day, an' it breaks me heart to see the way they walk about, like two little waifs, yet she's always decked up to the nines. It ain't just me as is sayin' it, either. She's the talk o' the whole village. I'm tellin' yer, the way things are goin' I wouldn't be surprised to see them two kids took off her.'

He nodded slowly, secretly agreeing with her. 'Well, there's nowt we can do about it, love,' he said wisely. 'You've lived next door to Karen McMullen long enough now to know that. Stubborn as a mule, she is. Just like you. That's probably why there's no love lost between the two o' you.'

Mary Tolly grinned, knowing that he was right before becoming serious again. 'Don't keep frettin' over this job-huntin', Sid. Somethin' will turn up in the end, you'll see.'

He grunted. 'Huh, I'd like to think you were right. But there's nowt turned up till now, is there? Soon as employers hear yer age, they don't want to know. To tell yer the truth I'm beginning to wonder if I'll ever work again.'

It hurt Mary to hear him so low. Sid had always been a hardworking man, proud to hold his head up and pay his way. But lately she had seen a change in him. His shoulders seemed to have a stoop to them that hadn't been there before, and the light in his eyes had dulled. She felt guilty about gossiping and determined that she wouldn't burden him with her worries about Claire and Tracey again. Having so decided, she stood up with the solution to all their problems. 'I'll brew us a nice cup o' tea,' she said and hurried away to put the kettle on.

As she walked along, the fixed smile slid from Claire's face and her foot-steps dragged. Worriedly, she took the money from her pocket and in the light from the street-lamp she counted it. She quickly worked out that after buying a pie for tea and some cereal, she would barely have enough left to keep them in bread and milk for two days, and yet here she was, promising Tracey chocolate. Still, she comforted herself, her mother had said that she might be home tomorrow and if she was, then at least she wouldn't have to worry about it. Besides, why shouldn't Tracey have a treat now and then?

She found herself thinking of the lunchboxes she sometimes glimpsed at school. They seemed to be crammed with treats, crisps, chocolate, fruit and sandwiches containing all manner of tasty fillings, whereas she and Tracey lived on jam sandwiches, which didn't even have margarine in them half of the time. And they wouldn't even have those if she didn't make them, because most mornings their mother was still in bed when they left for school. And now this; to just go off and leave them. Claire was terrified at the responsibility that was weighing on her shoulders. She had realised a long time ago that their mother wasn't the best in the world. And she was realising it more and more of late. But even so, Karen was the only mother they had, and up until now, at least she had been there for them.

The girl was still in a very sober mood when she reached the little village shop. The light from its well-stocked windows spilled onto the pavement, and as she entered, a little bell tinkled musically above the door. Mr Graham, the portly shopkeeper, beamed a welcome at her.

'Hello, love, yer mam got you runnin' errands again, has she?'

Claire nodded, avoiding his eyes.

'Well, what can I get fer you tonight then, pet? You're only just in time. Another ten minutes an' I would have been shut.'

'I'd like a packet o' Sugar Puffs an' a steak an' kidney pie, please,' Claire answered politely, and nodding, Mr Graham lifted the box of cereal down from a shelf high above his head and placed it on the counter.

'I'll only be a second, love. I'll have to slip into the back room an' get yer pie out of the fridge.' Whistling merrily, he bustled away to a door on his right and disappeared. While he was gone, Claire eyed the tempting display of chocolate bars. Again she fingered the coins in her pocket then, without being able to help herself, her hand shot out and closed around a large Milky Way. Within seconds it was safely tucked deep into her other pocket as a guilty flush flooded her cheeks. Instantly, she regretted her action. But it was too late to replace it now because Mr Graham came back just then, his warm smile making her guilt intensify.

'There you are then, pet, you'll enjoy that.' He placed the pie next to the box of cereal as Claire thrust the money at him, so flustered that she would have left without her change if he hadn't called her back.

'Hold up there, pet, is there a fire somewhere? Look, you're going without your change.'

Gulping, Claire snatched it from his hand and in her haste to be away, she nearly stumbled and fell. The chocolate bar, resting against her thigh, seemed to be burning her; it rustled, and every second she expected to feel his accusing grip on her shoulder.

'Th . . . thank you,' she stuttered, as Mr Graham stared after her, bemused.

It was not until she had rounded a corner and the shop was safely out of sight that she dared to slow down. Leaning against a lamp-post, Claire felt as if her legs had turned to jelly, and despite the cold evening air she was sweating profusely.

'I'm a thief,' she whispered in despair to the deserted street, and tears of shame pricked at her eyelids sharp as needles. But then she drew in a gulp of air. Pull yerself together, she scolded herself. So what if I have nicked it. Tracey deserves a treat an' Mr Graham has so much money he won't miss one blooming Milky Way. Besides, if I'm as worthless as me mam keeps tellin' me I am, then why shouldn't I steal?

An icy gust of wind whipped around the street corner, moulding her worn coat around her thin frame. She shrugged deeper into it and with her head bent low, she made her way home.

The two girls lay together on the sagging sofa. The heat from the fire and the drone of the television set was making them comfortably drowsy and oblivious to the outside world. Popping into the kitchen, Claire felt in her coat pocket, then returning to the living room she presented the bar of chocolate to Tracey with a flourish. The younger girl grabbed it greedily. Her stomach was already agreeably full, but even so her eyes lit up at the sight of the treat. She tore the wrapping away, but before biting into it she stared at Claire and asked, 'Where's yours?'

'Oh, I didn't fancy one.' The lie slipped easily from Claire's lips and as she watched Tracey enjoy the treat, any guilt that she had felt melted away.

Much later that evening, Claire awoke and stretched out her cramped legs. Tracey was fast asleep beside her on the settee and Claire shivered. The fire had burned low and the television was buzzing. She switched it off and hugging herself, hurried across to the window and drew the curtains. The brief feeling of wellbeing that she had experienced earlier was gone now, to be replaced by fear. She hastily shot home the bolts on the back door, then, hurrying into the small hallway she checked that the front

29

door was securely locked too. Somewhere far away a cat was howling a chorus to the night and Claire felt goosebumps form on her arms.

Scurrying back into the living room, she stood for some seconds looking around. It was a bleak sight. Torn lino, a settee that had long since seen better days, and a chair that didn't match it. Cheap curtains hung at the windows and equally cheap ornaments were dotted along the mantelshelf amongst her mother's make-up. Sighing, she stared down at Tracey. Her sister looked so peaceful that Claire was loath to disturb her, but it was way past their bedtimes so she lifted her into her arms. Tracey's small body had always appeared to be very frail, but now as she struggled up the stairs with her, one painful step at a time, the girl seemed to be very heavy. By the time Claire had deposited her none too gently on the bed, she was breathless, and Tracey roused briefly. But then when she saw Claire's familiar face leaning over her, she sighed contentedly and snuggled further down into the cold sheets.

Claire crept back down the stairs. She knew that she ought to throw some coal onto the fire but the coal-scuttle was empty and the thought of having to go out into the dark to the coalhouse was just too frightening, so again she checked the bolts on the doors. And then, when at last she was satisfied that everything was safely switched off, she stole away to her own bed. She knew every inch of her bedroom and yet tonight for some reason it seemed to be a sinister place. She was aware of every single sound, and the chink of light that peeped through the curtains only seemed to intensify the dark shadows that lurked in the corners. She began to tremble and soon she had convinced herself that the howling wind, that was making the ill-fitting front door rattle in its frame, was someone trying to get in.

Every ghost story that she had ever heard or read sprang to mind as she kept her eyes tight shut, too terrified to open them. Her bladder was uncomfortably full but she decided that she would rather wet the bed than make the long trek down the landing. So instead she lay there, feeling totally alone and vulnerable, cursing her mother.

'Oh Mam, Mam, why did you have to go off and leave us?' she whispered to the darkness. Only the sound of the wind answered her. She was used to being alone in the house. Her mother often came home long after she and Tracey had gone to bed, but to know that she wouldn't be coming home at all was strangely terrifying. Her mother often had some man in tow and that in itself usually caused Claire to quake with fear in case he found his way into her room as Don had once done. But tonight she had no need to fear the tread of footsteps on the landing, only the all-consuming loneliness that engulfed her. Tears slid down her cheeks and dampened her pillow until at last exhaustion claimed her and finally she slept.

Chapter Five

The sound of something being dragged across the living-room floor early one Saturday morning woke Claire with a start. For some minutes she lay listening, trying to determine what it was. Eventually she swung her legs from the warm bed, shivering as her feet touched the cold floorboards. Within seconds she was downstairs and gazing in utter amazement at the sight of her mother heaving the furniture flush against the walls.

'What yer doin', Mam?'

Karen paused to wipe a stray lock of hair from her eyes. 'I'll tell yer what I'm doin'. I'm making a bit more space, because tonight, young lady, I'm having a party.'

Claire's mouth gaped. 'What sort of a party?'

The woman laughed. 'Well, what bloody sort o' party do yer think? A party's a party, ain't it? Drinkin' and dancin' an' havin' a good time.' Struggling, she finally managed to position the settee where she wanted it. Then, turning back to Claire who was still silently watching her, she waved at her impatiently. 'Well, go on then, don't stand there like the cat's got yer tongue. Go an' put the kettle on an' make us a cup o' tea. There's a lot still to be done.'

Dutifully Claire went into the kitchen and filled the kettle. As she waited for it to boil she stared from the kitchen window. She supposed she should be excited at the prospect of having a party, and yet instead she found she was dreading it. The kettle whistled, disturbing her thoughts, and when she eventually carried her mother's tea into her, she found Karen sitting on a chair eyeing the room with satisfaction.

'That's better,' she remarked approvingly. 'It's made a bit more space fer dancin', that has.' She drew deeply on a cigarette then exhaled and stared at Claire through a cloud of smoke. 'What's up wi' yer then? Yer look as if I've just told you yer goin' to the dentist instead of to a party.'

'I err . . . was just wonderin' how we was goin' to afford it, that's all, Mam,' Claire replied cautiously. 'I mean, to have a party – a *proper* party – you have to lay on food, don't yer? An' there ain't much in the cupboards.'

Her mother grinned. 'You needn't worry about that. Ian's given me the money for the food. I'll be makin' you a list an' yer can fetch most of it from the corner shop. Ian will be supplyin' all the booze an' all. I'm tellin' yer, this is goin' to be *some* party.'

Claire said nothing. Instead she went to wake Tracey and tell her to get dressed. When she told her about the party, Tracey's face was almost ecstatic and her reaction totally different to Claire's.

'A party, a party,' she chanted excitedly as Claire tried to tug a brush through her hair.

Claire grew annoyed. 'Oh, for God's sake stand still!' she demanded peevishly and instantly Tracey did. 'Sorry – didn't mean to snap at you,' Claire said contritely. 'I just don't want yer getting too excited, that's all. I doubt we'll even get to see much of it anyway. We'll probably be sent to bed.'

Tracey looked crestfallen, but in a second or two she was smiling again. 'Oh well, even if we do, there's bound to be some nice things to eat. An' Mam might let us have some for our supper, mightn't she?'

Scraping Tracey's hair into a tight elastic band, Claire patted her pony-tail and smiled. 'Well, yes, there is that in it,' she admitted and the younger girl scampered happily away.

The day seemed to pass in a blur of activity. Ian arrived at lunchtime, just as he had promised, and soon after, Claire made the first of three trips to the shop.

Mid-afternoon, Ian departed again. 'I'll be back with the booze later,' he promised.

Beneath her breath Claire muttered, 'Good riddance.'

By teatime the kitchen table was piled with sandwiches, crisps and all manner of treats, and it was all that Claire could do to keep Tracey away from them. When Ian returned, loaded with cans and bottles, Tracey helped him to stack them all onto the draining board as she stared up at him adoringly.

'Will I be allowed to have some crisps an' things, Uncle Ian, before me an' Claire get sent to bed?' she pleaded.

He nodded. 'O' course yer will, me darlin'.' He winked at her and Claire turned away, afraid that he would see the dislike she felt for him in her eyes. He had been a regular visitor to the house for weeks, and up until now he had never so much as touched her. Yet still Claire felt uneasy in his presence.

'I bet yer sister wouldn't say no to a few treats an' all,' he grinned at Tracey, but his eyes addressed Claire.

Bristling, she glared back at him. 'I'm not hungry, thank you.' The words were polite but her tone made the false smile slip temporarily from his face.

'Suit yerself. There'll be all the more for you an' me, won't there, darlin'?' As his arm slid around Tracey's slender shoulders Claire again had the urge to snatch her away from him. Instead she managed to control herself before turning on her heel and, without giving him so much as a backwards glance, she strode from the room.

Once in the privacy of her bedroom, she flung herself onto her bed and glared at the bare wall. Her stomach was rumbling with hunger, but while Ian was there she was determined not to eat a thing. In the next room she could hear drawers opening and closing as her mother selected the clothes she was going to wear for the party, and slowly the light in the room faded as the early evening gave way to night.

Claire went to stand by the window and soon she saw the first guests arrive: a tall man whom she had never seen before, with an overweight woman who stumbled up the weed-strewn path on precariously high heels. Despite her dark mood, Claire found herself stifling a giggle. There was a knock on the front door, and seconds later, she heard her mother admit the guests with a gushing welcome. The sound of the record-player started up, piercing the silence, and loud music began to echo around the house. Claire grinned as she thought of the effect it would have on Mrs Tolly next door.

More guests arrived and despite her resolve not to go downstairs, Claire tiptoed to the bedroom door. Opening it slightly she listened to the sounds of merry-making. It sounded as if the party was in full swing, so Claire stealthily crept along the landing and peeped down the stairs. The sight of people laughing and joking, walking about with plates piled high with food made her stomach complain rebelliously, and she longed to go down and eat her fill. But instead she stubbornly stayed where she was. Some time later, Tracey appeared at the bottom of the stairs and Claire scurried back to her bedroom. Seconds later, the girl opened the door and entered bearing a paper plate full of sandwiches.

'I thought you might be hungry,' she said solemnly. Claire shrugged, as Tracey clambered onto the bed and sat beside her, carefully placing the plate between them.

'I got yer some salmon sandwiches an' some crisps an' pickled onions. Look, all yer favourites. Ain't yer goin' to eat 'em?'

Claire felt her determination slipping away. 'Well, I might try just one,' she sniffed, lifting a sandwich. Somehow just one turned to two and in minutes she had cleared the plate.

'I thought you'd be hungry,' Tracey grinned, snuggling up to her sister.

The music from downstairs was so loud that they could hardly hear themselves speak, so for some time they simply sat quietly, happy in each other's company.

The shower that had started some time ago had turned into a downpour, and the rain was throwing itself at the bedroom window as if it was trying to outdo the thumping volume of the music. Eventually Tracey peeped at Claire from the corner of her eye and asked gravely, 'Why didn't yer come downstairs to the party, Claire? Is it because yer don't like Uncle Ian?'

Claire pondered on her answer for a while. Then, choosing her words carefully, she got off the bed and crossed to the window. 'I just didn't want to, that's all,' she mumbled. 'And as to whether I like Ian or not, well . . . I'm not sure.' She preferred to lie rather than shatter the illusion Tracey had of him. Tracey came to stand beside her and for some time they watched, fascinated, as the water gushed down the gutters to disappear into the drains in the road.

Eventually, Claire patted Tracey's bottom. 'Come on you,' she grinned. 'For you the party's over, it's way past your bedtime. Let's go an' get washed, eh?'

Obediently Tracey trotted along the landing behind her and soon Claire was tucking her into bed.

'I won't be able to sleep, not wi' all this noise goin' on,' the little girl grumbled.

Claire smiled as she settled the blankets under her chin. 'Well, that's a joke that is, coming from you. You could sleep through an earthquake. Tryin' to get you up in the mornin' is like tryin' to wake the flippin' dead.'

Tracey giggled and after they'd exchanged a goodnight kiss, Claire went back to her own room. The party seemed to go on and on with no sign of ending. Claire tittered when she heard Mrs Tolly next door hammering protests on the neighbouring wall.

'Bugger off, yer miserable old sod,' she heard her mother shout in reply, and she had to smother her laughter beneath the blanket. She snuggled down into a more comfortable position and closed her eyes, and soon she had slipped into a doze. Some time later, she started awake. Her mouth was dry and she needed the toilet.

After climbing out of bed she inched the bedroom door open, and seeing that the landing was deserted, she padded along to the bathroom. On the way back, she paused outside Tracey's bedroom door, and when the sound of her sister's rhythmic breathing reached her, she nodded with satisfaction and moved on to hover at the top of the stairs. It was there that thirst got the better of her and tentatively she crept down them. A glance at the clock in the hallway showed that it was almost two o'clock in the morning. As she reached the bottom of the stairs she saw her mother standing at the front door saying goodbye to some of her guests. She glanced in Claire's direction but then pointedly ignored her so Claire made her way to the kitchen intent on getting herself a drink. The first person she saw when she entered was Ian leaning against the sink with a half-empty glass of beer in his hand.

She flushed with embarrassment as he eyed her up and down, deeply conscious of the fact that she was dressed only in a thin nightshirt. 'I've . . . er, just come down for a drink, that's all,' she stammered, feeling that she needed to offer some explanation.

Grinning, Ian handed her an empty glass and stood aside so that she could reach the tap. She filled it quickly, annoyed with herself when she found that her hand was trembling. Then, turning away, she hurried back up the way she had come, cursing herself for having ventured down in the first place. By the time she reached her room, half of the water had slopped over the side of the glass and tears of humiliation were threatening. But she blinked them away and climbed back into bed, hating Ian all the more.

The sound of car doors slamming as more of the guests departed reached her, and then at last the music was turned down to a more reasonable level and she felt her eyes grow heavy again.

It was the silence that woke her, and an awful sense of foreboding. She was astonished to realise that she had slept at all and lay rigid, straining her ears into the darkness. For some time there was nothing to be heard except the hoot of an owl in a nearby tree, but then it came to her; the muted sound of whispering outside her door. Just as she had feared, it slowly creaked open to reveal three people staring in at her. She blinked, willing her eyes to adjust to the bright light on the landing. In that time, the three people entered her room, bringing with them the pungent smell of alcohol. It was her mother, Don, and Ian.

Don instantly crossed to her bed, and sitting down beside her, he began to stroke her leg familiarly through the blanket. 'Well then, schweetheart, have yer missed me?' he slurred, and as he lowered his head to kiss her, Claire put out her hand and brutally pushed him away.

'No, I *ain't* missed you, so why don't you just go away an' leave me alone?'

Don laughed. 'Now then, Claire, that ain't very nice, is it? An' besides, yer don't *really* mean it, do yer? You and me have had some good times together, ain't we? As I've been tellin' Ian.'

Claire turned her head, just in time to see Ian reach out to steady her mother, who seemed to be having difficulty in standing.

'What's the matter with me mam?' she cried.

Don grinned. 'She's just had a drop too much o' the hard stuff, that's all. I'll let Ian go an' tuck 'er into bed, eh? Then he can come back in here and yer can show him how much you've missed me.'

Claire shook her head frantically, but Don only smirked as he turned back to Ian. 'Go an' get that one into bed then we'll have us a bit o' fun.'

Ian nodded, and gripping Karen's elbow, he steered her from the room. As Ian led her away, Claire realised that her mother seemed to be genuinely unwell. The girl had seen her drunk numerous times before but couldn't recall ever seeing her look as ill as she did right now. Her eyes looked strangely vacant and she barely seemed to know where she was. But Claire was not allowed to dwell for long on her mother's state, because Ian had only just left the room when Don began to peel off his shirt and Claire's main concern was for herself. Before Don had even had time to get undressed, Ian was back and began to take his clothes off too.

'Oh no – no *please*.' Claire began to whimper. Both men totally ignored her until eventually they stood before her naked. They made no attempt at small talk now. They simply advanced on her menacingly, as she stared at them horrified.

'Right then, get that nightie off *now*,' Don ordered, and when Claire did not obey, he caught it by the hem and tore it from bottom to top in one single movement. The girl gasped and began to sob, but Don merely grabbed her arm and flung her flat on her back. 'Don't come the little Miss Innocent wi' me,' he ground out. 'You've been askin' fer it. Ian told me how yer came downstairs earlier on, paradin' about half-naked in yer nightie. Yer nothin' but a little pricktease so lie still an' enjoy it – yer know yer want to.'

Claire didn't fight him. She knew there was no point. She merely turned her head away from his slavering lips. She was not strong enough to prevent him from violating her body, but she would rather have died than allow him to kiss her. The man took her roughly, with no attempt at tenderness. And all the time Ian looked on, doubling her humiliation until at last Don's lust was spent and he rolled off her.

Once his breathing had resumed some sort of normality he winked at Ian. 'There yer go then. She's all yours. I told yer she were good, didn't I?'

Ian's eyes were glazed as he stood excitedly stroking himself. As Don climbed from the bed, Ian eagerly took his place. Claire stared up at him, her hatred written all over her face. Bringing his arm back, Ian smacked her cheek with the flat of his hand. 'Don't you *dare* look at me like that, you little bitch,' he threatened. 'You come downstairs flauntin' yerself, then when yer get what you've been askin' for, yer decide to play hard to get. Now lie still, else I'll make you wish as you'd never been born.'

Claire lay unresisting, the livid marks of his fingerprints standing out on her cheek. But that was nothing compared to the pain she was feeling inside. There were no tears, no hope of anyone helping her, she had learned that a long time ago. And then at last her ordeal was over and she looked up at him with contempt.

The two men began to laugh and joke with one another as they gathered up their clothes. And then thankfully they were gone and Claire was finally alone with her misery. Eventually she dragged herself to the edge of the bed and gripped it tightly as giddiness washed over her. It was then that the sound reached her, and her own misery was temporarily forgotten. The sound came again and her stomach turned over. It was Tracey, calling for her!

Sprinting across the room, and trying to ignore the pain that burned between her legs, she ran along the landing and threw her sister's bedroom door open. When she saw what was happening, she drew to a shuddering halt. Tracey was sobbing uncontrollably as Don held her down, whilst Ian stood over her naked. For a second everyone froze as all heads turned to stare at her.

The silence was broken by Tracey's terrified voice, imploring her faintly: 'Claire, help me, *please*.' Claire felt a rage so intense that for a second it rooted her to the spot, rendering her speechless. But then it erupted from her throat in one single word.

'*No!*' Launching herself at them, she lashed out at the two men with every ounce of strength she possessed.

Momentarily taken off-guard, the men tried to lean away from her, and Claire felt a thrill of satisfaction as her fingernails scored Ian's cheek. She kicked out wildly and her eyes gleamed as she caught Don squarely between his legs. He gasped with pain and doubled up, sliding from the bed in an attempt to escape Claire's flailing fists. Tracey was screaming hysterically and suddenly their mother, who had been disturbed by all the noise, appeared in the open doorway.

'What the bloody hell's goin' on in here?' she slurred. But then as realisation dawned, she crossed unsteadily to the bed and slapped her daughter hard on the face.

'Can't you see what they're goin' to do to her?' Claire screamed, holding her face. 'They're goin' to hurt Tracey. You've got to stop 'em!'

'Oh, for Christ's sake, stop bein' so bloody dramatic!' her mother grumbled. 'She's got to learn about sex sometime, ain't she? Now get back to bed else I swear you'll be sorry.'

For the first time in her life, Claire didn't obey her. Instead she stood up and faced her mother squarely. 'I'm not goin' to let this happen, Mam. I ain't been able to stop it happenin' to me, but I *won't* let it happen to Tracey. If you don't do something, I'll go and find me dad an' then you'll be sorry.'

To her horror, her mother threw back her head and laughed scornfully. 'Huh, so you think yer bloody dad 'ud stop it, do yer?' she sneered.

Claire's chin jutted defiantly as she nodded.

Leaning towards her, Karen began to jab her viciously in the shoulder. 'Well, let me tell you somethin' then. Somethin' as I should have told you a long time ago. Your bloody dad wouldn't give a *toss* what happened to her. An' do yer know why not? Well, I'll tell yer. He wouldn't bloody care 'cos Tracey ain't his. That's why he left us. Oh yes, yer think he's a bloody saint an' the sun shone out of his arse, but Robbie McMullen weren't man enough fer me, else I wouldn't have had to look further afield, would I?'

As the meaning of her mother's words slowly sank in, Claire felt vomit rise in her throat and she shook her head in disbelief. 'No, no, you're lyin',' she sobbed, but her mother just laughed, a cold mirthless laugh that was chilling.

By now, Don had pulled himself back to sit on the edge of the bed. 'She's bloody mad, she is,' he muttered, and Ian nodded in agreement as little rivers of blood trickled down his cheek.

Karen grabbed Claire by the arm, digging her sharp nails in spitefully. 'Now get yerself back to yer own bed, yer stupid little bitch, an' mind yer own bloody business,' she warned, but still Claire refused to budge, which only infuriated her mother all the more.

Behind them, Don and Ian turned their attentions back to Tracey and the child began to tremble, making Claire feel even more desperate. 'I won't go until they do!' she screamed.

Just for a second, she saw her mother waver – but then Don grabbed Karen's arm and pushed her towards the door. He then crossed back to Claire and grasping her arm, he flung her out onto the landing to join her mother then slammed the door on both of them.

'Mam, *please*! You have to stop them,' Claire sobbed.

Again, Karen looked indecisively back at the door but then suddenly she too began to cry as she hissed, 'It's all right for you – you don't know what it's like to be lonely, do yer? It's *me* as has to go to a lonely bed each night. If I stop 'em, Ian will leave me an' I'll be on me own again. They ain't goin' to hurt her. Now get to your room.'

'No – no, I won't!'

'Oh yes, you damn well will.' Grabbing a handful of Claire's hair, the woman began to drag her kicking and screaming along the landing. Claire stumbled and fell, and before dragging her to her feet, her mother rained blows down on her. At one stage, Claire was sure that she felt something snap as her mother's foot connected with her ribcage. But her fury was so great that for now, the stabbing pain could be ignored. And then at last the journey was over and her mother shoved her breathlessly into her own room.

'Now get into that bed and don't let me hear another peep out of yer, do you understand?' Even though her words were harsh, tears were raining down her face and Claire felt totally bewildered.

Claire didn't understand and knew that she never would. 'How can me own mam let this happen?' she asked herself over and over again. But there was no answer, only the terrified cries of Tracey calling out for her.

As Claire crawled painfully into bed she slowly became aware of every bruise on her body. And when her sister's screams became more than she could bear, she blocked her ears with the threadbare blankets so that she no longer had to hear them, feeling more worthless and useless than she had ever felt in her life.

Much, much later, when Claire was quite sure that the two men had gone, she sneaked along the landing and into Tracey's room. Pulling aside the bedding, she lifted the broken child into her arms.

'They hurt me, Claire,' Tracey whispered.

Too heartbroken even to cry, Claire carried her little sister to the bathroom and soaped her body clean, and washed the tears from her face. Dressed in a clean nightie, with an old cardigan and a holey pair of socks for extra warmth, the little girl went back to bed, lying on a clean sheet, clutching a soft toy and a hot-water bottle Claire had made her.

After a long time, when the child's shivering body had become drowsy, Claire whispered a warning to her. 'You know, you mustn't tell anybody about what happened tonight, not anybody.'

'Wh . . . why not?' the little girl whispered, half-asleep.

'Because if you tell anybody, they'll take us away from our mam an' our home.'

'*Good!*' Tracey shot back, waking up. 'I wish they *would* take us away, an' then it could never happen again.'

Claire sighed as she tried to think of a way that would convey the seriousness of the secret that they must keep. 'Look – they won't just take us away from Mam. At this minute I don't care if I never see her again. But they'll split *us* up too. Is that what you want?'

'No, o' course it ain't.' Tracey started to cry. 'Uncle Ian told me that if I tell anyone about what he did, the bogeyman would come in the dark an' get me. Do yer think he will, Claire?'

Claire gulped. 'No, there ain't no bogeyman,' she whispered dully, and for some time they were silent.

Eventually Tracey's voice came from the darkness again. 'Claire, why did me mam let them do the bad things to me?'

'Cos she's lonely, I think, an' frightened that if she don't let 'em do what they want, she might be all alone again.'

'But she'd still have us.'

'I know . . . but that ain't the same.'

The image of the happy family Claire pretended they had once been, the image that she had tried so desperately to cling onto, became tarnished and died in that moment as she realised that her father was never coming back.

'From now on, we ain't got nobody else – only each other,' she murmured as she cradled Tracey protectively in her arms. 'But I promise yer this, you'll always have me and I'll never go away and leave yer.'

Slightly consoled, Tracey eventually fell into an uneasy doze, but Claire lay wide awake until at last the first cold fingers of dawn streaked the sky.

Chapter Six

Claire woke and blinked in the grey light then, turning awkwardly, she winced with pain. It had been three weeks now since the night of the party. Her bruises had faded from an angry purple and black to a dull yellow and blue, but it still hurt her to breathe, and she was convinced that something inside her had been damaged forever. At her side, Tracey stirred and shifted restlessly, and Claire grimaced as she became aware of the cold damp sheet beneath her. Cautiously she rolled to the edge of the bed and painfully climbed out. Plodding to the window, she drew the curtain aside.

Spread out before her was a crisp white world, and for the first time in what felt like a very long time, the girl found herself smiling. Overnight the snow had fallen, making everything appear clean and bright. The drab grey roofs of the council houses seemed to sparkle and Claire stared with fascination at the long black icicles that dripped from their sooty eaves. She stood entranced at the sight of a solitary robin who was furiously thrusting his beak in and out of the snow as he searched for food, his red breast standing out in stark contrast to the white lawn. But eventually the sound of the bed creaking drew Claire's attention back into the room.

'I've wet the bed again,' Tracey whimpered, her cheeks burning with shame, and instantly Claire dropped the curtain and went to her.

'It doesn't matter,' she reassured her. 'I'll go an' get a dry sheet in a minute but first come with me an' have a look outside.'

Tracey followed her to the window and Claire pulled back the curtain and pointed. 'Look . . . it's been snowing. Everywhere looks all brand new.' She stared at her sister expectantly but Tracey merely shrugged before crossing back to the bed where she began to strip off the wet sheet.

'You won't tell me Mam, will you?' she pleaded.

Claire shook her head. 'O' course I won't. Don't worry about it. When Mam goes out I'll wash it an' we'll dry it by the fire on the clotheshorse. All right?'

Tracey nodded and without another word, she left the room and went to the bathroom. Claire watched her go and after a time, she sank down onto a dry patch of the bare mattress and buried her face in her hands. Tracey had changed so much over the past three weeks that sometimes Claire could barely recognise her. Almost every night now she would creep into Claire's bed, and almost every morning the bed would be wet. Sometimes she would waken Claire as she screamed, lost in a terrible nightmare. And as Claire held her tight and comforted her, the guilt she felt was unbearable because she knew that it was all her fault. Ian had told her so and she believed him.

Christmas came and went. Ian bought Tracey a beautiful doll, which she unwrapped and then ignored, and he bought Claire a gaily-printed nightshirt, which she pushed deep into the bottom of a drawer and refused to wear.

It was New Year's Day when Claire answered a knock at the door to find Jane, Tracey's schoolfriend, standing there in bright shiny Wellington boots and a colourful hat and scarf.

'Is Tracey coming out to play?' she asked cheerfully.

Claire called over her shoulder, 'Tracey, come here. It's Jane come to see if you want to go out for a while. An' look, she's got her sledge with her.'

Tracey joined them at the door but shook her head. 'I'm not comin' out, I don't feel like it,' she muttered.

Jane peered at her, her small face concerned. 'Aren't you feelin' very well, Tracey?' she asked. 'You look a bit pasty.'

Tracey shrugged. 'I'm all right, I just don't feel like it,' she repeated, and then turning away she returned to the lounge without even saying goodbye.

Once Jane was gone Claire stood in front of the television set and glared at her. 'That was downright bloody rude,' she scolded. 'That poor girl has been round for you nearly every day over the Christmas holidays. I wonder why she even bothers. You're barely civil to her.'

Tracey stared resentfully into the fire as Claire dropped down beside her and took her hands in hers. 'You can't go on like this, Tracey,' she said in a softer tone. 'You've got to get out sometime. A bit o' fresh air would do yer good. In fact, it would do us *both* good. Come on, get your coat on an' we'll go for a walk.'

Tracey opened her mouth to protest but Claire pulled her to her feet. 'I said get your coat on, an' I meant it, so come on, get crackin' else I'll leave yer here on yer own.'

Immediately Tracey fetched her coat, too afraid of being left alone to argue, and soon they were in Claire's favourite spot, high on top of the valley, looking down across the village. Far below them, they could see children throwing snowballs. Others were building a snowman and their cries of glee floated to them on the air. They stood watching them for a long time and then Claire asked softly, 'Are you all right?'

For some minutes Tracey didn't answer her, then slowly she slipped her hand into Claire's. Her sister squeezed it. 'Things will turn out all right, you'll see,' she promised.

Tracey shook her head. 'No, they won't.' As she looked forlornly at Claire, the girl became aware of the large dark circles beneath her eyes.

'I've got something to show you,' Tracey whispered, and Claire raised her eyebrows. She watched as Tracey fumbled about in her coat pocket then slowly withdrew something that glinted in the reflection from the snow. It was a syringe.

Claire stared at it, appalled. 'My God . . . where did you get that from?'

'I found it under the settee the other mornin'.'

'Bloody hell, whose do yer think it is?'

'I know whose it is – it's me mam's. I saw her stick it into her arm . . . an' Ian did it too.'

Claire could hardly believe her ears.

'I came down one night for a drink,' Tracey explained, 'an' that's when I saw 'em. Mam stuck it in her arm an' then Ian filled it up again an' stuck it in his arm too. They don't know I saw them though 'cos I hid behind the door. Not long after that, they started to act all sort of funny but I went back to bed then. What do yer think they were doin'?'

'I don't know,' Claire admitted, shuddering. 'I can't think of any reason why anybody would want to stick a needle in themselves unless they had to, an' Mam ain't been poorly, has she?'

'Well, what should we do with it?' Tracey asked.

Claire scratched her head. 'I reckon we'd be best to bury it and then say nothin' about it to no one,' she decided eventually, and so together they bent and began to claw away the deep snow. When they finally reached the frozen earth they pushed the syringe in as far as it would go and then patted the snow back into place.

'That's the best place fer that,' Claire declared as she blew onto her cold hands, and Tracey nodded in agreement.

'Come on, now we're up here we may as well go an' have a look at the Blue Lagoon,' Claire urged, suddenly feeling the need to be away from here. Falling into step, the girls made their way towards the woods. Once they reached the Blue Lagoon they sat for a while in silence enjoying their freedom.

After a time, Claire said quietly, 'I'm sorry about what happened on the night of the party. I did try to stop them, Tracey, but I couldn't.' Tears began to roll down her cheeks unchecked. The sisters had never really spoken about it before but now Claire felt that she must.

Tracey looked back at her, her eyes deep wells of fear. 'Will it happen again?' she asked, and after a pause Claire answered her as honestly as she could.

'I don't know, but if it does you'll have to be brave, an' I meant what I said about yer not telling anyone. You mustn't – not ever.'

'But *why*?' Tracey wailed. 'If you'd only let me tell my teacher she'd stop it, I know she would.'

Claire snorted in disgust. 'Oh yes, she'd stop it all right. But she'd also make sure that you an' me were split up. She's a grown-up, ain't she? An' they're all the same . . . even your precious teacher. They all pretend to care but they don't. All they do is poke an' pry. I'm tellin' you, Tracey, we can't trust no one . . . only each other. Just try an' be brave for me and I promise you that one day I'll get us away when I'm old enough. Away to somewhere where they'll never be able hurt us again.'

It was as they were sitting there, each trapped in their own gloomy thoughts, that the girls heard a noise in the woods behind them. Turning, they saw two small boys emerge from the trees tugging a sack between them as they headed towards the pond. Tracey and Claire watched curiously as the larger of the two boys began to break the thin ice at the edge of the lake with the heel of his shoe. Dragging Tracey to her feet, Claire gripped her hand tightly and sauntered towards them. She would have passed without speaking but as she drew near she was sure that she saw something in the sack move.

'What have you got in there?' she asked suspiciously.

'Ain't none o' your bloody business,' the taller of the two boys retorted cheekily.

Claire frowned at him as alarm bells began to ring in her head. 'Well, I'm makin' it me business,' she told him threateningly. 'So open that sack now or else you'll be sorry.'

Suddenly swinging the sack with an ease that belied his small size, he threw it at her feet. 'Here, then, if yer so bloody interested, yer can have it.' He laughed. 'It'll save us the trouble o' havin' to drown it.'

He and his young accomplice then scampered away, leaving Claire and Tracey to stare bemused at the wriggling package at their feet. Bending, Claire quickly untied the rope that secured the sack and was nearly bowled over as a tiny energetic puppy emerged and launched itself at her. Almost as if he realised that Claire had saved him from a watery grave, he began to lick her furiously, and for the first time in weeks Tracey smiled as she stared at his fast wagging tail.

'The little sods them,' Claire muttered, staring after the boys who were just disappearing into the trees. Then, turning her attention back to the pup, she now managed to hold him at arm's length. 'Blimey, you ain't no pedigree, that's for sure, are yer?' she observed, taking in his gangly legs and lopsided ears. He cocked his head to one side and stared appealingly at her.

'Ooh, Claire, ain't he lovely?' Dropping to her knees in the snow, Tracey began to stroke him.

Claire nodded in agreement. 'Yes he is, but the problem is now, what do we do with him? If we take him home, Mam will go mad. But if we leave him here we might as well have let them drown him 'cos he'll die o' cold anyway.' As she hugged his skinny body to her, Tracey stared at her in alarm.

'I don't want to leave him to die,' she whispered tremulously, and instantly Claire made a decision.

'He ain't goin' to die. We're takin' him home with us,' she said resolutely. 'An' if me mam don't like it, then she'll just have to bloody well lump it.' Standing, she tucked the puppy into her coat to keep him warm. Then, smiling at Tracey with a bravery she was far from feeling, she told her, 'Come on, let's go an' get it over with.' Turning about, the two girls began to make their way home.

As they neared the house, they saw that Ian's lorry was parked outside and glanced anxiously at each other. They knew then that their mother was home. Tracey frowned fearfully but Claire squared her shoulders and winked at her.

'Come on, let's go an' face the music,' she grinned, as together they entered the kitchen. Her mother and Ian were sitting at the table, and when her mother first caught sight of the wriggling puppy in Claire's arms, her eyes widened with horror. 'What the bloody hell is *that*?' she demanded angrily as she stabbed her finger towards the puppy.

Claire stared back at her. 'It's a puppy,' she stated flatly. 'He's mine an' I'm goin' to keep him.' Something about Claire's determined stance made her mother stare at her cautiously.

'We can't afford to feed a dog,' she pointed out but Claire stood her ground.

'I'll worry about feedin' him,' she answered. 'He won't cost you a penny. I'll get meself a job, a paper round or somethin', if I have to.'

Her mother tutted disapprovingly as she eyed the animal with distaste. 'It ain't the prettiest o' creatures, is it?' she remarked scornfully. 'It's a bleedin' Heinz 57 if ever I saw one.'

Sensing victory, Claire began to relax a little. 'Actually, I think he's lovely and I don't much care what you think of him. He's mine an' I'm goin' to call him Tinker.'

Her mother sniffed. 'You can call it what yer like, but I'll tell yer now, the first time the bloody thing gets under me feet, it's out.' Then returning her attention to Ian, she ignored the girls and the puppy as if they weren't even there.

Claire was true to her word, and for weeks Tinker ate anything that she could beg, steal or borrow. She soon discovered that it was easy to be allowed out of class at school to visit the toilet, and easier still to detour to the cloakrooms and fill her pockets as she raided the lunchboxes. Tinker dined on everything from ham to tuna and soon began to grow. Unfortunately, the teachers soon realised that there was a thief amongst them and one morning as Claire was taking sandwiches from a lunchbox she was caught red-handed.

'What's the meaning of this?' demanded Mr Brindley, her maths teacher, but then as he looked into Claire's pinched face his voice softened as he asked, 'Are you hungry, Claire?'

She lowered her head. 'No, sir,' she admitted. 'The . . . they're for me dog.'

Mr Brindley gaped at her in amazement. In all his years of teaching he had never come across a situation quite like this. He knew that he should march her off to the office, but something about the weary stoop of her shoulders stopped him. He paused, at a loss as to what he should do, but then after making his decision, he addressed her sternly. 'If I have your assurance that this will never happen again, I am prepared to overlook this incident. Do I have that assurance, Claire?'

'Yes, sir,' she muttered miserably.

Mr Brindley nodded. 'Very well then, you may go and we'll say no more about it.'

'Thank you, sir.' And the girl turned and scuttled away, leaving the schoolmaster to scratch his head in bewilderment.

After that incident, Claire knew that she would have to become more cautious.

'But how are we goin' to feed Tinker now?' Tracey asked one night as they snuggled together on the settee before going up to bed.

The older girl sighed. 'Don't go worryin' about that, there's more ways than one to skin a cat. I'm gettin' a dab hand at shopliftin' now. Where do you think I get yer chocolate from?'

Tracey peeped at her fearfully. 'But ain't it wrong to steal, Claire?'

Claire nodded. 'Yes, it is, but what other option is there? Most days I can manage to lift a tin o' dog food from the shop fer him. An' when I can't, well . . . then he'll have to share my dinner with me. That is, if we've got any. I just wish me mam would stop moanin' about him all the time though. Do yer know what she said the other day? She said she didn't know why I don't just take him for a walk an' leave him somewhere. Huh! As if I would ever do that.'

Tracey was appalled at the very idea; she knew how much Claire adored Tinker.

'But what will happen to you if you get caught pinchin'?' she whispered fearfully.

Claire sniffed. 'There's no chance o' that, so stop frettin'. I'll make sure as Tinker is fed one way or another, you'll see.'

Reassured, Tracey sighed with contentment as she nestled further into Claire's side. If her big sister said that things would be all right, then she believed her.

'Come on, Sleepyhead,' Claire said softly after a time, 'let's be havin' you up them stairs. Mam will be back soon an' she'll be none too pleased if we're still up. We don't want to give her another reason to let rip at us.'

The girls reluctantly rose from the settee and hand-in-hand they headed for the stairs door with Tinker close on their heels. Claire was feeling better than she had in a long time, because ever since the night of the party, not only had Ian left Tracey alone, he had left her alone too. She was feeling almost cheerful as she tucked Tracey in, and hurried away to her own bed. Tinker hopped up beside her, as he had taken to doing, and she fondled his silky ears lovingly. As he licked her face with his soft wet tongue she cuddled him to her. 'Give over, yer sloppy mutt you,' she giggled. Obediently he dropped his head onto his paws, and stared up at her from soulful brown eyes. Unable to resist him, Claire planted a kiss on his nose. 'Do you know somethin', Tinker?' she confided. 'Since I had you, everything's got better. I've got somebody I can talk to now. Before you came, I had to keep everythin' bottled up inside, but now I can tell you all me secrets 'cos you understand, don't yer?'

Contentedly she drew him closer, and very soon both she and her beloved friend were fast asleep.

It was some time later when Tinker woke her again by licking her face. Peering at him sleepily from half-closed eyelids she grinned as she watched him jump from the bed and pad towards the door. 'Oh, so yer want to go out, do yer?' she grumbled as she swung her legs out of the warm blankets. 'Well, come on then.'

After opening the bedroom door, she followed him out onto the landing, but instead of going down the stairs as she had expected him to, he ran to Tracey's bedroom door and began to bark loudly.

'Give over, will yer?' she hissed. 'You'll wake Tracey up, yer daft dog.' Instead of obeying her as he normally did, Tinker ignored her and began to scratch furiously at the door. Claire had just bent down to lift him into her arms when the door was suddenly flung open and Ian appeared and kicked him viciously in the ribs. Yelping with pain, he scurried back to Claire's side, his tail between his legs, and confused, Claire stared into Ian's furious face.

'What you doin' in Tracey's room?' The words were laden with suspicion, but before he could answer, her mother appeared from her bedroom. Swaying unsteadily, she pulled her dressing-gown across her sagging, naked breasts. It was then that Claire heard Tracey whimper, and ignoring her mother and Ian now, she roughly elbowed past them and barged into the room with Tinker close on her heels.

Ian followed, and as she stormed into the room he glared at her, growling, '*Get out.*'

Claire stood her ground. 'No, Ian, I ain't goin' nowhere,' she informed him coldly, 'but *you* are.'

His mouth dropped open with amazement at her daring, and when her mother made to grab her arm, Claire shook her off and faced her too. 'I wouldn't do that if I were you.'

Something in the tone of her voice made her mother be still.

Claire looked calmly from one to the other of them and then her voice sliced through the silence that had settled on the room when she said, 'I'm going to tell you both something and you'd better listen. I want you to get out o' this room right now, else first thing in the mornin' I'm goin' straight to my teacher an' tellin' 'er about what's been goin' on here. An' what's more, I'll be takin' the syringe we found under the settee wi' me, an' you can explain that, an' all.'

Claire watched with satisfaction as her mother paled, and for the first time in her life, she felt power – *real* power – rush through her. 'I must admit when Tracey first found it I couldn't understand what it was for,' she went on, 'but then we had a policeman come into school to talk to us about drugs an' I realised what you were doin'.'

'Where is it?' her mother rasped as her hands clenched into sweaty fists.

Claire looked at her scathingly. 'It's somewhere you'll never find it,' she bluffed. 'But *I* could – an' then what are yer goin' to do, eh?'

A tense silence descended on the room until Ian suddenly sprang off the bed. 'Oh, I've had enough o' this,' he declared in disgust. 'I'm off. These bloody pair ain't worth getting into trouble wi' the law for.'

Karen clung to his arm as he made to pass her, but he shook her off roughly. 'Get out o' me way, woman,' he snarled, and as he clattered away down the stairs Karen turned and shook her fist at Claire.

'*Now* look what you've done!' she screamed. 'I'm tellin' you somethin', me gel, you're goin' to live to regret this night. You just mark my words.' And with that she ran from the room to try and catch up with Ian.

Claire sagged against the wall. She had never had any intention of disclosing what had happened to her, or Tracey, for that matter – she was too terrified of the thought of them being separated. But thankfully, neither her mother nor Ian had realised that they were empty threats. From now on, she felt that she would have a weapon to stop the abuse from occurring again, if only she could stay strong.

Two days later, glad to escape the tense atmosphere of the house, Claire took Tinker for a long walk and eventually found herself in the very spot where she had rescued him. Sinking down onto a convenient log, she hugged him to her, enjoying the feel of his silky fur in her fingers.

'Do yer know, I don't know what I'd do now if I didn't have you to talk to,' she confided, and slowly the bravado she had displayed for two whole days slipped away and she began to cry. Tinker whined and licked her face with his warm wet tongue as Claire smiled through her tears.

'Things are just about as bad as they can be at home, ain't they? But yer know, it won't always be like this, you'll see. One day, when I'm old enough, I'm goin' to take you an' Tracey a long, long way away from here where no one will be able to find us or hurt us again. An' you won't have to live on scraps any more then. Tracey will stop havin' nightmares an' wettin' the bed. We'll have a big posh house, an' no one will be allowed to come in unless we want 'em to.' Tinker wagged his tail as if he understood every word she was saying, and for a time as they sat there, Claire became lost in her dream.

Almost one week later she arrived home from school and pushed open the rickety gate. She looked about the overgrown garden expecting Tinker to bound towards her as he normally did. This afternoon there was no sign of him, so smiling she called, 'Tinker – here, boy. Where are yer, yer daft mutt?' Still he didn't come, so frowning now, Claire hurried up the path and into the kitchen and asked, 'Where's Tinker?'

Her mother glanced indifferently up at her from the magazine she was reading.

'Don't know,' she answered flatly. 'I ain't seen him all day, now yer come to mention it. Not since I put him out this mornin'.' She went back to her reading as Claire stared at her suspiciously.

'Tinker never goes off,' she muttered worriedly.

'Ah, well he has now. Still, not to worry. Happen he'll come back when he's hungry.'

Claire had a sinking feeling in the pit of her stomach as, snatching up the rope that she used for a lead, she headed back towards the door.

'You get back here! You've got to see to Tracey's tea,' her mother commanded.

'I'm goin' to look for Tinker, an' neither you nor nobody else is goin' to stop me,' Claire answered defiantly, and before her mother could say another word she was gone.

It was dark by the time she returned home and Tracey, who had been waiting for her, ran to meet her.

'Did yer find him?' she asked hopefully. When Claire wearily shook her head, Tracey's eyes filled with tears.

'I've looked everywhere for him,' Claire told her miserably. 'I must have walked for miles an' me legs feel as if they're droppin' off. But there ain't a sign of him anywhere.'

Tracey pulled her towards the table. 'Look, you sit down an' I'll make you a drink,' she offered, and shortly after she placed a mug of lukewarm tea in front of her sister.

'I'm sorry if it ain't very nice,' she apologised, 'but I ain't as good as you at makin' tea yet.'

Claire smiled at her gratefully and as she sipped the tea she tried not to grimace with distaste. 'Where's Mam?' she asked.

'She's gone out wi' Ian. Here – look, she left yer a note.' Lifting a crumpled piece of paper from the draining board, Tracey passed it to Claire.

'"Expect me when you see me", it says. Huh, that's all we ever seem to do.'

'Look, I'll go an' get meself washed tonight,' Tracey offered, sensing her despair. 'You don't have to help me, I'm gettin' big now. You stay here an' drink yer tea.'

When Claire didn't answer her, Tracey slowly made her way upstairs.

Much later, when Claire tucked her into bed, Tracey squeezed her hand. 'Don't worry, Claire,' she urged sleepily. 'Tinker will come back, you'll see. He's like yer shadow, he loves you and I'm sure he won't have gone far. He'd never leave yer.'

Claire nodded, then turning away she went back downstairs to keep her vigil at the window. Eventually the room grew dark and so, snapping on the light, she looked towards the dying fire. Sighing, she picked up the empty scuttle and headed for the back door. She hated going out to the coalhouse in the dark, but the room had grown cold and she reasoned that if she was going to wait up for Tinker, she might as well wait in the warm.

When her mother eventually came home she found Claire still standing at the window. 'What you still doin' up?' she asked abruptly, and before Claire could answer she sneered, 'I suppose yer still waitin' fer that bleedin' dog o' yours. Huh, there's times when I reckon you think more o' that bloody mutt than yer do o' me.'

Claire blinked to hold back her tears.

'Well, come on now, enough is enough. Get yerself off to bed, you've got school in the mornin'.'

Without a word Claire did as she was told but once she was in bed, she tossed and turned restlessly. 'Oh Tinker, where are you?' she whispered into the darkness, and loneliness engulfed her.

In the morning she was so pale that Tracey couldn't help but stare at her. As Claire pushed her cornflakes around the bowl, Tracey eyed them hungrily. 'Don't yer want them, Claire?' she ventured after a while, and when Claire shook her head she dragged the bowl across the table and cleared it in seconds.

It was as they were leaving that their mother appeared from the stairs and stopped them at the door. 'Ah, you two, I'm glad I caught yer.' She yawned. 'I'm off on a run wi' Ian today. Only fer one night though, so I'll see yer both tomorrer when I get back.'

The girls nodded. They were used to being left alone now and it no longer held any fear for them. It was as they stepped outside that Claire noticed that the toilet door next to the coalhouse was slightly open. She scowled; the outside toilet was never used, only for storing old bits and bobs, and she couldn't even remember the last time anyone had been in there. She let Tracey go ahead of her down the path and paused. Placing her hand on the rusty latch she was just about to close the door when something in the far corner caught her eye. Her heart began to thud as she opened it further, allowing the morning light to flood into the small confined space. The sight that met her eyes made her gasp with horror. Tinker was lying on the dirty floor, and oblivious to the filth, she dropped to her knees beside him. As she tried to gather him into her arms his head lolled to one side and his tongue hung loosely from his mouth. He was cold and Claire knew in that instant that he was dead. She heard Tracey behind her and swung around, her eyes wild with pain.

'*Get to school,*' she barked as grief washed over her, and when Tracey, who was obviously also deep in shock, didn't immediately move, Claire screamed at her, '*Go on!* Get to school, I said – we'll talk about this tonight.'

Tracey turned and ran as fast as her legs would carry her as tears streamed down her cheeks, and too deep in misery to care, Claire turned her attention back to Tinker.

'Come on, boy,' she whispered, as she hugged his familiar little body to her. 'Come on, please, *please* don't you leave me too. I love you.' She rocked him gently to and fro as if she were willing life back into his broken body. And it was there, sometime later, that her mother found her.

'Oh . . . so you've found him then?' The words were said softly but as Claire stared up at her, Karen was shocked at the raw hatred she saw shining in her daughter's eyes.

Nervously, her mother tried to explain. 'It happened yesterday mornin' just after you'd gone to school. He er . . . fell down the stairs, an' I didn't know how I was goin' to tell yer. So I put him in there. It were an accident, see.'

Claire continued to stare at her and angry now, her mother began to shout, 'Look, he were only a bloody mongrel. I can't see what all the fuss is about.'

Gently, Claire laid Tinker down, and standing, she faced her mother. 'Tinker would never have fallen down the stairs, Mam. He was like a little mountain goat.'

'What yer tryin' to say, then?' Karen blustered. 'An' don't look at me like that. Don't yer believe me? Are yer callin' me a liar?'

Without flinching, Claire nodded. 'Yes, I am calling you a liar. Yer never liked him, did yer? I don't think Tinker fell at all, Mam. I think yer kicked him or threw him down the stairs an' I'll never forgive yer, not fer as long as I live. 'Cos you see, he might have been just a mongrel to you, but to me he was everythin'. He were the only real friend I've ever had.'

Dry-eyed and deathly pale she now walked past her mother and climbed the stairs to her room. Once there, she sank down onto the bed and deep inside her a terrible resolve began to grow. 'I'll never *ever* love anyone or anythin' again,' she vowed silently. 'Every single person I've ever loved has left me, except Tracey. And now I've lost Tinker an' all.'

It was almost an hour later when her mother's voice floated up the stairs. 'I'm off then.'

Claire ignored her and sat deep in shock, too bereft even to cry. When sometime later she heard someone rap loudly on the front door, she ignored that too. But eventually the insistent knocking played on her nerves and irritably she made her way downstairs and flung it open.

'Yes?' she said shortly to the two women who were staring at her. One of them was quite young, fair-haired, tall and slender with a look of Farrah Fawcett-Majors about her. The other was an older woman with hair that was slightly greying at the temples; she was dressed in a drab grey coat and sensible flat shoes.

'You must be Claire,' the older woman smiled.

Suspicious now, Claire shrugged. 'What if I am?'

'Actually it's your mother we've come to see. Is she in, dear?'

'No, she ain't.'

Ignoring Claire's rude tone the woman went on, 'In that case we'd better speak to you then. May we come in?'

'Who are you?' Claire asked suspiciously.

'I'm a social worker, and this lady is my colleague,' the woman explained.

Claire's stomach began to churn. Reluctantly she opened the door a little wider and allowed them to enter. Once they were in the living room, the social worker smiled at her kindly whilst the younger woman remained silent, as she stared around the sparsely furnished room.

'Now then, Claire, my name is Jill Burrell,' the social worker introduced herself and held her hand out, but Claire pretended not to see it. 'And this is Jenny Seagrave.' Undeterred, the woman went on, 'What time will your mother be home?'

'I ain't got the foggiest idea,' Claire lied.

'Well, in that case, I'd like you to come with us.'

Claire's eyes stretched wide and quickly, Jill tried to reassure her. 'Don't look so worried, dear. It's only until we can speak to your mother and clear up a few things.'

'What things?'

Jill glanced uneasily at her colleague. 'We already have your little sister in a place of safety. She's with some very nice people – foster parents. I'm afraid she was very upset when she arrived at school this morning and she made certain er . . . disclosures that we need to look into. Her teacher was very worried about her. Do you know what I'm talking about, Claire?'

'No, I *don't*!' Claire screamed, and then pointing to the door she ordered shakily, 'Get out – go on, get out, both o' you. Go an' stick yer noses into somebody else's business an' just leave us alone.'

'I'm afraid we can't do that, Claire,' Jill explained sympathetically. 'Now come on, go and pack a few clothes and we'll take you to Tracey. You want to see her, don't you?'

Claire's shoulders sagged and knowing that she was defeated she went upstairs and began to push a few things into a carrier bag. Passing her mother's coat, that had been chucked untidily over the banisters, on the landing, she unpinned the brooch, a spray of green flowers that her mum kept on the lapel, and hid it in her bag. When she came back down, the two women were waiting for her in the hallway. Jill tried to place her arm around Claire's shoulders, but she shrugged her off angrily.

'Don't *touch* me,' she threatened. 'Just take me to Tracey.'

Nodding, they led her outside to a car.

Mr Tolly was out in his front garden, doing a bit of weeding, and before climbing into the back seat of the car, Claire crossed to the fence that separated the gardens. 'Mr Tolly, I . . . I need to ask you a favour,' she said brokenly.

'Well, ask away then, love,' he replied kindly.

'It's me dog, Tinker. He . . . well, he died yesterday an' he's out the back in the outside toilet. I've got to go away fer a little while an' I just wondered . . . do you think you could bury him fer me?'

As Mr Tolly looked into her pale, drawn face his heart went out to her. 'Of course I'll see to it for you, love. You just leave it wi' me.'

Claire smiled at him tremulously and then turning, she clambered into the back of the social worker's car. She looked round just once to stare out of the back window as it pulled away. Mr Tolly was standing where she had left him, his face a mask of concern. As she looked at her home she wondered if she would ever see it again and her heart ached. It might not have been much of a home, but it was the only one she had ever known and the thought of leaving it was frightening. Still, she tried to console herself, at least they were taking her to Tracey. At last the tears she had bravely held back erupted and spilled down her cheeks.

Chapter Seven

When Jill Burrell eventually drew the car to a halt outside a smart semi-detached house in Howard Road in Nuneaton, Claire stared at it curiously from the car window.

'This is where you'll be staying for now, Claire,' the social worker informed her as she climbed from the car and opened the back door.

Claire glared at her resentfully before slowly stepping out onto the pavement. The house was certainly a far cry from the one she had just left behind, she had to silently admit. The windows shone like mirrors in the late-afternoon sunshine and the small lawn that fronted it was neat and tidy. As the social workers positioned themselves one at either side of her and marched her up to the red front door, Claire began to feel like a prisoner being led to her cell. Jill had just lifted her hand towards the gleaming brass door-knocker when the door was opened and Claire found a tall dark-haired lady smiling down at her. Claire judged the woman to be around the same age as her mother. She was well-built and her face was kindly.

'Ah, you must be Claire. I'm Mrs Garrett, but you can call me Molly.' She extended her hand, but Claire simply looked away. 'Come on in then,' the woman said kindly, ignoring the slight. 'I'm sure Tracey is going to be pleased to see you.'

Claire stepped into a long narrow hallway that had wall-to-wall fitted carpets and pretty pictures on the walls. There were three doors leading off from the hall; Claire was soon to discover that they led to a sizeable lounge, a dining room and a kitchen, all of which were very tastefully decorated and furnished. She followed the woman into the lounge and her mouth gaped open. This room was decorated in red and gold, which made it look warm and inviting. Her eyes settled on a long mahogany

59

sideboard that was placed along one wall, so highly polished that even from where she was standing she could see her face in it. A huge hearthrug lay in front of a pretty tiled fireplace, and on either side of it were two matching armchairs upholstered in a rich red velvet. Her observations stopped there, however, for suddenly she heard a strangled sob as Tracey jumped off a settee and hurtled towards her.

'I'm sorry, Claire,' she sobbed as she wrapped her skinny little arms around her sister's waist. 'I didn't mean to tell the bad secret, honest I didn't, but . . . it just sort of came out.'

'It's all right.' Claire stroked her hair tenderly. 'Things will be fine, you'll see.'

There was a small bright-faced boy who looked to be about ten years old sitting in one of the chairs at the side of the fireplace, and as Claire caught his eye he flashed her a welcoming smile. Claire did not respond. She turned her attention back to Tracey, who was now staring fearfully at the two social workers.

'Wh . . . when will our mam be comin' for us?' she asked timidly.

Jill Burrell glanced at her colleague before telling her, 'I shouldn't think it will be too long. There are just a few things we need to talk to her about. Meanwhile, I'm sure that Molly here will take excellent care of you. That's Billy over there, Molly's son, and you'll meet Tom soon when he comes home from work. He's Molly's husband.'

Claire's face grew even darker as she clutched Tracey to her protectively.

'Right, how about I show you both up to the rooms you'll be staying in then?' Molly piped up, hoping for an excuse to break the tense atmosphere. Still tightly holding hands, Tracey and Claire followed her back into the hall and up a staircase onto a long landing. 'This here is the bathroom,' Molly told them. 'There should be everything you'll need in there but if there's anything I've forgotten, don't be afraid to shout up.'

Tracey's eyes stretched wide as they fastened on the soft fluffy towels that were neatly folded across the towel rail, but she stayed tight-lipped as Molly paused at another door. 'I thought you might like this room, Tracey.' She held the door wide for her to inspect it. Tracey's eyes positively bulged now as she looked at the soft pile carpet and the pretty quilt on the bed. The room was decorated in subtle shades of pink that made it look warm and inviting and flowered curtains hung at the window.

'B . . . but where will Claire be sleeping?' she asked falteringly.

'Oh, don't get worrying about that, love. She'll just be along here.' Molly led them to another room. This one was decorated in shades of lilac and looked just as nice as Tracey's, but Claire shook her head and refused to set foot in it.

'Me an' Tracey want to sleep together,' she declared obstinately.

'But there's only single beds in each room,' Molly pointed out. However, before she could say any more, Jill Burrell told her diplomatically, 'I'm sure they'll manage for a while. If they feel happier sleeping together it doesn't really matter, does it?'

'Well . . . no, I don't suppose it does.' Molly looked far from happy about the decision but went along with it anyway. After all, she had been caring for children long enough to know that they needed time to settle in. No doubt by the end of the week they would both be only too happy to have the privacy of their own rooms. Molly continued to chat cheerfully as she began to pack their things into a chest of drawers in Tracey's room. Once it was done, she then turned to them and suggested, 'How about I get you something to eat now, eh? I dare say you'll be hungry.'

Claire glared down at Tracey and pulled her closer to her side when she saw her lick her lips with anticipation. Tracey always seemed to be hungry. So was she, if she was to be honest with herself, but she was too proud to admit it. Soon they found themselves in a large kitchen that was as clean as a new pin. A delicious smell was wafting from the oven and despite her resolve not to eat a thing, Claire's stomach rumbled with antic- ipation. Especially when Molly lifted a steaming meat pie from it and placed it on the table.

Molly now ushered them both onto chairs as the two social workers prepared to leave with promises that they would be back very soon. Claire curled her lip and shrank away when Jill patted her shoulder, but some- what cheered now at the thought of the meal ahead, Tracey flashed her a smile and then the women left and Molly's son joined them. Their first day in their new foster home had begun.

It was much later that night, when they were tucked up in Tracey's bed with their arms wrapped around each other, that Tracey asked tremulously, 'Mam *will* be comin' for us soon, won't she, Claire?'

'O'course she will.' Claire's voice was confident. 'Soon as ever she gets back from her run with Ian she'll be round here like a shot, you'll see.'

Reassured, Tracey snuggled more closely into her sister and soon they were fast asleep.

It was two days later when the sound of someone hammering on the front door woke Karen McMullen from a deep alcohol-induced sleep. She had arrived home late the night before and tumbled into bed partially clothed, certain that the girls were in their own beds fast asleep.

'*Claire!*' Her voice echoed along the landing. 'Get the bleedin' door will you, before whoever it is knockin' has it off its hinges.'

When only silence greeted her, she cursed and dragged herself to the edge of the bed, moaning as the harsh morning light accosted her eyes. 'Bloody lazy little cow,' she muttered as she pulled on a faded old dressing-gown. 'I'll give her what for, ignorin' me like that.' She lurched unsteadily towards the open bedroom door. Her mouth felt like the bottom of a birdcage and there was the beginning of a hangover setting in. She flung Claire's bedroom door open, blinking with surprise when she saw that the bed was empty. Sighing, she tightened the belt on her gown and stumped her way down the stairs to the front door.

'All right, all right, keep yer bleedin' hair on,' she muttered as she fumbled with the lock, and then the door was open and she was confronted by two women.

'Well?' she spat. 'What the bleedin' hell do you pair want at this unearthly hour? It can't be much past nine o'clock.'

The older of the two women, who Karen now noted was a mean-looking sod, stared back at her coldly. 'Mrs McMullen? Mrs Karen McMullen?'

'What if I am?' The first flickering of fear sprang to life in Karen's stomach and that, added to the drink she'd consumed the night before, was making her feel queasy.

'We are here to talk to you about your two children.' The woman's voice was so icy that it made Karen herself feel cold.

'What about the kids? They're upstairs in bed where they should be at this ungodly hour.' She was on the defensive now without quite knowing why.

'I think you'll find that the children *aren't* in bed, Mrs McMullen,' Jill

Burrell informed her. 'Perhaps if you would allow us to come in, we could explain?'

'What do you mean, me kids ain't in bed? Where the bleedin' hell are they then? An' who are you?'

The social worker stepped past her and strode into the kitchen, followed by her colleague. Karen slammed the door shut and reluctantly followed them, noting the disdainful way the women looked around.

'So . . . spit it out then,' Karen snapped. 'Just what is goin' on here, eh?'

'Had you been here during the last two days you would have known what was going on, Mrs McMullen.'

Karen gulped deep in her throat and now alarm bells were ringing in her head.

'I am Jill Burrell and this is my colleague,' the woman introduced herself. 'We are social workers, Mrs McMullen, and we took your children into care two days ago.'

'*You did what!*' Karen sputtered as the colour drained from her face. Hastily reaching for a packet of cigarettes that was lying on the dirty table, she quickly lit one and drew on it deeply. The mascara that had streaked down her face stood out in stark contrast on her pale cheeks and it was all Jill Burrell could do to stop herself from shuddering with revulsion as she looked back at her.

'May we sit down?' she now asked.

Karen nodded numbly.

The woman perched on the edge of a chair and went on, 'The thing is, Tracey made a disclosure to a teacher at school and we had no choice but to remove the children to a place of safety until we could investigate, which obviously we couldn't as you weren't here.'

'I er . . . I had to go an' see me mam.' Karen was shaking now but the women looked back at her with not a trace of pity on their faces.

'Really? How very strange. Tracey told us that her grandmother had passed away some time ago.'

A dull flush now painted Karen's cheeks as she realised that she had been found out in a lie, and all the time her mind was working overtime. Why were they here? What had Tracey said? She'd skin the little sod's arse when she got her hands on her.

Deciding to take a different tack she now asked, 'So where *are* me girls?'

'Somewhere very safe, I can assure you, but I have to warn you, the disclosures Tracey made were very serious indeed and the police will want to interview you later in the day. She disclosed that certain men had sexually abused her.'

Panic took over now as Karen blurted, 'Yer don't want to go listenin' to our Tracey. She's a right little drama queen and a bloody liar into the bargain.' Then she sat down heavily on the nearest chair and made a big show of stubbing out her cigarette in an overflowing ashtray. She realised that she was going to have to be careful here, or she could find herself in serious trouble.

'Do I take it by your reaction that you were unaware that some of your boyfriends have abused your girls?'

'*Course* I were unaware,' Karen gabbled, intent on saving her own neck. 'What sort o' mother do you take me for? As if I'd let that go on knowingly. Me boyfriends . . . Well, it ain't easy bein' a single parent an' they've helped out wi' money an' such, but they've never . . . Our Tracey's lyin' – she must be.'

'Oh, I assure you she isn't.' Jill Burrell was struggling to keep the contempt from her voice. 'Both of the girls were given a full medical by a police doctor late yesterday afternoon, and the findings of that medical substantiated what Tracey had said.'

'But it can't be true . . .'

Karen could see by the looks on the women's faces that they didn't believe a word she was saying but she carried on regardless. The way she saw it it was all very well for them to sit there all smug and self-satisfied. They probably had blokes waitin' at home for 'em, whereas she . . . Tears of self-pity stabbed at the back of her eyes as she suddenly thought back to the night her husband had walked out on her. Everything had seemed to go wrong from then on, and all because she had slipped up and had one little affair. The fact that Tracey may have resulted from that affair didn't give Robbie the right to leave her, she thought bitterly. The bastard! And things had gone downhill ever since. How could these two know what it was like to feel lonely? To feel that you would give anything to have somebody love you again, even if it meant sacrificing your kids? And the girls hadn't been hurt, had they, so what was all the fuss about?

'Look,' she said shakily, 'I don't know what Tracey has told you, but if you'll just go an' fetch 'em back I'll make sure as whatever it was she said happened don't happen again.'

'I'm afraid it isn't that simple.' Jill's voice was stern. Without the mother admitting to knowing what had been going on, it would be her word against Tracey's if it came to court – and she would probably get away scot-free. So would the men, because even if they were arrested, they simply had to deny it – despite the physical evidence – and there would be no proof that they were responsible for the girl's injuries other than what Tracey, a mere minor, was saying. Jill Burrell sighed deeply. It was days like this that made her wonder why she had ever become a social worker in the first place.

The girls had been in their foster home for almost a week when Karen finally paid them a visit. They arrived home from school to find her sitting on Molly's settee with a cup of tea in her hand, looking very uncomfortable indeed.

'*Mam!*' Tracey's whole face lit up as she charged across the room and flung herself at her mother.

'Hello, love.' Karen was deeply conscious of Molly and Jill Burrell who were watching her closely, and kept her smile fixed firmly in place as she made a great show of being pleased to see her girls.

'I *knew* you'd come for us,' Tracey said excitedly. 'Didn't I tell you she would, Molly? Have you come to take us home, Mam?'

Karen was saved from having to reply when Jill answered for her. 'Not just yet, dear. There are still a few things we need to sort out.'

The child's face fell a foot. Why couldn't they just go home now? 'Well, when *can* we go home then?' Her voice was trembling now and Claire glared at her mother. What was the point of her coming, if she didn't intend to take them home?

'You're all right here for now, ain't yer?' Karen asked, hoping to defuse the situation.

'How would *you* know?' Claire shot at her. 'Or even care, if it came to that!' The girl's voice was so loaded with bitterness that for a moment Karen was speechless.

Eventually she stuttered, 'Don't get lippy wi' me, me gel. I'm here, ain't I? Can't that be enough for now?'

Claire thumped herself down into a chair with a face like thunder as Tracey began to cry softly. The little girl was looking very pretty in a new school dress that Molly had bought for her, and her hair was washed and shiny. Claire, on the other hand, was still in the clothes she had arrived in, despite all Molly's efforts to encourage her into her new uniform.

'Don't want nothin' off you,' she had declared sullenly, on the day that Molly had presented her with new clothes. 'Me mam will be comin' to fetch us soon so you may as well take 'em back to the shop where you got 'em from.' And now here was her mam, but it was obvious that she had no intention of taking them home. Not just yet, at least.

'Look . . . couldn't I just see the girls on their own for a while?' Karen now pleaded, and as Molly looked towards the social worker for an answer, Jill Burrell nodded.

'Very well then. Molly and I will go into the kitchen, but we'll be leaving the door open. I'll give you ten minutes.' Jill turned and walked stiffly away with Molly close on her heels and now Karen addressed the girls again.

To their mother, it looked as if her daughters had fallen on their feet here. The house was lovely and she had never seen Tracey looking so nice. Karen was feeling slightly easier now because the social workers had been forced to inform her that the case was unlikely to go to court. She had flatly denied knowing anything about what was going on, and as Claire had thankfully refused to say a word when questioned, the police, despite the medical reports, had insufficient evidence to take the case to court. Over the last few days, the selfish young woman had realised that it was quite nice to have the house to herself without the girls to worry about, so surely it wouldn't hurt them to stay here for just a while longer?

As if she could read her mother's thoughts, Claire now snapped, 'So – are we goin' to be comin' home or what then?'

'Well . . . the thing is, there are enquiries going on at the minute so it might be for the best if you were to stay here,' Karen answered cagily.

Claire's lip curled. She could read her mother like a book. What she meant was, she was too busy off enjoying herself to want them back.

'Don't look at me like that,' Karen warned the girl. 'I didn't 'ave to come, you know. I just wanted to check that you two were all right.'

'So now you have, you can go about your business wi' a clear conscience, can't yer?' Claire retorted. Deep down she wanted to fling herself into her mother's arms and beg her to take them home, but she was too proud.

'Right – I don't 'ave to listen to this,' Karen said huffily as she pushed

Tracey aside and stood up. 'Perhaps it would be best if I were to go an' come back when you've 'ad time to calm down a bit.'

'Yeah, that's right – you clear off an' leave us,' Claire shot back as Tracey scuttled over to her and hid against her chest. 'We're all right, ain't we, Trace?'

Karen flounced past them, and as they listened to the door slam behind her, Claire buried her face in Tracey's sweet-smelling hair and sobbed as if her heart would break. She had the strangest feeling that she might never see her mother again.

Chapter Eight

'Do you know Tom, I sometimes feel like I'm banging my head against a brick wall with Claire. It doesn't matter what I do, I just can't seem to get through to her. She's been here for ages now and yet she still treats me like a stranger.' Molly Garrett sighed as she sipped noisily at her cup of hot chocolate.

Tom nodded and stretched his feet towards the gas fire. 'I know what you mean, love, but we knew when we took Claire and Tracey on that it wasn't going to be easy. The poor little devils have been to hell an' back, and then to find that their mother didn't want them . . . well, it doesn't bear thinking about, does it? I think it's going to take Claire a very long time before she trusts anybody again.'

Molly knew that he was right and smiled sadly at him. 'I hear what you're sayin' but it doesn't make it any easier. Still, at least I'm getting somewhere with Tracey. She'll let me give her a bath and wash her hair now without insisting that Claire's in the room.'

'I reckon our Billy's helped there,' Tom chuckled, as he thought of his mischievous ten-year-old son. 'He and Tracey are getting to be inseparable, although I do think it's beginning to make Claire feel a little left out.'

'You're right,' Molly agreed. 'I just wish that Claire would make a few friends of her own age, but she's so standoffish it's no wonder nobody bothers with her. And then there's the matter of her personal hygiene. She doesn't wash her hair from one week to the next, let alone get in the bath no matter how I try and persuade her. And all those lovely clothes we bought her were a waste of time as well. She just seems to grab the baggiest most shapeless thing she can lay her hands on. The only time I ever see her smile is either when she's talking to Tracey or the blessed cat.

Do you know, Copper's even taken to sleeping on the end of her bed now?'

'There's no harm in that if she finds comfort with him,' Tom told her. 'Let's face it, after what people have done to her, it's no wonder she only trusts animals, is it? Animals have never hurt her, have they? As for her personal hygiene . . . well, I reckon when she starts to gain a bit of confidence, she'll take more of a pride in herself – but it has to come in her own time.'

Deeply impressed, Molly stared at him. 'Do you know, Tom Garrett, sometimes you can be clever without even knowing it,' she said. 'I'd never thought of it like that, but you just could be right.'

Tom grinned as he sipped at his drink. 'There you go then. An' you know what they say: "Time is a great healer". Claire is bound to be protective of Tracey. From what we've heard, she had to take on the role of mother, so it's no wonder she resents you. We've just got to be patient with her, that's all.'

'Oh Tom, I do hope so.' Molly stared into her drink. 'Because, you know, on the rare occasions when Claire does smile, *really* smile I mean, her whole face seems to light up. If she tidies herself up she'll be a real beauty in a couple of years' time. In fact – I reckon we'll have the lads queuin' at the door.'

Her husband nodded in agreement. 'Have you given any more thought about what the social worker asked us?' he enquired.

Molly nodded. 'To be honest, I haven't thought about much else. It's a big commitment though, isn't it? If we do decide to keep them both long-term, that is.'

'Yes, it is, love, and at the end of the day I'm going to leave the final decision to you, because in fairness, it's you that has to do the lion's share of the work with them. I mean, I can't go into Tracey in the middle of the night when she's having a nightmare, can I? And it's you who has to strip her wet bed nearly every morning because I'm already at work.'

Molly then took his hand. 'I think I *have* made my decision,' she admitted. 'I realise it's not going to be easy, but you know, Tom, I'd feel that I was letting them down if I allowed them to be moved on to another foster home now. Especially if they had to be split up.' She shuddered at the thought. 'I reckon that would be the final straw for Claire. She puts a brave face on, but I know it hurt when her mother decided she didn't want them back. No, I can't let that happen. So as long as you're happy about it, I'm going to tell Jill Burrell that we'll keep them long-term.'

'Our Billy will be pleased.' Tom grinned. 'And so will Tracey. As for Claire . . . well, she might not show it but at least she'll see that we're ready to stand by her – and who knows? – that might be all it takes to bring her out of her shell.'

'I don't think it's going to be quite that easy, but at least we'll be taking a step in the right direction and then . . . well, we'll just have to wait and see, won't we? Like you said, time is a great healer.' Molly smiled at him and then, content with their decision, they lapsed into a compatible silence.

Almost a week later, Claire and Tracey arrived home from school to find their social worker waiting for them. Molly and Tom were standing behind her and Billy was playing on the hearthrug with the cat. In the middle of the room the table was piled with party fare, and Claire glared at them all suspiciously as she gripped Tracey's hand.

'What's this, then?' she asked shortly. 'Packin' us off, are yer, an' havin' a party to celebrate?'

'Actually, Claire, it's quite the reverse.' Jill led her to the settee and Tracey followed apprehensively.

Once they were both seated, Jill smiled at them. 'Right then, girls, I have something to tell you and I hope you'll both think it's good news. I know the past months have been difficult for you, but hopefully, from now on things will get better.' She nodded towards Molly and Tom. 'As we all know, it hasn't been possible for you to return home to your mum and we're all aware that this must have been very hard for you both. The Department has become responsible for your well-being and we've had lots of meetings to try and decide what will be best for you. Obviously, our main concern has been to try and keep you both together, and Molly and Tom have come up with the ideal solution because they have agreed that you can both stay here. So, from now on this will be your home.'

Tracey responded immediately by flashing Molly and Tom a brilliant smile before asking excitedly, 'Does that mean we can stay 'ere for ever and ever?'

Delighted at her response, Molly beamed, 'Yes, love, you can stay for ever and ever – and even longer than that if you want to.'

Tracey ran to Molly and hugged her around her ample waist. Claire stood up and stared at her indifferently, then turning she walked towards the door leading to the hallway.

'Molly's prepared a bit of a party for you – Claire, aren't you going to stay?' Jill asked.

Claire simply shrugged. 'I'm not very hungry,' she said quietly, then feeling that something was expected of her, she looked towards Molly and Tom. 'Thanks for lettin' us stay,' she mumbled, and without another word she made her way up to her room with the cat close on her heels, leaving Molly to stare sadly after her.

Once upstairs, she lifted Copper gently onto the bed and began to pace up and down restlessly. Her feet made no sound on the deep pile carpet as she stared around her. She knew that this house was worthy of Nob's End. Her bedroom boasted every luxury she had ever dreamed of, but it wasn't home. It would never be home, and she hated every inch of it, just as she hated Molly and Tom. Oh, they might pretend to be kind but Claire could see right through them. They were adults, and as far as she was concerned, adults were not to be trusted. Not a single one of them. Already they were taking Tracey away from her. And as for Jill . . . Claire's face flushed with temper as she thought of her downstairs playing the do-gooder. 'Silly old cow,' she muttered to the ginger cat, then dropping heavily onto her dressing-table stool she glared at her reflection in the mirror. 'I'll show 'em,' she promised herself. 'One day I'll show 'em all. Never mind this silly *from now on this will be your home* business. The day I'm sixteen I'll be out o' here like a shot an' I'll take Tracey with me, whether they like it or not.'

Her face crumpled as she thought of Tracey, and angrily she brushed the scalding tears from her cheeks with the back of her hand. Last night she had crept along the landing to kiss her sister goodnight, only to find Molly already there, reading her a story. Claire had crept away unnoticed, feeling strangely rejected and acutely aware of how much Tracey had changed. She had gained weight and laughed a lot more now. In fact, she seemed to be happy again, and Claire could only watch with resentment as she saw the bond between her younger sister and her foster family grow. Claire wondered why Tracey couldn't see through the Garretts as she could. They were false, she was sure of it. But they would never hurt her, ever, because she was determined that she would never grow close enough to allow them to.

71

Crossing to the bed, she lifted the cat and cradled him against her as tears coursed down her pale cheeks. 'Someday soon they'll *all* start to pay,' she vowed to him. And the day came sooner than she expected.

It was perfect weather in the first three weeks back at school after the summer holidays, a real Indian summer. This lunchtime, Claire was sitting in a secluded corner of the playground, just wiping the sweat from her forehead, when from around the corner Melanie Wilson's voice carried to her. Unobserved, Claire became still as a statue and listened intently.

'Oh God, ain't he just to *die* for?' Melanie swooned.

Careful not to be seen, Claire peeped around the corner to try and see the target of Melanie's affections. On the school playing-field, a group of boys were playing football, and as Claire watched, she saw Melanie's eyes follow one particular boy's every move.

'Huh,' one of Melanie's friends giggled, 'you've got about as much chance o' gettin' off with Craig Thomas as pie in the sky. There ain't a girl in the whole school who ain't got their cap set at him.'

Melanie sniffed, offended. 'I could have him if I wanted,' she retorted, and as Claire settled back into her corner, an idea began to form. She thought back to all the times that Melanie had taunted and humiliated her, and a smile played around her lips. 'Right then, Miss Melanie bloody Wilson, now it's *my* turn,' she whispered, as the bell rang for afternoon lessons.

That evening when everyone else was in bed, Claire locked herself into the bathroom, stood under the shower and washed her hair, as well as methodically scrubbing every inch of herself. When she was done she stole back to her bedroom and sat at her dressing-table. After drying her hair with the little drier Molly had given her, she pulled the brush through it until it shone and spilled across her slim shoulders. Her long blond hair looked gorgeous, and she grinned. Next she opened the box of make-up that Molly had bought her for her thirteenth birthday last year and which, up until now, had remained unopened in a drawer. Now she applied it just as she had seen her mother apply hers a million times. When she was satisfied with the result, she peeled off her dressing-gown and stared in awe at her developing breasts as they pushed against her nightshirt. Normally she kept them hidden beneath layers of baggy clothes, even on the hottest of days. But now, instead of eyeing them with repugnance she saw them as a means of wreaking her revenge, and she could scarcely wait for the next morning to arrive.

Tracey was eating her breakfast when Claire entered the kitchen the next morning, and her eyes almost popped from her head, as did Molly's. 'My God, Claire, what have you done to yerself?' Tracey gasped. 'You look beautiful!'

Claire tossed her head cockily. 'I'm doin' what I should have done ages ago,' she replied. 'I'm makin' the best o' meself.'

Molly placed a bowl of cereal in front of her. 'You look lovely,' she said tactfully, 'but don't you think you ought to tone the make-up down just a little bit? After all, you are going to school, not to a disco.'

Claire shrugged defiantly. 'If you don't like it then you'll have to lump it,' she said insolently. 'You're always on at me to smarten meself up an' then when I do, you moan about it.'

Frowning, Molly turned away. The rest of the meal was eaten in silence and when Claire eventually left for school Molly watched her go through the kitchen window, still amazed at the transformation.

Her arrival at school caused heads to turn and Claire was pleased with the effect her new image was having. Boys who had never even looked at her before suddenly stopped to stare appreciatively as she boldly sauntered past them. At break-time, instead of hiding herself away in a corner, she positioned herself on the edge of the football field. Soon, just as she had hoped, she saw Craig Thomas and his friends heading towards her. She walked directly into his path and when he was no more than an arm's length away, she suddenly dropped her bag, spilling its contents all over the grass. Craig, who had been deep in conversation, glared at Claire, ready to make a harsh comment, but it died on his lips.

'Oh, I'm sorry,' she apologised charmingly, bending to gather her belongings, and immediately he stooped to help her, his football game temporarily forgotten.

'It's all right. Here – let me help you.' Within seconds the spilled items were retrieved and as they stood back up, he said, 'I haven't seen you before, have I?'

Claire shrugged. 'I should think so, but you're in Year Eleven and I'm in Year Nine so you probably haven't noticed me.'

'Huh, I can't believe I wouldn't have noticed *you*,' he muttered, and as Claire spotted Melanie Wilson on the touchline glaring at her in disbelief, she experienced a thrill of pure pleasure and wished that the moment could last for ever.

As she began to move towards Melanie, Craig fell into step. 'What are you doing tonight?' he asked.

It was all Claire could do to stop herself from laughing aloud as she replied, 'I'm not doing anything in particular. Why, what did you have in mind?'

By now they were almost adjacent with Melanie, and Claire grinned at her spitefully as they passed.

'I thought perhaps you might like to come out with me?'

Claire had the satisfaction of seeing Melanie turn a puce colour.

'What time do you have to be in?' the boy went on, moving past Melanie as though she was invisible.

Claire sniffed. 'Whenever I like,' she lied, then after arranging a meeting-place, she flashed him a smile and strolled away.

After the evening meal, Claire opened her wardrobe door and began to sift through her clothes, many of the items as yet unworn. She had just selected a pair of jeans and a top when there was a tap on her bedroom door and Molly entered.

'Off out then, love, are you?' She was pleased that Claire was finally making the effort and yet apprehensive all at the same time.

Claire nodded but said nothing.

'Well, where are you off to then? Somewhere nice, is it?'

Claire rolled her eyes. 'Look, it's no big deal – I'm just goin' to see a friend, that's all. I would have thought you'd be pleased. You've been naggin' me long enough to get out an' about.'

'Oh, I *am* pleased, love,' Molly assured her quickly. 'But just be careful, eh? An' don't forget it's school tomorrow, so be in for nine.'

When Claire ignored her and carried on getting ready, Molly turned and left, closing the door quietly behind her.

Twenty minutes later, Molly heard the front door slam and beckoned Tom to follow her into the kitchen.

He rose from the dining-room table where he was helping Tracey and Billy with a jigsaw puzzle. 'I'll be back in a minute, kids. The boss is callin' me.' He winked at them, and turning, he hurried after his wife.

'Right then, woman, what's up?' he demanded when the door was closed behind him.

Molly gulped. 'I don't know what's up really. It's just . . . Did you see Claire just now when she went out? She looked so . . . so, well . . . grown up.'

He sighed with exasperation. 'Come on, love, what do you expect? She is nearly fourteen, you know. It's perfectly normal at her age to want to go out with her friends, an' dress up a bit. I can't understand you. You've been telling her long enough to do it, an' now she is, you're fretting.'

'I suppose you're right,' she admitted. 'It's just me worrying for nothing, I expect. I can't wrap her in cottonwool, can I?'

'No, you can't, love.' He smiled at her. 'So come on, let's get back to this jigsaw. She'll be in for nine, you'll see.'

It was almost half-past ten when Claire eventually did arrive home to find Molly pacing up and down the kitchen.

'Just where the hell have you been?' she demanded, the second Claire put her foot through the door. Claire simply stared insolently back at her.

'I hope you know, young lady, that I've been worried *sick*. Don't you *ever* do this again, do you hear me? When I tell you to be in for nine, I *mean* nine.'

As Claire made to pass her, Molly put her hand out to halt her. Her anger and worry were already being replaced by an overwhelming sense of relief that the girl was safe, but Claire didn't care about Molly's feelings and her eyes flashed angrily as she confronted her.

'Don't you dare try tellin' me what I can an' can't do,' she snapped. 'I'll do as I please. You ain't me mam an' you never will be.'

There was so much hatred in her voice that Molly's hand dropped to her side as Claire stalked past her and clattered up the stairs. She threw open her bedroom door then banged it to behind her. Copper stirred and stretched lazily, then flexing his claws he curled into a ball on her pillow and went back to sleep.

Claire was in turmoil as she began to stride up and down her room. As she caught sight of herself in the mirror, her lip curled with contempt.

'Well, that's it then. I've done it,' she told herself, and a huge choking lump began to form in her throat. Crossing to her bedside drawers, she withdrew the diary that Molly had bought her last Christmas and the small key that would unlock it. Sinking onto the end of the bed she snatched up a pen and began to scribble.

Tonight I had sex with Craig Thomas. She paused. Usually, being able to write her feelings down brought her a measure of peace. But tonight they were so confused that they refused to transmit themselves onto the paper so eventually she flung the diary back into the drawer in frustration. Standing back up, she hastily began to undress and toss her clothes about the floor. She surveyed her naked body in the mirror, shivering with revulsion as she remembered the feel of Craig's hot eager hands, and the awful wave of nausea that had risen in her when he had tried to kiss her. She screwed her eyes tight shut, trying to block out the image, but no matter how hard she tried, the feeling of being unclean and worthless remained, and she knew then that it always would. In her head she heard Melanie Wilson taunting her: '*You can't make a silk purse out of a sow's ear.*' Perhaps Melanie had been right, but now it was Claire's turn for revenge. She knew that tomorrow, word would sweep around the school about what had happened tonight, and that at least would afford her some satisfaction. But the price of revenge had cost her dearly, because tonight she had realised that she would never be able to love anybody ever again. The pain she was experiencing was so intense that she longed to find relief in tears. But none came, and as she stood there, the self-loathing and a feeling of wicked injustice magnified. At last she dragged herself away from the mirror, unable to bear looking at herself a minute longer. She might as well go to bed.

Her eyes fell on the open bedside drawer and as she moved close to it, something in its far corner glittered and caught her attention. Lifting it, she carried it to her dressing-table, and sat on the stool, studying it. It was her mother's brooch. Claire had unpinned it from her coat on the day that she and Tracey had been taken into care. The spray of green flowers was cheap and garish, and seemed somehow to sum up Claire's whole life. As she fingered it scornfully, she laughed. A terrible laugh full of bitterness and disillusionment.

'*You've done this to me, you cow,*' she swore, as if the brooch could somehow conjure up the person who had worn it. '*You've ruined me whole life, an' then walked away an' left me. But you can't hurt me now. Nobody can, not ever again. You bitch, I hate you. I'm so screwed up I can't even cry now, do you know that?*'

Slowly she undid the rusty clasp and lifted the sharp bent pin to the soft skin of her inner arm. She scraped it down and watched with satisfaction as the superficial wound opened and leaked scarlet drops. '*I hate you, I hate you,*' she chanted over and over. '*I wish you were dead.*' Again and again she tore at herself until at last crimson rivulets of blood coursed down her arm and dripped like tears onto her dressing-table.

Copper, sensing Claire's distress, jumped off the bed and began to rub against her legs and purr with agitation, and it was he that pulled her back from her trance-like state. Suddenly flinging the brooch across the room, she gathered him into her arms and then at last she cried, great tearing sobs that racked her body.

'From now on, Copper,' she swore, 'whoever wants me can have me – but by God, they'll pay. You mark my words, they'll pay, every last one of 'em.'

Still naked, she crept into bed and the big ginger cat watched in silence as her tears fell to mingle with the tears of blood that oozed from her arm.

Chapter Nine

'Ooh, Claire, the lights were lovely, weren't they?' Tracey whispered. It was dark in her room, and the time showed – 10.05 – on her luminous bedside Mickey Mouse clock.

Claire nodded as she tucked the blanket around Tracey. 'Yes, they were, but you know what, I'm gettin' a bit sick of hearin' about them. Anybody would think we'd been on a bloody Caribbean cruise instead of a week in Blackpool. We've been back for three weeks now an' you ain't hardly stopped talkin' about it.'

Tracey pouted. 'I'm sorry. It's just . . . well, the seaside were so much better than I ever thought it would be. An' Molly an' Tom have said that next year we can go to Yarmouth. They've been there before an' Billy says it's great.'

'Yes – well, next year's a long way away, so for now I suggest you get your head down an' get some sleep.'

Instead of doing as she was told, Tracey pulled herself up onto her elbow and stared at Claire intently. 'Why are you all dressed up?' she breathed. 'Molly an' Tom went to bed ages ago an' it's really late. You ain't goin' to sneak out again, are you?'

Claire flushed angrily. 'What do you mean, sneak out? What are you on about, Trace?'

Her sister grinned knowingly. 'I know you go out, 'cos I've heard you. An' sometimes I hear you come back in, an' all.' She yawned. 'One o' these days Molly will hear you too, an' then you'll be in trouble.'

'That's for me to worry about, not you,' Claire said tightly. 'So just mind yer own business an' get off to sleep, eh? What Molly don't know can't hurt her. An' I ain't doin' nobody any 'arm.'

'I think you're bein' unfair,' Tracey declared. 'Molly loves us, but all you ever do is be horrible to her. Why can't you be nice to her?'

'Oh, just go to sleep!' Angry now, Claire headed for the door, and as Tracey heard it close behind her, she snuggled down into the bed and sighed sadly.

At breakfast the next morning, Molly opened her purse and scratched her head in bewilderment. 'I could have sworn when I left this on the table last night that it had a five-pound note in it.'

Claire felt Tracey's eyes on her and glared at her across the table. Tracey immediately looked down and began to push her Weetabix around the bowl.

Completely oblivious to the tense atmosphere, Billy scraped his chair back from the table and snatched up his schoolbag. 'I'm off,' he declared. 'Are you comin', Tracey?'

Grateful of a chance to escape, she nodded and joined him as Molly handed them both their tuck money and kissed them, and in seconds they were gone.

'Have a good day, kids,' Molly called after them and she was answered with two big warm smiles. Once she and Claire were alone, she looked at the girl tentatively. 'I don't suppose you'd have any idea where the money might have gone, would you, Claire?'

Claire rounded on her as she shrugged into her coat. 'How should *I* know where your money's gone? What you tryin' to say – do you think that *I've* had it?'

'No, no of course I don't think that,' Molly hastily assured her. 'But it is strange, isn't it? That's the third five-pound note that's gone missin' in the last two weeks.'

'Well, tough. I ain't had it, so if I were you I'd get me facts straight before I started accusin' people.'

'But I'm not—' Molly's words fell on deaf ears as Claire swung about and slammed out, leaving the woman to stare after her.

It was a bitterly cold day in February 1986 when Jill Burrell struggled up Molly's path through a sheet of driving rain. Once inside, she and Molly sat in the lounge with a tray of tea in front of them and laughed as Jill's damp clothes began to steam in the heat from the gas fire. As Jill noted the dark circles under Molly's eyes she asked quietly, 'So how are things then?'

Molly ran her hand distractedly through her thick dark hair. 'If I was to be perfectly honest, I'd have to say that things are going from bad to worse,' she admitted. 'Last year, I reckon Claire must have gone out with nearly every lad in the school. She treats them like muck. She won't come in when I tell her, and if I try and ground her she just laughs in me face. She's a law unto herself, that young madam. An' her language . . . Huh! It's enough to turn the air blue.'

Jill listened sympathetically as Molly continued, 'As if that wasn't bad enough, she's now taken to going out with older chaps – mostly lorry drivers that she picks up down at the lorry park in town. She was so drunk when she came in last night that I had to get Tom to help me get her up the stairs. I've tried talking to her but she just blanks me out. And to tell you the truth, I don't know what to try next. I just feel so . . . so useless.'

'You're not useless and it's not your fault,' Jill reassured her. 'You're doing all you can. Up until now Claire has refused any sort of counselling that I've suggested. Unfortunately that can only come when she's ready for it. She has to come to terms with her past in her own mind before she can talk about it to anybody else – and you and I both know that sometimes that can take a very long time.'

Molly nodded. 'I do know that, Jill, but my worry is what could happen to her in the meantime.'

The two women looked at each other and for the next hour they spoke of Claire, Tracey, and Billy, and of how Molly was trying desperately to turn them all into a family unit, because to Molly and Tom, that was what they were now. A family – and she loved each and every one of them.

Winter gave way to spring. Tracey and Billy were bickering light-heartedly over breakfast one morning when Molly interrupted their banter to ask, 'Where's Claire, is she up yet? She'll need to get a move on else she'll be late for school again.'

Swallowing a mouthful of soft-boiled egg, Tracey looked up. 'She's bad,' she told Molly solemnly. 'I heard her bein' sick in the toilet an' then she went back to bed.'

'Ah well, if that's the case, then bed is the best place for her. Best leave her be. Now come on, you two, shake a leg. When I've got shot of you little monsters I'll go up an' see if she needs anything.' Molly kept her voice light but inside she felt uneasy.

It was as the children were leaving for school that Tracey became serious and paused to look at Molly from troubled eyes. 'Claire will be all right, won't she?' she asked fearfully. 'She was bein' really sick when I heard her.'

'Ugh,' groaned Billy in disgust, and Molly laughed as she shooed them through the door.

'Of course she'll be all right,' she said cheerily. 'She's probably just picked up a tummy bug, that's all. Now come on, off with the pair of you.'

Pacified, Tracey skipped away, leaving Molly to clear the dirty pots into the sink. Shortly afterwards she crept upstairs to check on Claire and finding her fast asleep, she went away again, reluctant to disturb her.

Claire was sick again the following morning so once more Molly kept her off school and begged Claire to let her ring the doctor. Claire adamantly refused to see him, but when she was no better the following morning, Molly would not allow her to put it off any longer.

'Right then, young lady,' she said in a stern voice, 'this has gone on for quite long enough. I've made us an appointment with the doctor for eleven o'clock this morning. So here, slip this on an' go an' get yourself washed and dressed.' Unhooking Claire's dressing-gown from the back of the door, she tossed it onto the bed.

'I'm not goin',' Claire declared, staring back at Molly from red-rimmed eyes.

Molly placed her hands on her hips and stared back at her. 'Right then, fine, I'll give you a choice. Either you get dressed right now and come with me, or I'll ring the doctor and ask him to come here. But I'm telling you, Claire, one way or another you are seein' that doctor today whether you like it or not.'

Claire groaned as she pulled herself up onto the pillows. 'Oh, all right, all right, piss off an' let me get dressed then.'

Molly was so relieved that she chose to ignore her bad language. 'That's better. Now while you're getting dressed, would you like me to make you a bit of breakfast?'

At the mere mention of food, Claire felt vomit rise in her throat again. 'I don't want anythin',' she gasped, and flew past Molly, arriving at the bathroom only just in time to deposit the entire contents of her stomach down the toilet.

Molly raised her eyes to the sky. 'Oh, dear God, please don't let what I'm thinking be right,' she prayed.

Her prayer went unanswered and she and Claire made the return bus ride home from the doctor's later that morning in total silence, each shocked at the news he had imparted to them. Once they were back in the privacy of the kitchen, Claire sat down heavily at the table. Her face was as grey as putty and Molly bustled away to put the kettle on.

It was only when she placed a mug of tea in front of Claire and sat down opposite her that she finally spoke. 'Are you all right, love?' she enquired kindly.

Claire, who had been waiting for Molly to start screaming at her, began to cry. 'O' course I ain't all right. How can I be? I'm bloody pregnant, ain't I?'

Molly's heart went out to her. 'Well, love, it's not the end o' the world,' she said softly. 'You're not the first an' I'm sure you won't be the last. Would you like to tell me who the father is?'

But Claire folded her arms across her chest and remained stubbornly silent.

Molly sighed and went on, 'The dilemma you have to face now is what you're going to do about it. As the doctor explained to you, you've got three options. There's abortion, although that would worry me sick if you decided to take that path, with you being so far gone. There's adoption, or you can have the baby and keep it. I know none of them are easy decisions but I'll tell you now, whatever you decide, Tom and I will stand by you – an' if you decide that you do want to keep the baby then it will be as welcome here as you are.'

Claire had the urge to throw herself into Molly's arms, but fighting it she pushed her tea away and stood up. 'I'm goin' to me room,' she said shortly, and as Molly watched her go, her chin sank onto her chest and she cried at this latest injustice.

Three days later, Claire made her decision known. Molly and Tom were seated in the lounge watching television when Claire walked in and faced them.

'I've decided,' she told them coldly. 'I'm goin' to give the baby up for adoption as soon as it's born.'

Molly's heart seemed to turn a somersault in her chest. 'Oh, Claire. Look, love, you don't have to decide just yet. It's such a big decision. If you give this baby away, you might regret it for the rest of your life.' She would have said more but Tom squeezed her hand to silence her. Unknown to Claire, Tracey had followed her into the room and had heard every word she said. The younger girl had been struggling to come to terms with the fact that Claire was really going to have a real live baby, but now as she listened to Claire's harsh decision she began to cry softly and added her protests to Molly's.

'You can't just give the baby away, Claire.' She stared at her sister, distraught. 'I'll help you look after it, if that's what you're worried about. Honest I will, an' you'll help too, won't you, Molly?' She sidled up to Molly who stroked her hair soothingly, but Claire was unmoved.

'I've made me decision,' she said callously. 'An' nothing you lot, the social workers or a million bloody counsellors can say will make me change me mind. So that's the end of it.'

Turning on her heel, she then stamped out of the room, leaving them all to stare after her open-mouthed.

During the following months Claire watched her waistline thicken with a sense of revulsion. She felt as if this thing growing inside her was the ultimate violation of her body, and could hardly wait to be rid of it. She stayed in her room, only venturing out when she had to, even refusing to attend ante-natal classes, though Molly constantly begged and bullied her to try and get her to go. The school sent her home-work to do weekly but it was flung into the back of a drawer and forgotten.

When Jill came to see her, which was regularly, Claire refused to speak to her and Molly became more and more frustrated as she saw Claire effectively shutting herself off from the world.

Thankfully the pregnancy passed uneventfully until, one calm September night towards her due date she was woken by a dull throbbing pain in the small of her back. Cursing, she dragged herself from the bed and began to pad up and down the room. The cramping sensation increased and Claire began to swear at the pain of it. Suddenly she felt a warm gush of liquid flood from between her legs. Appalled, she stared at the pool of water beneath her that was slowly sinking into the carpet. 'Oh Christ, now look, I've gone an' wet meself,' she muttered, and at that moment there was a tap on the bedroom door.

Pushing it slightly open, Molly peeped around it to ask, 'Is everything all right, love? I heard you up and about and I wondered if . . .' Realising what was happening at a glance, she stopped mid-sentence. In a second she was across the room as Claire hung her head in shame.

'I've wet meself, Molly, I'm sorry,' she said miserably.

Molly grinned. 'You haven't wet yourself at all, love. Your waters have broken.'

Claire looked back at her with fear in her eyes. 'What does that mean?'

Molly patted her hand reassuringly. 'It means that this baby is well on its way. Now you just get back on the bed and lie still. I'm going to run and get dressed and call an ambulance. And don't look so frightened – everything's going to be all right, you'll see.'

The ambulance arrived within minutes, and as Molly helped Claire towards it, Tom, who was still in his dressing-gown, watched them from the doorway.

'Good luck, love,' he called.

As Claire looked back at him, she had an overwhelming urge to run back into the house.

Tom waved to them until they were out of sight. 'May God help her,' he muttered. 'The poor little sod's going to need all the help she can get.' Sadly, he then went back up to his lonely bed, where he spent the rest of the night tossing and turning.

The next morning, Molly phoned him from the hospital to report that as yet, the baby still seemed to be a long way from being born. Tom listened with concern before going to rouse Tracey and Billy, who plagued him with questions.

'Claire will be all right, won't she, Tom?' Tracey asked fearfully.

He flashed her a false smile. 'Of course she will,' he promised, but as soon as he had seen the kids off to school, the smile slid from his face. He rang into work to take the day off, then hovered by the phone, waiting anxiously for news.

The morning passed slowly. In the delivery room, Molly constantly mopped the sweat from Claire's brow and encouraged her. 'That's it, love, you're doing fine, just fine. It won't be long now.'

Claire barely heard her as one terrible contraction followed another. At last she turned her tortured face to Molly's. 'I . . . I can't do this,' she whispered.

Molly shook her head. 'Oh yes, you bloody well can,' she told her firmly as she stared into Claire's pain-filled eyes.

Just then the midwife exclaimed. 'One more big push now, there's a good girl! I can see the baby's head.'

Molly gripped Claire's hand. 'Now then, you heard that. Come on, hold on tight to me and push.'

Gritting her teeth, Claire clutched Molly's hand so hard that her knuckles turned white.

'*That's it, that's it!*' Molly shouted encouragingly, and with a last desperate effort Claire pushed with all her might. Seconds later, the sound of a newborn baby's cry rent the air and tears of joy and wonder spurted from Molly's eyes as Claire sank back exhausted onto the pillows.

'Oh, Claire,' she whispered in awe. 'Look . . . you've got a beautiful little girl.'

The midwife lifted the tiny infant and placed her onto Claire's chest, and Molly held her breath as the new mother surveyed her baby for the first time. For months, Claire had prepared herself for this moment. But what she hadn't prepared for was the rush of emotion that surged through her. The baby was perfect in every way, and as Claire gazed at her, she stopped crying and lay content on her mother's breast.

Molly's eyes were soft as she witnessed the bond between mother and daughter, but then suddenly to everyone's surprise, Claire looked away, her face hardening.

'Take her away, I'm not keepin' her,' she ordered.

Molly gasped. 'Oh Claire, you can't mean it?'

'I *do* mean it. I told you I didn't want her an' I meant it. Now take her away . . . *please*.'

Gently the midwife lifted the infant and wrapped her in a towel, then passing her to a waiting nurse she beckoned Molly from the room.

'Give her time,' she urged.

Molly nodded, but knowing Claire as she did, she was afraid that she had made her final decision.

In the room next door, the young nurse who was bathing the baby looked up as the midwife joined her. 'She's a hard one, isn't she?' she muttered. 'Fancy having a lovely little baby like this and then giving her away.'

The midwife sighed. 'I think you've still got an awful lot to learn yet, Nurse, and I'm not just speaking from a medical point of view.'

The young nurse paused to raise her eyebrows questioningly. 'What do you mean?'

'Sometimes mothers can feel pain far worse than any labour,' the older woman said wisely. 'That girl in there is little more than a child herself, and Molly is her foster mum, which leaves us to ask, where is her real mum? Oh, I know Claire is putting a hard face on, but didn't you see the look in her eyes when I laid the baby on her chest? I think she really wants this baby, but perhaps something in her past has made her feel unable to keep it. I don't know, of course – all I'm saying is that sometimes in this job you need to stand back and look a little deeper.'

The nurse nodded slowly as she lifted Claire's baby from the water and began to gently pat her dry, thinking on her superior's words.

Much later that night, when silence had descended on the ward, Claire climbed painfully from her bed. She crept along the corridor and paused outside the nurses' staff room. On the other side of the door she could hear the women laughing and chatting as they enjoyed a well-earned tea break; satisfied, she hurried on to the nursery. Once there she peered through the window at all the tiny cribs then, with a furtive glance across her shoulder, she carefully inched the door open and stole inside. She found her baby within seconds and stood gazing at her with a look of wonder on her face. Claire was sure that she was easily the most beautiful baby in the room, and unable to resist the temptation any longer, she plucked her gently from the crib and cradled her in her arms. The child awoke and stared up at Claire with eyes that were exactly the same colour as her own.

'Hello, sweetheart.' The baby stared back at her solemnly as if listening to her every word. In her short life, Claire had felt tremendous pain but it was nothing at all compared to the pain that she was experiencing now, for she knew that this would be the only time she would ever hold her baby, or ever see her again. 'I'm sorry I can't keep you,' she said brokenly, and her tears ran freely and dripped onto the baby's shawl. 'But you see, I've got nothin' to offer you. I'm bad. An' I know out there somewhere is a *real* mum an' dad who will love you an' see that you never want for nothin'. You'll have everything I never had.' She nuzzled her face into the soft skin of her tiny daughter's neck. 'But wherever you are, I'll think of you every single day,' she promised, and she knew then that when she signed the adoption papers she would be signing away a tiny part of herself. Tenderly she laid the child back into the crib. 'Goodbye, Yasmin.' She felt as if her heart was breaking. 'Have a good life, an' always know that I love you.'

She crept back the way she had come. Unobserved, the young nurse who had condemned her earlier watched her from the sluice room.

'Well, I'll be damned,' she muttered as she noted Claire's tear-drenched face, and as she continued with the unenviable task of washing out the bedpans, she thought back to the midwife's words. So she was right, she told herself. I won't be so quick to judge in future. As she continued with her task she realised that she had just learned a very valuable lesson.

Chapter Ten

Three days later, Claire was discharged from hospital. As Molly drove her home in the car she made a few half-hearted attempts at conversation, but they met with no response so eventually she lapsed into silence. When she reversed the car onto the drive, Claire got out and made her way inside.

The first person she saw was Tracey, who stared at her coldly. 'So you left her then?' she said accusingly. 'How *could* you, Claire? How could you just give a baby away as if she were nothin', especially knowin' how we felt when we found out our mam didn't want us?'

Claire's eyes flashed as all the pain she was feeling surfaced. 'Oh, grow up, Tracey!' she hissed. 'How could I have kept her? Would you want her to have the sort o' life we did?'

'Huh, don't make that an excuse,' Tracey retorted. 'We ain't got that sort o' life now, have we? We've got Molly an' Tom, an' we'd all have helped you to look after her. We told you often enough we would. And I'd have been her auntie.' The girl's lip trembled.

'Yes, well at the end o' the day she was my baby, not yours, or Molly's – or Tom's for that matter! I made the decision, 'cos do you know what? I'm sick o' people runnin' me life. This time I'm doin' what *I* want to do, an' if you don't like it, then you'll just have to lump it, won't you? You're only ten years old so how would you know what's for the best?'

With that, Claire ran up the stairs and locked herself into her room. She barely came out for six whole weeks, until eventually the day came when Jill Burrell arrived with the papers to be signed that would release the baby for adoption.

Claire stared at them spread out before her on the coffee-table.

'Are you quite sure about this, Claire?' Jill asked gently and silently the girl nodded.

Reluctantly, Jill handed her a pen and Claire hastily scribbled her name. Now there could be no going back. It was done.

'You can rest assured that we'll find your baby a wonderful home,' Jill promised as she collected the papers together, then suddenly rememenbereing something, she reached into her briefcase and withdrew a plain brown envelope. 'I almost forgot. The young nurse at the hospital who attended the birth asked me to give you this.' She held it out and when Claire made no attempt to take it, Jill placed it on the coffee-table and rose. 'I'll be off now then,' she said quietly, and nodding at Tom she followed Molly to the door.

Claire lifted the envelope and went to her room, where she slit it open. Inside was a photograph of Yasmin fast asleep in her crib, and as she stared at it, the tears that had been threatening throughout the long day suddenly spurted from her eyes.

'What have I done?' she whispered brokenly as she rocked to and fro. But then with an almightly effort she calmed herself and pushed the photograph into her diary. 'It's done now, no more chance to weaken,' she told herself, and her heart hardened. 'Now I can get on with the rest o' me life.'

Claire quietly inserted the key into the lock and crept into the dark kitchen. The light suddenly clicked on and she blinked as Molly and Tom confronted her. Molly was absolutely furious and made no attempt to hide it.

'Do you know that it's almost three o'clock in the morning, miss?' she hissed. 'Just where the *hell* have you been again?'

Claire stared back at her boldly. 'I should have thought that were as plain as the nose on your face. I've been out,' she quipped defiantly.

Molly's head bobbed. 'Yes, that's more than obvious, and no doubt you've been with that Mark again. I'm telling you, no good can come of you behaving like this, Claire. He's too old for you. Does he know that you're only just sixteen and still at school?' Thank God their doctor had put Claire on the Pill, she thought. At least there would be no more babies.

'Yes, he does,' Claire lied, her fury matching Molly's, and Tom, who had uttered not a word, glanced nervously from one to the other.

Molly thumped the table in her frustration. 'Oh Claire, can't you *see* what you're doing to yourself? Look at you! I hoped that being in a new school, making a fresh start, you'd knuckle down a bit. You've only got a few months to go, and then you can leave an' get a job. You should be doing your homework and studying for your GCSE exams, not carrying on like this. You're deliberately wrecking all your chances. And there's another thing. Don't you realise how much danger you're putting yourself in?'

Claire laughed – a cold hard sound. 'Ain't nobody can hurt me,' she bragged, and as Molly's anger slowly dissolved she sank onto a chair.

'Look, Claire,' she tried to reason, 'me an' Tom, well . . . I'll tell you the truth, we're about at the end of our tether. You've pushed us to the limit and I don't know how much more of this we can take. Nothing we do seems to get through to you. I know you've been missing whole days off school to go off on runs with your lorry-driver boyfriend, and I also know that it's you that's been stealing from my purse; I'm having to hide it now. Why, *why* do you do it when you know that if you want anything, all you have to do is ask?'

'So, what you sayin' then? Are you plannin' on sendin' me away, is that what you're tryin' to tell me?' Claire was suddenly fearful when Molly didn't deny it.

'All I'm saying is this.' Molly dropped her eyes and sadly shook her head. 'Things can't go on like this. Your behaviour is beginning to have a bad effect on Tracey and Billy now, not to mention me and Tom. And somewhere along the line, if you don't at least try, well . . . then we'll have no choice but to say enough is enough.'

A terrible silence descended on the room as Claire absorbed Molly's words, and then Molly made a final desperate effort as she told her, 'Claire, we don't want to lose you. We love you and we just want to be a family, that's all. All we're asking is that you just toe the line a bit. Show us a little respect and come in when we tell you.'

But the damage was done and indignantly, Claire flounced away without another word. Once in her room she crossed to the window and gazed out. *So this is it*, she told herself. *Now they're gonna get rid of me an' all.* She tried to ignore the little voice in her head that whispered, *Serves you right.* And it was then that a frightening realisation dawned on her. Despite all the promises that she had ever made to herself, she found that she *loved* Molly and Tom. But now, just like every other adult that she had ever loved, she was about to lose them too. She ached to throw herself into

Molly's arms and tell her that she was sorry. That she couldn't seem to help the way she was behaving. But her pride, and the barrier she had built around herself, would not allow her to do it.

Her thoughts turned to her baby, Yasmin, and the pain deepened. And then she thought of Tracey, sleeping peacefully along the landing. When they had first come here, Tracey wouldn't even allow Molly to bath her without Claire being present, but even she didn't need her any more. Nobody did – and in that instant, the girl knew what she must do. She would run away where nobody would ever find her. Better that than suffer the indignity of being just another disruptive placement, being shipped off from one foster home to another. She would go somewhere where she could become anyone she wanted to be. Not Claire McMullen, used, abused and unloved. With her mind made up, she crept into bed and began to make her plans.

The next day after school, Claire hurried home to change, and without even waiting to eat the meal that Molly had prepared for her, she rushed away to meet Mark. It was a half-mile walk from Molly's home into Nuneaton town centre, and as Claire crossed the Cock and Bear Bridge, her thoughts were deep and troubled. However, when she arrived at the lorry-park, her mood lightened as she saw Mark's lorry parked in its usual place. She had been seeing Mark Blake for some weeks and loved being able to brag that she was going out with an older man. He was so much more mature than the boys at school and she had learned quickly that if she played her cards right he was also very generous with his money.

Mark was leaning against the cab smoking and chatting to a group of men. As Claire approached him she revelled in their admiring glances. Mark's eyes lit up when he saw her and he eyed her up and down appreciatively.

'Hello, darlin',' he welcomed her. 'Just finished work, have you?'

Claire didn't even bat an eyelid as she nodded. His friends began to disperse, winking at her as they went.

'I can't stop for long tonight,' she told him. 'I just called by to see where you were off to tomorrow.'

'I'm going to London,' Mark informed her. 'I'll be able to have a couple o' nights in me own bed.'

Delighted with his answer, Claire grinned. 'I don't suppose you could lend me a fiver, could you?' She ran her finger teasingly down his chest, and instantly he dipped his hand into his back pocket and pressed a note into her hand.

'It must be great to have your own flat,' she said enviously as she tucked the money into her bag. Nodding, he pulled her towards him. He knew better now than to try and kiss her on the lips, so instead his eager tongue flicked around her neck as his hands roamed hungrily up and down her body. Claire basked in the feeling of power that his response evoked in her.

'That's it then, that's all you're getting for now,' she told him eventually.

His face echoed his disappointment. 'Ain't yer got time to climb in the cab fer a while?' he pleaded.

Claire shook her head. 'No, I ain't right now.' She disentangled herself from his arms. 'I've got something to do as won't wait. But don't worry – you'll be seein' me again sooner than you think.' With a final wink she swaggered away, leaving him to sigh with frustration.

She walked briskly until she came to the outskirts of Nuneaton and there she took the short-cut across the fields that separated her home village from the town. The plans she had made were falling into place, but before she could implement them there was something that she felt she must do. She needed to see her mother just one last time. Although the social workers had written to Karen to inform her of Claire's pregnancy and the adoption, there had been no reply, no contact whatsoever. It was months and months since Karen had even bothered to visit them, but tonight Claire was determined to see her.

The fields were dark, and more than once, Claire almost fell as her foot caught in a pothole. Still she hurried on. The darkness held no fear for her now. The darkness was her friend; in its shelter, she could allow her tears to fall unseen. And there had been so many of them. She had shed tears for her grandmother, who was only a fading memory now; tears for a father who had deserted her; tears for Tinker who had been the only loyal friend she had ever had. Tears for Tracey, who no longer needed her; tears for the baby she had loved too much to keep. Tears for her mother, who had not loved her enough to protect her. Tears for Molly and Tom, the substitute parents who just like everyone else she had ever loved were now about to send her away. And finally the bitterest tears of all; tears for the childhood of which she had been deprived. But there would be no more tears – of that Claire was determined. Tonight she would confront her mother for the very last time and tomorrow, her new life would begin.

In her mind she tried to picture their reunion. She intended to tell her mother just what she thought of her; of all the pain she had caused her. The girl imagined her mother grovelling and begging for forgiveness . . . She was so lost in thought that she was almost surprised when she found herself standing in front of her old home. She blinked in surprise, for the shabby council house looked so different that she could scarcely recognise it. The overgrown front garden that she remembered was now laid out with a neat lawn and borders, and looking beyond it she saw with amazement that there were pretty flowered curtains framing the living-room window. The light was on, and she could see the front room, lit up like a stage. A man sat in a chair by the fire reading a newspaper. As she watched, she saw a woman appear from the kitchen, followed by two children. Claire was bewildered. Where was her mother, and who was this family in her old home?

She nearly jumped out of her skin when someone suddenly placed a hand on her shoulder. Swinging around she found herself face to face with Mrs Tolly.

'Well, I'll be,' Mary Tolly gushed warmly. 'I thought it was you, Claire, but until I got a bit closer I couldn't be sure. Why, look at you – you're all grown up.'

Claire tried to answer her but was so confused that the words stuck in her throat.

'So what you doin' in this neck o' the woods then, love?' Mrs Tolly prattled on, then seeing the confusion on Claire's face she asked worriedly, 'You didn't come hoping to see yer mam, did you?'

'N . . . no,' Claire stuttered.

Mrs Tolly relaxed a little. 'Oh, that's good then, 'cos as you obviously know, she's been gone a good few months now. Word has it she buggered off wi' one of her fancy men – an' good riddance, that's what I said.' Her hand flew to her mouth. 'Oh, I'm sorry, love, I shouldn't have said that, I could bite me tongue off. She is your mam, after all.'

'It's all right, Mrs Tolly,' Claire assured her, but her stomach was turning over as the woman's words sank in. So that was why her mother hadn't written to them for so long, why she had never bothered attending any of the endless meetings or reviews, never known about the baby. She had simply walked away and forgotten all about her girls as if they meant nothing.

Mrs Tolly studied the girl's pale face in the light from the street-lamp. 'Look, pet, why don't you come in an' have a cup o' tea, eh?' she asked kindly. 'It's enough to freeze the hairs off a brass monkey out here. An' I know me old man would be tickled pink to see yer. Many a time he's asked after yer. In fact, we both have. Are you an' little Tracey all right? You're both living in Nuneaton now, ain't you?'

'Tracey's fine, thanks, Mrs Tolly,' Claire told her quietly. 'We both are. An' yes, we are livin' in Nuneaton but I . . . I can't stop now. If you don't mind, I have to get off.' As she started to back away, looking extremely uncomfortable, Mrs Tolly watched with sympathetic eyes although she did nothing to restrain her.

'All right, love, I won't keep yer. But it's been lovely to see you again. You're a good girl, Claire. Oh, and by the way, just before yer go – Mr Tolly buried Tinker for yer, just as he promised he would. He put him in our garden underneath the apple tree, all proper like.'

Unshed tears glistened on Claire's lashes and the need to be away was suddenly so strong that she had to fight the urge to turn and run.

'Thanks, Mrs Tolly,' she gulped, and as she turned away her heart felt as if it was breaking.

She found herself climbing the hill that rose from the valley, and then she was walking through the woods. At last she emerged onto the banks of the Blue Lagoon and her footsteps finally slowed.

She gazed up at the starlit sky. It was a cold, calm night. The surface of the lake stretched away like a sheet of glass before her and a million stars reflected on its surface. This was still her favourite place, the place where she and Tracey had always come to find peace of a kind. But tonight there was no peace; only a terrible constricting bitterness that threatened to choke her.

A picture of her mother's face swam before her eyes and hatred rose like burning bile in her throat. 'You bitch,' she sobbed to the silent trees, and as her nails dug painfully into the palms of her hand she felt the warmth of her blood. 'You didn't even care enough to come an' say goodbye to us, did you? You just wanted shot of us. Well fine, we don't need you now. I hope I never see you again. In fact, I hope you rot in hell where you belong, but I'll tell you somethin' – you ain't runnin' my life any longer. After tonight I'm gonna be in charge of me own destiny, an' one day I'm goin' to be somebody. Not the worthless sod you always told me I were, but somebody who people will take notice of. You just see.'

Composing herself with an enormous effort, she looked around at what had always been her special place, knowing that she would never come here again. And then slowly, weary to the bottom of her soul, she returned to Molly's to sleep in her comfortable bed for what she knew would be the very last time.

Chapter Eleven

The next morning at breakfast Claire made a valiant attempt to eat, but the food seemed to lodge in her throat and so in the end she gave up.

Molly sensed that something was wrong, but wisely said nothing.

Claire's feelings were a mixture of excitement, apprehension and sadness, and she found it hard not to stare at Tracey. She watched as her sister and Billy bickered and giggled, and it came to her again just how much Tracey had changed since coming to live with Molly. She was happy now, almost as if the past life and the things they had endured at the hands of their mother's boyfriends had never existed. Thankfully the meal was finally over and they all lined up at the door as Molly fussed over them and handed them their packed lunches.

'Right, you two, mind you behave now,' she grinned, addressing Tracey and Billy. Standing on tiptoe they kissed her. When she handed Claire her box, Molly placed her hand lightly on the girl's arm. 'Look, love, if you're still upset about what I said the other night, all I can say is, I'm sorry. Happen I was a bit hard on you but things will work out, you'll see. I'm not about to give up on you just yet.'

'No, Molly, it's me that should be sorry,' Claire mumbled. Molly was so shocked that she could think of nothing to say. Instead she opened the back door and herded them all outside. 'Right then, you horrible lot. Be off with you and let me have a few hours' peace.' She winked at them as she said it, and laughing, Tracey and Billy ran down the drive with Claire following behind. At the end of the road where they would go their separate ways, Claire suddenly drew Tracey to a halt and pulled her into an awkward embrace.

'You just be good now an' be happy. Do you hear me?'

Embarrassed, Tracey wriggled from her arms. 'Give over, Claire, I'm only goin' to school, not the other side o' the world. Anybody would think you were never gonna see me again, so gerroff.'

Billy giggled as he and Tracey ran off with a final wave to Claire, who watched them until they were out of sight. Her determination to leave began to waver, but then she straightened her shoulders and hardened her heart. She hovered on the corner of the street for a while then furtively retraced her steps, praying that Molly wouldn't see her as she darted back up the drive. Once she was safely hidden behind the garage she relaxed a little and waited impatiently for Molly to leave the house. It was Friday and Molly always caught the nine-thirty bus into the town to do her shopping. Restlessly, Claire listened and at last her patience was rewarded when she heard the front door slam. Peeping around the edge of the wall she saw Molly walking away down the drive.

After waiting another few minutes just to make sure that she wasn't coming back, Claire then stole around to the back door and let herself in with the spare key that she had pocketed the night before. Within minutes she had changed from her uniform into jeans and a sweatshirt, and hastily now she began to push things into a rucksack. She pulled a parka jacket over her head and into the deep pocket on the front she slipped her diary, her mother's brooch and two photographs, one of Tracey and the other of Yasmin.

Lifting the bag, she looked around the room for the last time. She knew that Molly and Tom would take good care of Tracey as they had of her, and she wished that things could have been different. But their loving had come too late. Too much had happened, and Claire was convinced that she was doing the right thing. They would all be happier without her.

Creeping back down the stairs, the girl crossed to a tin on the corner of the kitchen shelf and lifted it down. This, she knew, was where Molly hid her bill money. Inside was almost fifty pounds. She pocketed it quickly, feeling no guilt whatsoever, and returned the tin to its rightful place. Next she raided the piggy banks belonging to Tracey and Billy, adding another twenty-five pounds to her pocket. At last she lifted the rucksack onto her shoulders. Everything was going to plan. Hopefully it would be evening before Molly and Tom even realised that she was gone. By then it would be too late.

⋆   ⋆   ⋆

She made the journey to the lorry-park in record time and arrived there breathless. Relief flooded through her as she saw Mark's lorry laden and ready to go. Almost immediately she spotted him talking to another driver and stayed out of sight until he raised his hand to his colleague and headed back towards his own wagon. Unobserved, Claire smiled to herself. He was a handsome man in his twenties and Claire knew that he was totally besotted with her. Over the last weeks she had learned that there was financial gain to be made simply by being free with her favours. And she could see no reason why it shouldn't continue. For the first time in her life, her future looked bright.

She waited until Mark was in his cab and had started the engine. Then, sprinting across the lorry park, she stretched up to rap on the passenger door. When he opened it, she tossed her heavy bag inside, and hastily scrambled up behind it.

Mark's face broke into a wide grin. 'Why – what's this, eh?' he asked.

'It's a long story, just drive and I'll tell you as we go along.'

Intrigued, but also a little bit concerned, Mark obediently swung the huge lorry expertly out of the lorry-park and onto Queens Road. For some minutes neither of them spoke but as they neared the outskirts of the town, he pulled into the side of the road, turned off the engine and demanded, 'Right then, perhaps now you'd like to tell me exactly what's going on?'

She noticed that he was no longer smiling.

'I did tell you that I was going to be gone for a few days at least,' he went on grimly, 'so just what game are you playing? I shan't be back in Nuneaton until the middle of next week at the earliest.'

'Good, that'll be just fine,' she told him. ''Cos, you see, the thing is, I have no intention of comin' back here.'

His eyes stretched with amazement, but he said nothing. Instead he frowned and after restarting the engine, he pulled back onto the road. As they reached the by-pass that would lead them to the motorway and London, Claire allowed herself one last look back at the familiar town. Back there was everyone she had ever cared about. But before her was a new life, and so she tore her eyes away and stared ahead. Mark was unusually quiet and there was a deep frown on his forehead. They had gone some miles before he finally spoke again.

'I think you'd better tell me what's happened,' he said, none too pleasantly.

'Don't look so serious,' Claire giggled as she slid along the seat towards him. 'I meant what I said back there – I ain't comin' back.'

Mark dragged his eyes away from the road for a second to glare at her. 'Well, where are yer goin' then? And where are yer goin' to live?'

'With you, of course.' Her answer caused him to swerve.

'What do you mean, with me?' he demanded.

'Look, we get on well, don't we?' she faltered. 'I've had enough of me life back there, so I've decided to come and live with you.'

When Mark shook his head in disbelief, the first flutters of panic began to stir in Claire's stomach.

'Don't you think you should have asked me first?' he said.

'I . . . I thought you'd want me to,' she whispered, close to tears.

'Look, love, it ain't that simple.' His voice had softened as he ran his hand uncomfortably through his hair. 'Yer see, I've only got a bedsit. If I let anyone stay there, the landlord would have me out.'

Relieved, Claire grinned up at him. 'Is that all you're worried about? Well, that's easy then. You can move out and we'll find another place where we can be together.'

Sighing deeply, Mark Blake turned his attention back to the road, his mind in turmoil. How could he tell her that he was married with a mort-gage and two kids? He'd looked forward to his stays in her hometown; after all, Claire was a pretty girl and more than free with her favours. But he had never thought of her as anything more than a bit of fun and now he was panicking. What if his missus was to find out? She'd kill him for sure, and the thought of losing her and his kids for a girl like Claire terri-fied him.

Claire, meanwhile, was staring at the countryside flashing past the cab window, her mind full of plans. It was exciting to think that soon they'd be in London and flat-hunting. But more exciting still was knowing that once she was there, she could become anybody she wanted to be. A brand new person with a brand new start. Admittedly she wished that Mark could show a little more enthusiasm, but once he'd had time to get used to the idea, she was sure he would be as happy about it as she was.

Tracey and her past life all suddenly seemed a million miles away, and contentedly she sank back into her seat. They were almost in Oxford when Mark finally pulled into a service station. Confidently, Claire hopped down from the cab and followed Mark into the café. It was teeming with lorry drivers, and at Claire's entrance a dozen pairs of appreciative eyes turned her way. Mark wished to God that one of the blokes here would take her off his hands, for the nearer to London they got, the worse he felt. In fact, right now he was wishing he had never set eyes on her.

Claire, who was totally unaware of his feelings, slipped into a chair at a rare empty table, and soon Mark returned and placed a steaming mug of tea in front of her. She smiled at him but the frown never left his face, and he stared down into his own mug miserably. He'd only taken a few sips of his drink when he suddenly stood up abruptly. 'Look, I'll go an' get yer bag out of the cab then yer can freshen up while I diesel up an' visit the gents,' he told her, avoiding her eyes.

'But what about your tea?'

Mark merely shrugged and hurried away, his head down. Minutes later he was back and he dropped her heavy bag down at her side. She smiled at him trustingly but he looked away, ashamed. After all, she wasn't much more than a kid. But then, as he thought of his family, he knew he had no other choice.

'I'll see you out the front in fifteen minutes,' he told her, and turning on his heel he strode away.

Enjoying all the admiring glances she was attracting, Claire sat and leisurely finished her tea, before making her way to the ladies' toilets. After washing her hands and running a comb through her hair she smiled at her reflection in the mirror. 'Right then, gel,' she muttered to herself. 'Let's get this show on the road.' Swinging up her heavy bag and whistling merrily, she left the toilets with a spring in her step. Once outside, her eyes swept the huge lorry-park but at first glance there was no sign of Mark's lorry. He must have pulled round by the exit, she thought to herself, and hoisting her bag further onto her shoulder she made her way there. The lorry wasn't there either and Claire frowned. 'He *must* be in the lorry-park,' she said aloud. 'I must have missed him.' Turning round, she hurried back there.

It was almost an hour later and Claire had walked up and down the lines of parked lorries three times already. Still she clung to the hope that she had just not spotted him yet; the alternative was too terrible to contemplate. 'He wouldn't leave me, he wouldn't,' she kept telling herself. But even as she tried to convince herself, a dull acceptance was settling on her.

Finally, she made her way to the edge of the lorry-park, sank down onto the kerb and, dropping her head into her hands, she began to cry. Now she was forced to accept that Mark was no different to anyone else she had ever cared about. He had betrayed her and abandoned her too. But this time she had no one left; no one to turn to. She was all alone and the thought terrified her. She didn't know how long she sat there, she only knew that numerous times men approached her and offered her lifts. Her answer to them was always the same. 'Bugger off,' she would spit, and eventually they left her alone.

As the late afternoon gave way to dusk, she finally pulled herself together a little and weighed up her options. The way she saw it, she could either go back cap in hand to her foster parents, and be shipped off to God knows where, or she could go on and make a new life for herself as she had planned.

Underneath, she knew that she didn't really have an option, since her pride would never allow her to go home. Drying her eyes, she began to wander amongst the lorries. She didn't have to wait long before a dark-haired man approached her. Tall and well-built, he looked to be in his mid-thirties.

He eyed her up and down appreciatively. 'Are you lookin' for a lift then, love?'

She noticed he had a broad Cockney accent. 'I might be,' she said cautiously. 'It all depends on where you're goin', an' what you're chargin'.'

Grinning at her in happy anticipation, he rubbed his hands together. 'I'm goin' to London, as it so 'appens, an' as for what I'm chargin', well . . . I'm sure we'll fink o' somefin'.'

'Sounds all right to me.' Forcing a smile, she followed him as he hurried back to his lorry. His hand was shaking so much that he could barely get the key in the lock, but at last the door swung open and Claire clambered up before him into the cab. Behind the seats was a bunk and there were curtains at the windows. It smelled of stale cigarette smoke and sweat – a smell that evoked unpleasant memories. However, it was warm and so Claire entered without a qualm. Once he had followed her in, the man produced a bottle of gin and two plastic tumblers from beneath the seat, and after pouring out two generous measures he passed one to Claire and slid his arm around her shoulders.

'There, girl, get that down yer, it'll put hairs on yer chest,' he ordered as he drew the small curtains across the cab windows.

Claire obediently took a great swallow, and as the fiery liquid burned its way down her throat, she coughed. He laughed loudly and thumped her on the back, and after a few moments of spluttering, Claire giggled too. Once it had gone down, it gave her a nice warm feeling inside and she held her tumbler out for a refill. She could never remember how she ended up on the bunk, but soon they were lying side by side on the thin mattress, and his rough hands were all over her. She put up no resistance and in no time at all they were both naked. Sometime later he rolled off her and lit a cigarette. He offered it to Claire, but she was already fast asleep. Grinning with satisfaction, he lay beside her in the darkness.

When Claire woke she slowly opened her eyes and found to her amazement that she was naked. The driver was at the wheel of the lorry humming to himself as they trundled along. When he spotted Claire sit up in the mirror, he grinned. 'Mornin'', he said. 'How yer feelin'?'

Claire groaned; her head hurt and she felt sick. 'What time is it?' she asked.

Pointing at the clock on the dashboard he told her amiably, 'It's four in the mornin' – we'll be in North London in ten minutes or so.'

Struggling to sit up in the confined space, Claire began to search about for her clothes, and pulled them on as best she could. Then, holding firmly to the back of the seat, she scrambled clumsily over it to sit in the cab beside him. He flashed her a grin and slapped her knee. 'I'll tell yer what, there's a transport café just up the road. How's about I treat you to a nice fried breakfast, eh?'

Just the thought of it made Claire want to vomit, but feeling too ill to argue, she nodded and minutes later he swung the lorry off the road onto a gravelled car park.

'Right then, let's get somefin' inside us, eh? It's surprisin' how much better everyfin' looks after a good hot breakfast.' He hopped nimbly from the cab, leaving Claire to step down gingerly after him. Although the thought of food had made her feel ill, in fact, with a cup of hot tea inside her she began to feel better, and before she knew it, she'd cleared the plate of food he put before her.

Joe, as he had introduced himself, smiled at her. 'There then, weren't I right?'

Claire nodded. 'Yes, you were,' she admitted, and after he'd paid the bill, they returned to his lorry. Once they were back on the road again he peered at her curiously. 'So where exactly are yer headed then, gel?'

Claire shrugged. As far as she was concerned, anywhere in London would do. She imagined it to be a place of glamour and excitement, so surely one part of London would be much like another? However, her first glimpse of it was not at all what she had expected. Although it was still very early, there seemed to be traffic everywhere and she noticed that the walls they passed were covered in graffiti. Soon, Claire screwed her eyes up tight, sure that something would plough into them at any minute. Joe laughed at her nervousness and after a time he drew the lorry to a stop.

'That's it then, girl.' He grinned. 'This is as far as yer go.'

Claire gazed up and down the dismal street he had parked in. A sign-post read *Pentonville Road*. 'Where are we?' she asked nervously.

Serious now, Joe wagged a finger at her. 'You're on the edge of the red-light district, love, so be careful. The pimps'll have their hands on yer in the blink of an eye, so you just take care now, eh? There's plenty of caffs open at this hour, so you go in and get yourself a nice cup of coffee eh?' He pulled out a tenner and handed it to her. Gawd, in this light, she looked no more than a kid, he thought.

Claire nodded as reaching over the bunk, she dragged her heavy bag onto the seat beside her. 'Thanks, Joe,' she said quietly.

He felt a pang of sympathy for her. But, he reasoned, she seemed to know what she was doing, and as she jumped down from the cab he raised his hand.

'Look after yourself now.'

Smiling weakly, Claire slammed the cab door. There was a whistle of air as he let off the brake, then the lorry pulled away and in a minute disappeared around a bend in the road. She stood there for some seconds, surveying this unknown place, then swinging her bag onto her shoulder; she set off to explore.

Chapter Twelve

Claire had been tramping the streets for hours now, and her feet were beginning to ache. It was late morning and felt like another world here to the one she had left behind; everything was hustle and bustle and it being Saturday, people were milling everywhere, having come into the West End to do their shopping and have fun. Claire clutched her bag fiercely to her and hurried past them all, scared of pickpockets, of people knowing that she was a stranger here, seeing how lost she felt.

Earlier, after wandering into the unsavoury streets of Soho, she had seen tartily-dressed women standing on street corners, and occasionally, Claire saw them get into cars with men who pulled up at the kerbs. Claire hurried past them with her eyes downcast. More than once, a car pulled alongside her, attracted by her blond hair and waiflike appearance, but she walked quickly away without even looking at the drivers, and after a few moments they moved off in search of easier prey.

Now she trudged on, with no idea at all of where she was going until eventually she found herself in Trafalgar Square. The rest of the day passed in a blur as she took in the sights that she had only ever seen in books and on television. She walked down the Mall to see Buckingham Palace, then came back up to see Big Ben and the Houses of Parliament. After looking in awe at the interior of Westminster Abbey, she dragged herself and her rucksack across the road to the pleasant gardens overlooking the Thames, and watched the activity on the river. A strange sort of happiness washed over her. However, by teatime, her aching feet and grumbling stomach made her find her way back up towards the dingier streets off the Charing Cross Road, for the cafés and restaurants elsewhere were far too expensive for her to afford. It seemed a long, long time now since that breakfast with Joe.

At last she found a fish and chip shop, and taking the greasy packet of food and a drink outside, she found a quiet stretch of road and sank gratefully onto the pavement. Leaning her back against a wall, she hungrily tucked into her feast. The fish was piping hot. She was almost halfway through when she saw a small thin mongrel staring at her pleadingly. Her heart missed a beat as just for a second his sad brown eyes reminded her of Tinker's. He was actually nothing at all like her Tinker when she looked at him closely, but even so she felt sorry for him. His ribs were showing though his mangy coat and Claire guessed immediately that he must be a stray.

'Are you all alone too, boy, eh?' she asked, as his sorrowful brown eyes stared back at her. Lifting a large chip from the bag on her lap she threw it to him and grinned as he gobbled it down before it even hit the pavement. 'Here.' She laid the bag in front of him. 'I reckon you need 'em more than I do.' As if he could hardly believe his luck, the dog eyed her suspiciously for a moment before bending his head to the bag. He wolfed the lot down hungrily, and when he had licked the greaseproof paper clean he sidled up to Claire and dropped down on all fours at her side.

Claire's arm slid around him and they sat there for some time, each drawing comfort from the other. 'I reckon you an' me are two of a kind,' she whispered to him. 'We're here in this great big city, yet we're all alone, though there are people all around us. There ain't nobody would care if we both died tonight.' As she said it, two fat tears rolled down her cheeks and the little mongrel stared back at her as if he understood every word she had said. At this moment, Claire McMullen felt more alone than she had ever felt in her whole life – but there was no going back now. She had made the break and from now on she was on her own for better or worse.

After a while she stood up and, staring down at her little friend, she said gently, 'Goodbye, boy.' Hoisting her heavy bag back onto her shoulder, she set off up the dimly lit street. Her friend, however, had no intention of being left behind and trotted along beside her. After going a few yards she stopped to wag her finger at him sternly. 'Look . . .' Her heart ached at the expression in his sorrowful brown eyes. 'I can't take you with me, as I've nowhere to go, an' I don't know how I'm going to look after meself let alone you, so stay there. Good boy – *stay*!' she commanded.

His tail stopped wagging at her harsh tone and turning determinedly, she strode away. At the end of the street she turned just once to look back at him. He was still sitting dejectedly where she had left him, staring after her. For a second she felt like running back to him; at the minute he was the only friend she had in the world. But she realised that she couldn't. All her life up to now it felt like she had been responsible for something or someone. Tracey, Tinker, even her mam, and the last thing she needed to saddle herself with right now was a mangy mongrel. Her mind made up, she hurriedly turned the corner and headed back towards the bright lights of the town, which reminded her of Christmas.

As she gazed into the brightly illuminated shop windows in Oxford Street, her spirits began to lift a little. No one gave her a second glance, and Claire was glad. Here she could be anyone she wanted to be. There was no one here to lay down rules and regulations. This would be the start of a new life and she was determined to make the most of it, but it had been a long day and now she was tired.

Realising that she needed to find somewhere to stay, she headed back in the direction of the river, following her instincts. Every penny she had was precious. Tomorrow she would start looking for a job, and she didn't envisage having any problems there. She knew that she looked at least eighteen, and although there were unemployment problems elsewhere in the country, with the miners' strikes and God knows what else going on, there were bound to be jobs going down here, in the capital city, even if it was only washing-up in a café. Tomorrow she also intended to find somewhere to live, a bedsit or a flat – anything for now. Tonight she hoped to find a hostel or at least a bed and breakfast.

After another hour of tramping the streets, Claire began to realise that this was going to prove harder than she had realised, for even the cheapest places she found were more expensive than she could afford. She was too afraid to stop anyone and ask for advice, and so she trudged on until she found herself down by Cleopatra's Needle on the banks of the River Thames. It was as she was sitting forlornly on a bench gazing at the opposite shore and shivering that she noticed an old woman pushing a rusty pram heading towards her. She was dressed in a ragged coat tied at the waist with a piece of rough string, and as she came up to Claire she stopped and stared at her.

'What's a young' un like you doin' out at this time o' night then, dearie?' she asked.

Claire stared back at her suspiciously. The old woman had on a ludicrous, bedraggled wide-brimmed hat that had long since seen better days and when Claire didn't immediately answer her, she grinned, revealing a set of broken teeth.

'I was looking for somewhere to stay,' Claire replied cautiously.

The old woman threw back her head and laughed loudly. 'You're new to the city then, are yer?'

Claire nodded.

The old woman shook her head and sighed. 'A runaway, eh? Expectin' to find the streets paved wi' gold, were yer?'

Claire bristled and stuck out her chin stubbornly. 'I can take care o' meself,' she stated proudly.

The old woman tutted. 'They all say that, when they first get 'ere. I've seen it a million times, but I'll tell yer now, dearie, only the fittest survive. If I were you, I'd turn right round an' go back where yer come from!'

Just then, a gang of youths rushed towards them, and as they passed, one of them made a grab for Claire's bag. In a second as Claire hung on to it for grim life the old woman had produced a large stick from the seemingly bottomless pram, and swung it at them. 'Be off wi' yer, yer buggers, else you'll feel the length o' this,' she threatened and to Claire's amazement they hurried on laughing.

'That's it, piss off the lot o' yer!' the old woman bawled after them, and when they'd gone she turned back to Claire. 'Now do yer see what I mean?' she demanded.

Suddenly, the girl's tired shoulders sagged, and to her shame, she began to cry. It was all too much.

The old woman's face softened. 'Look, I'm Nancy,' she said kindly. 'Yer can stay wi' me fer tonight, yer look dead on yer feet. It ain't posh where I stay, but it's under cover, an' at least you'll be safe from the likes o' them little bastards.'

Claire nodded gratefully through her tears, and as Nancy trundled the old pram on its way, she stayed close on her heels. After what seemed a long time they came to a slope going down under a bridge. Nancy headed down it with Claire close behind her. Ahead of them, a group of people were clustered around a roaring fire, and at Nancy's approach they all raised their heads. No one took any notice of Nancy; she was obviously a familiar sight, but as Claire walked past she could feel their curious eyes boring into her back. Nancy acknowledged them with a brief nod of her head as hurrying by them, she made her way to a corner of a high wall where a large number of cardboard boxes were stacked.

'Here y'are then,' she said, almost as if she had brought Claire to an upper-class hotel. 'Take yer pick. You'll be snug as a bug in a rug, duckie, once you get yourself tucked into one o' them.'

Claire gazed back at her in horror as Nancy produced a bottle of gin from her grubby coat pocket. The old woman laughed at Claire's expression. 'Now then, don't look like that, dearie. Beggars can't be choosers, yer know. You ain't goin' to find nowhere better tonight, are yer?'

Claire slowly shook her head, and taking a great swallow from the gin bottle, Nancy sighed happily. 'Well then, I'll say goodnight. Hold on to yer bag now mind, love. They's a thievin' lot o' buggers around 'ere. Slit yer throat fer sixpence they would, but don't you worry. Old Nancy'll look out fer yer tonight.' So saying, she disappeared into a huge cardboard box and began to cover herself with thick layers of newspapers.

Claire selected a box for herself, and after throwing her bag in first she crawled in behind it. Surprisingly, just as Nancy had said, it was warm, and too exhausted to think much now, within minutes she was fast asleep.

When she woke next morning, she panicked for a minute, but then as the events of the evening before came back to her, she stretched stiffly and peeped out of her cardboard shelter. It was a fresh, bright spring morning and, just for a moment, her spirits rose.

She seemed to be the first one awake, and the sight of Nancy's down-at-heel shoes poking out of the box next to her made her grin. The old lady was snoring loudly, so crawling out of her box quietly so as not to disturb her, Claire looked about her. There were tramps lying here and there, all fast asleep. The fire of the night before was now a pile of ashes and Claire looked around in amazement. This was poverty as she had never seen it, and it frightened her. She was hungry and thirsty and longing for the toilet and a wash. Reaching into the box, she dragged her bag out and after fumbling inside it, she pulled out her purse. Taking out a five-pound note she crept across to Nancy and tucked it securely into the old woman's pocket. Within minutes she was on her way again. She walked briskly for some time until she came to a public toilet. Hurrying inside, she relieved herself and washed as best she could. Feeling a lot fresher, she then went into a café and used some more of her precious nest-egg to treat herself to a cooked breakfast.

With a warm meal inside her she began to feel much better so she set off again, this time in search of work. All morning she tried cafés, restaurants and hotels – but although she was willing to do anything from cooking to cleaning, everyone turned her away. Mid-afternoon she went into a baker's shop and bought herself some bread rolls and sat on a seat outside to eat them. Then the job-hunting continued, but by teatime, Claire had still had no luck. She was worried now. Besides not being able to get a job, she still hadn't found anywhere to stay, and as her second night in London crept upon her, she began to realise that it wasn't going to be as easy as she had thought. She had walked for miles, crossing and recrossing the river, and had no idea now where she was.

The gangs were out in force again as darkness approached, and they glared at her threateningly as she hurried past. Eventually she slipped into a shop doorway and sank down to rest her aching feet. As she stared out, she could see part of Tower Bridge ahead. A vision of her cosy bedroom back at her foster parents' home sprang to mind and she had to bite down hard on her lip and blink rapidly to stop the tears from falling. She was cold, she was hungry and she was tired, and worse still, she realised that she was missing her foster mum. She was frightened too, for some of the people passing the shop doorway looked unsavoury, to say the least. Shrinking back further into the shadows, Claire wondered what she should do next. Deciding that at least here she was under shelter, she hugged her bag to her and eventually drifted off into an uneasy doze.

It was the early hours of the morning when she woke. Her legs had gone to sleep with the weight of her bag, and her neck hurt from the way she had been leaning awkwardly against the shop door. She was shivering with cold and bursting to use the toilet, so warily she emerged from the doorway. She might have been the only person left on earth; there wasn't a soul in sight. Hurrying along the deserted pavements, she searched desperately for a toilet. Eventually she knew that she couldn't wait a moment longer, so glancing up and down the deserted street to make sure that she was still alone, she crept into a stinking back alley and hastily undid her jeans.

Almost an hour later, she found a café open. The warmth when she opened the door welcomed her and she sank gratefully onto a hard chair.

Although she'd promised herself she would make every penny count, she was so hungry that she ordered a full English breakfast and soon was tucking into bacon, eggs, mushrooms, tomatoes and a plateful of toast. She ate ravenously, and her spirits began to lift a little. 'Things will turn out all right,' she promised herself. 'I'm *bound* to find a job today.'

With the meal devoured she sighed with satisfaction, then before leaving she slipped into the ladies' and washed and tidied herself up. Soon she was busily jobseeking again.

Once more the morning passed and she had no success at all. There were blisters on the back of her heels and she felt like she hadn't bathed for a year. Dejectedly she leaned against a wall near Tottenham Court Road tube station and hung her head, and it was as she stood there that a girl approached. She was heavily made-up and wearing the shortest miniskirt that Claire had ever seen in her life. Instead of passing by as everyone else had, she stopped and stared at Claire. The girl was smoking and as Claire stared back at her, she drew in a great lungful of smoke. At first glance she looked to be in her early twenties, but as Claire studied her she realised that underneath the heavy make-up she was probably actually only in her late teens.

'You lost, mate?' the girl enquired.

'I suppose I am,' Claire admitted. 'I've been looking for a hostel where I could stay till I can get a job, but I haven't come across one yet.'

The girl laughed humourlessly. 'Wouldn't do you no good if you did find one,' she told her. 'They're queuing up at them places before it even gets dark. And they're full of junkies and piss-artists.'

Claire gulped as the girl eyed her thoughtfully.

'You run away from home, is that it?'

Terrified of being found, Claire shook her head in denial. 'No, I ain't,' she muttered. 'Just wanted a change o' lifestyle, that's all.'

'Huh! You've certainly come to the right place then,' the girl replied bitterly. 'You'll meet the scum of the earth round here, I'll tell you. An' before you know it, some pimp will have you on the game.'

At Claire's startled expression, the girl's face softened a little. 'Look,' she said kindly, 'why don't you do yourself a favour an' get yer arse back where you come from? It can't be no worse than 'ere.'

'That's what you think,' Claire retorted indignantly.

The girl shrugged. ''Ave it yer own way then. Ain't no skin off my nose.' After transferring the great wad of chewing gum she had in one side of her mouth to the other she took another long drag of her cigarette and without another word tottered away on her high heels.

After another hour of trekking though the streets, past the British Museum, over Russell Square and down past Great Ormond Street Hospital, Claire found herself at the entrance to King's Cross tube station. She stared about her curiously. This was where her journey had started, nearly three days ago, when Joe had dropped her off. She had come full circle, achieved nothing. Her heart sank.

Outside the main entrance, some standing, some sitting, was a motley array of people, ranging from kids who looked even younger than herself to very old people – and they were all begging. Claire looked at them in amazement; this was something that she had never witnessed before. If she wasn't careful, she would soon be joining their ranks. Panic swept over her. She had to get away from here.

Breathing deeply, she looked across the road, to the bus-stop. A big red London bus was approaching – a number 10, its destination Shepherd's Bush. The name reminded her of the sleepy Warwickshire town that she had grown up in, and which now seemed a million miles away.

Dodging the heavy traffic on an impulse, her heart in her mouth, she reached the stop in time to jump on, before the conductor pulled on the cord that made the bell ping. She was on her way!

An hour later, she got off at the terminus, after a wonderful journey in the front seat on the top deck, drinking all the sights in while her throbbing feet enjoyed their rest. Now, though, Claire felt very low. She was limping; the blisters on the back of her ankles had burst and her trainers were rubbing her painfully. This horrible, dirty place was nothing like the countryside. Just for a moment she longed to phone home, and realised with a start that when she thought of home now, she thought of her foster parents.

Deep inside, she knew that it would only take a phone call and the Garretts would welcome her back and even allow her to stay if she would only agree to behave. But then pride took over, and even though she missed her sister so much, she knew that she couldn't. She had built a wall, albeit an unseen one, between herself and the rest of the world. Never again would she allow someone to get over or through it.

As she hovered uncertainly outside an old red phone box, a noisy gang of youths caught her attention. They were taking it in turns to kick an empty Coke tin before them and were shouting loudly, coming her way. A feeling of apprehension washed over her. She knew that they had seen her, but couldn't have run even if she'd wanted to, the back of her heels were raw. Deciding to brazen it out, she set off again hoping to walk straight past them, but it soon became clear that they had other ideas, and as they came abreast of her, they suddenly surrounded her and blocked her way.

Sticking out her chin, she glared at them angrily and said, 'Will you get out o' me way, please?'

One of them began to mimic her: '*Will yer get out o' me way, please?* Hark at Little Miss High an' Mighty, eh?' The others began to laugh and as they circled her, Claire felt trapped.

Not feeling quite so brave now, she muttered, 'Look, I don't want no trouble.'

'It weren't trouble I was plannin' on given you, blondie,' the same youth leered, and reaching out he tried to take her bag from her shoulder.

Claire slapped him hand away. 'Get yer hands off that,' she said, and made to push past him, but he gripped her arm tightly.

'Got somethin' in there worth havin' then, have yer?' His eyes were glittering like cold marbles.

Claire struggled, but it was useless, within minutes they had her bag.

'You're a right little wildcat, ain't yer, blondie?' laughed the ringleader. 'Just 'ow we like 'em, eh, lads?'

He began to undo the belt on his jeans, and as Claire realised his intention, she opened her mouth to scream. A dirty hand clamped across it. Two of the other youths had her firmly by the shoulder, and at a nod from their leader they began to drag her behind the phone box.

They flung her to the ground so roughly that for a minute she was winded. By the time she had enough breath to try to scream again, he already had his jeans about his knees. Desperate to get away, Claire kicked out with every ounce of strength she had, and purely by chance, one of her kicks landed on his shin. Howling, he brought his hand back and smacked her hard across the cheek. As her head spun around, her nose connected with the pavement and she felt warm blood trickle down into her mouth. Instantly she went limp as she realised the futility of her position.

'That's better,' he gasped breathlessly, and urged on by his cronies, he pulled her jeans and pants down and mounted her. Claire lay quite still, as tears of humiliation slid down her cheeks and mingled with the blood. At last it was over and he stood up, grinning broadly as he pulled up his jeans. Claire curled into a tight ball.

'Anyone else wanna go?' he invited and a fresh wave of terror swept through her. Thankfully the others only laughed.

'Nah, let's go an' have a gander at what she's got in this 'ere bag instead,' said one, and to her relief Claire heard them walking away. She lay there for some time, too terrified to move in case they came back. Eventually, when the street was silent again, she sat up and pulled her jeans back up with trembling hands. They had taken her bag, and in it was every penny she had and every item of clothing she owned. All she had left now were the things in her coat-pocket.

Too afraid to stay there any longer, Claire staggered to her feet, then leaned over the gutter and was violently sick. She was shaking with shock and dizzy, but she staggered on looking for somewhere that she could hide. Her nose was still gushing blood and she could feel one eye already beginning to close. She felt more terrified then she had ever felt in her whole life. Once again, just as always, things had gone terribly wrong, and Claire wished that she had never been born. It felt to her as if she had been born to be abused, for apart from the gang of thugs she had just encountered, she recalled again her mother's many menfriends. Men who had come to her in the night right from when she was just a tiny girl, and made her too frightened to tell. Men who had hurt her, raped her, stolen her childhood, her innocence, and also her soul.

Claire bent her head and wept for that child.

Chapter Thirteen

Claire walked until she felt she had put a safe distance between herself and the thugs, then she slipped into a shop doorway and cried herself to sleep. Thank God the milder weather had arrived, or she would have frozen to death. The next morning, she stirred painfully. Catching sight of herself in the shop window, she gasped in horror. One eye was black with bruises and completely closed, and the whole lower part of her face was smeared with dried blood. Her hair was matted and wild and she ached all over and was shivering with cold.

There was no optimism this morning. There was nothing to be optimistic about now. She didn't have a penny to her name, and as the hopelessness of her situation washed over her she shrank into the corner and hugged her knees miserably while her stomach rumbled with hunger. She knew that she couldn't stay there for much longer; soon the shop would open and the staff would usher her away. That didn't worry her now, though. Nothing did. She was past caring about what might happen to her.

Just then, a big shiny car pulled into the kerb next to the shop and a large black man climbed from the driver's seat. He was impeccably dressed in a smart cream suit, under which he wore a freshly laundered open-necked shirt made of brown silk that almost matched the colour of his skin. Heavy gold chains hung at his neck. His jet-black curly hair was cut close to his head and Claire noticed a large diamond ring glittering on his finger. Another diamond flashed in his ear. Claire judged him to be somewhere in his early thirties.

'Are you in some sort of trouble, girl?' he asked.

Claire hugged her knees tighter beneath her chin. 'What's it to you if I am?' she said rudely.

He grinned, and as the watery early-morning sun glinted off a shining gold tooth, he held out his hands as if to ward off a blow. 'Now then,' his voice was kindly. 'I was just concerned, that's all, and wondering if I could help.'

'Why would you wanna do that?'

As he shrugged his broad shoulders, Claire thought she had never seen such a handsome man in the whole of her life.

'You just look like you could do with a friend, that's all. Who did that to you?' A well-manicured fingernail pointed towards her swollen eye as Claire's hand self-consciously rose to her face.

She felt her anger ebbing away. It was nice to talk to someone who seemed to care for a change. 'A group o' lads attacked me last night, if yer must know. They took me bag wi' all me money in it an' they . . . he . . .' As the horror of the previous night's attack came back to her, Claire's lip trembled and she began to sob.

'Hey now, don't cry,' the man told her as he inched closer. Then, 'Look, how about I take you back to my place and let you tidy yourself up a bit? I daresay I could rustle you some breakfast up as well. What do you say?'

She glared at him suspiciously through her tears for a time, but then realising that she didn't have an awful lot of options, she painfully pulled herself up from the ground. 'All right, then . . . thanks. But as soon as I'm cleaned up I'll be off, OK?'

'Of course.' He opened the passenger door of the car. Claire clambered in and sank into the luxurious seat as the smell of new leather wrapped itself around her. He climbed into the driver's seat and once the engine had purred to life he drove it slowly away from the kerb and into the early-morning traffic on Hammersmith Road.

'So what's yer name then?' she dared to ask when he slowed down at some lights.

Taking his eyes from the road just long enough to flash her a smile, he replied, 'It's Marcus. Marcus Thackeray. And you are?'

She muttered, 'I'm Claire.'

'Claire what?'

'Just Claire.'

'That's fair enough,' he said, 'but don't look so worried, Just Claire. I'm only trying to help you. I'm not going to hurt you, I assure you.'

She felt herself beginning to relax a little. He did seem nice and he hadn't *had* to help her, after all. By now they were driving through the heart of London. Claire spotted the Albert Memorial, which she had seen from the top of the bus yesterday – and the sight calmed her. She still wasn't used to the volume of traffic, though. There seemed to be cars and huge black taxi-cabs coming at them from every direction. Claire screwed her eyes up tight, expecting to feel something crash into them at any second, but Marcus, as he had introduced himself, seemed completely at ease. After a time, she felt the car slow down and stop. Opening her eyes again she saw that they were outside an impressive block of flats that stretched up into the sky above them.

'This is home,' Marcus informed her. 'I have the penthouse apartment here.' As he spoke, he climbed from his seat and within seconds had walked around the car and opened her door for her. Claire looked about her in amazement as he helped her out onto the pavement.

'It's a bit posh round here, ain't it?' she remarked, and was rewarded with a toothy smile again.

'This is Knightsbridge, and yes, I suppose it is a nice area.'

Claire decided that, as well as being very handsome, Marcus must also be very rich. Taking her elbow, he led her towards shining glass revolving doors, and once they had passed through them she found herself in a foyer the like of which she had only ever seen in magazines. Shyly passing the uniformed concierge on duty, whom Marcus greeted, Claire followed him into a lift. When it stopped, she stepped out onto a landing with a large plate-glass window, and gasped as she stared at the panoramic view of London spread out before her.

'Blimey, yer could almost think you were on top o' the world here, couldn't yer?'

Instantly, Tracey's voice sounded in her head, saying almost exactly the same words as they had stood on the hill overlooking their home village. Claire forced the memory away and turned back to Marcus, who was now unlocking a door. When it swung open he courteously stood aside – and as she stepped past him into his apartment, she was dazzled. Everything seemed to be black and white and was ultra-modern: white walls and floors, great black leather settees and chairs dotted here and there, and an enormous television set in one corner.

'Why, it's . . . it's beautiful,' she choked.

He smiled, revealing gleaming white teeth again as he headed for a door which led into an impressive kitchen. After filling a kettle at a spotlessly clean sink he plugged it in to boil before turning back to her.

'I'm glad you like it. Come on, while we wait for the kettle to boil I'll show you around the rest of it,' he offered. His tour led her through two bedrooms, again done in the same black and white theme, and a bathroom that had her eyes stretching wide. A huge corner bath took up most of the space, and the floors and the walls were made of solid marble. Claire began to think that he must be a millionaire at least.

'You must be really rich,' she sighed enviously.

He was saved from answering when the kettle began to sing. 'Come on, let's get something inside you,' he encouraged. 'You look as if you could do with it.'

For the first time that day she smiled, making her lip split painfully open again as she followed him without a word. Soon she was tucking into great thick slices of toast dripping in butter and marmalade, all washed down with enough tea to sink a battleship. She wolfed it all down hungrily and when her appetite was at last sated she sat back and rubbed her stomach contentedly. 'Cor, that hit the spot.'

He smiled back at her over the rim of a bone-china cup. 'Good, now I think we ought to get you cleaned up a bit, don't you? I'll let you use one of my dressing-gowns and you can have a bath if you like. My cleaner will be in shortly and she'll wash your clothes for you if you haven't any clean ones.'

'I ain't – they were all in the bag them lads took,' Claire told him regretfully.

'Not to worry, we can soon sort that.' After leading her back through the lounge he pointed towards the bathroom. 'There should be everything you need in there,' he told her. 'Please just help yourself.'

'Ta.' Claire self-consciously edged through the door and firmly locked it behind her. She quickly ran the water into the bath, added some posh bath salts and sank gratefully into it. Then for the next ten minutes she finally allowed herself to relax a little as the warmth soothed away her aches and pains. Once she had thoroughly washed her hair and every inch of herself she clambered out of the bath and dried herself on huge fluffy white towels before slipping into a silk dressing-gown that was hanging on the back of the door. After collecting her dirty clothes into a pile she extracted her diary and other personal possessions from her coat pocket before joining Marcus in the lounge. An elderly lady was polishing a long sideboard that stood along one wall and when Claire appeared she glanced at her damaged face curiously. Marcus was on the phone but he quickly ended his conversation when Claire appeared and, taking her elbow, led her into one of the two bedrooms.

'I'll get Mrs Fielding to put these into the washer for you,' he said as he took the dirty clothes from her. 'Unfortunately I have to go out for a while now, but you're quite welcome to stay here until your clothes are dry.'

Claire nodded solemnly as with a final smile he turned and left, closing the door softly behind him. Alone now, she looked about the room. A huge bed took up most of the floorspace in the centre of the room. A pure-white fur throw lay across it and Claire saw that beneath it were black silk sheets. Her toes sank into a white wall-to-wall carpet that made her afraid to walk on it, and white curtains framed the window. She felt as if she had stepped into another world – the sort of world she wanted to belong to, not the sordid one she had known before moving in with the Garretts. Crossing to the window, she gazed down into the street far below, just in time to see Marcus step into his car and roar away. He had shown her nothing but kindness, and she could hardly believe her luck. Perhaps this would be the start of better things?

Deciding that she would like another drink, she went back into the lounge, and once more the cleaner eyed her curiously.

'Hello, I'm Claire,' she introduced herself.

The woman frowned as she noticed how young Claire looked. 'New to London, are you?' she asked.

Claire felt herself flush. 'I am actually. I er . . . got into a spot of bother, got beaten up last night and had me bag nicked, but then Marcus came along an' he's been really kind to me.'

'Huh! You might think he's being kind, but all I can tell you is, watch out for yourself.'

When Claire raised her eyebrows the woman stared at her then, glancing fearfully towards the door, she went on, 'How old are you, love?'

The closed look came across Claire's face again. 'I'm . . . eighteen,' she lied.

'Yes, of course you are and I'm a monkey's uncle,' the woman shot back at her. 'You've run away from home, haven't you?'

Claire didn't like the way the conversation was going at all. Flouncing about, she hurried into the kitchen and turned the kettle on, aware that Mrs Fielding had followed her and was standing in the doorway.

'Look, I know it must come across that I'm interfering.' The woman's voice was gentle now. 'But I've seen so many young girls like yourself. They come here thinking that life is going to be a bed of roses from now on, and then before they know it, they find . . .' Realising that she had said too much, she suddenly turned away and moved back into the lounge where she resumed her polishing as if they hadn't even spoken.

Curious now, Claire followed her. 'What did you mean, Mrs Fielding?'

'Never mind. It's none of my business what you do,' the cleaner snapped. 'Just forget I ever said anything, eh?'

Claire slowly returned to the kitchen where she made herself a cup of tea, and half an hour later Mrs Fielding left without saying so much as another word to her. Eventually Claire went back to the bedroom and lay on top of the bed, soon drifting off into a deep and healing sleep.

The sound of someone moving about the lounge brought her springing awake, and when she glanced towards the bedroom window she was shocked to see that it was dusk. Knuckling the sleep from her eyes, she clambered off the bed then cautiously inched the door open and peeped into the lounge.

Marcus was there. His suit jacket was off and she could see the muscles in his arms rippling beneath his short-sleeved silk shirt.

'Ah, you're finally back in the land of the living, are you?' he greeted her. 'You were out like a light when I peeped in on you earlier on and you looked so peaceful that I didn't like to disturb you.'

Claire was about to answer him when she noticed a woman sitting on one of the enormous settees staring at her.

'This is Sandra, a friend of mine,' Marcus told her.

Sandra acknowledged Claire with a nod of her head. On first impression she looked to be quite young, but on closer inspection Claire saw that there were lines around her eyes, masked by the heavy make-up she wore. Her hair was backcombed until it almost stood on end, and now Claire noticed the black roots beneath the matted mess. Yet still she managed to be strangely attractive, helped by piercingly blue eyes that were now looking Claire up and down as if she was a piece of meat on a butcher's slab. Sandra was dressed in a suit that looked as if it was quality, and her shoes and handbag also looked expensive.

'Actually, Claire, I think Sandra here just might be able to help you,' Marcus now told her.

Claire looked at him with suspicion shining in her eyes. 'Oh yeah – an' how's she goin' to do that?'

It was the woman who answered. 'Marcus tells me that you're a bit down on your luck at the moment,' she said smoothly. 'I run a little business not far away from here, and I could offer you a job there if you were interested. You'd get to live in too, so you wouldn't have to worry about finding somewhere to stay.'

Claire sank down onto the edge of a chair, never taking her eyes from the woman's face as she asked, 'What sort of a job?'

Both Marcus and Sandra had a glass of wine in their hands and now Sandra passed another glass that had already been poured out to Claire before answering, 'I run a massage parlour. You could perhaps do the reception work there – what do you think?'

Claire gulped at the wine, suddenly feeling very grown up. Molly had never allowed her to drink alcohol except on special occasions, yet here was this woman and Marcus treating her like an adult and offering her a job into the bargain. She was about to answer when the door buzzed, and with a sigh of irritation, Marcus rose to answer it. He had barely opened the door when a young girl pushed past him and came into the flat like a whirling dervish. Her face was flushed and at a glance Claire saw that she was shaking like a leaf. The skirt she was wearing was so short that it was almost indecent and she was plastered in heavy make-up. The second that Sandra saw her, she rose from her seat and with an apologetic glance towards Claire she quickly crossed the room, went out and closed the lounge door between them.

Claire strained her ears to try and catch the muttered argument that was going on in the hallway. She could only hear muted words, but as the girl's voice rose she heard her shout, 'I want my fix *now*. You promised, Marcus! I've been out all day and done as you asked, so now give me what I'm due.'

Marcus's voice now rose too and then suddenly Claire heard the girl gasp as if she had been hurt and it all went very quiet. She took another swig from her glass, enjoying the warm feeling that was creeping through her. For the first time in as long as she could remember, nothing seemed to matter and she felt as if she were floating on a cloud of well-being. Damn the girl who had just arrived. Claire had enough problems of her own at the minute without worrying about hers. She heard the penthouse door slam and the next minute Sandra and Marcus walked back into the room with broad smiles on their faces as if they had never been interrupted.

'So,' Sandra addressed her. 'What do you think of my job offer then, Claire?'

'I think it shounds great,' Claire slurred and then she giggled. 'When would you like me to ssstart?'

'Well, now seems like just about as good a time as any.' Sandra smiled at Marcus. 'Why don't you get dressed, dear, and you can come along with me now.'

Claire lurched unsteadily to her feet with a grin on her face that stretched from ear to ear. Entering the kitchen, she lifted her washed and ironed clothes from where Mrs Fielding had left them. Then, hurrying back into the bedroom, she struggled into them, laughing as she swayed from side to side like some drunken belly dancer. I don't know what that drink was, she thought to herself, but I wouldn't mind a bottle full of it.

Sandra was waiting for her when Claire re-entered the lounge. 'Right then.' She took Claire's elbow to steady her. 'We'll be on our way, shall we?'

'Yesh.' Claire grinned at Marcus. 'Thanks for . . .' She would have said more, but for some strange reason her tongue didn't seem to be doing what she told it to, and now the room was starting to swim around her.

'You'd better help me get her downstairs and into the car,' she heard Sandra tell Marcus, and the words seemed to come from a long way away. He nodded grimly, then half-led, half-carried Claire out of the flat and into the lift.

The next thing Claire knew, she was sitting in the back of a car with Sandra driving her through the crowded London streets. She sighed contentedly. This was the beginning of the new life she had yearned for; she could feel it in her bones. Letting her head fall against the back of the seat, she soon slipped into a deep slumber.

Chapter Fourteen

'Ouch!' Claire groaned as her eyes struggled open. Her head was thumping as if there was a sledgehammer inside it and her mouth felt as if it had been stuffed with cottonwool. Pulling herself up onto her elbow, she tried to figure out where she was. She was lying on a bed in a small room that looked none too clean at all. A window was set in one wall with the curtains drawn across it. On another wall was an ugly wooden wardrobe with one of the doors hanging drunkenly open. The only other furniture was an equally battered bedside table. The floor, she saw, was covered in old linoleum that was torn in places, and it didn't smell too good in there either.

Pushing her legs off the edge of the bed with an effort, Claire crossed to the window where she yanked the curtains aside. She was confronted with a big brick wall; down below, all she could see were dustbins in what appeared to be a small enclosed back yard. And then slowly it all started to come back to her. The last thing she remembered was being in Marcus's flat and there had been a woman there who had offered her a job. Now what was her name? She groaned as her hand stroked her forehead. Sandra – that was it. Perhaps she would give her a cup of tea to clear her head?

The first feelings of panic fluttered to life in her stomach when she discovered that the door was securely locked. '*Let me out, let me out!*' she screamed as she began to pummel on it with her fists.

After a few minutes she heard footsteps shuffling towards it and she stood back, red-faced and breathless. There was the sound of a key turning in the lock then the door inched open and a short dark-haired girl who looked to be about the same age as herself peeped into the room. There were dark circles beneath her eyes and she was painfully thin, her legs like two matchsticks peeping from beneath a short skirt that left little to the imagination.

'Ah, you're awake then, are you?' she said quietly.

Claire clenched her fists as she glared at her. 'Who are you? An' where's Sandra? Why did you lock me in?'

'One question at a time.' The girl stared back at her solemnly. 'First of all, I'm Sabrina. At least, that's my name when I'm here. Secondly, Sandra will be up to see you in a minute. And thirdly, till they learn to behave, all the new girls get locked in.'

'What do you mean – *all* the new girls?' Claire was totally bewildered. 'I came here to be a receptionist at the massage parlour.'

The girl laughed bitterly now. 'Oh, that's what they told you, is it? Oh well, perhaps it's for the best that you didn't know what you were getting yourself into.'

'What's *that* supposed to mean?' Despite her anger, Claire couldn't keep the note of fear from her voice.

The girl glanced across her shoulder, then lowering her voice she told Claire, 'This is a brothel.'

Claire's good eye sprang open as if it was on a stalk; the other one was too swollen to follow suit. 'It's a *what*?'

'Ssh, someone will hear you an' then we'll both be in for it,' the girl whispered, then told her, 'Don't look so scared. It ain't as bad as you think, once you get used to it. And it's better than being out on the streets.'

'But I . . . I don't want to live in a brothel,' Claire whimpered pathetically. She had run away from home because of her feelings about having been abused, and now it looked as if it was about to start all over again.

'Look, I'll go and get you a drink, eh?' Sabrina offered. 'You'll feel better after that when the drugs wear off.'

'Wh . . . what drugs?' Claire faltered.

'The drugs Marcus would have slipped into your drink to get you here,' the girl told her patiently. 'How do you think he keeps us all here, and workin' the streets for him?' Lifting her sleeve, she showed Claire her arm. It was covered in tiny bruises and needle-marks. Seeing the look of horror on Claire's face, the girl shrugged. 'It's all very well, you pulling a face and looking down your nose at me, but he'll soon have you as hooked on smack as us lot are.'

'He will not,' Claire spat, feeling as if she had slipped into a nightmare. Surely she would wake up in a minute and all this would have been no more than a bad dream? Marcus had seemed so kind, and so had Sandra.

As if she could read her thoughts, Sabrina told her, 'Marcus is the pimp. He runs nearly all the girls in Shepherds Bush and Soho. Sandra is the madam of the brothel. It ain't so bad, as I said. Once they can trust you not to run away or steal your takings, they won't lock you up and he'll let you work the streets.'

Claire shuddered at the thought. Sabrina was backing out of the door now and just before she closed it, she promised, 'I'll be back as soon as I can with a drink for you. Try to keep your pecker up, eh? If you do as you're told, you'll be all right.'

As the door clicked shut and Claire heard the key turn in the lock, despair washed over her and she began to cry. How could she have been so gullible as to get into this mess? Hadn't she promised herself she would never trust anyone again? And now here she was, completely out of her depth. Looking back, she realised how foolish she had been to go with Marcus in the first place. After all, she should have realised he would have some ulterior motive for helping her.

Wiping her nose on her sleeve, she attempted to pull herself together before crossing back to the window and peering down into the yard below. Undoing the metal catch, she shoved at the bottom window with all her might. It slowly rose until she had just enough room to poke her head out of it. She saw at a glance that there would be no escape route there. It looked a frighteningly long way down to the ground and there wasn't even a drainpipe for her to cling on to. Sighing, she heaved the window down again and went back to the bed where she sat cross-legged, pondering on the latest dilemma she found herself in and trying to think of other ways she might escape.

Some time later, she switched on the bare overhead light bulb and then wished she hadn't, for the room instantly looked even worse than it had before. The bright light revealed wallpaper that looked as if it had been flowered at some time but had long since faded to a dingy brown. The curtains were so thin that they were falling into holes, and the grubby sheets on the bed made her shudder. But she wouldn't be here for long, she was determined about that, and now her fighting spirit was returning. She had escaped the abuse and humiliation she had been forced to endure at home, and she would escape from here too – or die in the attempt.

★   ★   ★

By the time the door finally opened again, Claire was calm. Sandra came in, balancing a plastic tray with a plate full of what looked like some sort of meat pie and a mug of tea on it.

'How are you feeling?' she asked, for all the world as if she cared.

Claire stayed tight-lipped and so Sandra prattled on, 'I've brought you some dinner – look. You must be hungry.'

Again only silence answered her, so now she shrugged as she placed the tray on the bedside table and backed towards the door. 'Have it your own way,' she sniffed. 'This can be as easy or as hard as you want it to be. It's up to you at the end of the day.'

Once the door had closed behind her, Claire stared at the food longingly. Her stomach was rumbling with hunger, but after the drugged drink they had given to her in Marcus's flat she was too afraid to touch it. What if the food or the tea was drugged too?

Her eyes settled on the tray. The gravy that had covered the pie was cold and congealed now, and lifting the whole sorry mess, she flung it against the wall. As the plate shattered and crashed to the floor, her eyes followed the fork as it spun away under the bed and an idea sprang to mind. Dropping to her knees, she fumbled in the fluff and dust until she found it, then tucking it into the waistband of her jeans she threw back the vile sheets and slithered inside them, pulling them up to her chin. And then she waited; her heart pounding and her eyes tight on the door. Beyond it, she heard music start up and then the sound of footsteps walking along the landing outside. There was a high-pitched giggle as a door slammed, and then within seconds the guttural sounds of someone having sex. It was as if the silent house was slowly coming to life. Trying to shut out the sounds, Claire kept her eyes fixed ahead. After what seemed a lifetime she heard other voices, talking outside the room she was locked in. The key grated in the lock and Marcus strode into the room. She sighed with relief when she noted that he didn't lock the door behind him.

His eyes immediately flew to the food and the tea spilled across the floor, and he tutted with annoyance. 'That was a silly thing to do,' he scolded. 'I shall have to teach you a lesson now, shan't I?'

Claire quivered with fear but said nothing as he took off his jacket and hung it neatly in the grotty wardrobe. Next he unbuttoned his shirt and did the same with that, and she found her eyes fixed on his bulging biceps.

'The thing is, my dear,' he told her as he now started to unbutton his trousers and slither out of them, 'I like to know that the men who use my establishments are getting value for money, so I try out the goods first, if you get my meaning.'

Claire got his meaning only too well and panic began to grip her as she clutched at the fork under the covers. In no time at all he was standing before her naked.

'I think it's about time you and I had a little fun, don't you?' He held himself erect, proud of his fine physique, and then slowly he began to advance towards the bed as if he was a model on a catwalk.

It was all Claire could do not to fly at him there and then, but she knew she had to gauge the right moment or she wouldn't stand a chance against him. Lifting the sheet, he slithered in beside her, cooing with excitement as his great hand closed across her tender young breast. It was then that she lunged forward, and with every ounce of strength she possessed, she plunged the fork into the tender skin of his private parts. The cry that issued from him might have been that of a wounded animal as his hands dropped away from her to stem the blood that was spurting from the wound. Knowing that there was not a moment to lose, Claire flung herself from the edge of the bed and snatching up her coat, she sprinted towards the door as his screams echoed in her ears.

She almost cried with relief when she found herself out on the landing – and then she was pushing her way through people in various stages of undress who were appearing out of doors as she ran for her life. When she came to a curving staircase she almost fell down it in her haste to escape.

'*Hey, you!*' Sandra's voice sounded from behind her as Claire fumbled with the key in the enormous front door, but she didn't waste a second in looking behind. Every moment she expected a hand to clamp down on her shoulder, and the hairs on the back of her neck stood to attention as adrenalin flooded through her. Suddenly the door was open and the wind was like a slap in the face as she flew down the steps and began to run along the road as if the hounds of hell were at her heels. She had no idea where she was going and didn't much care. All she knew was that she must get away.

Only when the stitch in her side was causing her to double over with pain did she allow her steps to slow, and she leaned painfully against a wall. By then she had managed to put a considerable distance between herself and the brothel. Straining her ears into the darkness, she sucked air into her burning lungs. And then the tears came as a vision of Marcus's face twisted in pain floated in front of her eyes and she looked about her helplessly. It was late now, she could tell by the sounds of the drunken men rolling out of public houses as they lurched unsteadily home, and she didn't have a penny to her name.

Forcing herself to move on, she eventually came to a sign that pointed towards Soho. Once again she was tired and dirty, and the bruises and black eye she had sustained from her encounter with the thugs were hurting. On top of everything else it had started to rain, so eventually she sheltered in the filthy doorway of a cinema, only to find that it 'belonged' to another street person, a wild-eyed tramp with two cans of Special Brew. In central London, it seemed that every doorway had its owner. Finally, in desperation, she sat on a gravestone in the churchyard, wet, cold and miserable, and hiding from the police when they walked past in pairs. Eventually she dozed off.

It was the following morning, when she was sitting there wondering forlornly what to do, that someone hurried past then slowly retraced their steps to stand and stare at her through the railings. Claire raised her head and stared back. It was a young woman. Her hair was tied back, and she was clutching a loaf and a pint of milk. She was dressed in old jeans and a baggy jumper, and Claire frowned, for there was something about her that was vaguely familiar.

'Bloody hell!' exclaimed the girl. 'I recognised you by your coat and hair. You've been in the wars by the look of it, mate, aincher!'

As she spoke, Claire suddenly realised that this was the same mini-skirted girl who had stopped to speak to her the other night. She looked completely different without her heavy make-up.

'I got mugged,' she said huskily as fresh tears welled in her eyes. 'They took me bag, me money . . . everythin'. And then they pulled me behind a phone box and they . . . they . . . An' then this man offered to help me an' I found meself . . .' She lowered her head at the horror of it all and was unable to go on.

In a second the girl had clanged through the churchyard gates and was sitting on the tomb beside her. Hesitantly she put her arm around Claire's shaking shoulders. 'You silly little mare, you,' she whispered, but her voice was kindly. 'I told yer to get yer arse off home, didn't I?'

Claire nodded and sniffed loudly.

'What are we going to do with you, eh?' The girl chewed on her lip thoughtfully as Claire carefully wiped her sore eyes.

'Look, I'll tell you what – you can come back to my place and get cleaned up a bit,' she suggested. 'I don't live in Soho – just come here to see a mate – but I'm on the way home. We'll get the 73 bus from Tottenham Court Road – right?'

Claire didn't answer because after her encounter with Marcus she was suspicious of everyone.

'Come on,' the girl said encouragingly, helping Claire to her feet. 'You can't stay here. You'll get piles sitting on this damp stone, and you don't want them, do you? Horrible things, they are, piles ...' Clutching her groceries in one arm and Claire's elbow with the other she set off along the pavement.

As she began to walk, Claire's blisters started to bleed again and she limped painfully. Her eye was tender and she smelled – of sweat from her running, of the stale odours from the nasty little room that had been her prison cell, of her night sleeping rough. It was then she realised that she had hit rock bottom. She couldn't sink any lower now.

Getting off the bus at King's Cross, the girls walked up a street of seedy hotels to a big square of Georgian houses. Most of them were in a state of disrepair, and all had been divided into bedsits. Eventually they came to a four-storey townhouse that was a far cry indeed from the luxury apartment where Marcus lived. Fumbling in her jeans pocket for a key, the girl made her way down some steep steps to a shabby door that was set below pavement level, and Claire followed her slowly. Once inside, she stared about her; she was in what appeared to be a small one-bedroom flat that smelled strongly of bleach and disinfectant. It was very basic and sparsely furnished, but surprisingly clean and tidy.

Claire's eyes began to smart and the girl grinned. 'It ain't much,' she admitted, 'but it's comfortable enough for now, and it's better than a blooming tombstone, ain't it? Sorry about the smell. I use disinfectant to keep the cockroaches at bay. It's the damp, see. It attracts them. I should charge them rent, shouldn't I?' she joked.

Claire suppressed a shudder. 'Where am I?' she asked.

'This is King's Cross, or if you wanna be posh, you can call it Bloomsbury. We're off the Gray's Inn Road. Now why don't you sit down while I put the kettle on?'

Wearily, Claire did as she was told. As she pulled her trainers off she found that her socks were stuck to the back of her heels. When they came off, the blistered skin came with them, and she gasped with pain. Minutes later, the girl placed a mug of tea in her hands and Claire sipped at it gratefully as she bustled away again. However, she kept a cautious eye on her rescuer who was now bending over the grill of a small oven that had been hidden behind a long curtain in the corner of the room.

'I'm Cindy, by the way,' the girl threw over her shoulder, then giggled. 'To tell the truth, my real name's Deirdre Kennedy, but I call myself Cindy 'cos it's a bit more glamorous, ain't it?'

Despite herself, Claire managed a smile.

Minutes later, Cindy handed her a plateful of hot buttered toast. 'There, get some of that down you,' she ordered. 'There's Marmite or strawberry jam to go with it.'

After all that had happened, Claire's appetite had fled, but even so she nibbled at the toast obediently.

In the meantime, Cindy opened a door to reveal the smallest bathroom that Claire had ever seen, and she started to run a bath. When she emerged she eyed Claire's empty plate with satisfaction. 'Well done,' she praised. 'Now we'll get you in the tub and soon you'll be feeling as good as new.'

'Why are yer doin' all this for me?' Claire wanted to know.

For a second Cindy paused. 'Let's just say that once I was in your posi-tion, and somebody helped *me*,' she replied quietly. Smiling, she crossed to an old-fashioned cupboard and reaching inside, pulled out a large towel and a clean nightshirt.

'Look, go and get yourself cleaned up. There's everything in there you'll need and I'll take the things you're wearing to the launderette with my washing later on.'

Claire needed no second telling; the thought of a bath sounded like heaven, and within minutes she'd thrown off her clothes and was immersed in hot soapy water. She sank back thankfully. Through the closed door she could hear Cindy softly humming 'Imagine' by John Lennon to herself as she cleared away the supper things, and so she lay there letting the hot water soothe her aches and pains.

Just as Cindy had promised, she did feel a lot better after her bath; as if she had washed away the drugs and the stinking sheet in the brothel; when she eventually emerged, Cindy smiled at her. She was busily pushing dirty washing into a large laundry bag, and after scooping Claire's dirty clothes up off the bathroom floor, she added them to the rest. A good judge of character, the older girl had no qualms about leaving this lass alone in her flat. She was no thief, that much was obvious.

'Right then, I'm off to the launderette to get this lot washed and dried,' she told her. 'You put your feet up while I'm gone an' when I get back in a couple of hours we'll have a talk, eh?'

Claire nodded and with a cheery wave, Cindy was gone.

Cindy returned almost two hours later to find Claire fast asleep on the settee. She felt sad as she stared down at her. Claire reminded Cindy of herself when she had first run away from Kent three long years ago. Like Claire, she too had had big plans, but what had become of them? Nothing! She had been abused like Claire, but in a different way. She had suffered a drunken bullying father who had beaten her and belittled her at every opportunity. On the day she was sixteen she had left home with her head full of dreams and her heart full of hope, but once she got to London, all the dreams had soon been knocked out of her, and now she was nothing more than a common street girl.

Sighing for her lost dreams, the older girl crossed to her bedroom, pulled a blanket off her own bed and tucked it around her guest.

Chapter Fifteen

By the time Claire stirred, it was evening and she blinked sleepily, taking a moment to recall where she was.

Just then, Cindy came out of her bedroom, dressed as she had been when Claire first met her. 'Ah! So you've joined the land of the living again, have you?' she grinned as Claire looked back at her sheepishly. Pointing towards the curtain that hid the kitchenette, Cindy now told her, 'I've got to go to work, but there's some soup on the stove. It just needs warming up.' She nodded to the back of a chair. 'Your clean clothes are there, but you may as well stay here for tonight. I don't suppose you've anywhere better lined up, have you?'

Claire shook her head as Cindy headed for the door.

'Well, I'm off then, duty calls. Expect me when you see me.' She flashed her a friendly grin then left, closing the basement door softly behind her.

It was almost two o'clock in the morning when she got back in, and seeing that Claire was once again fast asleep on the sofa, she tiptoed past her and slipped into the bathroom.

The next morning, late, it was Cindy's turn to be waited on as Claire presented her with tea and toast in bed.

Cindy looked at the tray. 'Blimey, if you make a habit of this, I might keep you here for good,' she joked.

Claire was feeling much better today after a good rest, and was more grateful to Cindy than she could say. 'I don't know what I would 'ave done without you,' she admitted.

Cindy waved her hand at her. 'It was nothing. I'm just glad to see you looking a bit chirpier again.'

Rising from the foot of the bed, Claire backed towards the door. 'Well, anyway, thanks for everythin'. I'd better get dressed an' be on me way now.'

Cindy frowned. 'And just *where* were you planning on going?'

'I suppose I'll go job-huntin' again,' Claire muttered.

'Look, finding jobs hereabouts is like looking for a needle in the proverbial haystack,' Cindy warned her. 'Believe me, I've been there, done it and got the T-shirt. Why do you think I went on the game?' She patted the bed. 'Look, kid, why don't you just do yourself a favour and get yourself back home?'

As Claire sat back down, her eyes filled with tears. 'I ain't got no home,' she replied miserably. They sat in silence for some minutes, each recognising the loneliness in the other until eventually Cindy asked, 'How old are you?'

Claire sniffed and hesitated before answering, 'I'm eighteen.'

'Oh yeah? You ain't a day over sixteen if I'm any judge, and I'm being generous at that.' Seeing Claire bristle, Cindy said gently, 'Look, I don't want to come across as nagging you, but believe me, London ain't no place for a kid your age all on her own. Surely whatever it is that's wrong at home could be sorted with your folks?'

When Claire sadly shook her head, Cindy tried another tack. 'You'll only end up going back sooner or later, you know. Surely you've realised by now that jobs around here are like gold dust.'

'But there must be *somethin'* somewhere that I could do.' For a time they lapsed into silence.

As a thought suddenly occurred to Claire, she stared at Cindy with excitement shining in her eyes. 'Perhaps *I* could go on the game?' she suggested.

Cindy choked on her toast. 'Here, hold on a minute,' she gasped. 'It ain't quite as simple as that. You step on anybody's patch round here and the toms are likely to claw your eyes out – and then there's the pimps. They'll have you in their clutches in the blink of an eye if you ain't up to their tricks – and I should know . . .' She stared thoughtfully at Claire before asking, 'This bloke you met who said he was going to help you – what was his name?'

'Marcus,' Claire told her, keeping her eyes downcast.

'*Marcus!* Not Marcus Thackeray, a big black man?' Cindy had paled to the colour of putty. Claire nodded. 'Bugger me, I don't believe it,' Cindy muttered, taking a swig of tea. 'He runs most of the girls and the brothels in West London and in Soho. It was him that got hold of me when I first came to London.'

Claire was shocked but had no time to comment, for Cindy went on, 'Did he take you back to his flat?'

'Yes, he did, but only for a few hours and then this woman came – Sandra, he called her – and they gave me some wine.' Claire frowned as she tried to remember the details of what had happened. 'She told me that I could have the job as a receptionist in a massage parlour and after that, everything went a bit fuzzy. Next thing I knew, I woke up in this dirty little room. They'd locked me in and wouldn't let me out.' She shuddered now as the memories came pouring back. 'A girl brought me some food but I didn't eat it in case they'd put anything in it. Then later that night Marcus came back and he . . .' She gulped deeply before going on. 'He undressed and got into bed with me. He was going to . . . Well, it doesn't matter what he was going to do 'cos I stabbed him with a fork and then made a run for it. I ended up back in Soho and that's where you found me.'

Cindy shook her head in amazement. 'I can't believe the very same bloke who tricked me got hold of you too. That Marcus Thackeray should be locked up, and they should throw the key away. He's ruined so many young girls' lives it's unbelievable.'

'So why *don't* they lock him up then?'

Cindy snorted with derision. 'They don't lock him up 'cos he has friends in high places. The Tom Squad never bother Marcus Thackeray. He could get away with murder – in fact, he probably has. But if you've already had dealings with him, how come you still want to go on the game?'

'I'd do it because I was doing it from choice,' Claire told her. 'And not because someone like Marcus Thackeray made me.'

Cindy looked at her sympathetically. 'Whether you do it for yourself or for a pimp, this life ain't no bed of roses, you know,' she said. 'Are you quite sure that this is what you really want to do?'

As Claire could see no alternative, she nodded miserably.

'I'll tell you what I'll do then, I'll let you stay here for another couple of days, just while you have a think about it, eh? If you're still in the same mind after that, then we'll see. As long as you stay away from Marcus's patches and stick to King's Cross, you should be OK. The pimps have an unspoken law that they don't poach each other's girls. But being a tom ain't something you go into lightly.'

Relieved, Claire smiled at Cindy. 'Thank you.' She had dreaded the thought of tramping the streets again, and whilst Cindy's flat was hardly what she could term a palace it was somewhere safe to hide for a while at least, even if it meant sharing it with the occasional cockroach.

Cindy waggled a finger at her. 'It's only for a couple of days,' she warned. 'And if you take my advice, you'll let me lend you your train fare and you'll get yourself off home.'

The closed look settled on Claire's face again. 'I've told you, I haven't got a home,' she muttered resentfully.

Cindy shrugged. 'Have it your own way. I haven't got time to sit about here chatting – I've got to get ready for work – I'm doing an afternoon shift for a change. I suggest that while I'm gone, you have a good think about it, because I'll tell you now, if you *do* decide to stay, you might well live to regret it.' And with that she swept into the bathroom to change.

The next morning, Claire set off job-hunting again bright and early, but by the time she arrived home late in the afternoon, she had still had no luck at all in finding employment of any description. She was beginning to realise that Cindy had spoken the truth about jobs being hard to come by, and her spirits were at a very low ebb indeed.

'It's useless,' she told her new friend sadly.

Cindy nodded in agreement. 'What did I tell you?'

Still, Claire was determined not to go home. 'Is there no chance of me working with you?' she asked.

Cindy laughed bitterly. 'Look – I've already told you.' She sighed. 'You don't know the first thing about this game; you wouldn't last a single night.'

Claire shook her head in denial. 'I would,' she insisted. 'I'm tougher than I look an' you could teach me . . . I'd listen to what yer said, honest.'

Cindy stared towards the small window and now her voice was low as she told Claire, 'Some of the poor cows I know out there are enough to break you heart. There's little Moll, she's just seventeen but to look at her you'd take her for thirty. Two little kids she's got already, and she goes on the streets just to keep a roof over their head and clothes on their backs. She leaves 'em locked in a grubby little bedsit night after night, all on their own. Then there's Jenny. She came to London much like you, with stars in her eyes till some pimp got his claws into her. Now he's got her so hooked on heroin she'd sell her granny for her next fix. How's it sounding up to now? Still fancy it, do you?'

Claire gulped deep in her throat but there was a determined light in her eye.

Cindy could see now that she meant it, and eyed her shrewdly. 'You *have* got the looks,' she admitted slowly. 'In fact, I reckon you'd be in great demand. The punters like 'em young and pretty. But I still think you'd be making a big mistake.'

Claire was staring at her hopefully, and realising that she meant to do it, Cindy shrugged in defeat.

'You've got a lot to learn,' she warned. 'For a start, there's the prices; they vary depending on what the punters want.'

When Claire frowned, Cindy couldn't help but smile. 'You haven't got a clue what I'm on about, have you?' she asked. 'Right, then I'll try to explain,' Cindy said patiently. 'If they just want a hand job, it's a tenner. If they want a blow job, it's twenty quid.'

Claire blushed but Cindy went on relentlessly, hoping to put her off. 'If they want the works – full sex, like – it's between thirty and forty quid. You'll learn to suss out those who are willing to pay a bit more. But for a start it's best to just charge thirty, then it doesn't get confusing. And by the way, make the dirty buggers use a johnny. There's no way you want to catch anything off them, especially not this AIDS thing.'

Claire nodded obediently as for the next hour Cindy advised her of the dos and don'ts of prostitution. At the end of it, the girl's head was spinning. At her age, Claire should have been studying for her GCSEs at the end of this school year. Instead, here she was, learning all about a subject that was most definitely not on any school curriculum.

Cindy eyed her thoughtfully. 'You know,' she said, 'I reckon with your looks, you could make a high-class call girl eventually. With the right clothes you'd be a knockout, and then you'd be talking *real* money. But of course you'd have to do something about that Midlands accent of yours.'

Claire was astounded. 'What – yer mean they earn even more than you?'

Cindy chuckled. 'What I earn is peanuts compared to them,' she said.

'How come you're not one o' them then?' asked Claire, and now Cindy threw her head back and laughed aloud.

'Like I told you, they dress the part. They wear designer clothes, they look like models, and they talk proper too! How do you reckon I'd do, with this London accent, eh? At least you've got the looks, and you could do somethin' about the voice.'

Claire giggled, knowing that Cindy had a point.

'Anyway – are you still up for it then?' Cindy asked.

'Yes.' In truth, Claire felt that she didn't have much choice. Anything was better than having to swallow her pride and run home, even if it meant resorting to prostitution. If she could do as Cindy told her, this might be the means of her being able to stand on her own two feet. She would never need to be dependant on anyone again.

'Right then.' Cindy's eyes twinkled with mischief. She was still convinced that Claire would run a mile at the sight of the first punter. 'You can't go anywhere for at least a couple of days, with your feet and your face in that state, can you? But there's nothing to stop us having a dress rehearsal, is there? Come on, we'd better find you something suitable to wear. There's no way you could go out in those clothes.' The older girl was hoping that if she went along with this mad scheme, Claire would chicken out and come to her senses.

The girls spent the next half an hour rummaging through Cindy's wardrobe. Once they'd selected an outfit, Cindy made up Claire's face, dabbing gently on the bruises, and did her hair for her. As Claire stared at herself in the mirror, she could hardly believe the transformation. It was just like the time she had decided to seduce Craig Thomas. She was wearing a tight miniskirt and a skimpy top that barely concealed her midriff, but showed off her firm young breasts, and she guessed that anyone looking at her could have easily taken her for at least twenty years old.

Her hands began to tremble as the full significance of what she was planning to do came home to her. She was about to sell her body for money. But then, she reasoned, would it be so very different to what she had done with Mark? She had played him like a fiddle, sucking every penny she could out of him for favours – until he had abandoned her, that was, at that service station on the way to London. Resentment washed over her in a wave. At least this time *she* would be calling the shots. And it couldn't be that bad, surely? It was only sex.

Sensing her waver, Cindy now said, 'You never go off with anyone you don't like the look of. There's many a pro gone missing and never been seen again. This is a hard business to be in. And don't think you won't take the odd beating. It's all part of being a tom, so be warned. *Still* want to go ahead?'

Claire nodded when Cindy sighed. 'Then just remember everything I've told you,' she warned. 'Else you won't last a single night.'

Claire shivered, suddenly nervous and excited all at the same time. At least she still had the rest of her month's supply of the Pill, she thought. Those thieving youths hadn't got them and her precious photos out of her coat. She'd better get herself to a clinic and order some more, she thought. There must never be any more babies . . . For a second, her heart cried out, '*Yasmin!*' and the pain was excruciating.

'Come on,' Cindy said, sensing that the girl's mood had changed. 'We'll have us a nice stiff drink an' listen to the news before I get my arse into gear. No point in going out too early – the punters are still at home with their wives and kids at this time of night.'

Grinning at her own joke, she pottered away to fetch a cheap bottle of wine and two glasses from the small teak sideboard that stood against one wall as Claire switched the television on. When Cindy rejoined her, she nodded at the screen as she took a long slurp from her glass.

'Looks like Maggie Thatcher is only hanging on by the skin of her teeth now if you ask me. That's two Cabinet Ministers have resigned this month, first Leon Brittan an' now Michael Heseltine. Not that I'm that much into politics, to be truthful.'

Seeing that Claire wasn't listening to a word she was saying, Cindy switched the television off and placed her hand gently on her arm. 'There's still time to change yer mind.'

Claire's head wagged from side to side.

'Then just remember everything I told you.'

'I will,' Claire said, and it was like making a promise to herself.

Two nights later, with half a bottle of white wine inside her to give her courage, Claire followed Cindy out of the basement flat and along to the dimly-lit back streets near King's Cross station.

They passed many girls, all obviously prostitutes, and some of them eyed Claire suspiciously. Luckily, Cindy was well-known to them and because Claire was with her, thankfully they left her alone. Along the way, Cindy stopped to talk to one or two of her friends.

'Hello, Blue,' she said to one girl who was leaning against a lamp-post smoking a cigarette.

'Hello, Cindy.'

Claire was shocked as they drew close to the girl to see the great dark circles under her eyes and the bruises all down one side of her face. She looked to be little more than a child and was painfully thin.

'Had a good day, have you?' Cindy asked cheerfully.

The girl shook her head and Claire saw that her eyes had a glazed look about them. 'Awful up to now. Bill'll swipe me when I get back if trade don't pick up soon.'

'Well, it's still early yet,' Cindy told her encouragingly.

'What happened to her face?' Claire asked, once they were out of earshot. Her own bruises were hidden under panstick, and her swollen eye had been skilfully disguised. Even the sore patches on her heels were feeling comfortable enough in a pair of Cindy's silver slingbacks.

'Huh! Bill's her bloke – or should I say, her pimp. She hands over her money and he keeps her in drugs. Poor little sod needs them, to help her with what we have to do out here.'

As visions of the girl's pale face flashed in front of her eyes, Claire fell silent and they moved on. When they finally approached a particular street corner, Cindy stopped abruptly.

'Try to steer clear o' those two girls over there,' she said. 'They've been arrested by the Tom Squad so many times they could probably find their way to the nick in their sleep.'

'Why's that?' Claire asked innocently.

''Cos they're both into clipping and rolling.'

When Claire looked at her blankly, Cindy explained patiently. 'Rolling is when you take a punter down a back street to do the business but have your boyfriend or a pimp waiting for you. The bloke then gets mugged and the girls never have to do the business. Clipping is much the same thing, except while the girl is giving the punter a blow job and his mind is otherwise occupied, she lifts his wallet herself and then does a runner.'

Claire tried not to look shocked. It seemed there was a lot more to being a prostitute, or a tom as Cindy referred to them, than she had thought.

'You've also got to look out for the Tom Squad,' Cindy went on. 'Sometimes they're in plain clothes, sneaky bastards and if you proposition them they'll have you in the paddy wagon in no time. Now I ask again, are you still *quite* sure you want to go through with this? You can clear off back to the flat now – just say the word.'

Not trusting herself to speak, Claire nodded.

'Right then. This is it.' Deadly serious now, Cindy looked at Claire. 'Don't forget what I told yer. Don't *ever* attempt to work any other stretch than here. The girls are very protective about their patches an' if you do move in, they'll have your guts for garters. Go beyond here and you're likely to bump into Marcus an' all.' She sighed. 'One more thing. Watch out for the squealers.'

'Squealers?'

'The blokes who make you do the deed then refuse to pay. That's why you *always* ask for the readies upfront, OK? Finally – have you got your condoms?'

Claire nodded.

'Right then – and don't forget: you ask them what they want *first* and it's money upfront, OK? Watch me,' she said calmly. Cindy now walked a short way away from her and stood on the kerb, her chest stuck out and one hand playing with her hair. Traffic was whizzing by and people were streaming out of the entrances to the tube station. Everywhere seemed to be hustle and bustle. Within minutes, a car pulled up beside Cindy and Claire watched her lean into the driver's window, exchange a few words with the driver then straighten up and walk around the car to the passenger door. Just before climbing in she flashed Claire a reassuring wink then the car pulled away and Claire was alone.

She was suddenly terrified and her knees were almost knocking with fear. But she had barely had time to even miss Cindy when a car pulled up beside her. This is it, she thought, and remembering Cindy's words she swaggered up to it with a false smile fixed on her lips.

A middle-aged bald-headed man leered at her from behind thick-lensed glasses. Claire's stomach did a somersault but she managed to smile at him seductively as Cindy had shown her.

'Looking for work are you, sweetheart?' He was surprisingly well-spoken and Claire was glad of the darkness that hid her blushes. When she nodded, he reached across and swung the passenger door open for her. On legs that no longer seemed to belong to her, she walked unsteadily around the car and almost fell into the seat beside him.

She sank back into the plush leather seat as the car glided almost noise-lessly away from the kerb, suddenly seeming to have lost her tongue. Thankfully, the man seemed far more intent on watching her legs than worrying about any conversation she might make, and so for the first few minutes they were silent as Claire admired the car. It was spotlessly clean and from what she could judge, worth a small fortune – which, if what Cindy had told her was right, meant he might be a good payer.

'Err . . . what was it yer were wantin' then?' she asked eventually, desperately trying to remember everything that Cindy had told her. As he glanced away from the road to smile at her, the eyes behind the thick lenses seemed to gleam like a cat's and his hand strayed from the gear-stick to stroke the soft skin of her inner thigh.

'Oh, I think we might manage the works, don't you?'

Claire gulped and lapsed into silence again as the car cruised along. It was some time later when he pulled into a small deserted yard. It had obviously been a factory yard of some sort at one time, but now as Claire gazed around she saw that the buildings inside it were derelict.

The man turned off the engine and suddenly the silence was deafening. 'Shall we get into the back?' he said. 'There's a little more room in there and we want to be comfortable, don't we?'

He switched off the car headlights and Claire blinked as her eyes tried to adjust to the pitch dark. When he flung the car door open, a gust of cold wind caused her to shiver. They might have been in the middle of nowhere instead of on the outskirts of the capital city, for everywhere was as silent as the grave.

He climbed out of the car and seconds later opened her door for her. He's a gentleman, Claire thought, as he took her hand to help her from the car, but seconds later when he flung her roughly onto the back seat, she changed her mind.

'Right then, you bleeding little whore, let's get on with it, shall we?'

She saw him fumbling with his flies, and remembered her instructions.

'It's er . . . it's sixty quid,' she managed to say as she struggled to remember all that Cindy had told her. 'Upfront.'

Cursing, he thrust his hand into his jacket pocket and the next second some notes fluttered onto her lap.

'Not cheap, are you?' he complained. 'I just hope you're worth it, you fucking little trollop. Now . . . can we get down to business?' Suddenly his hands were all over her and his slobbering mouth was seeking hers as he lowered his heavy weight onto her. The gentleman she had thought him to be only moments before was gone, to be replaced by a wild, foul-mouthed animal. He cursed and called her all the vile names he could think of, and she chewed on her lip to stop the scream that was lodged in her throat from erupting. She was suddenly back in her little bedroom in Gatley Common calling for her mother, and instead of the car roof, in her mind's eye she was staring up once again at the cracked ceiling. Thankfully it was over in minutes and he rolled off her and stood outside the car as he hurriedly dressed himself. Claire felt around in the dark until she found her knickers on the car floor, then quickly pulling them on, she joined him as shame and humiliation washed over her.

'That was very enjoyable, my dear.' He patted her hand as if they had just shared a cup of tea together. 'Now we had better get you back, hadn't we?'

Claire nodded and swallowed the lump of pure misery that had lodged in her throat. This was to be her life from now on, for the foreseeable future at least.

When she returned to the flat that night with a tight little bundle of notes clutched fiercely in her fist, Claire knew that Cindy had been right. This was certainly no bowl of cherries and she wondered if she could bear it. But then again, what other choice was there? From where she was standing, men still ruled the world – the whole rotten lot of them – but not one of them, she thought fiercely, *not one of them*, is man enough for me!

Cindy followed her in almost an hour later and took in Claire's red-rimmed eyes at a glance. 'How did you do?' she asked gently.

Claire held the money out to her.

Cindy counted it quickly, then handed it back. 'That's really good for your first night,' she said encouragingly. 'And don't worry, it does get easier.'

Claire had grave doubts about that. If she had to do this, then she wanted to make it really pay, like the high-class call girls that Cindy had told her about. That would be the only thing that could make her stay at it, the thought that some day she could become someone else. Someone who could stand on her own two feet, not answerable to anyone. Already in her mind she was beginning to plan how she could make it happen.

Chapter Sixteen

Claire had now been living with Cindy for almost a week and was worried about over-staying her welcome, yet she had no idea how to go about finding a place of her own. She told Cindy so as they were getting ready for the streets one night.

'To tell you the truth,' Cindy admitted, 'finding a place round here is almost as hard as finding a job. When I first arrived in London I lived off the Fulham Road, but I had to get out of there quick. I got sucked in good and proper, you see, just like you did. Ended up with a pimp on my back – Marcus – the same one that picked you up. I reckon he must spend half his life looking around for girls like us who are down on their luck. And he's a mean bastard, I don't mind telling you. He worked me into the ground and took almost every penny I earned. If I didn't earn I got beaten up – it was as simple as that. For a time I took it because I were green back then. I thought he cared about me, but I soon realised that if I didn't get out, he'd end up killing me.' She shuddered. 'I left that flat with nothing but the clothes I stood up in. Did a moonlight flit with not a penny to my name. That's how I ended up here, and even this dump costs an arm and a leg. Everywhere does in London. The rent's due on Monday, that's why I've been doin' overtime.'

'How long did you stay with him?' This was the first time Cindy had really ever spoken of Marcus and Claire was appalled yet fascinated all at the same time.

'A couple of months or so.' Cindy's eyes grew moist as she thought back to those days. 'I'll never forget the first time I set eyes on him. I thought he were the most handsome bloke I'd ever seen. I'd just arrived in London from a little village in Kent, much as you did, with my head full of big ideas. Huh! They didn't last long. My first night was spent under a railway bridge. The next morning I was tramping the streets when I met Marcus. He was just coming out of a shop and there I was, crying my eyes out on the pavement. He was kind and took me to a café for a drink. Next thing I know, I'm pouring my heart out to him and he took the time to listen. Smooth-talking bugger he was.' She sighed. 'Big, black and beautiful. Trouble was, he was also the biggest bastard on two legs, though I was so wet behind the ears then that I couldn't see it. Anyway, eventually he offered to let me stay at his place for a while, and muggins here went with him like a lamb to the slaughter. His penthouse apartment was one of the best in Knightsbridge, and I remember thinking to myself, You've landed on your feet here, mate. He bought me some decent clothes, and in no time at all I was totally besotted with him. But then one night he comes back with this bloke. "Be nice to him," he says, and you don't have to be the Brain of Britain to work out what he meant, do you? When I refused, he gave me a black eye and it was all downhill from then on. This went on for a couple of weeks and then he tells me that he's found me somewhere else to live. The somewhere else turned out to be a rat-infested brothel in Soho, sharing with six other girls who he'd treated exactly the same as me. He were coining it in between us, but I got to the point where I couldn't take it any more. The other girls were reliant on him because he'd got them hooked on drugs. That was one thing I put my foot down about. My best mate died from a heroin overdose, you see, and no way was I gonna let him turn me into a junkie. Eventually, one of the other girls helped me to get away. She gave me her night's takings and with what I'd made too it gave me enough to do a runner. That's how I come to be living here.'

Claire stared at her in horror before asking, 'Didn't he come looking for you?'

Cindy shrugged. 'Oh, I've no doubt he looked. He wasn't one for letting his girls go easily. But thank God, he has never found me – or at least, what I should say is he ain't found me *yet*. But it will be God help me if he ever does. It'll be God help you, an' all.'

Claire plucked up her courage and put a suggestion to her. 'I know that you said I could stay for just a couple of nights, and the time is going on, Cindy, but I wondered if you'd mind very much if I stayed on for a bit longer? I'll pay my fair share o' the rent an' the bills, an' I don't mind sleeping on the sofa.'

'You're more than welcome,' Cindy said kindly as she pulled herself together with an effort. 'To tell you the truth, it's been nice having someone to talk to.'

Claire struggled to stop the tears of relief that were threatening to fall. She'd soon found out that being alone in London was desperately hard, and Cindy had been like a port in a storm. Despite the cheerful front the other girl presented, Claire suspected that she was very lonely too. Only the day before, she had found a bottle of tablets lurking in the bathroom cabinet and when she took them out, Cindy had flushed and snatched them off her.

'They're not what you think. I am *not* into drugs,' she had snapped as Claire looked at her enquiringly. 'If yer must know, they're Valium. I just take them when things get a bit on top of me.'

Claire had wisely not commented, but from then on she had known that Cindy hated kerb-crawling just as much as she did.

For her part, Cindy knew from the glasses of cheap vodka Claire had to swallow every night before she went out just how much *she* hated what she was doing. Claire insisted that it was just to keep out the cold, but Cindy guessed otherwise. She was forced to admit that the kid had guts. They both did.

The following day, Cindy took Claire to Leather Lane Market, where she chose some new clothes. They were cheap and tarty, and Claire hated them – but soon, she promised herself, I'll buy myself some classy clothes.

For the first time she went out that evening wearing her own things. Up until now she had been forced to borrow Cindy's clothes, but the new ones she had bought with her ill-gotten gains did nothing for her confidence. Smartly-dressed women looked down their noses at her crotch-length miniskirts as they passed her on their way home from work, and Claire felt her cheeks burning with shame and humiliation.

Within minutes of standing on the street corner, a car pulled into the kerb and a repulsive little man who looked old enough to be her grand-father leered at her and asked, 'How much, sweetheart?'

Claire tried to drag her eyes away from the spots on his chin as she stuttered, 'Thir . . . forty quid to you, darlin'.'

He hesitated but then reached across and flung the passenger door open. 'Not cheap, are you, so let's just hope you're worth it, eh? Get in.'

Every instinct she had told her to run away as fast as her legs would carry her, but then commonsense took over and she knew that she would be a fool to turn down a punter. As he steered the car away from the kerb, Claire watched the street-lights reflecting off his bald head and swallowed the revulsion that was rising in her throat. Just think of the money, she told herself over and over again, and that is exactly what she did. When he dropped her off almost an hour later, she fingered the crisp notes in her pocket and blinked away her tears as she wondered how she had ever allowed herself to sink so low. But then it won't be for ever, she promised herself, as yet another car drew into the kerb, and flashing him a radiant smile, she leaned towards the new punter.

Claire was already in when Cindy arrived back at the flat that night. The girl was huddled in front of the small electric fire with a large vodka and tonic in her hand, and Cindy saw at a glance that she had been crying.

'Everything all right, is it?' she asked casually as she hurried past to switch the kettle on.

Claire nodded speechlessly, when Cindy crossed to her and gave her an impulsive hug. 'I did warn you that it was no picnic out there, didn't I?'

Claire returned the hug. She didn't know what she would have done without Cindy, and as time passed she found herself growing more and more fond of her. She never probed or asked questions that Claire was unwilling to answer, and Claire accorded her the same respect. There was no front to Cindy: what you saw was what you got, and at the moment she was the closest thing to a friend that Claire had in the whole world.

'Look, why don't you let me tip that down the sink and make you a nice hot cup of tea instead, eh?' she said now. 'That stuff could strip paint, and too much of it ain't gonna do you no good at all.' Cindy gently took the drink from Claire's shaking hand. 'Ain't no point getting reliant on the bottle. That's how half them poor bitches out there have ended up on drugs – to help 'em face what we have to do. I don't want to see you like that.'

Without another word she went to make the tea as Claire hugged her knees and stared miserably towards the fire. Today, for some reason, she had found it hard to push thoughts of her baby to the back of her mind. Would Yasmin's new parents be looking after her properly? Would they give her a good life? Earlier on, she had also seen a young girl who had reminded her of Tracey, and ever since then the day had seemed to go from bad to worse. Still, she consoled herself, it would be bedtime soon. At least when she was asleep she didn't have to think.

The next day, Claire walked into the city centre. The Oxford Street stores were bustling with crowds, mainly young people wearing acid-washed jeans, torn T-shirts and faded leather jackets that Michael Jackson and the Sex Pistols had made so popular. She wandered along, eyeing the dress shops eagerly.

Eventually she entered a classy department store and began to browse along the racks of expensively tailored clothes. For as long as she could remember, men had used her, but now she was determined that she would use *them*. She had no intention of standing on street corners for the rest of her life. In order to command the fees that the high-class call girls earned, Cindy had told her that she needed the right wardrobe to look the part; unfortunately, Claire couldn't afford to buy it as yet. However, she intended to have it anyway. As she stood there wrestling with her conscience, her eyes settled on the most beautiful cocktail dress she had ever seen. To steal this would be quite different from stealing the odd tin of dog meat or chocolate bar for Tracey. But then, why shouldn't she have it? she reasoned. No one apart from Cindy had ever helped her, so why shouldn't she help herself?

By the time she left the department she had the dress tucked securely inside her jacket. Next she visited the lingerie section and added some expensive underwear to it. The shoes proved more difficult to steal as they were not displayed in pairs so she decided to leave those until another time. Even so, she was thrilled with her day's work and could hardly wait to get back to the flat to try the new things on. On the way home, she made her only purchase that day – a little book on elocution called *How to Speak the Queen's English*.

'So where have you been then?' her friend asked. 'I was just beginning to get worried about you.'

'Oh, you know, here and there,' Claire replied cagily. 'I thought I'd do a bit o' window shoppin'.' Suddenly the things she had stolen were burning her and she felt ashamed.

Cindy carried on getting ready and was just about to leave when Claire asked, 'What time will yer be back?'

Cindy shrugged. 'How long is a piece of string? It all depends how

146

many customers there are about, and how much money they want to part with.' As she was heading for the door she winked at Claire over her shoulder. 'I'll see you later.'

Claire knew that she should be getting ready to join her, but first she couldn't resist admiring her new clothes, even if she was slightly ashamed of the way she had come by them. But then, she thought, these will be my ticket to becoming the person I want to be. Taking them carefully from her jacket, one by one, she laid the items out across the back of the sofa and gazed at them. They were perfect, and she could hardly wait for the day when she would be able to wear them.

After a time she folded them neatly and put them all away in a drawer that Cindy had cleared for her. The underwear was made of pure silk, not the cotton sort that she usually wore; along with the bra and panties she had stolen was a suspender belt heavily trimmed with black lace, and two pairs of silk stockings with beautifully soft lace tops. She tried to imagine how they would feel next to her skin beneath the classy little shift dress . . . and as she closed the drawer on them, she had to force herself to put on the other tarty gear, ready for walking the streets.

Within a month or so, the girls of the neighbourhood begrudgingly accepted her, and Claire was paying her way. She and Cindy went shopping and purchased a small settee that folded out to make a bed; Claire could now sleep in comfort. The savings that she had stashed in her underwear drawer was a sum beyond her wildest dreams, and she showed it to Cindy with delight. Yet still she hated every single minute she spent with her customers, and dreamed of the day when she would no longer have to do it.

Cindy still nagged her constantly, warning her to keep her guard up. 'Remember what I told you,' she said. 'If you come up against a nasty character, you steer clear. One beating and you may not be able to work for days, so just take care of your money while it's coming in and everything's running smoothly.'

Claire nodded, but as her savings grew so did her confidence. She knew that what they were doing was considered to be wrong, but then, she reasoned, wasn't what she had suffered as a child wrong? No one had cared then, and no one cared now, except Cindy, so why should she? Sometimes in the dead of night, Claire would hear Cindy crying into her pillow, and it made her feel sad. She herself was no stranger to tears in the night and it hadn't taken her long to realise that beneath Cindy's hard exterior beat a soft and tender heart.

It was on such a night, when Claire had gone into Cindy's room to waken her from a nightmare, that Cindy began to confide in her. Claire discovered that before Cindy had run away from the little village in Kent where she had been brought up, she'd had a boyfriend. When she spoke of him, her eyes filled with tears.

'So why did you run away then?' Claire asked, baffled.

'Because of my dad. He was a right bullying bastard and it got to the stage where I couldn't take it any more.'

'But why don't you go home then, if you still care about your boyfriend so much?' Claire pressed. 'Your dad couldn't hurt you now; you needn't even live at home.'

Cindy shuddered at the thought. 'Oh yeah?' she said, and her voice was heavy with bitterness. 'And do you really think Jimmy would still want me now if he knew I'd been on the game?'

'He would if he loved you,' Claire said gently.

Cindy hung her head. 'No . . . it's too late now.' Her voice was sad. 'I couldn't look my mum in the eye. She'd die of shame if she knew how I was earning a living.'

'Well, at least you've got a man who cares about you.' As Claire thought of her own mother, her heart broke afresh. She often thought of the people she had left behind and missed them much more than she had thought she would. But at least she found comfort in knowing that Tracey was settled and loved. Yasmin, too. As always, thoughts of her baby were never far from her mind, and one night when she was feeling particularly vulnerable, she broke down and confided everything to Cindy. Everything, that is, except the abuse she had suffered at the hands of her mother's boyfriends. That was a hurt and shame that went too deep to ever confide to anyone; even Cindy.

Cindy could hardly believe that Claire had given her baby away. She gaped at her sympathetically. 'Gawd, that must have been awful for you.'

As a tear slid down Claire's cheek she nodded. 'It was, but I don't regret it. What sort of a life could I have offered her? At least now she's gone to someone who'll give her the best.'

Cindy couldn't argue with that, but all the same she wondered at the injustice of life.

'Where did she go?' she asked.

Claire shrugged her shoulders. 'I don't know. I was just told that a Lancashire couple were going to adopt her, that's all.'

After that night, the bond between them grew even stronger. They were both victims of abuse. Different kinds of abuse, but each equally painful, and they both bore scars inside that would never heal – and they knew it.

Claire practised her grammar at every opportunity, and one day when Cindy caught her talking to herself in the mirror she fell about laughing.

'Bloody hell, who do you think you are? Eliza bleedin' Doolittle?'

Seeing the funny side of it, Claire laughed too. 'You won't think it's so funny when I'm earning more with one punter than I do now with half a dozen,' she told her friend. She had now added a pair of Italian leather shoes to her wardrobe and a beautiful pure wool coat, and for the first time in a very long while she was beginning to feel in control of her own life. Her seventeenth birthday came and went uncelebrated in the autumn of that year, 1988; she didn't even tell Cindy about it. It was time to try and forget the past, even her own birthday.

Sometimes when a customer, or punter, as Cindy always called them, was groping and pawing at her, a wave of nausea would pass through her, but then she would remember the money and the new lifestyle it would bring her, and she could bear it. After all, she decided, it was she who was using the men now, and soon, very soon, they would pay dearly for the privilege of access to her body.

As Christmas approached, she began to look forward to it. Whilst Cindy was out one day, she went to a small local shop that was selling Christmas trees and bought one. By the time Cindy arrived home, it was bedecked with fairy-lights and baubles.

'Ooh, Claire!' Cindy gasped with delight. 'It's lovely!'

Claire grinned with satisfaction at the other girl's reaction. 'This is going to be the best Christmas *ever*,' she promised, and arm-in-arm the two friends stood back to admire her handiwork.

The next evening, as darkness approached, they left the flat together as usual, and within half an hour of reaching their pitch, had gone their separate ways. Cindy had a busy night, and when she finally descended the steps to the little basement flat in the early hours of the morning, she was tired but almost a hundred pounds richer. She was longing for a bath and a mug of hot chocolate, and pushed the key into the lock thankfully. However, she was barely inside when the sound of muffled sobs came to her from the darkness. Her eyes bulged from her head as she snapped on the light.

Claire was huddled into the corner of the sofa, clutching a hot-water bottle.

Cindy guessed what had happened immediately. 'One o' the punters turn nasty, did he?' she enquired. When Claire nodded, instead of being sympathetic, Cindy tutted with annoyance. 'I thought I told you never to go with anyone you didn't like the look of,' she snapped.

'He looked all right,' Claire said indignantly. 'He just cut up rough all of a sudden, punched me in the guts and slapped me around. He wouldn't pay either so the whole night was all for nothing.'

'I did warn you to get the money upfront, didn't I?' Cindy said. 'Still, it ain't the end of the world. We all come across a squealer at some time or another in this game. With luck, from now on you'll be a bit more careful.' Hurrying over to Claire, she tilted her chin up and surveyed her swollen face. 'Oh well, at least it ain't too bad,' she comforted. 'A bruise or two. A few days and you'll be good as new. Mind you, you'd best not go out till the swelling's gone down and until your guts stop hurting. You ain't going to get many punters looking like that.'

'I'm not walking the streets again *ever*,' Claire said flatly.

'Everybody feels like that, the first time they get a slap,' Cindy told her. 'You'll get over it. Now, do you want me to get the quack in, to check where that bastard punched you?'

Claire gazed back at her stubbornly. 'No, I'll be all right. I've taken some painkillers. But Cindy, I've told you, I'm finished on the streets and I mean it.'

'You know,' Cindy said, 'it's all very well saying you're finished, but you've got to live, and in case you hadn't noticed, there aren't too many options open to girls like us.'

'I didn't say I was *finishing*,' Claire told her calmly. 'I just said I wasn't going back on the streets.'

Cindy was totally confused. 'And what's that supposed to mean?'

'It means I'm going upmarket.'

Cindy's mouth gaped open, and a note of admiration crept into her voice. 'You're serious, aren't you?' she said. 'You know, I reckon you could bloody well do it an' all.' She stared at Claire's swollen face before saying thoughtfully, 'Let me make a few enquiries. I know a couple of girls who've gone upmarket. I'll pick their brains for you.'

Claire looked at her gratefully as Cindy crossed to put the kettle on. Her brain was working overtime now as she considered the opportunities that might be open to her.

Cindy was true to her word, and three days later she produced an address. 'There you go.' She had just come in from the streets and her nose was glowing red with the cold. 'This is the address of an escort agency. But be warned – this ain't going to happen overnight. If you want to go upmarket you've got to look, sound and dress the part, so we've got a lot of work to do.' As she surveyed Claire critically she tapped her fingers on the table in time to Robert Palmer who was belting out 'Addicted To Love' on the radio.

'First of all, I reckon we ought to get you signed up for some of those elocution lessons,' she stated. 'It shouldn't be too hard to find somewhere that does them in the Yellow Pages. I doubt they'll come cheap but then you have some savings now and it'll be an investment in the long run. Then we need to get you dressed to look the part . . . and then, with any luck, it'll be all stations go.'

'An escort agency's no good to me,' grumbled Claire. 'I want to go on my own.'

Cindy rolled her eyes in exasperation. 'God, you don't understand *anything*, do you? The agency gets you your bookings, then when the booking's over, *that's* when you make your money. Do you understand now?'

Claire flushed as comprehension dawned.

Cindy shook her head. 'God, you are thick at times.' She grinned. 'Mind you, I shouldn't phone them just yet, not looking like that. They'd have you out the door soon as look at you.'

'I think you might be right,' Claire agreed, wincing, and crossing to the oven, she took out the shepherd's pie she had prepared. In the end, she decided to wait until after Christmas and take Cindy's advice. She ventured out only once and that was to buy Cindy a Christmas present. Her bruises and slow gait attracted more than a few curious glances, and she was relieved to get back to the privacy of the flat.

The two girls spent a pleasant Christmas together, grateful that they had each other for company because it helped to keep their minds off the families they were missing. Cindy bought a small turkey, which Claire cooked to perfection, and in the afternoon they snuggled down on the sofa, ate chocolate and cried at the old movies on television. Cindy loved the gold locket that Claire had bought her. Her gift to Claire was a beautiful silk dressing-gown to add to her rapidly growing store of expensive clothes. Claire gasped with delight when she saw it, and swore that it was far too nice to wear.

Deciding to take a few days off, since the punters were 'all at home playing Happy Families', as Cindy quipped, the two friends visited the Zoo, Hampstead Heath, went skating at Queensway ice-rink and queued up for the sale at Harrod's, to see how the other half lived. It was a time of relaxation and fun, doing all the kinds of things that other girls of their age took for granted.

1988 had been a year of tremendous upheaval, Claire thought, and from now on, things could only get better. In 1989, she would do her utmost to ensure that they did.

Chapter Seventeen

Once the New Year was over, Cindy went back on the streets. By now Claire was almost completely better and she knew that it was time to get down to business. After poring through the phone book, she eventually dialled the number of a retired teacher called Miss Melody Finch, who did elocution lessons from her home in Mayfair; she gasped when the woman told her how much it was going to cost. Even so, she was determined to see it through and so the very next day she dressed carefully in a skirt and blouse and set off for her first lesson. The woman lived in an apartment within a smart, three-storey townhouse off Berkeley Square. Claire felt very nervous as she stood on the imposing marble steps and rang the bell. It was answered almost immediately by a tiny, immaculately dressed woman. She had grey hair, scraped back into a tight bun on the back of her head, and piercingly blue eyes.

'Ah, you must be the young lady who made the appointment yesterday. Miss er . . . what was it now?'

'Hamilton, Claire Hamilton, Miss Finch,' Claire said quietly. She had decided that was the name she would use from now on, as it sounder somewhat grander than McMullen.

'Yes, yes, of course. Well, do come in, my dear. From the sound of that dialect, the sooner we get started the better.'

Claire followed the woman through a door into a spacious hallway and then into a ground-floor flat with a beautiful sitting room.

The woman walked around her, eyeing her up and down as Claire nervously clutched her bag.

'Well, my dear, you certainly have the looks, but the posture and the voice leave a lot to be desired.' She tapped her chin thoughtfully. 'I can see that you are going to be quite a challenge, but then I always did love a challenge. Very well – shoulders back, chin up. Shall we begin?'

When Claire left an hour later, her head was reeling, but surprisingly she had enjoyed herself. Miss Finch had given her lots of exercises to prac- tise. Claire thought that the woman's name suited her to perfection; she was like a little bird flitting here and there as she constantly flapped her hands and trilled, 'No, no, *no*, my dear. It is *how now brown cow*. Not, *'ow now*. Let us begin again, shall we?'

That night, Cindy fell about laughing as Claire stood in front of the small mirror above the fireplace rolling different letters around her tongue. Although Claire had confided a lot about her past in the months they had been together, Cindy still felt there was more that she didn't know about. Claire had built up a barrier that no one could penetrate, not even herself. Yet she knew Claire well enough by now to know that she would confide no more until she was good and ready. Cindy was happy to wait and watch as Claire battled to better herself. She guessed that this was her friend's way of trying to leave her past behind. But could she do it? Cindy doubted it, but admired her all the more for trying.

Soon after that, Claire also joined up for evening classes at a college in the Angel, Islington.

Cindy was greatly impressed. 'So what will you be doing?' she asked.

'Learning bookkeeping. I intend to have my own business one day, so if I can do my own books it will save me money,' Claire informed her. Already Miss Finch's lessons were paying off, and the girl's voice was taking on a more refined tone.

'Phew! Well, I've got to take me bleedin' hat off to you,' Cindy told her admiringly. 'The only thing is – how are you gonna pay for all this? The old dear charges an arm and a leg, and evening classes cost a few bob too.'

'I know,' Claire agreed. 'I suppose I'll have to get back out to work again for the time being. My savings ain't . . . I mean *aren't* . . . bottom- less.'

Cindy grinned, and then both girls burst out laughing.

Two months later, Claire walked wearily down the basement steps. Earlier in the day, she had had an elocution lesson with Miss Finch. From there, she had gone straight to her evening course at college, and then rushed home to change before taking up her usual position on the street corner. Now, in the early hours of the morning, she was so tired that she ached in every limb. Halfway down the steps, she paused to fumble for her key in the dim light of the street-lamp, and heard something that made her blood turn to ice. Someone was down there by the door, in the dark shadows. She looked around for help but the street was deserted with not a soul to be seen. Thankfully, just then a watery moon climbed above the black clouds that were scudding across the city. The peeling paint on their front door was momentarily lit with silver light and she saw a figure huddled against it, whimpering. It was Cindy.

Forgetting her fatigue, Claire clattered down the steps and throwing aside her bag with no thought for the hard-earned money inside it, she fell to her knees beside her friend.

'Cindy?' There was a catch in her voice as she fought off panic. 'Come on, let's get you inside.' Her hand shook as she tried to get the key into the lock but at last she succeeded and clicked on the light. It spilled past the door and onto Cindy, who looked as if she had bathed in blood.

'Oh dear God.' With a strength she didn't know she possessed, Claire managed to hook her arms under Cindy's and half-dragged, half-pulled her into the safety of the tiny flat. Once she had manhandled her onto the settee she then rushed back and locked the door securely before turning to Cindy, who looked as if she had done ten rounds in a boxing ring.

'I'll call an ambulance,' she said, but Cindy caught her arm.

'No, Claire, please d . . . don't. I don't want the police here. It'll only make things worse.'

'But—'

'I said no! If you think anything of me at all, please don't call anyone,' Cindy whispered. 'It . . . it was Marcus, and if you call the cops he might get to find out where I'm living. It's not as bad as it looks – really. Just help me get cleaned up and you'll see.'

Claire hurried away to get a bowl of warm water and some towels. Thankfully it was as Cindy had said, and once she was washed and changed, it appeared that she had suffered nothing worse than cuts and bruises. One of her eyes was already beginning to close and there didn't appear to be an inch of her that wasn't turning a nasty purple colour, but at least nothing appeared to be broken.

'I dread to think what you're going to look like in the morning,' Claire commented.

Cindy laughed weakly. 'I reckon you're right, but it could have been worse. The bastard could have killed me – I think he would have done, if a car hadn't come along when it did.'

'How did he find you?' Claire questioned as she threw the bowlful of bloody water down the sink.

'I had a punter earlier on who took me into Marcus's neck of the woods,' Cindy croaked. 'When we'd done the business the lousy bugger left me there. And who should come by in his car just as I was making my way home but Marcus. Cindy flinched as she shifted her weight on the settee before she went on. 'I'd nearly got to Shaftesbury Avenue an' there he was, as large as life. Oh, he was lovely to start with. Told me he'd missed me an' gave me all the bullshit, but then when he saw I was having none of it, and I told him to piss off, and all,' she chuckled hoarsely, 'he turned nasty. Luckily a car came by and slowed down when the driver saw what was going on, and Marcus hopped into his motor and scarpered. I got a taxi and asked them to drop me off here. I didn't want to go to hospital. I reckon I must have blacked out when I got down the steps.'

'Are you quite sure that he didn't follow you home?'

'Nah. If he had, he would have finished what he'd started. But I don't mind telling you, it's put the wind up me. I reckon from now on, I'm gonna have to be more careful.'

Claire made Cindy a hot drink, then helped her into bed. The clothes she had been wearing were covered in blood. Even her mousy-coloured hair was caked in it, but she looked too weary to worry about having a bath tonight. That could be done in the morning.

'Just call if you need me in the night,' Claire told her, and Cindy nodded gratefully.

Once she was alone in the small living room again, Claire paced up and down with a frown on her face. She had no doubt at all that by the next morning, Cindy would be black and blue, which would mean she would be out of action for at least a couple of weeks. She sighed. That meant that there would only be her money coming in to pay the bills and the rent, plus her own tuition fees. Ah well, she thought, Cindy helped me when I needed it and now it's my turn to help her for as long as she needs me, even if it means doing overtime.

Strangely, she felt a glow of satisfaction as she switched off the light and made up her bed on the sofa.

The next morning, just as Claire had expected, Cindy could hardly move. She looked a very sorry sight indeed. For the next two weeks Claire worked every minute she could between her elocution lessons and her college course to support them both. Eventually the bruises faded, but Cindy made no effort to get out and about again. She would come up with some excuse even if Claire just asked her to go to the corner shop and back; she seemed reluctant to set foot out of the door. It didn't take long for Claire to realise that her confrontation with Marcus had frightened the other girl far more than she would admit.

Claire began to feel real concern. Cindy almost jumped out of her skin if someone so much as tapped at the door, and she lost weight. She was tearful and edgy, and smoking like a chimney, and Claire wondered where it would all end. Her savings were dwindling at a rapid rate, and yet she was reluctant to bully Cindy into going out again because she could well remember what it was to feel real fear.

She'll go back out again when she's ready, she told herself and eventually Cindy did, but now she tended to stay close to home, choosing her clients with care and only working enough to pay her share of the bills. Previously, the two girls had gone out for a drink together on the odd nights when they didn't work, but now Cindy preferred to stay indoors and Claire didn't mind; she stayed in to keep her company.

On a bright afternoon in June, Claire sat sipping tea from a delicate china cup in Miss Finch's elaborate living room. As always, the tutor was watching her closely and it was clear that she liked what she saw. Placing her own cup back onto the saucer and delicately dabbing at her lips with a napkin, she smiled at Claire kindly.

'You know, my dear,' she said, 'I am beginning to feel that I am taking your money under false pretences. You have been a most willing student, but I feel there is little more I can teach you. I shall miss you, of course. But now, Claire, I feel that you could go anywhere and hold your own. You are a very beautiful young woman.'

When Claire flushed to the very roots of her hair and her cup rattled on its saucer, Miss Finch giggled girlishly.

'Do you mean that I don't need any more lessons?' Claire asked incredulously.

Miss Finch nodded graciously. 'That's exactly what I mean,' she told her. She had grown fond of Claire, although there was something about the girl that had always vaguely concerned her, without her being able to put her finger on why. She seemed to have an all-consuming need to better herself. Claire never, ever discussed her family or her personal affairs. She seemed withdrawn, and often Miss Finch had glimpsed a haunted look in her eye that played on her mind long after Claire had left each week.

But for now, Claire was glowing. She stood up gracefully and held out her hand.

'Thank you so much, Miss Finch.'

The woman shook her hand. 'Thank *you*, Claire. I can truthfully say it has been a pleasure. Now all that remains is for me to wish you good luck.'

Claire almost flew home to tell Cindy her good news. She arrived to find Cindy curled up on the sofa with a Benson & Hedges hanging out of the corner of her mouth, avidly watching the news.

'Look at that,' she said, stabbing her finger towards the screen. 'They've just given Princess Anne the title of Princess Royal. It must be nice to be born with a silver spoon in your mouth, mustn't it?'

Claire strode through a haze of cigarette smoke and clicked off the television impatiently. 'Never mind that now. Guess what? Miss Finch thinks I don't need any more lessons.'

Cindy stared at her blankly. 'That's great, but what are you getting so excited about?'

Claire sighed. 'Don't you see? Miss Finch said, and I quote: "*You could go anywhere and hold your own now*". It means I'm ready to go upmarket. Where's the address of that escort agency you got for me?'

Cindy thumbed towards the sideboard, which was covered in clutter. The flat was tiny, and since Claire had moved in, there never seemed to be enough space for them to put everything. 'It was in that drawer, the last time I saw it.'

Claire scrabbled about amongst the contents of the drawer, then flourished the address in the air. 'Right then, here goes. There's no time like the present. I'm going to do it now while I have the nerve.' When she rang, she introduced herself as Claire Hamilton and was delighted when the agency offered her an interview for the next afternoon.

Cindy immediately began to nag her. 'Right then,' she said sternly. 'Now you have to get this just right. The walk, the voice, the clothes, *everything*.'

'I know,' Claire admitted as nerves began to set in.

Chapter Eighteen

The next day, Claire got ready for her interview. She applied her make-up carefully then piled her long hair on top of her head in loose curls. Finally she slipped into a plain but smart day suit and high-heeled shoes. When she eventually stepped self-consciously from the little bathroom and gave a twirl, Cindy let out a low whistle of appreciation.

'Bloody hell, Claire,' she choked. 'You look bloody lovely.' Her face was full of admiration and Claire flushed.

She felt different dressed like this, and hoped that anyone seeing her now wouldn't guess that only a couple of nights ago, she had trodden the streets. Cindy was fussing over her like a mother hen, flicking imaginary hairs from the shoulders of her suit and beaming at her proudly. When the taxi that Claire had ordered pulled up outside, Cindy pushed her gently towards the door. 'Right then, my girl, you go and knock them dead,' she urged.

'I'll do my best,' Claire promised, and hurried out to the waiting cab.

Two hours later, she arrived back – and as soon as she came in, Cindy knew that the interview had been successful.

'They took me on!' Claire cried excitedly, hardly able to believe her good luck.

Cindy whooped with delight. 'When do you start?'

'Tonight.'

'Bugger me, they must have been well-impressed with you,' Cindy gasped as Claire took an address from her bag.

'I've got to meet my client there at seven-thirty,' Claire told her as she handed her a card and now Cindy's eyes widened even further.

'Christ, this is one of the poshest hotels in the West End.'

Claire giggled nervously. 'I know.'

★   ★   ★

By the time the taxi came for her that evening, Claire was shaking with fear.

'I can't do this,' she cried in total panic as Cindy gazed at her sternly.

'Oh yes, you bloody well can,' she insisted. 'Just remember, once men are stripped off they're all the same – one thing in mind. And if you don't get this right tonight, you'll never get another booking, so pull yourself together. You haven't come this far to back out now.'

Claire obediently pulled herself up to her full height.

'That's better,' Cindy praised her. 'Now off you go, and remember everything I've told you.'

'I will,' Claire promised.

As a uniformed doorman hurried forward to open the door for her, Claire had the sensation of stepping into another world. She was treated with courtesy, and shown into a luxurious cocktail bar to wait for her client. Heads turned as she entered. She looked stunning in a sequinned midnight-blue cocktail dress and strappy sandals. The eyes of the women who watched her progress across the room were envious, those of the men openly admiring. As she approached the bar, a sense of power washed over her. She had heard the expression *Clothes maketh the man*, and in that minute she believed it.

Settling gracefully onto a bar stool she smiled beguilingly at the barman, who almost tripped in his haste to hurry and serve her.

'A glass of dry white wine, please.'

'Yes, miss. Straight away.'

She felt like a different person and by the time her client joined her, she appeared poised and sophisticated beyond her years. This, she decided, beat standing on cold street corners hands down, and she determined to make the most of it.

Her client's eyes were fixed on her silk-clad legs, which she had crossed in order to show them off to their best advantage.

'Miss Hamilton?'

Claire swallowed her disappointment as she took in his fat stomach and his bald head. Keeping a seductive smile on her face, she nodded graciously.

'Edward Taylor,' he introduced himself and licked his lips with anticipation before shaking her hand and gesturing towards the door.

'No point in staying in here, my dear,' he said, with lust shining in his eyes. 'I'm sure we'll be *much* more comfortable in my suite of rooms.'

Claire walked sedately beside him as he gripped her elbow and led her towards a lift. Once again, Cindy had been proved to be right. Mr Taylor might be wealthy and well-spoken, but Claire had a feeling that once he got her to the privacy of his room, he would be just as lecherous as the men who picked her up from street corners. Suppressing a sigh, Claire kept her smile fixed firmly in place and tried not to think of the ordeal ahead. The fairy story was over and it was time to go back to work.

When she eventually left the hotel, she not only had her fee tucked into her bag, but a large bonus too, and a further date booked with the same client for the following week. She had earned more with one man in two hours than she did on the streets in a whole night and supposed that she should be feeling excited, yet all she could feel was revulsion and bitterness.

'So – what was he like then?' Cindy asked, the second she put her foot through the door.

Claire pulled the pins from her hair and kicked off her high-heeled shoes. 'He was bald, sweaty, pot-bellied and middle-aged. His name was Mr Taylor and he was extremely generous.' She waved a wad of money at Cindy. 'Do you know, I think I could get quite used to this. The dirty old thing was like putty in my hands. His name was Edward but I had to call him Teddy . . . and Daddy.'

As she suddenly saw the funny side of it, she wrapped her arms around Cindy and the two girls fell onto the settee in a giggling heap.

The very next day, the agency phoned her with another booking, and from then on Claire found herself in huge demand. She was young and pretty and earning more than she had ever dreamed of. But never once did she even think of leaving Cindy. She had big plans and now for the first time was well on her way to achieving them.

During her college course, Claire learned typing as well as bookkeeping, and within a year had skills that would have earned her any number of jobs. But Claire had no intention of working for anyone. She wanted her own business. She and Cindy were sitting together one night having their evening meal when she said musingly, 'I think it's about time I bought myself a car.'

'A car?' Cindy paused in the act of lifting a forkful of spaghetti to her mouth. 'Can you afford one?'

Claire grinned. 'Oh yes, I've been thinking about it for a while. It would be an investment in the long run. I'd save a fortune in taxi fares getting to and from my clients.'

Cindy sniffed enviously. She'd thought that the men she encountered on the streets were the lowest of the low, but since Claire had joined the escort agency she had told her tales that almost made Cindy's hair curl. Many of Claire's clients were very influential and much in the public eye too; they included top barristers, members of the police force and even men of the cloth. As she thought of them now she asked, 'Got a client for tonight, have you?'

Claire nodded. 'Yes, more's the pity. It's that awful hairy-backed solicitor I told you about. The one that likes to be whipped.'

Cindy shuddered. 'Ugh, it doesn't bear thinking about, does it? How do you manage it without laughing?'

'I don't have much choice, do I?' Claire retorted. 'That's what he pays me for, so I do it. As long as he doesn't want to whip *me* I don't much care. To be honest, I quite enjoy it. I can take all my frustrations out on his filthy little backside.'

'Do you hit him hard then?'

'Oh yes. I broke the skin last week, but the harder I hit him, the better he seems to like it. God knows what excuses he comes up with to his wife for the weals on his buttocks.'

'Huh, it's highly unlikely his wife ever gets to see his arse,' Cindy snorted. 'His sort only keep their wives to make themselves look respectable, and as long as the wives have plenty of shopping money they don't seem to care. Half of 'em have probably got toy boys, if truth be told. It makes you wonder how they manage to live like that, doesn't it?'

'I could,' Claire told her matter-of-factly. 'In fact, I intend to hook myself a nice rich man who'll give me respectability and the sort of lifestyle I want.'

'An' just where does love come into these plans of yours?' Cindy asked softly.

'*Love?*' Claire was looking at her as if she'd taken leave of her senses. 'There's no such thing as love – I learned that a long time ago. Women were born to be used and abused by men, but I intend to turn it around.

When *I* get married I intend to have my husband jumping through hoops for me and I'll treat him like dirt.'

'Oh, Claire.' There was a wealth of sadness in her friend's voice. 'You can't mean that, surely? Of course there are good men out there. My Jimmy was one of 'em. It's just that in this game, you get to meet the dregs.'

'You're not wrong there,' Claire quipped. 'But it will only be for as long as it suits me and then I'll pay them all back, every *filthy* last one of them.'

There was so much bitterness in her tone that Cindy frowned. She too longed to end the sort of life she was living, but when she thought of another life, she dreamed of one man who would love her, and a little house and two children. She continued with her meal as a silence settled between the girls, and for now the subject of their future lives was dropped.

For days Claire scoured the London forecourts until at last she found just what she was looking for. It was a sporty little red MG with a soft top, and Claire fell in love with it on sight. It was two years old and well within her price range. Besides going to college, she'd also been taking driving lessons and had recently passed her test. And so the day after spotting the car, she arrived back at the garage with a hefty wad of notes and drove it away. She could hardly believe that it was really hers and felt as if she could burst with pride.

When she got it home and parked it in the dingy square where she and Cindy lived, it looked strangely out of place, but Claire didn't care. Even after paying outright for her car, the money she had left still amounted to a healthy sum. Cindy oohed and aahed over the car and was touchingly proud of her, but still adamantly refused to let Claire pay more than her fair share of the bills although Claire was earning far more than she did. She was stubborn and proud, and eventually Claire gave up offering.

As another Christmas approached, Claire again took on the task of buying a Christmas tree and decorating it.

The two young women stood side by side admiring it one evening before they both went out, Claire looking elegant in her expensive clothes and far older than her years, and Cindy dressed in a tarty miniskirt and low-cut leopardskin sweater. In some ways they were now as different as chalk from cheese and yet for all that, the friendship and trust between them bound them together more firmly than any chains.

'Ooh, it looks lovely, doesn't it?' Cindy sighed as the fairy-lights twinkled.

Claire nodded in happy agreement.

'I'll tell you what,' Cindy suggested, as excited as a child. 'Let's both stop work tomorrow, eh? Just until after Christmas. We had such a great time with our little holiday last year.'

Claire had already decided to suggest the same thing. 'Sounds good to me,' she agreed.

When Claire arrived home just before midnight she hurried into the bathroom and ran herself a steaming hot bath. Tonight she had catered to a man who had a fetish for nurses and had spent half the night tripping round his hotel room in a ridiculously revealing nurse's outfit and high-heeled shoes. But even now that she was sleeping with the wealthy, she still felt dirty and always bathed after every client. Now as she sat there in the hot bubbly water she methodically scrubbed every inch of herself as her thoughts turned to Tracey. What would her sister be doing now? Would she be missing her, or would she have forgotten all about Claire? Loneliness closed in, wrapping itself around her like a cloak, and beneath the loneliness was the fear that was never far from the surface. Slowly she was turning herself into the sort of person she dreamed of being and yet it brought her no joy; inside, she felt dead and incapable of caring.

What about love? Cindy's words echoed in her head, but what *was* love? If love was the feeling she had felt for her mother and Tracey then she never wanted to feel it again. Love let you down; it betrayed and deserted you. A solitary tear slid down her cheek and plopped into the bathwater. Let Cindy look for love if that's what she wanted. She would never love again.

She was still in the same solemn mood when Cindy arrived home in the early hours of the morning. Normally Claire would have gone to bed but tonight there was something she needed to ask her friend.

'Jesus,' Cindy griped as she flung her coat across a chair. 'It's enough to cut you in two out there, and trust me to get a punter who wanted a knee-trembler in a back alley. I'm telling you, the wind was whistling down it. It's a wonder I haven't caught my death of cold.'

'Well, get this down you then.' Claire pressed a mug of hot cocoa into her hand.

'Ta.' Cindy took the mug and stared at her curiously. 'What are you still doing up, anyway?'

'Actually there was something I wanted to ask you. You see, the thing is, I need some documents. A birth certificate for a start-off so I can open a bank account. Do you know anyone who might be able to forge me one? If I can get a birth certificate I can officially go by the name of Claire Hamilton.'

'As it happens I know just the bloke, a mate of mine from Soho,' Cindy informed her as she slurped at her drink gratefully. 'Tommy Moran over near Marble Arch is the best forger you could come across. He's the one I got to fill in your forms so you could get your provisional licence. He can forge anything – money included. Leave it with me and I'll have a word with him tomorrow for you, shall I?'

Claire nodded her thanks and wearily made her way to bed. Very soon now she would have a new identity, and then she could say goodbye to Claire McMullen for ever.

Chapter Nineteen

As Claire manoeuvred her car through the traffic towards the hotel in St John's Wood, to keep her rendezvous with Mr Taylor the next evening, it started to snow. The streets looked dark and dismal, which matched her mood.

Of all her clients, Edward Taylor was her least favourite, although he was easily her best payer. He was totally besotted with her and had recently taken to showering her with expensive gifts. Only last week he had presented her with a diamond bracelet that almost made her eyes pop out of her head. She took everything he offered without so much as a word of thanks. After all, the way she saw it, she deserved the gifts.

She parked the car and swept into the foyer, a picture in her white fur coat and soft leather knee-length boots. Anyone seeing her might have taken her for a film star, for she held her head high and spoke as if she had been born with a silver spoon in her mouth.

'Has Mr Taylor arrived yet?' she asked the man on the reception desk imperiously, noting with satisfaction the look of admiration in his eyes. She could feel every man's eyes on her and basked in the feeling of power it never failed to instill in her.

'Y . . . yes, Miss Hamilton,' the man stuttered in his haste to answer her. 'He asked me to tell you that he would be waiting for you in the bar.'

Dipping her head in acknowledgement, she sailed past him. Edward was waiting for her perched on a high bar-stool, looking for all the world like some little red-faced, bloated Buddha.

'You're looking lovely, my dear,' he leered as she approached him. 'Would you like a little drink before we go to our room? If not, I've got some champagne waiting for us there.'

'Then I think we'll go straight to your room.' Claire fluttered her eyelashes seductively and he almost fell off his stool in his haste to follow her.

In the mirrored lift it was all he could do to keep his hands off her. Once inside his room, Claire waited for him to pounce on her as he normally did, but tonight to her surprise he crossed to a silver ice-bucket instead and withdrew the champagne.

'Claire, my dear . . . why don't you sit down. I er . . . I have something I'd like to ask you.' He popped the cork and quickly poured the frothing liquid into two crystal glasses before passing one to her.

Claire was sitting on the elegant chaise-longue that was placed in front of heavy velvet curtains, tightly drawn to keep out the chill night air. She stared at him curiously as he took a seat beside her before asking, 'Goodness, Teddy, whatever can it be that's so important?'

He cleared his throat and she noticed the sweat standing out on his forehead. Whatever it is he wants to talk to me about must be pretty important, she thought, but she remained silent as he began to fumble in his jacket pocket.

Eventually he placed his drink on the table in front of them and laid a small leather box down next to it. Claire's eyes sparkled greedily. Judging by the shape of the box it might contain a ring – and knowing Edward as she did, it would be an expensive one.

'Claire, I . . .' He suddenly rose from his seat and began to pace up and down before telling her, 'The thing is, I've seen a rather nice little town-house over in Chelsea today. It's quite delightful and I was wondering if you'd like to move in there? Oh, and this is for you.' As if suddenly remembering the gift, he lifted the small box and snapped open the lid to reveal a glittering diamond ring.

Claire's mouth fell open. 'Teddy, are you asking me to marry you?' she gasped, genuinely astonished.

Now it was his turn to gape. 'Oh no, no. Not *marry* me exactly. But I thought . . . perhaps you could live there and I could come and see you.'

An angry red stain crept into Claire's cheeks as he rambled on.

'You must know how I feel about you, and the thought of you with other men . . . Well, I can't bear it. If you were to move in, it could be just you and me whenever I could get to see you.'

'What you're trying to say is, you want me to be your kept woman.'

Claire's voice was as cold as ice and now he ran his hand through his hair distractedly.

'I wouldn't have put it *quite* that way,' he mumbled.

'Oh? Well, how *would* you put it then? What you're saying is, I'm good enough for you to hide away so that you can visit me whenever it suits you, but not good enough to leave your wife for?'

'It isn't like that at all,' he told her hastily. 'But you have to understand . . . I have children. I can't just walk out on them, can I? It won't always be like this, though. Perhaps when they're a little older?'

Claire judged him to be fifty if he was a day, which made her assume that any children he had would probably have left home by now, or be independent at least. What a liar!

He lifted the ring from the box, and as he pressed it into her hand, her first instinct was to fling it back into his face – but then commonsense took over. These were real diamonds, if she wasn't very much mistaken, and would fetch a pretty penny. She slipped the box into her handbag. There was no use cutting her nose off to spite her face. The bastard! Just like every other man she had ever met, he thought she was there for him to use whenever it suited him. Well, she'd show him. But not right now. The ring she had just received must be worth a small fortune, so for tonight at least she would try to please him.

With an effort she pasted a false smile on her face and told him softly, 'Very well then . . . I'll think about it. And thank you so much for the lovely ring, darling. It's beautiful.'

Standing slowly, she undid the buttons of her white fur coat, and it slid to the floor, leaving her standing there in nothing but her bra and skimpy silk knickers.

Edward's colour rose to such an extent that Claire wondered briefly if he was about to have a heart attack. His shirt buttons strained across his swollen stomach and one of them popped off and rolled away under the bed – then suddenly he was on her, his wet slobbering lips roving around her neck as she turned her face away. Tonight she determined she would make him pay double.

'The bloody *nerve* of the man,' she ranted to Cindy later that night as she relayed to her what Mr Taylor had suggested. 'As if I'd ever tie myself up with an ugly old thing like *him*!'

Cindy sat quietly letting Claire rave on until eventually she said, 'I can't understand why you're so angry. You don't even like him, let alone love him. What would you have said if he *had* been asking you to marry him?'

Claire gazed thoughtfully back at her before replying, 'I wouldn't have married him.'

'You wouldn't?'

'No, I wouldn't,' Claire snapped.

'Waiting for a bigger fish to come along then, are you? Or waiting for someone you *love* . . .'

'Oh, there you go with that word again,' Claire said irritably. 'How many times do I have to tell you – there's no such thing as love in this life! Fairytale endings don't happen for girls like you and me, and the sooner you get your head round that, the happier you'll be.'

With that she turned and flounced away to the bathroom, leaving Cindy to stare after her with a deep frown on her face. What could have happened to Claire to make her mistrust everyone so, she wondered. She knew that Claire had had a baby girl and give her up for adoption, and she also knew that before running away, she had been in a foster home. Some deep instinct told her that there was something more, something *much* more for Claire to be as embittered as she was. Claire was the best friend that Cindy had ever had, and she could only hope that one day, Claire would confide in her.

The following night, after a leisurely soak in the bath, Claire slipped into a comfortable towelling robe and brewed herself a pot of tea. Then, sinking down onto the sofa with a blanket and putting her feet up, she brought her diary up to date before settling down with a newspaper to wait for Cindy to come in.

It was daylight, filtering through the curtains in a murky grey dawn, that woke her. Blinking sleepily, she rubbed at the crick in her neck then peered at the clock. It was almost seven-thirty in the morning! Wide awake now, Claire frowned. She hadn't heard Cindy come in. Feeling concerned, she went to the girl's bedroom door and inched it open. As she saw the neatly-made bed, the first stirring of panic gripped her. Cindy hadn't come home.

Claire had never known her friend to stay out all night before. After chewing on her lip, she decided to go in search of her. She pulled on some warm clothes and within minutes was in her car, slowly cruising the streets in the heavy traffic.

All around her, people with briefcases were hurrying along the pavements, their coat collars turned up against the cold. Children were being taken to school, buses, cars and bikes filled the main road, but there was no sign of Cindy. After driving slowly past Cindy's pitch at least a dozen times, Claire realised that it was pointless. At this hour of the morning, the prostitutes had all gone. It suddenly occurred to Claire that Cindy might be trying to phone her. She drove the MG back to the flat, and sat by the phone, willing it to ring, but by lunchtime she had heard nothing.

By then she was deeply concerned, and unable to sit there a minute longer, up the basement steps she ran to the street and again began to search for Cindy, this time on foot. At last she spotted a familiar face turning a corner with a bottle of milk in her hand. It was one of the local prostitutes, washed clean of her heavy make-up.

'Hello, Kirsty. Have you seen Cindy?' Claire asked.

'No, I ain't,' the other girl replied. 'Why – ain't she come 'ome then?'

Claire shook her head and now the girl was concerned too.

'Look, word's goin' round that someone was beaten up last night,' Kirsty said quietly. 'I'm not sayin' it was Cindy, but whoever it was took a right fuckin' bashin'. A punter turned nasty by all accounts, and pushed the poor cow out of the car as it was going along.'

Claire was horrified. 'Where did they take her?' she asked, her heart pounding.

The girl pointed down the street. 'UCH. Off Gower Street. No one knows who it was as yet, but we're all bein' careful. Perhaps you ought to go there an' see if it was your mate?'

'I will,' Claire promised as she hailed a cab to the local University College Hospital.

'You had a girl brought in last night,' she gasped urgently to the straight-faced nurse at the enquiry desk. 'She'd been beaten up. Was her name Deirdre Kennedy?'

'Are you a relative?' the nurse asked.

'Yes. I'm her sister,' Claire lied.

Painfully slowly, the nurse began to go through a pile of papers in front of her on the desk. 'Ah, here we are,' she said at last. 'Wait there, please.'

With that she was gone. It seemed an eternity before she came back accompanied by a heavy-eyed young doctor.

When he saw how agitated Claire was he smiled at her sympathetically. 'Come this way.'

Claire began to follow him through a labyrinth of twisting corridors, the walls all appearing to be bleached white by the harsh fluorescent lights.

He nodded as they reached a ward door. 'Miss Kennedy is down there, third bed on the left,' he told her. Forgetting to thank him, Claire slowly walked towards the bed, dreading what she might see. It was afternoon visiting time, and no one took any notice of her. Just as she had feared, it *was* Cindy lying there, although Claire barely recognised her. Her face was swollen and bruised. One wrist was heavily plastered and bandages were wrapped tightly about her chest. Claire sank onto the chair at the side of the bed and gripped Cindy's hand. Hot tears poured down her cheeks as at her touch, Cindy's puffed-up eyes flickered open a fraction.

'Hiya, kid,' she said weakly through cracked lips.

Unable to utter a single word, Claire began to sob. 'Oh, Cindy,' was all she could say as her friend squeezed her hand.

'I'm all right,' Cindy croaked. 'But we're in danger. *You're* in danger.'

'Why?' Claire's heart sank. 'Was it Marcus?'

Cindy stared at the sky through the window at the side of her bed. 'Yes, it was Marcus,' she whispered. 'But worse than that, I . . . I reckon he knows where I live, an' he knows about you an' all.'

As Claire gazed at her in horror, a nurse approached. Seeing Claire's distressed state, she beckoned her away from the bed.

'Deirdre will be fine,' she reassured Claire kindly. 'Her injuries actually look much worse than they really are.' Claire gulped as the nurse went on, 'She's got a broken wrist and some cracked ribs. The rest is just cuts and bruises. A few weeks' rest and she'll be as good as new. But maybe you should warn your mother before she comes to see her.'

Claire thanked her and went back to Cindy's bedside. And now it was Cindy who was crying. She looked so young and vulnerable lying there, that Claire's heart ached.

'I want my mum,' she sobbed pitifully.

Claire swallowed the lump in her throat. 'Do you want me to phone her for you?' she asked gently.

Cindy nodded through her tears.

'I'll do it as soon as I get back.' Claire knew where Cindy kept her phone numbers back at the flat, but for now she had no intention of leaving her and sat silently by the bed gripping her hand in her own. Every time Cindy so much as moved, she winced with pain, and Claire was so concerned at one point that she called a nurse.

The nurse was reassuring. 'It's normal,' she assured Claire kindly. 'Cracked ribs are very painful, but they'll heal. In the meantime I'll get her some stronger painkillers.'

As she hurried away to get them, the nurse sighed. Cindy had told them that she'd fallen down some steps, but the nurse didn't believe her for an instant. She had seen this happen too many times to other young women, little more than children, who were forced by circumstance to go on the streets and sell their bodies to make a living. They were regularly beaten up and abused; it was a fact of life and there was nothing she could do about it. But at least this girl had someone who cared about her. Some of the young women who came in had no one except pimps, and the latter only wanted them well again so that they could get them back to work and earning.

Claire stayed at the hospital with Cindy until the end of visiting time. When she finally rose to leave, Cindy became agitated.

'Yer can't go back to the flat now, Claire. What if Marcus comes lookin' for us?'

'Huh! You just leave him to me,' Claire declared with a bravery she was far from feeling. 'If he turns up, I promise you he'll be sorry. I know how to handle his sort. You just concentrate on getting well and leave the worrying up to me, eh?'

Without Cindy, the tiny home they had shared felt unbearably lonely. Not only that – now there was the fear that Marcus might appear at any minute. Claire thumped the table as a strangled sob escaped from her throat. Once again she knew that she was about to lose someone she had come to care about, and how could Cindy stay here now? This was the second hiding that Marcus had dealt out to Cindy; she might not survive a third.

Claire stared about her, then with a vicious swipe she toppled the little Christmas tree to the ground. Tears poured down her cheeks as she searched through a drawer until she found Mrs Kennedy's phone number. She had a terrible feeling that once this phone call was made, life as she had come to know it would never be the same again. But she owed it to Cindy to make the call. The girl had helped her when no one else would, but now it was time to repay her and let go; so after taking a deep breath, Claire slowly dialled the number.

When she'd made the call, she eyed the smashed Christmas tree forlornly, then began to gather some toiletries and a clean nightshirt for Cindy to take for evening visiting at the hospital.

Cindy was propped up against the pillows when Claire approached the bed. The bruises, that seemed to be growing darker by the minute, had turned her face into a rainbow of blues, blacks and purples. She had obviously been sedated and was struggling to keep her eyes open.

At the sight of Claire she began to cry again. It was almost as if her spirit had been broken.

'I've had enough of this game,' she confessed, and Claire knew that she meant it. Cindy drifted in and out of sleep as Claire sat gently stroking her hand. There was no need for words; the girl seemed to draw comfort just from the fact that Claire was there.

Eventually a nurse approached the bed. 'You ought to go now,' she whispered to Claire. 'Your sister's in a lot of pain. I'm going to give her something to help her sleep more comfortably.'

Claire nodded, and rising, she planted a kiss on Cindy's swollen cheek. 'Mum will be here tomorrow,' she promised, and at that, the injured girl managed a weak smile as the nurse prepared her injection.

Chapter Twenty

When Claire arrived at the hospital the following afternoon, she paused inside the double doors at the entrance to the ward. At Cindy's bedside she saw a grey-haired woman sitting holding the injured girl's hand.

Her arms full of magazines, Claire walked towards them and the woman raised red-rimmed eyes and smiled at her. Claire guessed immediately who she was, for she looked like an older version of Cindy. This must be Mrs Kennedy who she had spoken to on the phone yesterday.

'Are you Claire?' The woman rose and held out her hand, and Claire warmed to her immediately. 'I'm Sheila Kennedy, Deirdre's mum. But then you probably guessed that. Thanks for letting me know about my daughter. You're a very good girl, to look out for her and help her as you have.'

Claire shook her head in quick denial. 'It's not like that, Mrs Kennedy. It was Deirdre who helped *me.*'

'Well, perhaps you've helped each other.' The woman's voice was heavy with regret. 'I just thank God I know where she is now. I've been almost out of my mind with worry since she ran away from home. Though it's as well I didn't know what she'd been up to. I couldn't have borne it, to think of her . . . Well, that doesn't matter now. She's told me everything and I just thank God she didn't come off worse than she did.'

Her voice was sincere, and turning to Cindy now, Claire smiled and placed the magazines she had bought for her within her reach. Although the other girl seemed much more her usual self today, if anything, she looked a lot worse. Even so, it was more than clear that having her mother there was doing her far more good than any medicine; she was clinging onto her hand as if it were a lifeline. The two of them obviously loved each other very much.

Claire too had a mum somewhere. But she knew that her mum wouldn't have flown to her side as Cindy's had, if she had been beaten up. There was someone else who would have, though. *Molly.* It was funny, but now that it was too late, Claire had come to realise that her foster parents had been the closest thing to a real family she had ever known. But she had blown it, and it was too late to make amends now. The thought made her sad. She was still sitting quietly, thinking of Molly, when the doctors arrived for their daily round. They reached Cindy's bed, and a tall, grey-haired doctor smiled at Cindy over the top of his glasses. After unhooking the charts from the foot of the bed, he began to study them before asking, 'How are you feeling today, Deirdre?'

Cindy winced with pain as she answered him through swollen lips. 'Not too bad, just sore all over.'

The doctor nodded. 'I'm not surprised.' He ushered Claire and Mrs Kennedy away while a nurse pulled the curtains around the bed. Some minutes later, he emerged and smiled at their anxious faces.

'It's good news,' he assured them. 'Luckily the X-rays have shown there's no internal damage. The wrist has been set, the cuts and bruises will heal, and though the cracked ribs will cause her a lot of pain for a time, I don't foresee any lasting damage. In actual fact, she's been a very lucky young woman.'

Sheila Kennedy let out a long sigh of relief.

'I'd like to keep her in for another couple of days for observation,' the doctor continued, 'but then if everything's healing well, I see no reason why she shouldn't go home.'

Cindy's mum was beaming. So was Claire, as with a final kindly nod, the doctor moved on to the patient in the next bed.

'Did you hear that, pet?' Sheila couldn't keep the delight from her voice. 'A couple more days and you'll be out of here.'

But Cindy's eyes were full of tears. 'I'm not coming home with you, Mum,' she whispered. 'I ain't *never* coming back to let me dad use me as a punchbag again.'

Her mother dropped back into the chair at the side of the bed and distractedly ran her hand through her greying hair. 'There's something I've been meaning to tell you ever since I got here, sweetheart. You see . . . your dad died last year. Massive heart-attack it was that took him. I couldn't let you know because you never put your address or phone numbers on any of your letters.'

Cindy's eyes almost started from her head with shock. 'Is this the truth?' she asked.

Her mother nodded. 'I wouldn't lie, Dee, not over something like that.'

'But . . . *that* was why I wouldn't let you have my address,' Cindy stated. 'In case *he* got hold of it.'

Claire suddenly felt in the way. Cindy and her mother obviously had a lot to talk about and a lot to catch up on. Taking a piece of paper from her bag, she hastily scribbled down their address. Now that she knew Cindy was going to be all right, she was suddenly exhausted. She had barely had a wink of sleep the night before and now it was all catching up on her.

'Here.' She pressed the piece of paper into Mrs Kennedy's hand. 'This is our address. You can stay at the flat with me tonight, if you like, unless you were planning on going home? I shall nip off now and do a bit of shopping – get some food in. You just come back when you're ready.'

The woman smiled at her gratefully. 'That would be a real help, love. Everything's so expensive in Central London, and I have to admit I'm a bit strapped for cash. I shudder to think what the hotels hereabouts must cost.'

Claire nodded and bending, she gently kissed Cindy's face. 'I'll be back this evening,' she promised. Cindy mouthed a kiss. At the top of the ward Claire paused to glance back at them. Cindy and her mother were already deep in conversation, their heads close together, and for the first time since Cindy had befriended her, she suddenly felt alone again.

She did some shopping on her way back to the little basement flat, then once she had let herself in and double-locked the door behind her, looked at the toppled Christmas tree with dismay.

Dropping the carrier bags onto the table, she crossed to the little tree and stood it back up. As she did so, something scuttled across the floor and she shuddered before stamping down on it. The cockroaches were a feature of life here that Claire had never got used to. She knew that Cindy wouldn't want her mother to see the flat in a mess, so although she was dog-tired, for the next hour she rushed about, putting every-thing to rights. She repaired the little Christmas tree, re-hanging the unbroken baubles and sweeping up the shattered ones, along with the dead cockroach. After a lot of fiddling she even managed to get the fairy-lights working again, and by the time she'd finished, although it looked a little bare, it was passable.

Next, she stripped the sheets from Cindy's bed and bundled them into the laundry bag before remaking it with fresh ones. She vacuumed and polished and finally slipped a joint of pork into the oven to roast as she looked about her with satisfaction.

It was around teatime when Sheila Kennedy got out of a taxi and descended the steps to the basement flat. Claire sat her at the table and quickly brewed them a large pot of tea.

As Sheila eyed the flat, she nodded her approval.

'It's as neat as a new pin,' she commented. 'Mind you, our Deirdre always was a tidy girl.'

Claire smiled wryly as she thought of how it had looked a few short hours ago, and also at the way Cindy's mother called her Deirdre. It was hard for Claire to think of Cindy by any other name now, but she didn't say so. She watched as Sheila drank her tea. The woman must have been very pretty once, but life had taken its toll on her and now she looked far older than her fifty years.

Plucking up her courage, Claire asked, 'Was it true what you told Cindy – you know, about her dad being dead?'

Sheila sighed despondently. 'Yes, it was, love.' Her face was full of pain. 'I'll tell you now, for years I lived between the devil and the deep blue sea. Deirdre never saw eye to eye with her dad and I seemed to be constantly having to get between them. But to think that she feared him enough to run away and resort to . . .' She pulled herself together and continued, 'I suppose she told you how he used to knock us about, did she?'

Claire nodded.

'He wasn't all bad,' Sheila said regretfully. 'When he was sober, you couldn't have met a nicer bloke. But when he'd had a drink it was God help you if you got in his way.'

'Why did you stay with him then? Why didn't you just leave and take Deirdre with you?' Claire found it hard to imagine why any woman would stay with a bullying man.

Sheila grinned bitterly as she read her thoughts. 'Eeh, pet, things aren't that simple when you've got kids to worry about feeding, you believe me. And anyway, in our day, once you'd made your bed you lay on it, for better or for worse. Not like nowadays. The newlyweds only have to look at each other the wrong way, from what I can see of it, and they're asking for a divorce.'

Claire stared into her tea thoughtfully as Sheila reached across to pat her hand. 'Anyway, on a brighter note, thank God for your phone call, Claire. At least I've found my girl again now – though I shudder to think what could have happened.'

Claire nodded in agreement. They ate their meal then rested for an hour before making their way back to the hospital for evening visiting time.

The Sister stopped them as they entered the ward. 'Look, you may find Deirdre a little upset this evening,' she warned. 'She insisted earlier on that we give her a mirror, and when she saw the state of her face she got very distraught.'

Sheila frowned as side by side, they made their way down the ward to Cindy's bed.

'How's my girl?' Sheila asked cheerily, trying to present a brave face.

Cindy stared at her through bloodshot eyes. 'I'm a ruddy mess, Mum,' she said brokenly.

Sheila wagged her head in angry denial. 'Oh no, you're not! The Sister's just told us it's just swelling and bruising. In a few weeks' time you'll be back to normal, and pretty as a picture again – you just wait and see.'

Claire nodded in agreement, hating to see her friend so low. But Cindy was not convinced and began to sob uncontrollably. Her ribs hurt, her wrist ached and her face felt like it was on fire.

'Look,' Sheila said worriedly, 'Jimmy Williams asked me to give you his love, when I met him on my way to the station. He ain't never so much as looked at another girl to my knowledge, not since you left, Dee. And he was really worried when I told him you were in hospital.'

Deirdre Kennedy's eyes flew to her mother's face at the mention of Jimmy's name, and her mind flooded with memories. She and Jimmy had been childhood sweethearts right through school and beyond. Everyone in the little Kent village where she'd lived had thought of them as a couple. She knew without a doubt that if she hadn't run away from Gordon Kennedy's bullying ways, they would probably have been married by now. For a long, long time she'd tried not to think of him; it hurt too much. But now, the flood gates opened and she burst into a fresh torrent of tears.

'Come on now, Dee, pet,' soothed Sheila, squeezing her hand lovingly.

Feeling in the way, Claire said quickly, 'I'll see you back at the flat Sheila. You can stay for as long as you like – it'll be great to have some company. I don't suppose you'll want to go home until you know Cindy, I mean Deirdre, is a lot better.'

The woman stared down at her daughter. 'What I'd love more than anything is to take you home safe and sound with me, Dee,' she whispered. 'There's nothing to stop you coming back now, you know, nothing for you to fear. But sleep on it, eh, and perhaps you can tell me what you've decided tomorrow. Thank you, Claire. It would be a great help to stay with you until Dee makes up her mind.'

A cold hand closed around Claire's heart. If Cindy did decide to go home with her mother, she would be completely alone again. In that moment she realised just how much Cindy had come to mean to her, and was annoyed with herself. Hadn't she *sworn* that she would never care about anyone again? When would she ever learn? Suddenly feeling the need for some fresh air she stood up and forced a smile to her face.

'Right then, I'll get off now and let you two catch up. I could do with nipping to the launderette. Will you make your own way back when you're ready, Sheila?'

'Of course I will, dear. We'll have a cup of tea together when I get back.'

Claire inclined her head, and hurried away down the ward feeling suddenly tearful.

That night, Sheila slept in Cindy's bed and Claire slept on her sofa-bed in the lounge, feeling safer knowing that someone else was there. She wondered if Marcus was really on their trail, and shivered as she thought of what he would do to her when he found her. Cindy's injuries would be a walk in the park by comparison. Sheila was impatient the next day wondering what Cindy would decide to do, if the doctors gave her the all-clear, so Claire let her go off to the hospital alone, promising to follow on later.

When Sheila arrived at UCH, she found that her daughter still hadn't reached a decision, and although her mother desperately wanted to take her home, she loved her too much to push her.

Claire made a brief visit to the ward in the evening. Now that Mrs Kennedy was here, she felt that she was intruding if she did more than show her face. The next day, Sheila had already left for the hospital when she got up. Claire hadn't worked for several days now, but had plenty of savings, so she decided to do some Christmas shopping. She jumped on a bus to Oxford Street, and when she arrived home over two hours later, was surprised and delighted to find Cindy propped up against cushions on the sofa, with Sheila fussing over her like a mother hen.

'Oh, Cindy!' Claire would have hugged her but managed to stop herself just in time. There didn't seem to be an inch of her friend that wasn't bruised or bandaged, and she was afraid of hurting her. She stood there beaming, until suddenly her eyes settled on a bulging suitcase at the side of the bedroom door, and the smile slid from her face.

Realising that the two girls needed a moment alone, Sheila bustled towards the bedroom.

'I'll just tidy up in here,' she muttered tactfully, and closed the door behind her.

'You're going home, aren't you?' As Claire stared at the girl who she had come to love as a sister, Cindy nodded.

'I'm so sorry, Claire, but I can't stay here now, can I? But don't be sad. You see, the thing is, Mum wants you to come home with us too.'

Claire's chin sank miserably to her chest. 'I can't – but I thank her from the bottom of my heart. And for what my opinion's worth, I think you're doing the right thing,' she said. 'Your mum loves you, anyone can see that, and if you've got a family that cares about you, it's only right that you should be with them. As for your face, that will heal with time. But I'll tell you now; it wouldn't make any difference, even if it didn't. You'd still be lovely ... because you're lovely inside. In fact, you're the only *true* friend I've ever had except for Tinker, and I'll never forget you.'

Cindy was crying too now. 'Why won't you come with us, Claire?' she asked.

Claire shook her head. 'I'll be all right on my own,' she said steadily. 'You just get back to where you belong and put this part of your life behind you.' It took more courage to say this than Cindy would ever know.

'But what about Marcus?' Cindy fretted. 'He has a good idea of where we live now. And how will you manage the rent on your own?'

Claire brushed aside her concerns. 'No problem. Mind you, I'm not intending to be here for much longer myself. I've got plans of my own.'

'But what if Marcus turns up?' Cindy said again.

'As I told you before I'm not afraid of him. He's hardly about to recognise me now, even if I bumped into him in the street, is he? So will you *please* stop worrying? I'll be just fine.'

The two girls embraced and were still in each other's arms when Sheila emerged from the bedroom some minutes later. She took in their tear-stained faces at a glance. The woman sensed a deep loneliness in Claire, this sophisticated young girl, and every instinct she had told her that Claire was hiding something awful deep inside. 'You're more than welcome to come with us, you know, love,' she said again.

Claire sniffed. 'I'll be fine here,' she promised, then rushed about helping Sheila to pack up the rest of Cindy's everyday clothes. The tarty outfits were chucked in a binbag.

'At least you'll get to sleep in a proper bed tonight,' smiled Cindy, trying to lighten the mood, and Claire grinned gamely back.

An hour later, the minicab that would take Cindy and her mother home to Kent pulled up outside and it was time to say goodbye. Sheila and Claire helped Cindy up the steps and into the car, and now Sheila was bossily ordering the driver about as he packed Cindy's cases into the boot. Claire had a huge lump in her throat, but she wouldn't cry now. She would save her tears for later.

'You take care now and write often?' begged Cindy.

Claire nodded.

The driver had finished packing the boot, and now as he got behind the steering-wheel, Sheila slipped in beside Cindy. Leaning over her daughter, she kissed Claire and told her, 'You've got the address. Come whenever you like.'

'I'm fine,' Claire said. 'You just get her home and have a wonderful Christmas and take good care of her for me.'

'I will,' Sheila promised as Claire slammed the cab door.

Suddenly she just wanted them to be gone; she didn't know how much longer she could bear it before she broke down. The minicab pulled away from the kerb and Claire waved until it was out of sight. Then, as she stood there, the tears that had been threatening for so long suddenly spurted from her eyes. It was Christmas, and once again she was alone.

Chapter Twenty-one

Claire paused to listen as the sweet sound of the choirboys' voices floated from the majestic church just off the Euston Road. The stained-glass windows cast a rainbow of colours onto the snow-covered graves. As if drawn by some unseen magnet, she passed into the churchyard and began to wander amongst the tombstones. She found herself envying the people who lay there, at rest. It was Christmas Eve. Behind her, a woman hurried up the path obviously intent on getting into the church for the special carol service, for which she was already late, but when she saw Claire she paused to enquire kindly, 'Aren't you coming in, dear? You'd be very welcome.'

'No, thank you. I haven't the time,' Claire lied.

The woman shrugged, wondering why such a young, immaculately dressed girl was all alone on Christmas Eve. Perhaps she was on her way to some family gathering or a party.

'Merry Christmas!' she shouted over her shoulder at Claire.

'Thank you – and the same to you.'

The woman disappeared through the large wooden doors of the church and Claire turned to make her way home to the shabby little basement flat. Now had that Cindy had gone, the seedy place had lost any appeal for Claire, and she knew she would have to start making some decisions. Thank God at least that it was Christmas, and Marcus would surely be otherwise engaged, rather than on trying to track her down.

Although she was warmly dressed, she was shivering by the time she approached the flat. She was just about to make her way down the steps to the door when something made her pause. She could have sworn she'd seen a movement down in the shadows.

'Hello? Is anyone there?' A worm of fear was wiggling its way through her stomach when a huge black face with startling white teeth suddenly appeared below her. It was Marcus. Her fear struggled with anger at what he'd done to Cindy. But she mustn't let him see she'd recognised him, so instead she stared at him coldly.

'May I help you?' she bluffed in her poshest tones.

He climbed the steps and was standing in front of her now – towering over her, in fact – and she was having to look up at him. The many gold necklaces draped around his neck glittered in the light from the street-lamp as he smiled at her disarmingly. He looked like a younger, slimmer version of Mr T from the *A Team* series on television, Claire thought, and almost grinned. She realised that he hadn't recognised her – thank God! It was hardly surprising, when she came to think about it. In her smart clothes and expensive make-up, she looked nothing at all like the bruised and battered waif he had once taken in off the streets.

She stared boldly back at him. 'Well?'

'Well, pretty lady, it might just be that you can help me, as it so happens. You see, an acquaintance of mine told me that a mutual friend lives here – a girl by the name of Cindy. Would they be right?'

Claire shook her head. 'I'm afraid your acquaintance is wrong. I purchased this flat recently, and *I* live here.'

'Alone?'

'I really don't see that that is any of your business,' she said crisply. 'But I can assure you that no one called Cindy lives here.' She kept her head high although her tightly clasped hands were shaking with nerves.

Marcus frowned. He had been tipped off that Cindy lived here with another little scrubber, but this young woman in front of him looked quite well-to-do, and she certainly didn't *sound* like a tom, though there was something about her that was vaguely familiar.

'Now, if you don't mind I'd quite like to get in out of the cold. My fiancé will be here at any minute and I have a Christmas Eve meal to prepare.' Claire swept past him with her head in the air as he stared after her bemused, wondering where he might have met her before. Maintaining her poise, the girl walked down the steps and calmly inserted her key into the lock. Then without so much as a backward glance, she disappeared into the flat leaving Marcus to scratch his head, out on the cold pavement.

Once inside, Claire hastily shot the bolts home and relocked the door before leaning heavily against it. Reaction set in and she began to shake as tears flowed down her cheeks. Crossing to the curtains, she twitched them aside and peered up into the street; sighing with relief when she saw that he'd gone. That had been a little too close for comfort, but she congratulated herself on the way she'd handled him. With luck, that would be the last she would see of him – if he believed her story. But where the hell had the bit about the visiting fiancé come from? Loneliness engulfed her.

Holding her hands out to the welcome warmth of the gas fire, Claire wondered what Tracey would be doing. She began to pace restlessly up and down the living room. Eventually she took her diary from the drawer and gazed at Molly and Tom's phone number. All she had to do was swallow her pride, dial a few numbers and she could be speaking to them. She would hear their familiar voices and might even be able to talk to Tracey. Hovering by the phone, she then thought of the consequences that might result and flung the diary back into the drawer. Through one single phone call they might be able to trace her, and Claire knew that if Tracey ever found out that she was a prostitute she wouldn't be able to bear the shame.

Unable to settle, she ran a bath and while she was waiting for it to fill she looked at the tablets and medicines in the bathroom cabinet. Suddenly, a vision of the graves she had visited earlier in the night floated before her eyes.

'It must be nice to be dead,' she muttered to the steam-filled silence. 'All tucked up cosy and warm beneath a blanket of earth feeling nothing.' Reaching into the cabinet she withdrew a bottle of pills and tipped them into her hand. 'All I need to do is swallow these, get into the bath and go to sleep,' she told herself. An image of Don and Ian and all the other men who had ever abused her swam before her eyes. Her skin began to crawl as she remembered the feel of their filthy hands on her body. Nothing was different now. Men *still* abused her. But now she made them pay for the privilege. Suddenly she knew that they hadn't paid enough, and angrily she swiped the tablets into the sink and turned on the taps.

'I won't take the easy way out,' she vowed. 'Else all of this would have been for nothing. I *am* going to be somebody. Somebody whom people will respect – and I don't care who I have to hurt to become that person. From now on, Claire McMullen is dead.'

She clambered into the bath, shocked at how close she had come to taking her own life. And as she slid into the hot soapy water, she smiled, a cold hard smile. 'It won't be long now,' she promised herself. 'I'll soon have enough money to be anyone I want to be and go anywhere I want to go – and I won't need anyone.' So thinking, she forced herself to relax and began to make her plans.

During the next year, Claire worked every moment she could. She afforded herself few luxuries apart from the expensive clothes that she needed to look the part for her clients, and continued to live frugally in the dingy basement flat that she had shared with Cindy, who still phoned her frequently to make sure that she was all right. She kept herself to herself, her only indulgence being the odd show, which she always went to alone. And she saved . . . and saved.

On a beautiful spring morning in 1991 Claire emerged from her bedroom to see a brightly coloured envelope lying on the doormat. Recognising Cindy's handwriting, she immediately tore it open, and found herself looking at a wedding invitation. Cindy and Jimmy were to be married in June. It was still very early in the morning, but Claire phoned Cindy immediately.

'Hello,' a familiar voice yawned.

Claire laughed aloud. 'Hello, Sleepyhead, you sound as if you've only just got up.'

'That's right, I bloody well have. What are you thinking of, phoning at this ungodly hour?'

'Oh Cindy, you never change, do you?' Claire chuckled. 'I just received your invitation and I couldn't wait to speak to you. I'm *so* pleased for you.'

'It is good news, isn't it?' the other girl said happily. 'I can still hardly believe it myself. Jimmy's been marvellous. Do you know, from the second I got back it was almost like I'd never been away. We just seemed to take up where we left off. I can't believe how lucky I am. I've made him wait for a while to be sure I was what he wanted, and I've told him everything. I didn't want us to start married life with secrets between us, and yet he *still* loves me. It's incredible, isn't it?'

'No, I don't think it's incredible at all,' Claire told her. 'I just think

Jimmy knows when he's on to a good thing and I'm sure you're both going to be really happy. You deserve it.'

Cindy's voice was emotional as she answered her. 'Thanks, Claire, I hope you're right. But what about you? I still worry about you, down there all alone. Isn't it time you went home too now? If I can do it, couldn't you?'

'No, I couldn't, it's different for me.' Claire's voice hardened. 'The difference between you and me, Cindy, is that you have a family who *wanted* you back. I don't have anyone. But don't worry, I don't intend to be here for much longer, I can assure you.'

'Where will you go?' Cindy asked.

'I'm not quite sure yet. Keeping my options open.'

Cindy suddenly giggled. 'Cor, you don't half sound posh. Those elocution lessons certainly paid off, didn't they?'

'I hope so – they cost enough,' Claire retorted. 'But I'm still the same inside. I just look and sound a little different, that's all.'

'Good, I'm glad to hear it. Just don't come to the wedding and outshine me, eh? Else my Jimmy just might change his mind.'

When Claire eventually put the phone down she felt more light-hearted than she had in a long time. She also felt unusually restless and after breakfast, she took her savings book from her bag and studied it. Not long now, and she could begin her new life. Again she looked at Cindy's wedding invitation. She was pleased that things had worked out for her friend, but would it be a good idea to go to the wedding? Since Cindy had left, Claire had cocooned herself in a little bubble that no one could penetrate. She treated her clients with contempt and yet it only seemed to make them want her more. That was just how she liked it. She never wanted to be reliant on anyone ever again, not even Cindy. She was no longer the young frightened girl Cindy had taken in off the streets. Claire McMullen was dead and now she was Claire Louise Hamilton. There would be no going back.

Later that day, she walked into the office of the agency that employed her and stood to her full height in front of the manager's desk.

'I want a rise,' she informed him coolly.

He stared incredulously back at her. 'But, Miss Hamilton, you've already had two rises since you started working for us. I really don't think I can sanction another one. You are already one of our highest paid escorts.'

'Very well then, I'll leave. Believe me, I'm more than aware that my clients will be willing to pay more for my services, but if you're not prepared to consider it then I'll go somewhere that will.' Shrugging her slim shoulders she turned to leave but the irate manager called her back.

'Now, Miss Hamilton, *please*. Don't let us be hasty. I'm sure we can come to some arrangement that we will both be happy with.'

Claire slid into the chair in front of his desk and smiled provocatively as she crossed her long, slender legs. 'I'm sure we can,' she said confidently.

From that day on, she worked until she was fit to drop. It seemed strange when her last client turned out to be Edward Taylor – considering he had also been her first.

They were once again in the hotel room in St John's Wood that he favoured. Claire had kept him dangling like a fish on a hook for many months now, and it was time to reel him in.

'Teddy . . .' Her voice was low and husky, making his flaccid member tremble with anticipation. 'What you asked about some time ago, you know, about me moving into a little house, and stopping working? Well, I've been thinking, perhaps it wouldn't be such a bad idea after all. I'd be more than happy to leave the renting of the house to you, but I *will* need some money to furnish it.'

'Of course.' Edward Taylor could scarcely believe his luck. 'Just tell me how much you want, my dear, and I'll write you a cheque out immediately.'

Claire raised herself onto her elbow, displaying an erect nipple that almost had him panting. 'Mmm . . . perhaps three thousand pounds for a start? I know that you have impeccable taste and I wouldn't want to fill the house with rubbish for you.'

He slid from the bed and hurried across to his jacket, setting his flabby thighs wobbling like a dish of jelly. Shortly afterwards he came back to the bed and handed her a cheque.

'Thank you, Teddy,' she simpered. 'How long do you think it will be before I can move in?'

'Well, I should have no problem at all in finding somewhere suitable,' he gushed, 'so shall we say two months at the very most?'

She smiled at him sweetly. That would give her just enough time to make her escape.

★   ★   ★

The following week, Claire finally gave her landlord a month's notice in writing and began to plan her new life. She had thought of staying in London, but dismissed the idea almost immediately. There were too many men here who might recognise her. She didn't give Edward Taylor a second thought. As far as she was concerned, he deserved all he got, the lecherous old pervert. And anyway, once she had given up her life as an escort, she wanted a completely new start. After much deliberation, she had decided that she *would* attend Cindy's wedding, after all. She owed it to her friend to be there. She would then take a holiday, and decide where to go from there.

Early one morning in June, Claire loaded all her belongings into the boot of her little red MG. Above her, the sun was struggling to slice its way through the smog that floated across the London streets, smelling strongly of exhaust fumes and grime. She then posted the keys of the flat through the letterbox and drove away from the grubby little basement without a second glance. It was hard to believe that she had lived there for so long, but now another part of her life was over. She felt no sorrow, only excitement as she closed the door on a chapter of her life that was best forgotten.

The drive to Kent was pleasantly uneventful. When Claire drew up outside Cindy's mother's terraced house, she smiled. It had a slightly faded and worn look about it, much like Sheila Kennedy herself, but it also looked welcoming as she did.

Cindy, who had been waiting in the window, ran down the path to meet her. They hugged each other warmly then Cindy held her at arm's length and exclaimed, 'Bloody hell, girl! What did you do, win the bloody pools? You look a million dollars.' She was shocked, for although she remembered Claire as being a pretty girl, the person who stood in front of her now had developed into a stunningly beautiful young woman.

'I have to say you don't look so bad yourself,' Claire grinned. 'Being in love suits you.'

Cindy squeezed Claire's hand. 'It does,' she admitted shyly. 'I never thought I could be this happy. I can't believe that this time tomorrow, I'll be Jimmy's wife. I keep thinking I'm dreaming and I'll wake up.'

Arm-in-arm, the girls walked up the paved path to the house. Sheila was as delighted to see Claire as Cindy was, and made her so welcome that Claire almost felt like a part of the family.

Claire liked Jimmy as soon as she met him. Tall and thin, he had somehow just missed being handsome. His mouth was just a little too wide and his nose just a little too large. He was also very quiet. But he did have beautiful, piercingly blue eyes, and every time they looked at Cindy, Claire noticed how they would soften. She knew that the couple were just right for each other.

That night, she slept in the spare bed in Cindy's room and the two friends chatted about their hopes and plans for the future until the early hours of the morning.

The wedding day dawned bright and sunny. Cindy was so nervous that Claire had to help her dress. She wore a calf-length suit and a pillbox hat trimmed with a short veil in a soft cream colour, and when she was finally ready, Claire thought that she had never seen a more radiant bride. Her face glowed with happiness.

The wedding took place in a tiny picturesque church in the small village. It was a modest affair, as Cindy had wanted it to be, but the love and sincerity which shone between Cindy and Jimmy as they took their vows brought a lump to Claire's throat. They were so wrapped up in each other that there might have been no one else present. Claire was envious. The reception was held at a small local hotel and Claire enjoyed every minute of it. But eventually the car that would take the happy couple on honeymoon drew up outside and the guests followed them out to it.

Cindy and Claire stood face to face, each sensing that this was the last time they would ever see each other. Cindy had a life in front of her with a loving husband now. Claire knew that she could only be a reminder of the squalid past that they had been forced to share, should they stay in touch.

'You take good care of yourself now.' Cindy's eyes were moist.

Claire nodded, too choked to speak. They hugged each other one last time, and as Cindy stepped away from her, she turned and tossed her posy high into the air. A ripple of laughter ran through the assembled guests, as it seemed to hover in the sky before dropping squarely into Claire's hands. A great cheer went up as Sheila slapped her firmly on the back.

'There you are then, love,' she laughed. 'It looks as though you're gonna be next.'

Claire blushed as Cindy scrambled into the car with Jimmy amidst a shower of confetti and rose petals, and then the car pulled away. The tin cans that were tied to the rear bumper clanked and clattered on the road, and long after the car had disappeared from sight around a bend they could still be heard.

Sheila put her arm around Claire. 'My little Deirdre made a lovely bride, didn't she?' she sighed happily.

'Yes, she did,' Claire agreed, and she meant it.

Cindy had gone through a bad time but it was over for her now and Claire was glad. They walked back to the house in silence. Once inside, Sheila kicked her shoes off and exclaimed with relief.

'Ooh, that's better, they were killing my bunions.' Then, becoming serious, she said, 'You don't have to go tomorrow, pet, not if you don't want to. You're welcome to stay here for as long as you like.'

'I know that,' Claire replied gratefully, 'but I'm thinking of just taking off and snatching a few day's holiday somewhere.'

'Where were you thinking of going?'

'To tell you the truth, I haven't decided yet,' Claire admitted, sipping at the tea that Sheila handed to her.

Soon afterwards they kissed each other goodnight and went to bed. Claire lay trying to decide where she should go. She'd considered Cornwall or perhaps Wales, but then as she pondered, it suddenly came to her.

Blackpool. She smiled into the darkness. Why hadn't she thought of it before? She had pleasant memories of the holiday she'd taken there with Molly, Tom, Billy and Tracey. There were the shows, the Tower, the pleasure beach, nightlife and everything that she could want. An added bonus was the fact that it was so busy there, she would be just another face in the crowd. It was perfect. Once she was there she could decide what to do next. When she finally fell asleep, her mind was full of happy thoughts, all jumbled together: Cindy, who she still struggled to think of as Deirdre, looking beautiful, and Jimmy looking proud. Blackpool. A holiday. And best of all, a future where she need never be abused again.

She left the next morning after being made to eat every scrap of the huge breakfast Sheila had cooked for her.

The woman became tearful. 'You look after yourself now, pet, and remember we'll always be here for you if ever you should need us.'

Claire's heart was full. Cindy and her mother had made her feel, just for a little while, a part of a real family, and she would never forget it.

But now it was time to move on, and so after hugging Sheila warmly, she got into the car and within minutes was leaving the little Kent village and her past behind her.

Once she was on the motorway north, her spirits lifted, and by teatime she was cruising along the Golden Mile. Everything was just as she remembered it. The pavements were packed with people and everyone seemed to be smiling. Young people in *Kiss Me Quick* hats were playfully pushing each other. Sticky-faced children half-hidden behind candyflosses and toffee apples were being towed along by long-suffering parents. Open-topped trams went to and fro, with high-spirited holidaymakers waving at anyone who would wave back. The whole atmosphere was electric and Claire felt as if she could have driven up and down forever just soaking it up, but eventually she headed away from the seafront and as soon as she could, parked her car in one of the narrow back streets. Then she strolled along viewing the many hotels that displayed Vacancies signs until she found one that she liked the look of. She could easily have afforded one of the plusher hotels on the seafront, but until she'd decided what she wanted to do with her life, she would make every penny count. Entering what looked like a modest but comfortable hotel, she rang the bell in the foyer.

The landlady appeared from the dining room. 'Looking for a room are you, dear?' she greeted her with a friendly smile.

'Yes, a single please.'

After asking her to sign the register, the woman led her upstairs and Claire looked at the room. Like the hotel it was small and modestly furnished, but spotlessly clean. The rates were ridiculously cheap compared to the London hotels and so Claire paid for a week in advance. Once alone, she changed from her expensive designer suit into jeans and a jumper then after hastily unpacking she went down to dinner. It was a delicious roast followed by a home-made apple pie and thick creamy custard, and she enjoyed every mouthful. She received a few curious stares from some of the other residents, for it was unusual to see a girl of her age on her own in Blackpool. Claire was too happy to care.

There was a small licensed bar in the corner of the lounge and after her meal Claire treated herself to a large glass of wine, which only added to her feeling of well-being.

That evening she strolled along the front, her hands tucked deep into her coat pockets as the wind from the sea whipped her hair into a mass of fair tangles. More than once men approached her and tried to get her into conversation, but she just eyed them disdainfully and walked on with her nose in the air. She didn't need to pander to men any more.

When she arrived back at the Seabourne Hotel, she was cold and tired but still in a happy frame of mind, and that night, after another glass of wine, she slept like a log. The next morning, after a hearty breakfast, she visited Madame Tussaud's where she eyed the waxworks with fascination. Next she went on a tour of the Sea World, and there she viewed every sea creature imaginable. In the afternoon she took a trip to the top of Blackpool Tower, and as she looked down on the people who swarmed like ants below her, she could almost believe that she was on top of the world, and was reminded again of all the times she and Tracey had looked down on their home village of Gatley Common from their favourite place. Hastily wiping the memories away, she took a trip on a pony and trap the whole length of the front and back.

The days passed in a pleasant blur. She visited the pleasure beach. She ate candyfloss and toffee apples. She went to the circus and the ice show, and through all these treats she kept herself strictly to herself. Occasionally her friendly landlady tried to find out where she was from but Claire remained tightlipped.

One evening at dinner, Claire glanced up to find the little girl who was sitting on the next table smiling at her. She smiled back, but her heart twisted in her chest. The child looked about five years old, the age her Yasmin would be now. Claire suddenly lost her appetite. For the first time in days loneliness swept through her, and that night she stayed in her room, locked in with her memories. She gazed forlornly at the only picture she had of her baby. It was grubby and dog-eared now from handling, but even so, it was still the most precious thing she owned.

She realised then that her holiday was over. For a few days she had almost managed to lose herself in the hustle and bustle of the seaside resort. But now it was time to make plans. That night as she lay in bed, an idea occurred to her.

Why not buy a hotel and live here in Blackpool? She turned the idea over in her mind. She could be her own boss, run her own business. Part of the secretarial course she had taken at college was on bookkeeping, and she wasn't afraid of hard work – so why not? Chewing thoughtfully on her lip, she tried to stem the excitement; after all, she had no idea as yet what a hotel would cost. Still, that was something she could put to rights first thing the next morning, and determined to do just that, Claire snuggled further down into the bed.

Chapter Twenty-Two

She was up at the crack of dawn, and one of the first down to breakfast, dressed in a smart suit.

Mrs Benton, the landlady, eyed her with approval. 'My, you look smart this morning,' she declared.

Claire smiled.

'Have you got some business on then?' the woman couldn't resist asking.

'Something like that,' Claire replied noncommittally, and with that Mrs Benton had to be content.

The first estate agent she visited had only just unlocked his door when Claire marched in.

'Good morning,' she said confidently, and began to look through his lists of hotels for sale and lease. She was pleasantly surprised at the prices, and by the time she left almost an hour later, she had a handful of brochures on properties that she was interested in looking at.

By lunchtime, and six estate agents later, she had an armful, so hurrying back to her room she began to pore through them.

By teatime, Claire had phoned and made appointments to view three properties the following morning. That night, she could barely contain her excitement as she prowled restlessly about her small single room.

Her first appointment at 'The Seaview' the next morning was for 9.30 a.m. and Claire was there on the dot looking every inch a business-woman.

The place was a huge disappointment. It had ten bedrooms, but smelled of damp, was dingy and depressing – and Claire couldn't get away quickly enough. The second one, 'Belle View', wasn't much better, and again Claire left as quickly as she could. The third, 'Towers Reach', was much better, but too far away from the front, so after lunch Claire returned to the estate agents.

In the next three days she visited eight more hotels, but none of them was quite what she wanted and she began to get disheartened. Her landlady noticed her sombre mood and commented on it as she was serving dinner that evening. 'Had a bad day, have you, love?' she enquired kindly.

When Claire nodded, Mrs Benton sighed. 'I have an' all, to tell you the truth,' she admitted. 'I'm finding it hard to keep this place going now my Fred can't help out so much.'

Claire frowned at her quizzically as Mrs Benton went on, 'It's his back, you know. It's really giving him gyp now, his arthritis. That's why we're selling up and getting us a nice little bungalow somewhere.'

Claire's ears pricked up with interest as she asked cautiously, 'Is this place up for sale then?'

'Yes, it is.' Mrs Benton looked about her sadly. 'It's been up for sale for the last ten months, but I haven't had a single person come to view it yet.'

Claire looked at the little dining room through different eyes. 'Do you mind me asking who's selling it?'

Mrs Benton laughed. 'Course I don't. It's up for sale with White and McKenzie.'

Just then a family came in and sat down at an adjoining table, so throwing Claire an apologietic grin, Mrs Benton hurried away to serve them.

Claire's mind was in a spin. 'The Seabourne' was just what she was looking for, but could she afford it? She knew it boasted twelve bedrooms, and up to now the biggest she had looked at had only had ten. There was only one way to find out, and she determined to do that first thing in the morning.

When she strolled into White & McKenzie, the next morning and enquired after the Seabourne Hotel, the estate agent's eyebrows rose in amazement. This lady seemed remarkably young to be interested in buying a hotel. Still, he had nothing to lose by giving her the information she was asking for and when she left, she had all the details tucked into her bag.

Claire hurried into the first café she came to and after ordering a cup of tea, she spread the details out on the table and began to look over them. She had put a ceiling on what she was prepared to pay and The Seabourne was ten thousand pounds above it. Disappointment washed over her, but then as she sipped her tea, she began to see it from a different angle. All the hotels she had looked at up to now had needed a lot of work doing on them, whereas The Seabourne was very acceptable as it was. Then there was her car. If she lived in Blackpool she wouldn't really need it, plus she could always put in a lower offer than the asking price. All was not lost.

At the third garage she drove into that afternoon she was offered a very fair price for her MG. It was a lot less than she had paid for it, but still it could bring the hotel within her reach. When she re-entered the estate agents he smiled at her cautiously.

'Would it be possible to see the books on this property?' she asked.

He nodded. 'By all means,' he agreed. 'If you and your husband are interested, that is.'

Claire gazed back at him boldly. 'I don't have a husband and I wouldn't be asking if I wasn't interested.' Her manner was cold, and realising that she meant it, he hurried away to make a phone call.

When he came back some minutes later, Claire was strumming her fingers impatiently on his desk.

'I'll have the books here first thing in the morning for you,' he promised.

Claire nodded and without another word swept from the shop.

The next day, a little bubble of excitement rose in her as she examined the neatly kept ledgers. The hotel was showing a healthy profit, and there were already bookings taken for the next season. In her mind she was doing rough calculations. If she sold her car and managed to knock Mrs Benton down a little on the price of the hotel, she would have enough left over to live frugally until next March when the new season began. Suddenly her mind was made up and she snapped the thick ledger shut. Pulling a piece of paper towards her she scribbled down a price and pushed it towards Mr McKenzie. It was seven thousand pounds below the asking price. She didn't think for a moment that they would accept it, but the way she saw it, it was a case of nothing ventured, nothing gained.

'Offer them that,' she told him firmly. 'And tell them it will be a cash sale.'

Mr McKenzie gawped at her in amazement. 'I'll do that,' he said hastily. 'Where can I reach you, Miss Hamilton, with the answer?'

'I'll be back first thing in the morning,' Claire informed him and, turning on her heel, she strode away, leaving him to stare open-mouthed after her.

'They're prepared to come down five thousand pounds,' Mr McKenzie informed her the next day. Claire beamed with satisfaction. That afternoon she drove into the garage and walked out with a cheque for her car tucked into her pocket. The next morning she visited a solicitor that Mr McKenzie had recommended and by the time she left, the wheels had been set in motion. She was on the way to owning her very own hotel.

Both Mr McKenzie and the solicitor were highly suspicious of her at first. After all, it wasn't every day that a young woman her age offered to buy a hotel outright. Claire sensed their misgivings and haughtily passed the solicitor her savings book.

'There,' she said coolly. 'As you can see, I have more than enough to make the purchase. My mother and father were killed in a car accident recently. I was their only child, and they left me very comfortably provided for.' The lie came easily to her, she had rehearsed it for a long time, and their attitudes changed immediately. By the time she left the office, she had them both eating out of her hand.

'You may send any correspondence to the Seabourne Hotel,' she informed Mr McKenzie.

His head bobbed up and down. 'Certainly, Miss Hamilton,' he fawned. 'May I say it's been a great pleasure to be of service to you, and I wish you well in your new venture.'

'Thank you,' Claire said politely as she picked up her handbag and left.

'A woman like that could almost make me wish I was twenty years younger,' Mr McKenzie sighed longingly to the solicitor as they watched her leave.

The elderly man laughed. 'I think she's out of both our leagues. I know what you mean, though. She's a bit of a mystery, is our Miss Hamilton, but obviously comes from the top drawer.'

Claire would have been delighted, could she have heard them, for she had created just the impression she had hoped to. She stayed on at the Seabourne Hotel for another five weeks. The pleasure beach and Blackpool's illuminations had long since lost their charm for her, and now she just longed for the hotel to be hers.

A week before she was due to sign the final contracts, she informed Mrs Benton that it was she who was purchasing the hotel. Up until then, Mrs Benton had had no idea at all and she stared at Claire incredulously.

'Well, you're a dark horse and no mistake,' she said. 'But are you sure you'll manage, love? It's hard work running a hotel, you know. And you're very young.'

'I'll be fine,' she assured her. 'Though I would be grateful if you'd ask the staff to stay on. I'll pay them whatever you do, and I'll need an accountant as well, if you could recommend one.'

'No trouble at all, love,' beamed the kindly landlady. 'I'll give you the address of mine before I go – he's handled our books for years – and as for the staff staying on, I'm sure they'll be glad to.'

Claire inwardly breathed a sigh of relief; it had all been much easier than she'd dared hope. Now the time for her to take over was drawing nearer, she was feeling nervous and excited all at the same time. But still, she had come this far and now there was no backing out. In a week's time, Mr and Mrs Benton would leave – and the hotel would be all hers. She could hardly believe it.

It was done, the contracts were all signed and sealed, and Claire Louise Hamilton was now the official owner of the Seabourne Hotel.

She stood in the foyer, hands on hips, proudly surveying her little kingdom. All the months and years of degradation at the hands of men in London were suddenly worth it. From now on, she intended her reputation to be unblemished. No man, or woman for that matter, would ever use her again. Respectability was something that Claire had craved all her life and now that she'd obtained it, she intended to cling on to it with all her might. She was Claire Louise Hamilton, the orphan and only child of wealthy parents. Claire McMullen was dead and from this day forward must remain so.

At the back of the hotel were modest living quarters: a small lounge that doubled as a study, a bedroom, kitchen and a tiny bathroom. Claire had already moved her clothes and the few possessions she had into there and though it wasn't plush by some standards, to her it seemed like a palace. The season was now coming to an end. There were still a few bookings in the register but not too many, and Claire was thankful for that. It would give her time to become used to her new way of life at a steady pace instead of being thrown in at the deep end.

Mrs Benton had employed two ladies to help her during the busy period. Betty, a plump middle-aged local lady, helped out with the bedrooms and the general cleaning, and Mary, a much older lady, helped out with the cooking and kitchen duties. Both of them had been delighted at Claire's offer of staying on, and Claire had even given them a small pay rise, which endeared her to them immediately.

However, they soon discovered that their new boss kept herself very much to herself. She was quite happy to let them get on with their chores and never interfered with them. She was more than fair and pleasant, but whenever they asked her anything personal, she carefully changed the subject and soon they got the message and stopped asking.

Claire took to her new life like a duck to water. She was up at the crack of dawn every day and breakfasts were served promptly and efficiently.

As Christmas approached, she came to the end of her bookings, so with fat bonuses in their pockets, Betty and Mary bade her goodbye until the start of the new season.

For the first time since she had been there, the hotel was completely empty. Claire didn't mind – in fact, she loved it. The slack period would give her time to make any small alterations or do any decorating that needed doing, and she strolled from one room to another with a critical eye. She spent Christmas Day painting her living quarters. There was no time to be lonely this year; she had far too much to do. She purchased a small settee and matching chair for her lounge, and then feeling frivolous treated herself to a pretty pair of chintz curtains to match.

After making sure that her finances would last her until the start of the new season, Claire then scoured the surrounding garage forecourts and eventually bought herself an old van. It was a far cry from the shiny MG convertible she had previously owned, but she knew it would prove to be invaluable for picking up food supplies and such. After bartering with the salesman, she managed to buy it at an unbelievably knockdown price.

By the time Claire reopened her doors in March, the Seabourne Hotel gleamed from top to bottom like a new pin. Every single pair of curtains had been taken down, washed, ironed and re-hung. All the carpets had been steamcleaned, and the huge airing cupboard bulged with fresh linen. Two gigantic freezers in the kitchen were stacked to the top with food and Claire was raring to get going.

The holidaymakers came in dribs and drabs to start with, but by mid-June every single room was taken and Claire had to hang her *No Vacancies* sign in the window for the first time. She kept her account ledgers meticulously and as the money poured in, her spirits rose. She was on the go from early morning until late at night, and sometimes when she fell into bed in the tiny bedroom in her living quarters, she ached from head to toe. But she didn't care. She was her own boss now. She answered to no one and that was just how she liked it.

Mary and Betty turned up to help her every day, and although Claire kept her past a closely guarded secret, they all got on reasonably well.

'She can be a bit standoffish, can't she?' Mary commented to Betty one day.

Betty nodded in agreement. 'I suppose she does tend to keep herself to herself, but then she's obviously been brought up different to us – posh like – so I suppose it's to be expected.'

The two older women went about their work, and between the three of them they soon had the hotel running like clockwork.

In mid-July, Claire rang the accountancy firm that Mrs Benton had recommended and made an appointment to pay them a visit. For the first time in months, she dressed in one of her expensive designer suits and took a little time over her appearance. She felt strangely uncomfortable after her months of jeans and jumpers, but it was a wonderful outfit and Claire knew that it suited her. It was navy with a beautifully cut knee-length skirt and a short tailored jacket; Beneath it she wore a crisp white blouse. Her long fair hair was drawn back into a chignon and on her feet were Italian leather high-heeled shoes.

When she descended the stairs, Betty, who was going to mind the hotel for her while she was gone, whistled with appreciation. 'Blimey,' she beamed. 'I hardly recognised you. You look like a film star.'

Claire blushed. 'Well, I thought I'd better make an effort,' she muttered.

'I know it ain't none of my business, but you stay in far too much for a young woman,' Betty scolded kindly. 'You should get out and about a bit more, mix with people your own age instead of being stuck in here all the time — it ain't natural.'

Claire knew Betty meant well. 'Don't fret about me,' she said. 'I'm quite happy doing what I'm doing.'

'Yes, well, even so, you're young and you need a bit of time to yourself. You know what they say, all work and no play . . .'

Claire looked at Betty's serious face before hurrying past her to collect her books from her desk. She mustn't allow herself to become close to the woman but even so, she was touched at Betty's genuine concern. It was nice to have someone show they cared.

Back in the privacy of her living quarters, she paused to stare about her. She had done what she'd set out to do and wrapped herself in a cloak of respectability. But sometimes, now that she'd formed a routine and the hotel was running smoothly, the deep loneliness that was inside her would surface and engulf her, and she would find herself thinking of Molly, Tom and Tracey.

'Oh, pull yourself together,' she said aloud. Just for a second she allowed herself to give way to self-pity as she thought of Cindy. She'd been the best friend that Claire had ever had, but apart from sending her one postcard, Claire hadn't been in touch with her since the wedding.

Cindy had a new life to lead now, as did she.

She found the offices of Smythe, Nightingale & Wainwright easily enough, and after she had waited for a few moments, a young secretary showed her into Mr Nightingale's office. He was busily writing at a desk as Claire entered, and when he looked up she was struck by his dark good looks. At first glance she realised that he was much younger than she'd expected him to be. He appeared to be in his late thirties, built like an athlete and devastatingly handsome.

Claire was obviously nothing like he had expected her to be either, and she noticed that he eyed her appreciatively as he extended his hand.

'Do sit down.' He beckoned her to a chair and Claire obeyed. Crossing her legs, she pulled her skirt down demurely as she placed her books before him. He flipped through them expertly as Claire sat silently watching, and after a few moments he raised his head to smile at her. 'You must have had some experience in bookkeeping,' he praised warmly.

Flushing, Claire nodded. 'Yes, I did,' she admitted. 'I did a secretarial course, and bookkeeping was part of it before I bought the hotel.'

For the next half an hour they went through the books together. By the end of that time, Gregory Nightingale was deeply impressed. This was a young woman who obviously knew exactly what she was doing and did it well, and he told her so.

'Well, everything appears to be just as it should be.' He smiled beguilingly. 'I can't see any problems at all here, and now I think we've both earned a coffee, don't you?'

Relieved, Claire smiled and nodded. Minutes later, Mr Nightingale's secretary entered and placed a tray before them. They were remarkably at ease in each other's company, and for the next twenty minutes as Claire sipped her coffee they chatted companionably. By the time Claire left, Mr Nightingale's next appointment was sitting waiting impatiently, but he didn't care. Gregory Nightingale was very taken with Miss Claire Hamilton, and before she descended the stairs from his office, he had made an appointment to call at her hotel and see her in three months' time.

It was a clear day and so Claire decided to walk back to the hotel. She made her way to the front and strolled along, enjoying the feel of the sea breeze on her face. She was almost home when, a short distance ahead of her, she saw someone emerging from one of the large seafront hotels. Sweat broke out on her forehead and her legs seemed to have developed a mind of their own as they threatened to dump her on the pavement. Pulling herself together with an enormous effort, she slipped into a shop doorway and watched the man walk to a waiting taxi. Her heart was hammering – she would have known him anywhere. After all, hadn't he been one of her most regular clients back in London? It was Edward Taylor. But what could he be doing here, in Blackpool? The briefcase he was holding suggested that he was on some sort of business; or could he be looking for her? She had left owing him three thousand pounds, after all.

The taxi cruised past her with just a pavement's width between them. Claire hastily turned her back and pretended to be looking in a shop window until she was sure that it had gone by. Then, with no heed for the high-heeled shoes she was wearing, she almost ran back to the sanctuary of her own hotel as if the very hounds of hell were at her heels.

Her worst nightmare had almost come true and it had affected her badly.

An hour later, Claire was back in her jeans and busily preparing vegetables for the evening meal at the huge sink in the kitchen.

'Ah, so you're back then, love.' Betty bustled in with an armload of dirty linen. 'How did you get on? Is everything all right?'

Claire nodded at her over her shoulder. 'Everything was fine,' she assured her. 'I met Mr Nightingale. He'll be the one who handles my accounts.'

Betty giggled girlishly. 'He's a bit of a dish, ain't he? Gregory Nightingale is a right heart-throb hereabouts.'

Claire could quite believe it, and trying her best to push thoughts of her close encounter with her past to the back of her mind, she shrugged.

Betty, who loved a bit of a natter, continued: 'The poor bloke's had a lot on his plate, though. He were widowed two years ago, you know? Terrible it were – his wife were a lovely woman.'

'How awful, what happened to her?' Claire asked. She'd made a point of not gossiping with the staff but was so curious that she couldn't help herself.

Serious now, Betty went on, 'To tell you the truth, it were all a bit hush hush.' She was well in her stride now. 'Everyone thought they were the perfect couple. She was stunning, used to be a model apparently before she met him, but a nicer girl you couldn't have wished to meet. They had a lovely little girl – about six or seven she'd be now – a big house in Bispham, posh cars, the lot. Then one night really late, the wife crashes her car up the North Shore – killed outright she were. But the strange thing was, she were in her nightie and she'd been drinkin'.' The woman tutted as she remembered it. 'Anyway, people could only assume they must have had a blazin' row over somethin' or other an' she jumped in the car an' crashed it when she was upset. Obviously, no one really knows, it's all hearsay, an' poor Mr Nightingale were left with a little daughter to bring up all on his own. A crying shame it is.'

Claire nodded, saddened at the thought of what the accountant must have gone through, but just then the phone rang and their little gossip came to an end as she hastily dried her hands and ran to answer it.

Chapter Twenty-Three

Over the next few weeks Claire was almost run off her feet as a constant stream of holidaymakers came and went. The days seemed to pass in a blur but she didn't mind the hard work; compared to what she had done for the previous five years she found it easy. Being busy also gave her a good excuse not to have to go out, for the glimpse of Mr Taylor had totally unnerved her.

Her bank balance, which had been almost completely depleted with the purchase of the hotel, steadily began to rise again and her spirits rose with it.

Now she had almost everything she had ever dreamed of – her own business, which was flourishing, respectability, and a new identity. What she hadn't as yet managed to acquire was peace of mind. The nightmares still haunted her and she still missed Molly, Tom and Tracey far more than she would allow herself to admit. She missed Cindy too and hoped that she was happy. Cindy had the one thing that Claire knew she could never have – and that was someone to love. But to love someone, you had to trust them, and Claire was determined to never trust anyone again. If she did, there was a chance that her past would come to light and then everything she had worked so hard to achieve would all have been in vain.

Late one night, Claire sank gratefully into the easy chair in the living room and kicked off her shoes. She'd cleaned the bar and laid the tables ready for breakfast, and now before she flopped into bed, she intended to enjoy a nice cup of cocoa. She'd just taken a sip of the steaming drink when she heard a noise in the yard. Instantly she sat bolt upright and held her breath, but now there was only silence. Beginning to think that she must have imagined it, she relaxed – and it was then that she heard it again. It sounded like someone in pain. On bare feet she warily approached the kitchen door and looked around for something to use as a weapon before she dared to open it. Her eyes lit on the rolling pin; snatching it up she cried with a bravery that she was far from feeling, 'All right then, whoever you are, be warned . . . I'm coming out and I'm armed!'

Plucking up every ounce of courage she had, she turned the key in the lock, then throwing open the door, she stepped into the dark yard.

For a minute she squinted as her eyes became accustomed to the darkness, then relief washed over her. There was no one there. It must have been a cat, she thought thankfully, when the noise, very close to her now, came again. Completely unnerved, she flew back to the safety of the kitchen doorway. She was almost there when her foot brushed against something. Staring down, she found two huge brown soulful eyes staring back up at her. It looked like a dog and it was obviously injured. Dropping to her knees without even thinking that it might bite her, she spoke to it reassuringly.

'Hello, boy. Been in the wars, have you? What's wrong then?' The little dog whimpered pitifully. It was so dark that she could barely see him out here, let alone help him, so scooping him up as gently as she could, she carried him into the warmth of the kitchen. He was surprisingly light and she could feel his bones through his fur. With one hand she snatched up a large fluffy towel, then after throwing it onto the floor, she laid him on it and stood back to survey him. What she saw didn't look good. He'd obviously been in an accident, probably a hit and run driver, she guessed, and his right back leg was sprawled out behind him at an unnatural angle. Unbidden, she remembered Tinker, the dog she had loved so long ago, and her eyes filled with sympathetic tears.

'Oh, you poor thing,' she crooned, stroking his grubby head. 'You need a vet.' Hurrying into the lounge she snatched up the phone directory and after running her fingers down the lists of vets' surgeries, she then stabbed her finger at a number at random and hastily dialled it. No reply. She tried the next one; again no reply. Impatiently now, she tried a third one. She was just about to replace the receiver when a sleepy male voice said, 'Hello?' Sighing with relief, she quickly explained what had happened.

'Right,' the voice told her. 'Keep him warm until I get there, but don't give him anything to eat or drink yet. I'll be with you in twenty minutes.'

With that, the phone went dead in her hand and Claire set about making the little dog as comfortable as possible.

Just as promised, almost twenty minutes later, an old van, not much better than her own, screeched to a halt outside, and a young man, looking like he'd just fallen out of bed, hurried up the path. His chestnut hair was tousled, and Claire found herself wanting to grin as she noticed that his shirt was buttoned up wrongly. However, he hardly gave her a second glance, but followed her quickly through to the kitchen. She was a little put out at his brusque manner, but forgave him immediately when she saw how his face softened at sight of the casualty.

'Poor thing you,' he said to the little dog, and the animal gazed up at him trustingly. 'Can I have a bowl and some hot water, please? And I'll want to put him on the table to examine him,' he said curtly. Claire quickly put a clean towel on the table and filled a bowl with warm water from the kettle.

'Mm.' The vet's voice was heavy with concern. 'His leg is badly broken.' He began to clean the injured limb. 'The cuts aren't too bad,' he said after a while. 'Nothing a few stitches won't put right, but as for the rest of him, well . . . he's in pretty bad shape. A stray, I'd guess.'

'What will we do with him?' Claire asked.

He shrugged. 'I suppose the kindest thing to do would be to put him out of his misery.' Seeing Claire's obvious distress he explained, more gently now, 'I can't tell you how bad the break is until I've X-rayed him, but if I'm right in what I'm thinking, he's going to need a pin in his leg, and even with that, he'd probably always have a limp. Plus he's so under-nourished he may not even survive the operation.'

Claire was openly crying now. 'Can't you at least *try*?' she sniffed.

He gazed thoughtfully at the little dog for a time before pointing out, 'His treatment's going to cost a fortune – and who will want him even if we do get him better?'

Claire's mind was made up in a second. '*I'll* want him.'

'Are you quite sure what you're taking on?' He was openly astonished. 'The bill for all the treatment he'll need could run into a few hundred pounds.'

Claire nodded adamantly. 'I don't care. I want you to try.'

'Very well then.' Underneath, the vet could understand how she felt; the dog was an appealing little chap. Ten minutes later they had him tucked into the back of the van, and suddenly realising that he hadn't introduced himself, the vet held his hand out to Claire.

'By the way, I'm Christian Murray.' The smile he flashed at her was so infectious that Claire found herself smiling back at him.

'Claire Hamilton.' They shook hands, and as their fingers met a queer little ripple passed through her.

'Ring me first thing in the morning,' he told her, businesslike again now. 'I can't promise anything mind, but I'll do my best.' Then he jumped into the van and with a final wave he was gone.

Claire was strangely unsettled as she entered the hotel. She didn't know who had distracted her the most – the dog or the vet. Within the space of an hour, she had become the new owner of an injured little mongrel. And as to Christian Murray . . . well. What was it about him that had attracted her? She couldn't understand it and the feeling made her vaguely uneasy. Still, with regards to the dog, she had no regrets, and as she finally nodded off to sleep, when it was almost time to get back up again, she prayed for the first time in a very long while that her new pet would pull through. Somehow, with Christian in charge, she had a feeling that he might.

The next morning, Christian Murray answered the phone on the second ring. He sounded unbelievably tired but when he recognised Claire's voice, his tone lightened. 'It's good news and bad news,' he informed her. 'Which do you want first?'

Claire sighed worriedly. 'I'll have the bad.'

'The break was just as bad as I feared,' he explained. 'I've managed to pin it, but whether it works or not is another matter. The good news is that he's come through it. He must be tougher than he looks. Plus he's just wolfed down a whole tin of dog food.'

Claire's spirits rose. 'Well done.' She was genuinely delighted, and after chatting for a few more minutes she promised to ring back again at dinner-time after the vet's surgery and hung up.

That morning, she zipped through her chores, humming merrily to herself. 'I must think of a name for him,' she said to herself, and as she worked she tried to think of one that would suit him.

Betty and Mary raised their eyebrows and winked at each other as they heard her humming. 'She's in a good mood this morning, ain't she?' Betty whispered as she passed Mary in the hallway with a tray full of dirty pots.

'Mm, I don't think I've ever seen her so chirpy,' Mary agreed, but when Claire told them both during their morning tea break about what had happened the night before, they stared at her as if she'd taken leave of her senses.

'Do you really think it's wise to have a dog in a hotel?' Betty asked with concern. 'You might find that the guests ain't too keen on having a mutt about the place.'

Claire visibly bristled. 'If the guests aren't happy then they'll have to go and find somewhere else to stay, won't they? Because I'll tell you now, no one – and I mean *no one* – is going to dictate to me who I can or can't have in here. This, in case you'd forgotten, happens to be *my* hotel, so if guests, or staff for that matter, don't like it then they needn't bother coming.' Then, turning on her heel, she strode away without so much as another word.

'Blimey. I reckon that's what you call bein' put firmly in your place. Hoity Toity little Miss. Problem with her is, you never know where you stand with her.'

'Mm.' Mary said. 'I think there could well be a reason for that. If you ask me, there's more to that little madam than meets the eye.'

'What do you mean by that?' Betty was all ears.

Glancing across the sea of starched white tablecloths in the dining room to the doorway to make sure that they couldn't be overheard, Mary murmured, 'Think about it. Claire's been here for months now and what do we actually know about her?'

'Well, we know that her parents were killed in a car crash, and—'

'Exactly – and! Have you ever heard her say where she actually comes from?'

'No – no, I ain't, now you come to mention it,' Betty admitted.

'And have you ever heard her talk once of any family she might have left? Or friends, for that matter? Think about it, most girls Claire's age have friends, don't they? What about her birthday a couple of weeks ago? We wouldn't even have known it was her birthday if she hadn't bought that cake and invited us into her living quarters for a slice. It was her twenty-first, for God's sake, an' not a single birthday card in sight. There's something else that's strange, as well. I've noticed that every week when we're due for the new intake of guests, she's like a cat on hot bricks, almost as if she's afraid who might walk through the door.'

The two women lapsed into temporary silence, which was broken when Mary suddenly whispered, 'It's funny that she doesn't go out anywhere as well, ain't it? I mean, the furthest I've seen her venture is to the cash and carry, and then it's as if she can't get there and back quickly enough. Do you reckon she's scared of bumpin' into someone?'

'But what could a young girl like her have to hide from?' Betty mused. 'I reckon you're barkin' up the wrong tree somewhere along the line. I have to admit, Claire does keep herself to herself, but then if she's recently lost her family she's probably still grievin', which would explain why she can be so prickly at times. An' also that haunted look you see in her eyes when she don't know you're watching her.'

'Have it your own way,' Mary sniffed as she stood up from the table. 'But I still say as there's more to her than meets the eye.'

'Well, there's one thing for sure, only time will tell,' Betty said wisely, and the two women went their separate ways.

Claire slammed the door to her private quarters and clenched her fists. Just who the hell did Betty think she was anyway, trying to tell her what she could and couldn't do in her own hotel? The anger dispersed almost as quickly as it had come and tears sprang to her eyes. She knew that she'd been a little harsh on the woman. After all, she had shown Claire nothing but kindness since she'd arrived. So had Mary for that matter, but perhaps that was the problem? Claire had become adept at putting her guard up if she became fond of anyone and she determined that from then on, she would keep a distance.

She supposed in fairness that Betty had a point. It probably wasn't ideal to have a dog there but nothing would make her change her decision now. She'd given Christian Murray her word and could hardly wait to have the dog home. The way she saw it, he would be company for her.

That afternoon, after ringing Christian again, she went out and bought a collar and lead, dog dishes, food, biscuits, a basket and anything she could think of that he might need. When she rang again at teatime, Christian assured her that he thought the dog was well enough to come home and offered to drop him off while he was on his rounds. It was as she was waiting for the vet to bring him that a name suddenly came to her. Cassidy. That's what she'd call him, as in Hop-a-long Cassidy. The more she thought of it, the more she liked it, and when Christian's van pulled up almost an hour later, she hurried down the path to meet him. Considering what the little mutt had been through, he looked unbelievably perky as she peeped through the van window, and her heart melted at the sight of him. Somehow, Christian Murray had found time to bath him as well as repair his leg, and he was almost unrecognisable.

'Oh, Mr Murray!' She was absolutely delighted. 'He looks wonderful. I think you've performed a miracle.'

He laughed. 'Look, call me Christian,' he insisted. 'I'm afraid you'll be seeing quite a lot of me over the next few weeks and Mr Murray sounds very formal. Meladdo's not out of the woods yet, not by a long shot, and as for performing a miracle, well . . . it's surprising what a bit of soap and water can do.' Reaching into the van, he lifted the dog out and followed Claire up the path. Once inside her lounge, he grinned at the huge new dog basket. Inside it, Claire had placed a pillow and a warm blanket. Christian placed him inside.

'Blimey,' he joked. 'Do *all* your guests get this treatment? If they do, I think I'll come and stay here.'

Claire smiled as they stood looking down on the cause of all the trouble. 'I'm going to call him Cassidy,' she announced.

Christian gazed at him thoughtfully. 'Do you know, I think it suits him.'

Cassidy wagged his tail as if in agreement. In truth, he wasn't the prettiest of dogs; he had a small body with short brown hair, but his ears were long and bushy like his tail. Even so, to Claire he was perfect, and she loved him already, which she found rather strange. She had become adept at distancing herself from people, yet could still not resist animals. She supposed it stemmed from her love of Tinker as a child. Finally pulling her eyes away from Cassidy, she was shocked to see how tired Christian looked. He hadn't gone back to bed after Claire had rung him the night before, and now after a long day it was telling on him.

'Sit down,' she insisted. 'I'll make us both a hot drink, and I'll bet you could manage a sandwich too, couldn't you?'

Christian nodded at her gratefully, and without needing to be told twice, sank wearily into the easy chair. Ten minutes later, Claire was back bearing a tray of ham sandwiches and a large pot of tea. But the sight that met her eyes made her stop dead in her tracks. Christian Murray was fast asleep, his long legs stretched out before him with one arm trailing over the arm of the chair, resting on Cassidy's head, who by now was fast asleep too. They made a nice picture, and for a second Claire stood there staring at them.

Christian wasn't the most handsome man she had ever seen by a long shot, but there was something about his kind nature and twinkling eyes that touched a chord in her. Tiptoeing back into the kitchen she placed the tray down quietly, then after wrapping the sandwiches in Clingfilm she poured the tea down the sink. I'll just let him have half an hour before I disturb him, she thought. He obviously needs it. But it was in fact two hours later when she gently woke him. As she tapped his hand, his startled eyes flew open and he stared at Claire in horror.

'Oh God, I didn't fall asleep, did I?'

'Yes, you did,' she said solemnly. 'So did Cassidy, and you both looked so peaceful I hadn't the heart to disturb you. I hope you didn't have any more calls to do?'

He was mortified and flushed with embarrassment. 'No, no. Thankfully I did the last one before bringing His Lordship home. I'm so sorry.'

Claire waved her hand at him. 'Stop apologising,' she ordered. 'If it wasn't for you and all the hard work you've done on our friend here, he wouldn't have pulled through. I've got you to thank for Cassidy.'

'You won't say that when you see the bill,' he warned.

Claire was completely unconcerned. 'I told you last night I didn't care what it cost and I meant it,' she said, and Christian could tell that she *did* mean it. Cassidy had dropped on his feet here, he thought, and no mistake.

Claire poured him a fresh cup of tea out and handed it to him with a large plate of the sandwiches. He tucked into them as if he hadn't eaten for a month and in minutes had cleared the plate.

'That was just what the doctor ordered,' he thanked her.

Cassidy was still fast asleep. His injured leg was in plaster and heavily bandaged, but Christian assured her that he would be able to hobble about on it. Claire was amazed at how easy Christian was to get on with, and by the time he left another hour later, they were chatting as if they'd known each other for years. He told her that he ran his practice from a place called 'Seagull's Flight' on the main road to Fleetwood. It was actually his grandmother's place, he explained. When his grandfather had been alive, it had been a farm. It seemed that Christian had inherited his love of animals from them. They had brought him up since he was a child, following his parents' deaths, and after his grandfather died his grand-mother had opened up a small dogs' home there. Claire sighed, thinking it all sounded wonderfully romantic, but Christian quickly disillusioned her.

'It's hard work,' he said. 'Gran takes in a lot of strays. The RSPCA give us a little towards their keep until we can find homes for them, and I look after them free of charge if anything is wrong with them. But mainly we have to rely on charity.'

Claire was deeply saddened at the thought of all the strays. A thought occurred to her.

'I was just thinking, the season will be over soon here and I'll have some spare time on my hands. Would there be anything that I could do to help?'

Christian chuckled. 'You might live to regret that offer. We're always glad of any help we can get. I'm not long out of vet school, so we're still struggling a bit. To be honest, there never seems to be enough money or enough hours in the day to do everything that needs doing.'

Claire promised there and then that she'd help out in any way that she could, and suddenly the cold winter days that lay ahead didn't seem quite so daunting.

When he finally left, Christian promised to call back in a couple of days and see how Cassidy was doing. As she watched his van pull away, loneliness closed around her again, and suddenly, totally confused, Claire slowly made her way back to her new friend.

Chapter Twenty-Four

True to his word, Christian was back two days later. By then, Cassidy was managing to hobble about. In fact, he'd become Claire's shadow and Christian was amused to note that he followed her everywhere adoringly.

Already the little mongrel was gaining weight, and the young vet eyed him with satisfaction. It was more than obvious that Claire already loved him, and he had a feeling that this was one little dog he would never have to worry about.

'He's doing fine,' he assured her. 'Another couple of weeks and we'll have the plaster off and see how his leg's healing.'

Despite their initial reactions, Cassidy soon had Mary and Betty pandering to him too. They became used to Christian popping in and out and would wink at each other when they were sure that Claire and Christian weren't looking.

'I wonder if it's the dog or Claire he's comin' to see?' Mary whispered one day as she passed Betty on the stairs with a pile of clean laundry in her arms.

Betty chuckled. 'Well, from the way her face lights up at the sight of him, I hope it's Claire,' she whispered back. With big grins on their faces the two women went about their work.

At last, during one of his visits, Christian declared that Cassidy was well enough to have his plaster removed. He intended to do it at Seagull's Flight and told Claire that he would pick him up the next day, but when he arrived, Claire insisted on going with him.

'Please let me come,' she begged. 'He might fret without me there.'

Christian agreed immediately.

They trundled along the seafront and soon they had left Blackpool behind them and were heading for Fleetwood. Claire was feeling strangely tonguetied. She supposed it was because this was the first time she had been alone with a man other than a client for years. Luckily, Christian didn't seem to notice so she sat cuddling Cassidy on her lap in silence. They were on a particularly busy stretch of road when Christian suddenly indicated and turned down what appeared to be little more than a dirt track.

'Welcome to Seagull's Flight,' he said.

Now she stared about her with interest. The track was incredibly long and winding, and as she saw the sand dunes directly ahead in the distance, she realised that they were heading for the sea. Suddenly they rounded a particularly sharp bend and there was Seagull's Flight.

It was just as Christian had described it, an incredibly old farmhouse almost nestling into the sand dunes onto which it backed. Claire fell in love with it immediately. Although it was off the main road, you could almost feel here that you were in the back of beyond. A long low building was built alongside it and Christian explained that it was here that they housed the dogs. He'd barely parked the van and turned off the engine when the door to the rambling old house burst open. A friendly, wrinkled-faced old woman, who was surprisingly agile on her feet, hurried out to meet them.

'You must be Claire, dear.' Holding out her hand in greeting, she beamed. 'I've heard all about you and how good you've been to His Lordship.' She nodded towards Cassidy, as Claire awkwardly shook her hand, wondering if it had been such a good idea to come here after all. Friendly people always made her nervous.

'Anyway,' the old lady went on, 'I expect you'd like to have a good look around. Christian's told me that you might be able to help out here from time to time, so I'll let him show you about, while I put the kettle on.'

As Christian watched her go with a fond smile on his face, he told Claire apologetically, 'Don't mind Gran. She loves a bit of company almost as much as she loves the dogs.' He then led her towards the dog pound. Just as Christian had said, Claire saw that there was a lot that needed doing here. But for all that, the building she followed him into was spotlessly clean and cosy inside. There was a long walkway all down the length of the building on one side; the other side consisted of a row of small enclosures. Every single one had a dog inside it. As she walked by them they yapped and stared at her mournfully, and by the time they'd reached the other end, Claire was choking back tears.

'How can people be so cruel?' She was shocked to see so many abandoned pets.

Christian shrugged. 'You'd be surprised,' he said bitterly.

Claire was tempted to take every single stray home; as she had learned long ago that animals couldn't hurt you, unlike people. By the time she followed Christian back to the farmhouse her spirits were at a very low ebb. His gran eyed her sympathetically.

'Don't get upset, love,' she urged. 'You'd be surprised at how many of them we find good homes for.'

Later, Christian showed Claire and Cassidy his surgery, which turned out to be little more than a lean-to built on to the side of the house.

'I did say it wasn't much,' he sighed. 'Mind you, Gran and I have got great plans for it. She scrimped and saved to get me through my training, and one day I intend to have the best practice for miles around.'

Claire hoped with all her heart that he would achieve his goal, as she lifted Cassidy onto the examination table. Christian carefully cut away his plaster and tentatively tried to bend Cassidy's leg. The dog let out a howl of pain, and if it hadn't been for the fact that Claire was holding him tightly, he would have plunged from the table.

Christian frowned. 'I think I'd best do another X-ray,' he said, and carried the dog into an adjoining room. Claire paced up and down the confined space until eventually Christian reappeared, his face grim.

'It hasn't worked,' he said bluntly.

She stared back at him in horror. 'Well, you'll just have to do it again then,' she blurted out.

Christian shook his head. 'No. It can't be done again.' Seeing that Claire was distraught he said carefully, 'The problem is, his leg is never going to mend. If we leave it as it is, there's every chance that it will become infected and if it does, we could lose him.'

Claire was still staring at him silently, waiting for him to offer a solution, and after a while he did. 'Unfortunately, it seems we're back to two choices; either we put him to sleep or we take his leg off and have done with it.'

Claire was totally appalled. 'But how will he manage with three legs?' she gasped.

'He'll be just fine.' Christian's voice was reassuring. 'And it's a much better option than letting an infection set in.'

Although she was deeply upset, Claire trusted Christian implicitly. 'All right then . . . do it,' she said.

'Are you sure?'

She nodded miserably; she couldn't bear the thought of losing this little dog that she'd come to love.

There was no point in delaying the inevitable, so after leaving Cassidy in his gran's safe hands, Christian drove Claire home. 'You'll be able to have him back tomorrow if all goes well,' he promised.

Claire nodded. They were both subdued on the journey home and as she stepped out of the van, Christian momentarily squeezed her hand.

'I'm sorry,' he muttered.

Claire shrugged to hide her true feelings. 'It's not your fault.' But she was missing Cassidy already, and as Christian drove away she slowly made her way into the hotel with a heavy heart.

That night, she cried herself to sleep, just as she had done so many times before. The night must have been made for tears, she thought. Once again she had allowed herself to care – and what had it brought her? Pictures of her mother, Tracey, Tinker, Yasmin, Molly, Tom and Cindy flashed in front of her eyes in quick succession. Once again she had broken all the rules she had laid down for herself, and this was the result.

To her relief, Cassidy came out of it all fighting fit. For a while he had a job balancing, but once he got the hang of hobbling about on three legs, he was soon following her around again like a shadow. Claire knew that she could never thank Christian enough, and when he eventually presented her with the bill, she not only paid it but also added a sizeable amount to it. Christian argued, deeply embarrassed, but Claire was insistent and eventually he took it gratefully. After that, there was no excuse for him to call around any more, and to her horror, Claire found that she was missing him.

Still, she consoled herself, another couple of weeks and the last of the guests would be gone. Then she could go and help out at Seagull's Flight. At least it would be something to do, to while away the time. Her spirits rose at the thought but almost immediately she changed her mind. Perhaps it would be better if she kept away? She had Cassidy to keep her company now. He would be enough.

On a cold frosty day in November, Claire closed the door behind the last guest of the year. Her first full season as the landlady of the Seabourne Hotel had been far more successful than she'd dared to hope, and to her relief, even after paying all her expenses and the staff's wages, she was still in profit. This year she would be able to pay a local decorator to do any jobs that needed doing during the winter months instead of having to struggle to do them all herself.

Throughout the season she had kept her account books religiously up to date, even if it meant working on them in the early hours of the morning. Two weeks after the hotel had closed, Gregory Nightingale phoned her, as promised, and made an appointment for her to come and see him.

She took particular pains over her appearance on the day she was due to visit him, and when she was shown into his office, his appreciative smile told her that the trouble she'd gone to had been worth it. He was even more handsome than she'd remembered and equally as much of a gentleman. They spent an hour going over her ledgers, and when they'd finally done, he looked up from the neatly kept books and smiled at her.

'Congratulations! You've done remarkably well for your first season, and the way you've kept your ledgers is a credit to you.'

Claire flushed at the compliment as Gregory Nightingale gazed admiringly at her. She was very beautiful, and yet seemed to be unaware of it, and she appealed to him as no woman had for a very long time.

When their business was concluded, he shook her hand – and Claire had the feeling that he held on to it for a fraction longer than was necessary. Gregory Nightingale was a very confident man; he had wealth, a respected position in the community, good looks and charm, and now as he led her to the door he said smoothly, 'Just leave everything in my hands – I can't foresee any problems. You'll be hearing from me again shortly, Miss Hamilton.'

Then, pausing with his hand on the doorknob, he said casually, 'How about coming out with me for a meal tonight to celebrate your first successful season?' He was oozing charm, and Claire was instantly on her guard although her smile never faltered.

218

'Why, thank you,' she replied coolly. 'Unfortunately, I do have other plans for this evening.'

The accountant was visibly startled; he wasn't used to being turned down. In fact, he knew women who would have queued to go out with him, and had assumed that Claire would be one of them.

'Perhaps some other evening then?' He hid his disappointment with a smile.

'Perhaps.' Completely in control of the situation, Claire flashed him a final smile, and swept from the office. She was amused; she had learned how to handle men in her former life in London, but luckily Gregory Nightingale couldn't know that.

When she arrived back at the hotel, Cassidy leaped all over her, and heedless of the expensive suit she was wearing, she dropped to her knees and cuddled him. It was a relief to change from her smart suit back into her comfortable jeans. She felt strangely out of place now in her expensive clothes. In the afternoon she took him for a long walk along the beach, and watched him chase the seagulls and run along on his three legs, as lively now as any dog with four.

When they got back to the hotel, Claire made them both scrambled eggs on toast. It was one of Cassidy's favourites, and although he was putting on far too much weight, Claire couldn't resist spoiling him. He was unrecognisable now from the thin bedraggled little stray she had taken pity on. His coat shone and his eyes when he looked at his mistress were full of trust. Claire loved him unreservedly as she felt she could never love a person.

That night, as the wind howled outside, they lay together on Claire's sofa in the lounge, while she ate chocolate and they watched a film on TV that reduced her to floods of tears. Cassidy licked them away with his warm tongue, and soon Claire was laughing and crying all at the same time.

The next morning they had a well-deserved lie-in; a pleasure that wasn't afforded them when there were guests staying. When the front-door bell rang at half-past nine, Claire cursed loudly. Pulling on her dressing-gown she clattered down the stairs with Cassidy close at her heels. When she threw the front door open, to her amazement she was confronted with the largest bunch of red roses she had ever seen. A delivery boy's face peeped over the top of them.

'Miss Claire Hamilton?'

Bewildered, Claire nodded. Without further ado, he pushed the flowers into her arms, then whistling merrily he headed off back down the path. Claire frowned. No one had ever bought her flowers before – ever – and she could hardly wait to see who they were from. Hurrying into the living room, she placed them on the coffee-table. Then, searching among the blooms, she found a small white envelope. She opened it and read the card inside. It said simply:

Well done on your first profitable season. Don't forget our dinner-date. Best wishes, Gregory Nightingale. xxx.

Disappointment swept over her. For a moment she had hoped they were from Christian, but then she scolded herself. She and Christian were just friends, and that's all they could ever be.

The roses filled two vases and Claire imagined they must have cost a small fortune. She wondered what Mr Nightingale would think if he could see her now, in her old dressing-gown with her hair all over the place. When the flowers were arranged to her satisfaction she washed and dressed and went about her daily business without giving them or Gregory so much as a second thought.

Three days later, a huge box of chocolates was delivered, again from Gregory Nightingale, and she found herself wondering, What would he do if he knew of my past? The thought made her shudder and she forced it from her mind.

By the Sunday of the following week, Claire was totally bored. During the season, when the hotel was full of guests, she was used to running about from morning until night, but now the days stretched before her endlessly. 'How about we take a ride to Seagull's Flight, eh?' she said to Cassidy. 'We could see if they need any help.' Deep down she knew that it would be safer to stay away and had promised herself that she would do just that, but now the need for human company was strong. And after all – what harm could it do?

Cassidy wagged his tail as if in agreement with the idea, and twenty minutes later they were in her old van heading along the coastal road. When they pulled onto the beaten track that led to Seagull's Flight, Claire experienced a strange sense of well-being. Dilapidated the place might be, but Claire had fallen in love with it at first sight. As she pulled into the yard, she noticed that Christian's van was missing, but felt sure that the old lady, his grandma, would be at home.

When Mrs Murray came out, she peered at the van curiously until, recognising Claire, she hurried forward to greet her.

'Hello there, love. Was it Christian you were wanting? I'm afraid he's been called out.'

Claire shook her head. 'Actually no, it wasn't. To tell the truth, I was at a bit of a loose end and I was wondering if I could lend a hand at anything?'

Mrs Murray chuckled. 'Don't go makin' offers like that unless you mean it. There's always somethin' around here that needs doin' believe me. There just never seem to be enough hours in the day.'

Claire hopped out of the van. When Cassidy followed her, Mrs Murray was amazed. 'God love us!' she exclaimed delightedly. 'That's never the poor little soul that was at death's door, is it?'

Claire nodded as Mrs Murray's eyes softened. Reaching out, she squeezed Claire's hand. 'You're a good girl. I know it cost an arm and a leg to get him right, an' there aren't many as would have thought a mangy little mongrel like him was worth it.'

Claire suffered a pang of conscience. No one had ever called her good before, and she knew that she was far from it, but she said nothing and as the old lady headed towards the dog pound, Claire fell into step beside her.

'I've got all the pens to clean out today,' she informed Claire. 'You could help with that if you wanted. But I warn you, it's a mucky job.'

'I don't mind, really,' Claire assured her, and they entered the pound together. As Mrs Murray opened the doors to two of the pens, two dogs, with their tails furiously wagging, leaped on them.

Claire watched as the dogs raced up and down the walkway with Cassidy, then she and Mrs Murray tackled a pen each. First they removed all the dirty straw and put it into black bin liners. They then swept the pens out thoroughly, disinfected the floors and put fresh straw in. Side-by-side they worked their way down the row. A gust of icy air as the door to the dog pound was flung open heralded Christian's arrival almost two hours later, when they had almost finished.

Claire was on her hands and knees wielding a dustpan and brush. A few strands of fair hair had escaped from her ponytail and curled about her face, and she was covered from head to foot in bits of straw. Beads of sweat stood out on her brow despite the harshness of the weather. Yet as he looked at her, he realised with a little shock how beautiful she was.

'What's this then?' He felt embarrassed as he realised how pleased he was to see her.

A blush spread across Claire's cheeks. 'Well, I promised I'd help out when the hotel closed, didn't I? So . . . here I am.'

Rolling his sleeves up, he joined them, and soon the pens job was finished.

'There,' said Mrs Murray as she straightened her back and stretched painfully. 'That's a good job out of the way.' She smiled at Claire. 'You will stay for dinner, won't you?'

Claire hashly shook her head. 'No . . . no, it's all right, really. I wouldn't want to put you to any trouble.'

Mrs Murray was highly indignant. 'It ain't no trouble, I've got a roast in the oven on low that would feed an army, and besides, I won't take no for an answer. You've worked your socks off since the second you arrived. The least I can do is feed you, so you're staying an' that's an end to it.'

Underneath, Claire was delighted to stay, and soon the three of them were sitting at an old oak table, eating a hearty meal of slices of roast lamb and creamy mashed potatoes all swimming in a delicious gravy.

When they'd finished, Claire sat back and sighed contentedly. 'I couldn't eat another thing. I feel as if I could burst,' she declared.

Christian laughed. 'I'll tell you what then – you can come and help me exercise the dogs. That'll walk some of it off.'

They walked the dogs, four at a time, through the sand dunes until they reached the beach where they let them off their leads. The dogs barked furiously and scampered about, delighted to be free. By teatime they had exercised them all and Claire was feeling pleasantly tired and happier than she could ever remember feeling.

In her past she'd had little to do with men apart from her many clients, but Christian was remarkably easy to talk to and she felt very comfortable in his presence. They talked about everything, from politics to nature, although Claire was careful to avoid anything personal. She cringed at the thought of him knowing of her past, and dreaded the look of condemnation that would surely cross his face if ever he did.

She found herself thinking of all the abuse she had suffered as a child behind closed doors. Of the desperation, the guilt and loneliness, and the prostitution, which had been the only way she could think of to rise above it and escape, and she knew that someone decent like Christian could never understand. No one would. Although she had carved a new life for herself, it had been bought at the cost of degradation and she knew then, that although she had tried to put it behind her, it was still there, just below the surface, too shameful to ever share with anyone. It was Claire McMullen who still scribbled away in her diary each night.

This realisation took the shine from the day and by the time they arrived back at Seagull's Flight, Claire was subdued. Mrs Murray took it as a sign of tiredness, and plied her with steaming tea and scones fresh out of the oven. After the huge dinner she'd eaten earlier, Claire felt that she would never eat again, but to please the dear old lady she made a valiant effort, counting the minutes now until she could be alone again with her thoughts.

'Gran's a great cook, isn't she?' said Christian as he buttered yet another scone.

Claire nodded in agreement. 'Yes, she certainly is. But look – I really ought to be going now.'

'Thanks for all your help, love,' Mrs Murray said as she rose from her chair to follow Claire outside. 'You've worked like a little horse today.'

'You're very welcome,' Claire told her sincerely. 'I've enjoyed every minute of it.' And she had.

By now it was dark. Christian and his gran stood framed in the light from the kitchen doorway and waved her up the lane. Cassidy, who was totally worn out, immediately fell asleep on the seat beside her, and as she headed for home, Claire promised herself that this would be the very last time she would come here. Happiness like this was dangerous.

Chapter Twenty-Five

The following morning, Gregory Nightingale returned her ledgers personally. Luckily, he phoned her to say that he was coming so Claire had time to smarten herself up. With the accountant she had an image to live up to; with Christian she could almost be herself and this disturbed her.

Gregory not only brought her books but another armful of roses, and was charm personified. As usual he was impeccably groomed, and during his visit he made it more than clear that he was becoming impatient for their dinner-date. Claire intrigued him. She was like no other woman he had ever met, and the more she refused to go out with him, the more he wanted her. But once again she stalled him with excuses. And once again he went away disappointed but even more determined to succeed.

By the time Christmas loomed, Claire had become a regular visitor to Seagull's Flight, despite the vow she had made to never go there again. Mrs M, as Claire now called Christian's grandmother, had become extremely fond of her. They were sitting at the kitchen table one day enjoying a well-earned tea break when the old lady peered at her out of the corner of her eye to ask, 'So, what are you planning on doing for Christmas dinner then, love?'

Claire shrugged.

'Why don't you come and join us?' the woman said and Claire was sorely tempted. She and Christian had just finished exercising the dogs on the beach. It was a bitterly cold, windy day. Her hair was full of salt spray and her cheeks were glowing. As Christian watched her over the rim of his mug he was thinking that she looked very pretty.

Mrs M was determined to have an answer about Christmas lunch. 'Say you'll come,' she pleaded. 'There'll only be the four of us.'

'Four?' There was a question in Claire's voice.

Mrs M nodded. 'Yes. Me, Christian, Lianne and yourself.' The old lady saw her puzzled look and quickly explained, 'Lianne is Christian's fiancée. I don't think you've met her yet, have you? She's away at university so they don't get to see too much of each other at present.'

The colour drained from Claire's face. 'I didn't know you were engaged,' she said, trying desperately to keep the accusation from her voice.

Christian avoided her eyes. 'Well, like Gran said, Lianne and I haven't seen much of each other lately.'

Claire felt as if the bottom had dropped out of her world, but she was an expert at hiding her feelings and turning now, she smiled at Mrs M.

'Well, it's very kind of you to invite me, but I've made other arrangements,' she said politely. Her heart was crying, but she would have died rather than show it. For the rest of the visit an uncomfortable silence settled between Christian and herself. She was glad to leave Seagull's Flight, and as the van jolted its way up the track, she cursed herself for a fool as tears poured down her cheeks. 'You idiot,' she wept. 'You almost let yourself get too close.'

When she arrived home, a huge bunch of roses was waiting for her on the step, yellow this time, and before she'd even opened the card she guessed who they were from. She let herself in with Cassidy, who was worn out, close at her heels, and read the card.

How about Christmas dinner? Gregory Nightingale had written. He had already asked her once before and she had refused him, but now, without allowing herself time to think, Claire dialled his number with shaking fingers.

He was delighted to hear from her and asked if she would care to visit his home and have Christmas dinner with him and his daughter. Claire felt it was a little soon in their relationship to meet his child, so tactfully suggested that they met for lunch on Boxing Day instead. After all, it didn't seem right to drag him away from his family on Christmas Day.

Gregory readily agreed. And so he picked her up at midday on Boxing Day and took her to the best restaurant in town. He was looking very smart in a grey pinstriped suit, and Claire was chic in an expensive designer dress that she had bought and worn during her time in London. They made a handsome couple and heads turned as they entered the restaurant. No expense was spared. They had a five-course meal and drank champagne, and as they were sitting over coffee and biscuits, Greg, as he insisted on her calling him, handed her a long midnight-blue velvet box across the table.

'Open it,' he urged, grinning charmingly, 'I think you'll like it, but if you don't, we can change it.'

Claire slowly opened the lid. Inside was a gold bracelet, set with amethysts, and she knew at a glance that it must have been very expensive.

'I . . . c–can't accept this,' she stuttered, but Greg took it from its velvet case and fastened it onto her wrist.

'There,' he beamed. 'It looks wonderful. You *do* like it, don't you?'

'How could I *not* like it? It's beautiful,' Claire whispered. In fact, she could hardly tear her eyes away from it. No one had ever bought a present like this for her without her earning it. 'Greg, you shouldn't have,' she scolded. 'You hardly know me.'

His eyes twinkled in the candlelight. 'I'm hoping to remedy that,' he said smoothly. 'And anyway, you're worth it.'

Claire felt uncomfortable. This was no inexpensive bauble: what would he expect in return? However, her fears proved to be unfounded. Greg had realised a long time ago that he would have to go slowly with this woman, and now that she had finally agreed to go out with him he had no intention of rushing things. He was the perfect gentleman right up until the moment when he dropped her off back at the Seabourne Hotel. She felt that she ought to at least invite him in for a coffee, but fortunately he explained that he should be getting home to his daughter.

'I have a wonderful woman, Mrs Pope, who doubles as a housekeeper and a babysitter whenever needed,' he told her. 'She's a widow who lives not far from me, but being as it's Boxing Day I'd better not push my luck.'

Claire was secretly relieved that she didn't have to ask him in, and flattered that he had left his daughter to have dinner with her on Boxing Day. She thanked him again for the wonderful meal and the gift, and still the perfect gentleman, he leaned over and kissed her chastely on the cheek. No more than that. She was amazed.

Cassidy leaped on her joyously when she let herself in and she cuddled him affectionately. It was nice to have him to come home to. She couldn't imagine life without him now.

As she was changing, her thoughts went back over her dinner-date. She laid the heavy bracelet back in its case and sighed. Despite herself, she had enjoyed Greg's company – but then, who wouldn't? He was intelligent, he had a sense of humour, he was generous, rich, and the most handsome man she had ever met. So why was it then that even now, a picture of Christian's unruly mop of hair and twinkling eyes kept popping into her mind?

Claire spent the rest of the day watching old movies, snuggled up next to her three-legged best friend.

The next day, Greg rang her and she was surprised at how pleased she was to hear from him.

'How are you?' he asked.

'I'm fine,' Claire assured him, but she was lying. She was bored sick.

'How about dinner on Wednesday evening?' he asked, after they had chatted for some minutes, and this time Claire accepted readily. When she finally put the phone down she felt lonelier than ever. Wednesday was two whole days away. She prowled about the hotel for a time but then, making a decision, she called Cassidy to her.

'Come on, we'll go and see if anything needs doing at Seagull's Flight.' His tail began to wag furiously as if he understood her. She hadn't meant to go there ever again, but couldn't help herself. It was almost like a magnet to her. But of course, she tried to convince herself, she was only going to see Mrs M and the dogs.

When she pulled into the yard she noticed a smart little saloon car parked next to Christian's old van, and guessed immediately that this must belong to Lianne, his fiancée. She hesitated, unsure whether to turn around and leave, but Mrs M had heard her pull up and hurried out to greet her. 'Hello, love.' She was obviously pleased to see her. 'Did you have a good Christmas?'

Claire nodded, and just then Christian stepped out of the kitchen door, closely followed by a stunning young woman. When they saw Claire, they came across to her van and Christian introduced them.

'Hello, Claire.' He looked vaguely uncomfortable. 'This is Lianne, my fiancée.'

The two young women shook hands, and Claire felt suddenly gawky and under-dressed. Lianne was very pretty; tiny and delicate with flame-red hair cut into a stylish bob, and deep, sea-green eyes. Her outfit looked as if it had come straight off a designer peg, and on her feet she wore expensive high heels that were completely out of place in the dusty yard. The women eyed each other warily and although Lianne smiled, Claire noted that the smile didn't quite reach her eyes.

'I hear you've helped a lot about the place lately,' Lianne said.

Unsure what to reply, Claire nodded.

It was Christian who broke the tension when he said, 'Oh well, I'd better get this into your car.' He pointed at an expensive leather suitcase and Lianne smiled up at him possessively as with a final nod at Claire she followed him to her car.

Claire and Mrs M made their way in silence to the dog pens.

It was Mrs M who spoke first. 'I shouldn't be saying this,' she admitted guiltily, 'but those two are as different as chalk from cheese. Don't get me wrong – Lianne's a nice enough girl, and from a very good family too. But I can't somehow see her settling down to be a vet's wife, can you? She doesn't even like animals.'

Claire was stunned. For most of the time she preferred animals to people. But then, she reasoned, it wouldn't do if everyone were the same, and in fairness after meeting Lianne so briefly she didn't feel that she knew her well enough to comment, so she wisely didn't answer.

When she and Mrs M had cleaned out almost half of the pens, Christian joined them. Claire was distressed to see that the number of dogs had grown.

'It's Christmas,' Mrs M said sadly, following Claire's eyes as if she could read her thoughts. 'People buy puppies for presents then soon as Christmas is over and the novelty has worn off, they turf them out.'

Claire was heartbroken. Again she wondered how people could be so cruel. But then she thought bitterly how she, more than most, knew first-hand just how cruel people could be.

Between the three of them they soon had the pens spick and span. Christian fetched some dog leads, and he and Claire then took four of the dogs down onto the beach. Cassidy was in his element, and Claire and Christian chuckled at his escapades. The wind was whipping the sand up into swirls and the waves were thundering onto the beach as the seagulls wheeled in the leaden-grey sky overhead. Despite herself, Claire experienced a feeling of coming home. She couldn't help but compare

Greg to Christian as they strolled along, their heads bent against the wind. Greg was everything she had ever dreamed of – a rich, successful businessman – while Christian was a struggling vet who never looked even remotely tidy. So why was she so attracted to him? It was a question she found impossible to answer as they strolled along in companionable silence.

They were just returning to the pens with the last of the dogs when they noticed that the door was open, and when they stepped inside, they found Mrs M walking the length of the run with a man, woman and two children. The latter were almost beside themselves with excitement and were racing from cage to cage, peering inside each one.

Mrs M smiled at Christian and Claire. 'This family have come to choose a pet,' she informed them.

'We don't want one too big now,' warned the father, and so the search continued. At last the two children paused in front of the same cage, and Mrs M lifted the latch and let the little mongrel come out to them. He was an odd-looking character, one of Claire's favourites, with soft brown eyes and a long shaggy coat. He leaped all over the children delightedly, licking any part of them that he could reach as they giggled noisily.

'Oh Daddy, *please* may we have this one?' they begged in unison.

Their parents exchanged a resigned smile.

'Well . . . he does seem to have a nice temperament,' the man admitted, and Mrs M was quick to agree with him. When they left, the dog was snuggled down between the children on the back seat.

The old lady sighed contentedly. 'There goes one that we won't have to worry about again,' she said.

Claire too felt a thrill of satisfaction. It was nice to think that the little dog had finally found a good home; it made Mrs M and Christian's efforts all worthwhile. She was feeling happy when she drove home that evening. She had forgiven Christian for not telling her about Lianne. After all, it had been she herself who had avoided talking of anything personal, and she had never encouraged him to do so either. But for some reason, the thought of Lianne still hurt and she couldn't understand why.

Greg rang her the next day, and the day after that he turned up as promised, exactly on time, to take her to dinner. She invited him in while she slipped upstairs to get her coat and bag, and when she came down she saw him gazing at Cassidy with amusement.

'Whatever breed is *that*?' he questioned.

Claire was instantly offended. 'He's a mongrel,' she declared, as if he was the winner of Crufts, and Greg chuckled. Cassidy bounded up to them, sensing that they were talking about him.

Greg put out his hand and tentatively patted him. 'Down boy, stay,' he ordered. 'I don't want dog hairs all over my suit.'

Totally ignoring him and the fact that she herself was dressed in a very expensive outfit, Claire bent to Cassidy and planted a kiss on the top of his head. 'I'll be back soon,' she promised, highly indignant at Greg's reaction to him, and she marched out, leaving Greg to follow her.

By the time they had reached the middle of the meal she had forgiven him. It would have been hard not to, for he was a witty and charming companion. And after all, she told herself, he probably wasn't used to dogs. She was wearing the bracelet he had given her on Boxing Day, and the amethysts sparkled in the light from the candle in the centre of the table. They were almost through the meal when he presented her with another, smaller box, identical to the one the bracelet had been in. When she opened it, she found matching amethyst earrings nestling in a bed of silk.

Claire was totally enchanted with them. 'Oh, Greg,' she whispered. 'You're spoiling me – you shouldn't, really.'

'Why shouldn't I?' he said airily. 'I enjoy spoiling you.'

Claire was deeply touched, despite her misgivings.

That night, when they arrived back at the hotel, she finally invited him in for coffee. She had enjoyed the evening and was in a mellow mood. Eventually they wound up on the settee, and Claire felt like a girl on her first date. He was undeniably handsome and it seemed ungrateful not to let him hold her after how generous he had been. However, that was as far she was prepared to let it go, and when he finally left, he was longing for her in a way that he hadn't experienced in a very long time.

When Greg invited her to a party at his home on New Year's Eve, Claire was more than happy to accept. She'd heard a lot from Betty and Mary about his luxurious home, Nightingale Lodge and his little daughter and was curious to see both. Her mind was full of what she should wear, as she carefully sorted through her wardrobe. Eventually she decided on a pure silk cocktail dress in a pretty shade of blue that would set off the amethysts to perfection. As New Year's Eve approached, she found herself looking forward to it. She assured Greg that she could make her own way there, but he insisted on picking her up personally. As usual, he was right on time. When she let him in he gazed at her admiringly and Claire was glad that she'd gone to so much trouble with her appearance.

His low-slung Porsche was a far cry from her rusty old van, and as they headed for his home in Bispham, Claire felt almost like Cinderella.

They eventually came to two huge wrought-iron gates and Greg guided the car easily through them onto a long, tree-lined drive. Seconds later they turned a bend and Greg's home came into view.

Claire's eyes stretched in amazement. Nothing Mary or Betty had said had prepared her for this; Nightingale Lodge was more like a little mansion than a house and she couldn't help but be impressed. After helping her from the car, Greg drew her arm through his and they climbed the steps that led up to a huge polished mahogany door. When Greg opened it and stood aside for her to enter, Claire could hardly believe her eyes. Her feet sank into a rich, deep-piled carpet and overhead, a huge crystal chandelier twinkled a welcome. Claire was no art critic but she knew enough to realise that the framed pictures on the walls were original oil paintings. In front of her, a beautifully carved staircase swept up to an imposing galleried landing and Greg smiled as he saw her looking about. He took her arm possessively and led her into the dining room, and Claire felt as if she had stepped into another world. There were people standing about in little groups chatting, and as Greg passed them and nodded, he held on to Claire proudly. Later that evening he took her on a guided tour of the house and she was even more impressed. On their way back to the party, a grey-haired woman with a kindly face stepped from the kitchen holding a little girl's hand. Claire guessed immediately that this must be Mrs Pope and Greg's daughter.

'Claire, this is Mrs Pope,' Greg introduced them. 'She's a godsend. I really don't know what I'd do without her.'

Mrs Pope flashed Claire a kindly smile, and the girl warmed to her immediately.

'And this,' said Greg, 'is my daughter, Nicole Michelle Nightingale.'

As he drew the little girl gently out from where she was trying to hide behind Mrs Pope's skirts, Claire's heart twisted painfully in her chest. She was the most beautiful child Claire had ever seen, and looked exactly as Claire pictured her Yasmin would look now. She had huge, deep blue eyes and blond hair that cascaded in loose curls down her back.

Claire had the urge to snatch her into her arms but restrained herself. 'Hello, Nicole,' she said softly.

The little girl looked up at her warily. 'I like to be called Nikki,' she said solemnly.

Claire nodded. 'That's a very pretty name.' For a few moments they stared at each other. 'How old are you, Nikki?' asked Claire eventually.

Without hesitation the child told her, 'I'm six – seven next November.'

Once again Claire's heart twisted. Yasmin would be seven in September of this year.

Mrs Pope now patted the child gently on the bottom. 'Come on, madam,' she said affectionately. 'It's way past your bedtime, so let's go and get you tucked in all nice and warm, eh?' With a final friendly smile at Claire and Greg she led the child away.

The rest of the evening passed in a blur of champagne, music and dancing, and Claire enjoyed every minute of it. Greg made her feel like the belle of the ball and never left her side. But through it all, Nikki's little face swam before her eyes and she could hardly wait to see her again.

The following week when Greg rang her, Claire suggested that they should take the child to the zoo. He agreed enthusiastically. Claire still hadn't allowed him to go any further than holding her. But he could feel her letting down her defences and had every hope that she would soon let him make love to her.

She was still going to Seagull's Flight, although not quite as often now, and sometimes felt that she was leading a double life. She intended to make the most of every minute; once the new season began, she knew she wouldn't have time for either Greg or Christian. But for now she was enjoying herself and pushed any thoughts of the future into the back of her mind.

The day out at the zoo was a resounding success, and by the time it was over Claire was forced to admit that the child had her wrapped around her little finger. She was a quiet little girl, and Claire commented on it to Greg.

'She's been like that since her mother died,' he informed her, and Claire was sad. Nikki was suffering, albeit in a different way, just as she had when she was a child. Claire better than anyone understood the loneliness she must be feeling. She was in a pensive mood when they all arrived back at the hotel, and insisted on Greg and Nikki coming in for tea and biscuits. Unlike Greg, Nikki took to Cassidy immediately and within minutes they were rolling about the floor together in a laughing heap.

'Have you ever thought about getting her a dog?' Claire asked Greg.

He shuddered at the thought. 'All those dog hairs all over the house!' he exclaimed, horrifed. Claire was sure that Nikki would come out of her shell if she were allowed a pet. But it wasn't her place to interfere and so she sensibly held her tongue.

Chapter Twenty-Six

As the beginning of the new season approached, Claire viewed it with mixed feelings. She was now invaluable to Mrs M at Seagull's Flight and loved every moment that she spent there, but she was now also seeing Greg at least three times a week. She had still not allowed him to go beyond kissing her, but just as she'd hoped, instead of it deterring him, he became even more attentive. She saw Nikki whenever she could, and brought her little presents, but the child still kept her at arm's length, and showed more feeling to Cassidy than to her.

Christian's practice was growing, slowly but surely, and Mrs M was proud of him. 'One day, this will be the best vet's practice in Blackpool,' she declared. Claire believed her. Christian's love and dedication to animals couldn't have it any other way.

In mid-February, Mrs M came down with a cold that developed into a terrible hacking cough and she looked desperately ill. Claire visited more often then, taking on a good deal of the workload until Mrs M recovered. The old lady was extremely grateful, but Claire was glad to do it and told her so.

In the mornings, Christian held a surgery for domestic pets. In the afternoons, he visited farms and smallholdings tending everything from chickens to cows, pigs and sheep. If Claire was still there when he got home, he would pitch in and lend a hand, and between them they kept Seagull's Flight running smoothly.

'Hmm, seems like I'm not needed,' Mrs M teased, but they were both quick to assure her that she was. Christian obviously adored his gran and Claire found it touching when she saw them together, although it made her even more aware of what she had missed out on. Neither Christian nor Claire ever mentioned Lianne, and sometimes Claire could almost believe that she didn't exist. They'd slipped back into an easy friendship, content in each other's company.

One afternoon as she was cleaning out the dog pens, it began to snow, and soon it had turned into a blizzard. By the time she'd finished, Claire could barely see her hand in front of her. The wind was howling and although it was only five-thirty in the afternoon, it was dark as pitch. She struggled through the snowstorm with Cassidy close at her heels, and by the time she pushed the kitchen door open and almost fell inside, she was blue with cold.

Christian had just come in, and he stared at her with a look of concern on his face.

'Come and sit by the fire,' he urged, drawing her forward.

Dragging herself out of the fireside chair, Mrs M went to put the kettle on. 'You're staying for tea, my girl,' she insisted. 'And I'm telling you now, if it don't slow down soon, you're staying the night, so just make your mind up to it.'

'I can't,' Claire protested, but Mrs M was adamant.

Claire had a dinner-date with Greg tonight, and catching sight of herself in the mirror above the fireplace, she wondered what he would think if he could see her now. She looked like a bedraggled haystack, and knew that if she were to be ready on time, she should be leaving now. But instead of easing, the snow began to fall even more thickly.

Claire glanced at the clock. 'Look, I really *must* be going now,' she said at six-thirty.

Mrs M glared at her indignantly. 'You're going nowhere, Claire! I'd never forgive myself if anything happened to you on the way back home. It's fit for neither man nor beast to be out in this.'

Resigned to staying, Claire wished that she could at least phone Greg and make an excuse, but she hadn't brought her address book and so there was nothing she could do.

Oh well, she thought, I'll phone tomorrow and make my peace, and settled down to spend a night at Seagull's Flight. She had a lovely time. Mrs M fell over herself to make her feel welcome. They ate beef stew and light fluffy dumplings, followed by home-made apple pie and thick creamy custard. It was a far cry from the à la carte meal she would have shared with Greg, but Claire ate every morsel. After the meal she helped Mrs M to wash up, then struggling into a huge pair of Wellington boots that Christian had found for her, she put on her coat and accompanied him back to the dog pens to bed the animals down. They had to hold onto each other on the way back to the house. It seemed as if the swirling snow was intent on blowing them off their feet, and they slipped about laughing like children. When they finally got back to the warmth of the kitchen they found Mrs M cuddling a hot water bottle and heading for the stairs. She was slowly on the mend but still far from well, and she tired easily.

Gazing at them standing there, with their faces glowing, the old lady thought what a handsome couple they made, and she couldn't help but wonder what might have been if it weren't for Lianne.

'You two will have to entertain yourselves,' she told them. 'My old bones are weary and I'm off to my bed.'

'I'll bring you a cup of tea up later on, Gran,' Christian promised.

Mrs M nodded. 'There's a bottle of wine and a bottle of sherry in the sideboard left over from Christmas,' she informed them. 'Help yourselves. You look frozen to the bone – it'll warm you up a bit.' Then with a final fond grin she was gone.

Christian built the fire up and soon it was blazing up the chimney, casting a cheery glow about the room. He poured them both a large glass of sherry, and they sat contentedly, their feet stretched out to the fire, listening to the wind howling outside. It was peaceful, warm and cosy, and Claire felt as if she were in heaven. She could never remember being this contented before in her whole life. The sherry was making her all warm inside, and when Christian's arm slid around her shoulders, it felt like the most natural thing in the world.

'I don't know how to thank you for all your help while Gran's been ill,' he said.

'It's been my pleasure.' She meant every word. He was staring at her intently, and she suddenly became embarrassed. 'I must look a right sight,' she muttered, raising a hand to her tangled hair.

Christian shook his head, his eyes tender. 'You look beautiful,' he said softly, and when he bent his head to Claire's and their lips met, it felt right.

A rush of emotions swept through her, emotions that she had never known. She had slept with so many men, but that was sex. She suddenly realised that this was love – and it was wonderful. She had never given herself to anyone willingly before, and became lost in the sensation. She could hardly stop tears springing to her eyes at the sheer joy of it.

When he eventually laid her down on the carpet in front of the fire and gently eased her clothes from her, she was powerless to stop him. Claire had never guessed that making love could be so beautiful, and when their bodies finally joined she clung to him fiercely and wished that it might never end . . . but eventually it did and they gazed at each other in sheer wonder. Huge snowflakes stuck to the window pane outside as if they were trying to peep into the room and witness the love that was growing. Christian was lying beside her, the firelight washing over his face, and for the first time in her life Claire felt fulfilled and loved. She didn't feel guilty, she didn't feel dirty, only incredibly happy. And as he stroked her face with his fingertips, tenderly, she gazed up at him with wondering.

'I've wanted to do that since the very first time I set eyes on you,' he confided.

Claire didn't answer him. Her heart was too full to allow her to speak.

'You are the most beautiful, kindest woman I've ever met.' His voice held such sincerity that Claire suddenly started to cry. The logs on the fire crackled and cast dancing shadows on the lovers.

What have I done? she thought fearfully. I'm not beautiful or kind, and if he knew who I really was, he wouldn't look at me twice. She began to cry even harder and instantly, Christian was concerned and embarrassed.

'Oh God, Claire, I'm so sorry,' he whispered, suddenly horrified at what he had done, and the moment was spoiled. 'I shouldn't have let that happen.' Hastily sitting up, he began to pull his clothes on.

Claire was out of her depth. How could she tell him why she was crying without shattering the illusion he had of her? Once again, her past had reared up to haunt her, and even as she realised that she loved him, she knew that she could never have him. She loved him too much to deceive him, and too much to tell him of her sordid past. He deserved someone better, someone like Lianne who was clean and good and honest.

'It's all right,' she tried to reassure Christian, but now there was a distance between them, and the magical time they had briefly shared was gone. Claire knew that if she stayed, she would end up telling him everything, and then she would see his face twist with distaste – and she wouldn't be able to bear that. She dressed miserably, as he carefully averted his eyes. Then, calling Cassidy to her, she headed for the door, the keys to the van in her hand.

'You can't go home in this,' Christian objected.

Claire paused to stare back at him miserably. She owed it to him to leave. She was a lie, her whole life was a lie, and he deserved the best. His eyes as they stared at each other were full of pain, but she deliberately hardened her heart.

'Say goodbye to your gran for me.'

He nodded numbly as, opening the door, she stepped out into the freezing blizzard. She never knew how she got home, the windscreen wipers could barely cope with the onslaught of the weather, and tears were spurting from her eyes, distorting her vision. But eventually she reached the hotel, and after turning off the engine, she fell across the steering-wheel and sobbed as if her heart would break as she thought how it had felt when Christian kissed her. He was the only man she had ever allowed to do that.

Once inside, icy cold and hugging Cassidy to her, she noticed that there were a number of messages on her answerphone, and she stabbed the button that would play them back. Every one was from Greg, and he sounded worried.

Where are you, Claire? I've been worried sick about you. Please call me as soon as you get in.

But tonight, Claire couldn't bring herself to speak to anyone.

The phone woke her when it was barely light. She snatched up the receiver, and Greg's voice came to her across the line.

'Thank God you're all right. Where *were* you?' he demanded frantically. 'I was ringing all night, I was worried sick.'

Claire made an excuse about the van breaking down and having to wait for the repair truck, and apologised for standing him up.

He sighed with relief. 'I don't know,' he said softly. 'I think you need someone to take care of you. How about marrying me and letting it be me?'

'All right,' Claire whispered dully.

For a while there was a shocked silence on the other end of the line.

'What did you say?' he asked in disbelief.

'I said all right . . . I'll marry you.' A knife was twisting in her heart but Claire knew that she was doing the right thing. She didn't love Greg, but married to him she would have everything she had ever dreamed of and she would make him a good wife. Plus, there was Nikki; she would have married him for her alone.

Greg could hardly believe his good luck; his voice was ecstatic. 'Oh darling, you won't regret this,' he promised. 'I'll be there in an hour.' Laughing, he slammed down the phone.

Claire showered slowly, then took great pains with her make-up and dressed in a smart day suit. By the time Greg appeared, she was back in control of herself. She was pale and her eyes were red-rimmed, but he put that down to the late night before.

For once, Greg was late. When she let him in he apologised straight away, and she soon found out the reason why.

'I called in at the jeweller's,' he explained, after kissing her soundly on the cheek, then he produced a tiny box from his overcoat pocket. After flipping open the lid, he drew from it the most perfect diamond ring that Claire had ever seen. It was a huge princess-cut solitaire and she gasped at the sight of it. He proudly slipped it onto her finger and drew her into a fierce embrace.

'There,' he whispered. 'It's official now. Soon you'll be Mrs Gregory Nightingale.'

Even though Claire returned his hug her heart was heavy and the urge came on her to cry again.

Chapter Twenty-Seven

From the second that Greg slipped the ring onto my finger, I've felt as if I'm on a roller-coaster, Claire wrote in her diary in February 1993. *Things are moving much more quickly than I'd planned, and I feel powerless to stop them. Greg wanted to put an announcement in the papers this week but I managed to discourage him. I told him that it might appear disrespectful to his late wife, and thankfully he agreed to wait a while. He's insisting on an engagement party though. It's going to be a very grand affair with a band and outside caterers. I told him that I'd rather just celebrate with the three of us going out for a quiet meal or something – but he's insisting on a party, with gold-embossed invitation cards. He's already sent them out and told me that everyone who's anyone will be there. That's what worries me. This is me – Claire McMullen – the kid from a council house who never used to know where the next meal was coming from. Of course, I can't tell Greg that. I can't tell anyone. He's marrying Claire Hamilton, an image, and somehow I've got to maintain that image now for the rest of my life. If Christian weren't . . .*

'Oh *damn!*' Claire slammed the diary shut and threw it onto the bed. She felt more than a little tearful. This should have been the happiest time of her life, so why was it that nothing felt right? She wandered into the deserted hotel dining room and peered out into the equally deserted street beyond.

So much had happened to her since she'd come to live in Blackpool. Perhaps it was fate that had brought her here? But then she had to be honest with herself and admit that fate had nothing to do with it. Deep down, she'd always known that she would end up here, because Yasmin was in this area. She didn't know exactly where or who she was with, she'd just been told that a couple in Lancashire were adopting her. For all

Claire knew, she might already have passed her a dozen times on the street. Most of the time she managed to push thoughts of her baby to the back of her mind; but at other times, she found herself staring at little girls who looked to be about Yasmin's age and wondering. And yearning.

The weather was still awful, with blinding snow and gusting winds. At one point towards the end of February the whole of the seafront was closed to traffic and Claire felt shut off and alienated from the world. She missed her visits to Seagull's Flight. She missed walking the dogs on the beach. She missed Mrs M. But most of all, she missed Christian. Betty and Mary popped in for a cup of tea occasionally, although they weren't due to start work again until the beginning of the next season. Claire found herself grateful for their visits. They had both been good to her since she took over the hotel, and she knew that once she was married, she would miss them too. When she told them of her engagement, Betty danced her around the living room in her excitement, eyeing Claire's engagement ring enviously.

'Oh love, I'm so pleased for you. Gregory Nightingale, eh? You've dropped on your feet there and no mistake. You'll be the envy of every woman in Blackpool. And that ring! By heck, I've never seen a diamond as big. It's like a bloody light bulb.'

Claire smiled at Betty's reaction. She had a big body and a big heart to match. Mary congratulated her too, but more cautiously, and when Betty eventually bustled away to put the kettle on, she asked Claire, 'Are you sure you're doing the right thing, love?'

Claire flushed. 'Why do you ask that? Of course I am,' she snapped.

Mary didn't look convinced. 'It's just that I thought there was something between you and that young vet. He's such a lovely young chap. Not wealthy like the other, admitted, but you know, money can't buy love.'

Claire became indignant. 'I don't know whatever made you think that, Mary. Christian and I were never more than friends.'

Mary wisely dropped the subject. 'Well, you know best, pet,' she agreed placidly. But privately she disagreed.

When the two women eventually left, Claire prowled about the hotel restlessly, and suddenly, for the first time, a thought occurred to her. The hotel: what was she going to do with it? It was modest compared to the luxurious home Greg lived in, but it was hers, earned with humiliation and tears.

As she paced from room to room, she began to wonder if she could bear to leave it.

When she voiced her concerns to Greg later that night she found that just like everything else, he had thought of that too.

'The way I see it, we've got two options,' he informed her. 'We can put it on the market and sell it, or you can keep it on and we'll put a manager in to run it.'

Without hesitation Claire decided that she preferred the last option and Greg promised to sort it out. At least that way it would still be hers; the thought was comforting.

The first disagreement they had, and by far the worst, was about Cassidy. Claire commented innocently one evening how much Nikki would love having the little dog about.

Greg stared at her open-mouthed. 'You weren't seriously thinking of bringing that mongrel with you, were you?' He was obviously appalled at the thought.

Claire's eyes flashed fire. 'It's a case of love me, love my dog,' she informed him heatedly. 'You don't get one without the other. What did you think I was going to do with him?'

A picture of his pure wool, wall-to-wall carpets covered in dog hairs flashed before Greg's eyes, and he groaned inwardly. Glancing across at her, he saw that Claire had flushed and her chin was set with determination. This was one argument he felt he had no chance of winning. 'All right then, I suppose he'd better come,' he muttered in defeat.

Claire's face instantly brightened. 'You'll get used to him,' she promised.

Greg nodded, but underneath he doubted it very much.

As news of their engagement spread, Claire was treated almost like a celebrity. Everywhere they went, Greg's acquaintances went out of their way to congratulate the couple, and cards began to arrive by the dozen. Soon there were only two days to go until the party. Claire had been shopping all day, scouring the shops for just the right outfit. She'd almost given up, when at last she came across it in a small select boutique in the town centre. It was a scarlet satin cocktail dress with a becoming halter neck that showed off her figure to perfection. It was simple but classy and Claire knew that it was perfect. She'd just arrived home clutching her purchase when the phone rang. Thinking that it would be Greg, she snatched it up.

'Hello, Claire.'

At the sound of Christian's voice she paled with shock and her heart began to race.

'I was just wondering if you were all right,' he went on. 'We haven't seen you for a while and we . . . we've missed you.'

The urge came on her to cry, to tell him how much she had missed him too, but she managed to keep her voice steady and cheerful. 'I'm fine,' she assured him, and steeling herself for what had to be said she went on, 'I meant to ring you, but I've been so busy organising the engagement party that I haven't got round to it.'

'Engagement party?' His voice was confused. 'Who's getting engaged?'

'I am.' She kept her voice light. 'To Gregory Nightingale.'

The silence seemed to stretch for ever until finally he spoke again. 'I wish you well.' His voice was dull. 'I had no idea that you were in a serious relationship but I hope you have a good life – you deserve it. You're a lovely person, Claire. I just hope he knows what a lucky man he is.'

She was glad that he couldn't see the tears that were trickling from her eyes. This was the hardest thing she had ever had to do.

'Thank you,' she whispered. 'You be happy too.'

He gently replaced the phone and was gone, and for the first time in a long, long time, Claire felt totally bereft.

She rang Greg and pleaded a headache, and that night she lay in bed wrapped in self-pity. Over and over she relived in her mind the night she had made love to Christian in front of a roaring fire at Seagull's Flight. It had felt so right, so natural. But come morning, she was resigned. Happy endings were what you read about in books. Not for people like her. And besides, from now on she would have Nikki to think about. The thought cheered her. When she married Greg she would gain not only a husband but a daughter, and she intended to make what was left of the little girl's childhood happy. Not like hers had been.

She tried to imagine what it would be like living in Greg's house, reading Nikki bedtime stories, tucking her in each night with a kiss, taking her shopping and helping her to choose her clothes, and brushing her long fair hair. If only for Nikki's sake she suddenly knew that she was doing the right thing.

As Greg's wife she would have achieved her ultimate goal. Respectability, wealth, a family – and perhaps even more children? The thought made her tingle with excitement, and by the time he called that evening to take her to dinner, she had pushed all thoughts of Christian and the brief time they had shared together at Seagull's Flight firmly to the back of her mind.

She had suffered humiliation and degradation to get where she had, and was determined that nothing should spoil it. Even a struggling tousle-haired vet, whose smile could light her day.

Because of the atrocious weather conditions, almost a third of the people invited to the engagement party had to phone with apologies. Even so, Greg's sumptuous house seemed to bulge at the seams with guests. It was a party that would be remembered by all who attended, for Greg had spared no expense and the very finest champagne flowed like water.

Claire looked breathtakingly lovely and by far outshone any other woman there. Every woman envied her, and every man envied Greg.

She slipped into the role of hostess as if she had been born to it, and Greg's eyes followed her triumphantly whenever she left his side.

Halfway through the evening, she managed to slip away unheeded. After sneaking upstairs, she tapped on Nikki's bedroom door. Silence answered her knock, and thinking that the little girl was asleep, she inched the door open cautiously. A bedside lamp threw a circle of light onto the child's bed and Nikki's eyes peeped fearfully across her duvet at her. At sight of Claire, she visibly relaxed.

Claire crossed to her and perched on the side of her bed. 'Is the noise keeping you awake?' she asked. Nikki nodded. The house was so large that the merrymakers could barely be heard from here, but Claire had needed an excuse to visit her.

'Are you feeling all right about your father and me getting engaged?' Claire went on.

Nikki shrugged noncommittally.

'Well, I'll promise you this.' Claire gripped her hand in her own. 'Once we're married, you and I will be the best of friends.' The child didn't appear convinced and Claire guessed that now wasn't the time to press the point. That, plus the fact that she would soon be missed downstairs, made her rise and smile kindly. 'I'll tell you what, I'll try and get over here in the next couple of days, and you and I can take Cassidy for a run on the beach, eh? He loves the snow.'

244

For the first time since she'd entered the room the little girl's eyes sparkled and she grinned.

Bending to place a gentle kiss on her forehead, Claire grinned back. 'Right, that's a date then,' she whispered, and hurrying from the room she pulled the door to quietly behind her.

There was something about this child that had touched a chord deep within her, and she prayed that once she and Greg were married, Nikki might eventually accept her as a substitute mum. She already loved Nikki deeply and could only hope that one day, the little girl would return the feeling.

The rest of the evening passed in a pleasant blur. It had been agreed beforehand that Claire would stay the night, along with quite a few of the other guests. But even though they were now engaged, she still insisted on a room to herself. She had her image to maintain, and had no intention of letting it slip – or of giving Greg a chance to change his mind once he had sampled the goods, if it came to that. When Greg saw her to her bedroom door, she found it hard not to laugh. He obviously had the impression that she was a virgin, and she guessed rightly that this made her even more desirable to him.

So be it, she told herself. If that's what he thinks he's getting, then that's what he'll get. And she didn't feel even remotely guilty at the deception.

As promised, two days later she battled her way through the drifting snow to Greg's, with Cassidy. The old van coughed and spluttered for most of the way, and sometimes Claire thought that they wouldn't make it. When she eventually arrived, Nikki's smiling face more than made up for the treacherous journey. After wrapping the child in layers of warm clothes, the three of them ventured onto the beach, and soon Claire was laughing at Nikki and Cassidy's antics. The snow was so deep in places that sometimes it was impossible to see that Cassidy only had three legs. Nikki chased after his furiously wagging tail laughing unrestrainedly. They built a snowman, which Cassidy immediately flattened. They threw snowballs and chased the waves, and by the time they arrived back at the house, blue with cold and breathless, Claire couldn't remember a time when she'd enjoyed herself more for a long, long time.

The friendly housekeeper fussed over them and made them hot chocolate and toasted crumpets dripping with butter, and Nikki's face was alight as she breathlessly told Mrs Pope of the fun they'd had on the beach. Claire eventually loaded a somewhat bedraggled Cassidy into the van for the homeward journey. When Nikki waved them away, Claire's heart was light. For the first time today, the girl had let down her guard a little and Claire hoped that this was the beginning of something special between them.

She was radiant that evening when Greg picked her up in his shiny Porsche. Cassidy was fast asleep in his basket, worn out with his day's exertions, but Claire was glowing from the time spent in the fresh air. Greg had never seen her look more lovely, and unsure how much longer he could restrain himself with her, he suggested a June wedding. Claire agreed immediately. There were those that would whisper at the speed of it, but she didn't care what people said. She had made a positive decision now to become Mrs Gregory Nightingale, and as far as she was concerned, the sooner it happened, the better.

The wedding list was decidedly one-sided, made up of Greg's friends, distant relatives and business acquaintances. On Claire's side there was just Betty, Mary and their husbands. Claire insisted they were the only guests she wanted, and when Greg tried to question her about her family she faked tears and told him that it was still too painful to talk about. Not wishing to upset her, he hastily changed the subject. Her heart ached to invite Cindy, but she couldn't allow herself to weaken. Sometimes she also pictured Tracey and her foster parents there too, but again she pushed the thought from her mind. She mustn't think of her past when everything she had ever dreamed of was within her grasp.

Claire McMullen, to all intents and purposes, was now dead and buried. When she walked down the aisle, she would be Claire Louise Hamilton, which was the name on the fake birth certificate Cindy had supplied her with. She adamantly refused all offers of a white wedding, not wishing to be a hypocrite. But after a lot of persuasion from Greg she did eventually concede to a church wedding. She was touched when Mary's husband, Tom, offered to give her away. Nikki was to be a bridesmaid, and the little girl was almost beside herself with excitement. As it was to be a June wedding, they decided to have a marquee erected in the grounds of

Nightingale Lodge and hold the reception there. Claire was happy to leave all the arrangements for that to him.

In March the weather began to improve and that was when Claire hit the first snag. Up to now, all Greg's attempts at finding a manager to run the Seabourne Hotel had been fruitless. Claire already had guests booked in for the new season, and rather than let them down, she reopened the hotel herself. Greg was far from pleased but Claire refused to be swayed. He renewed his efforts to find someone suitable to run it, but by the beginning of May he had to accept defeat. He had interviewed no one vaguely resembling what Claire was looking for, and suggested to her that perhaps they should put the place on the market after all.

At first, Claire refused but the wedding was rapidly drawing nearer and eventually she had to admit that perhaps he was right. The day that the estate agent came to value the hotel she was miserable. She followed him from room to room, as he peered into corners and took notes, and by the time he left she was at a very low ebb indeed. She had been so busy running the business that she still hadn't as yet even looked for a wedding outfit, and Mary and Betty began to nag her relentlessly.

'Get your skates on, girl, else you'll be gettin' married in your jeans,' warned Betty.

Claire knew that Betty was right, and so the search began, but it was sad to shop for her wedding outfit alone. The custom was for the bride's mother to accompany her on this trip, but Claire shopped alone, trying on one outfit after another, but finding fault with each one. The wedding was now just a month away, and she began to panic. At this rate, she fretted, Betty would be right. She would be getting married in her jeans.

Much to her relief she finally found just the right outfit in a tiny back-street boutique. It was an ivory two-piece suit with a fitted jacket, lace sleeves and a calf-length lined lace skirt with a scalloped edge. It was perfect, and when the sales assistant topped it off with a wide-brimmed hat with a becoming veil, Claire was suited. She bought strappy gold sandals and a gold bag, and when she got home, spread her purchases out before Betty and Mary.

'Eeh love, that's beautiful,' said Betty, fingering the heavy lace. 'You'll look a picture in that.'

Claire hoped that she was right. The next day, she picked Nikki up and they went shopping for her bridesmaid's dress. The little girl oohed and ahhed at the selection and tried on one after another. Claire enjoyed shopping for Nikki's outfit far more than she had for her own, and watched indulgently until Nikki finally found the one she wanted.

Claire was thrilled at her choice. It was a rose-pink satin ballerina-length dress, with a wide sash at the waist, pretty puffed sleeves, and a scalloped hemline caught up with tiny rosebuds. She looked wonderful in it and Claire smiled at her fondly.

'We'll get you some satin ballerina slippers and a basket of pink rosebuds to go with it,' she promised.

Nikki beamed excitedly. Although Claire had refused a traditional white wedding dress for herself, Greg insisted on top hat and tails. The day he fetched his suit from the tailors he tried it on for Claire and she was impressed, to say the least. He looked stunningly handsome and she had to pinch herself to believe that all this was really happening. So why was it then, when all her wildest dreams were about to come true, that Christian's face kept suddenly flashing before her eyes?

Just two weeks before the wedding Greg finally found a manager who was prepared to run the hotel until it was sold. It was a huge relief for Claire, and the day the manager moved in she went over the bookings with him and gave him a tour of the hotel from top to bottom. He seemed a competent man, and Claire felt that she would be passing her business into safe hands. Greg suggested that she move in with him and Nikki until the day of the wedding but Claire wouldn't be persuaded. Instead she moved upstairs into one of the hotel bedrooms, although she did transport most of her clothes and belongings to her new home in readiness for when she would join them.

She and Greg were to honeymoon in the Bahamas. Claire had never flown or been abroad in her life, and she talked about the honeymoon even more than the wedding, much to Mary and Betty's amusement. Everything was going to plan and Claire prayed that it would stay that way. Three days before the wedding, Greg presented her with an eternity ring. It was a full circle of diamonds and Claire was awed at the sight of it.

'No beginning and no end, just like our love,' Greg told her romantically as he slipped it onto her finger, and in that moment she prayed that she would be able to go on with the deception.

Greg had just celebrated his fortieth birthday, but he was a very hand-some man, and many women would have jumped at the chance of being in Claire's shoes – so why then, she wondered, could she not love him? Until recently she had thought herself incapable of loving anyone, but the time she had spent with Christian had taught her otherwise. However, she then thought of Nikki, and Greg's lovely house, and the wonderful life she would have with him – and she smiled at him and told him, 'Thank you, darling.'

The dream that had kept her walking the streets of London was almost within her grasp now, and she must allow nothing, not even herself, to spoil it.

It was agreed that Mary and Tom would stay at the hotel with her on the eve of the wedding. Claire was more than glad of their company. By now she was sick with nerves. Mary adamantly refused to let her see Greg at all that day, insisting that it was bad luck, and so they spent the evening in the bar of the Seabourne, drinking wine and chatting. Mary had proved to be a tower of strength to Claire over the last weeks and Claire had grown fonder of her than she cared to admit.

When Greg phoned at nine o'clock that evening, Mary grudgingly allowed Claire to speak to him, mumbling that she supposed it would be all right, just so long as she didn't see him face to face. Claire found this highly amusing and broke into a fit of giggles brought about by a combi-nation of a little too much wine and a severe case of pre-wedding nerves. Greg was delighted to hear her sound so happy, and by the time he put the phone down he could hardly wait for their wedding day to dawn.

By bedtime the happy mood had worn off and Claire tossed and turned until the early hours of the morning until at last she sank into an uneasy sleep.

It was Mary who woke her the next morning with breakfast on a tray. She was as excited as if Claire had been her own daughter. After depositing the tray on the bed, she threw open the curtains, allowing the early-morning sunshine to stream into the room.

'There,' she grinned. 'We couldn't have asked for a better day for the wedding even if we'd ordered it. They say the sun always shines on the righteous.'

If Claire seemed a little quiet, Mary put it down to nerves.

After she'd finished breakfast, which she only managed to peck at, Claire had a long leisurely soak in the bath and then began to get ready. Mary fussed over her but surprisingly, now that the big day had finally arrived, Claire was very calm. She ushered Mary away, insisting that she could manage on her own. By the time Mary reappeared in a smart blue two-piece suit and hat, bought especially for the occasion, Claire was almost ready.

Mary's eyes filled with tears at the sight of her. 'Eeh, love,' she whispered, 'I've never seen such a lovely bride.' She meant every word. Claire looked truly beautiful, apart from the haunted look in her eyes. Mary supposed that was because the girl was wishing her mother and father could be there.

When they went downstairs, Tom was as enchanted with her as Mary had been. 'Do you know, love,' he teased, 'you look that lovely, I've a good mind to keep you meself instead of giving you away.'

Mary playfully clipped his ear. 'You keep your eyes to yourself, you dirty old sod,' she scolded him, and Claire was suddenly overwhelmed at their kindness and the love that was obviously between them.

A taxi picked Mary up eventually and she waved goodbye excitedly. Ten minutes later a long white limousine, trimmed lavishly with flowers and ribbons, arrived to take Claire and Tom to the church. By then he was tugging at his cravat, which was uncomfortable. As soon as the car arrived he handed Claire her posy. It consisted of tiny pink rosebuds and gypsophilla.

'This is it then, gel. There's no going back now.' Offering her his arm, Tom proudly led her out to the car.

The service at the church was short and simple, as Claire had requested. Nikki looked adorable in her bridesmaid dress clutching her basket of pink rosebuds that perfectly matched Claire's posy, and Claire's heart swelled with love at the sight of her. Throughout the service the little girl stood solemnly behind her and Greg. Every now and then Claire managed to flash her a reassuring smile. And then they were all outside and cameras were flashing and confetti and rose petals were floating around them.

This should have been the happiest day of her life – so why then, Claire wondered, did she just feel like crying her eyes out?

Chapter Twenty-Eight

If the wedding had been simple, the reception that followed was far from it. A huge, silk-lined marquee had been erected at the back of Greg's house on gently sloping lawns that ran down to the dunes. Greg had spared no expense, and waiters in crisp white jackets welcomed them with crystal glasses of champagne served on silver trays. At one end of the marquee a full band was ready and waiting to play, following the meal. The tables were set with the finest silver and china, with huge candelabras dotted along them. There were large bowls of fresh cut flowers everywhere, and the scent of them filled the air. Everyone who was worth knowing was there, and as Claire stood at Greg's side and greeted them, she looked as though she had been born to this life. The meal, all seven courses of it, was perfection. Once the wedding cake had been cut, the speeches given and photos duly taken, the tables were cleared efficiently away and the band began to play. Greg led Claire onto the dance floor and after the first dance they then began to mingle with their guests.

Some time later, Claire hurried into the house to make sure that all was well with Mrs Pope, Greg's housekeeper-cum-nanny. She had kindly agreed to move in and take care of Cassidy and Nikki whilst the newly-weds were on honeymoon. Claire found her in the huge kitchen with Cassidy curled up beside her on a small settee. The two had obviously taken an instant shine to each other and Claire sighed with relief. Cassidy's tail began to wag furiously at sight of his mistress and Claire grinned.

'You've met Cassidy then?' she asked.

Mrs Pope nodded. 'I have that, and don't worry, love, I'll take good care of him and Nikki while you're away.'

Claire believed her, and after a few minutes, she left to make her way back to the marquee. It was as she was crossing the lawn that from the

251

corner of her eye she saw a man making a beeline for her. Knowing the effect she could have on men, she quickened her steps.

'Hello, Claire, fancy meeting you here.'

The voice made her stop dead in her tracks, and the colour drained from her face.

Gulping deep in her throat she turned to find Edward Taylor leering at her. He was balancing a crystal flute full of champagne on his protruding stomach. Time stood still. Surely she was in the grip of a nightmare? She would wake up in a minute to find that this had all been a bad dream. But she didn't wake up and now Edward advanced on her. Taking her elbow, he led her unprotesting around the side of the marquee.

'So,' his voice was dripping with sarcasm. 'We meet again, eh?'

Claire found that she was speechless. He was obviously enjoying himself immensely at her expense, but what could she do?

'Done well for yourself, haven't you?' He looked grimly back at Greg's impressive house. 'A far cry from a little love nest in Chelsea, isn't it?'

'Edward . . . Teddy, I . . . I can expl—'

'*Save it!* I've heard quite enough lies from your lips, thank you.' His eyes were flashing fire now as he struggled to control his temper. 'And then, of course, there's the little matter of the money you owe me.'

'I'll pay it back – every single penny,' she gabbled.

His lips curled back from his teeth. 'Oh, I know you will, my dear. In one way or another, I can guarantee it. But never let it be said that I'm an unreasonable man. It is your wedding day after all, so we'd better get back inside before we're missed. We wouldn't want your husband to come out looking for you, now would we? Perhaps we could have a little get-together when you come back off your honeymoon, eh? It shouldn't be too difficult, seeing as I'm a business colleague of Gregory's. Hence I get to come into this neck of the woods on a fairly regular basis.'

Claire felt faint. How could this have happened on the very day that she had thought she was about to achieve everything she had hoped for? She had worked so hard, degraded herself and pandered to perverts to gain respectability, and now here was her past ready to slap her in the face again.

Mr Taylor, who was looking hugely pleased with himself, steered her back into the marquee, where they instantly saw Greg, who strode towards them with a wide smile on his face.

'Ah, so you've met my lovely bride then, have you, Edward?'

'I have indeed,' Edward simpered, and Claire felt herself blushing furiously.

'You're a very lucky man, Greg.' Mr Taylor's eyes were undressing her and she felt herself shrink before his gaze. 'But now if you'll excuse me, I'd better get back to my wife.' With that he sauntered away and the knot that had formed in Claire's stomach slowly unwound. So much for starting a new life. It was ruined before it had even begun.

When Claire began to tremble uncontrollably, Greg put his arm protectively around her, which only made her feel even worse. For her the whole day had been ruined, and each time her fearful eyes met Mr Taylor's, she found him staring at her with a sinister grin on his face. Her mind was working overtime. She was now Mrs Gregory Nightingale and nothing must spoil that. Nothing. Once the honeymoon was over she would deal with this problem somehow, just as she had dealt with everything else that life had thrown at her.

By the time darkness fell, late that June night, everyone was in a merry mood. Claire and Greg left their guests drinking and dancing and went into the house to change into their going-away outfits. Claire felt strangely shy, undressing in front of Greg. Still, they were married now and he had every right to see her this way. She began to dread the night ahead, but she needn't have worried. Soon the car that would whisk them off to the airport arrived and she spent her wedding night on a plane to the Bahamas.

Their union, when it eventually came about, was far easier than she had hoped. Greg was so eager for her that the lovemaking was over in minutes, and for the remainder of the honeymoon she was so delighted with the places she saw, that she actually endured it happily. Greg had given her respectability and that was something she had always craved. Allowing him the use of her body seemed nothing in comparison. She felt as if she had stepped into another world as she lay on the silver sands beneath swaying palm trees. Each evening they sauntered along the beach as the sun sank into the brilliant blue sea. She dined on fish caught fresh from the sea and by day they visited places that she had only ever read about in books. Had it not been for the fact that she was missing Nikki and Cassidy, and was terrified at the prospect of being exposed by Edward

Taylor, she could quite happily have stayed there for ever. But all too soon it was time to return.

Greg was touched when she cried as they packed their cases. 'Don't worry, darling,' he whispered affectionately. 'This is only the beginning.' But his kind words only made her cry all the more

The newlyweds received a rapturous welcome when they arrived home. Cassidy threw himself at them but Greg brushed him away, worried that he would end up with dog hairs on his expensive suit. Nikki eyed Claire shyly, and Claire hugged her fiercely as she produced a beautiful doll she had bought for her. Mrs Pope hadn't been forgotten either and gasped with delight at the expensive perfume Claire presented her with. Suddenly Claire was pleased to be home. She'd missed Nikki and vowed there and then that they would never go on holiday without her again.

During the next weeks, life fell into a pleasant routine. During the day, Mrs Pope continued to come to do the housework, and although the older woman protested, Claire insisted on helping her. When Nikki was dropped off by coach from the small private school she attended, Claire would take her stepdaughter and Cassidy, weather permitting, down onto the beach. There they would spend a pleasant hour, Claire laughing as Nikki, dressed in old clothes, and Cassidy gambolled in and out of the surf and rolled on the sand. Greg was attentive as ever, and each night she made sure that by the time he returned home, she looked her best. They gave extravagant dinner-parties, at which Claire was the perfect hostess, and he still took her out frequently for romantic candlelit dinners for two.

Her bond with Nikki strengthened, and one day, two months after the wedding, as she sat in the kitchen enjoying a tea-break with Mrs Pope, the woman commented on it.

'I haven't seen that lass so happy for a long time.'

'She does seem to be coming out of her shell, doesn't she?' Claire agreed. 'Though I think she must still miss her mum; she's never even mentioned her to me.'

'Grieving affects children differently,' Mrs Pope muttered. 'Her mother was a lovely woman, but just between you and me, I don't think things were all as they should have been here.'

When Claire gazed at her in confusion, Mrs Pope chose her words cautiously and continued, 'I've worked for them since they moved here, when Nikki was just a baby. Up until she was about four years old everything seemed fine, then suddenly her mother started to hit the bottle.'

'But why?'

'I've no idea,' Mrs Pope admitted. 'But things seemed to go from bad to worse from then on, and the night she died, well . . .' She shrugged at the memory. 'Who's to say why she should have taken the car out in her nightdress after she'd been drinking?'

They lapsed into silence; each lost in their own thoughts.

Eager to lighten the mood again, Mrs Pope smiled. 'Anyway, all's well that ends well, eh? You're here now, and I reckon you'll be just what the doctor ordered for that little girl. She'll trust you in time, you'll see.' And on that optimistic note she took up her duster and bustled from the kitchen.

At the beginning of November Greg put an idea that had been growing in his mind to Claire. 'It's Nikki's birthday soon,' he told her. 'How about we do a party here for some of her schoolfriends?'

Claire's face lit up at the idea. 'She'd love that,' she grinned. 'What date is her birthday?'

'November the fourteenth,' Greg replied, and Claire had the sudden urge to cry as she thought of Yasmin. She assured Greg that it was a marvellous idea, and then, making her excuses, she hurried from the room. By the time he joined her in their bedroom sometime later she had composed herself.

There was nothing she could do for her own child but she determined that she would make Nikki's birthday one that she would never forget.

She thought of hiring a Bouncy Castle but then decided that the weather wasn't right for an outside party so engaged a clown instead. With a little help from Mrs Pope, Claire made her stepdaughter a huge cake with a figure seven iced on it, and Nikki beamed with delight when she saw it. Greg had offered to order one, but Claire had particularly wanted to make it herself and Nikki seemed to appreciate this.

There were trifles and jellies and fizzy drinks in abundance, and once the party was in full swing, one little boy who had over-indulged was violently sick, which Nikki found highly amusing. It was a birthday she

255

would never forget, and seeing her happy face, Claire's hard work seemed worthwhile and strengthened the bond that was growing between them.

As Christmas 1993 approached, Claire began to feel a little easier about things. She'd seen neither hide nor hair of Edward Taylor since the day of the wedding and was daring to hope that he'd decided to leave her in peace. It was round about then that she and Greg had their first major row. They were enjoying a pre-dinner sherry one evening when he casually mentioned that they'd been invited out on the following Thursday with an important business colleague of his.

'I'm sorry, Greg,' Claire said, 'but I'm afraid I won't be able to make it.'

He frowned at her. 'Why not?' he demanded.

'Because Nikki's an angel in the nativity play at school and I promised I'd be there to see her.'

His face relaxed into a smile. 'Is that all? Then you'll just have to explain to her that you can't manage it.'

Claire shook her head. 'I won't do that, Greg. I've promised her I'll be there and I will be.'

When he saw that she meant it, he slammed his glass down pettishly. 'Sometimes I think you care more about her than you do about me,' he said, a note of jealousy creeping into his voice. Then, with his face set, he strode out of the room. Minutes later, Claire heard his car start up and roar off down the drive.

It was the early hours of the morning by the time he returned, and by then the meal she'd cooked for them was no more than a burned offering. Even so, she had no intention of going back on her promise to Nikki. Once, a lifetime ago, she'd been in a school play, and even now she could remember how much it had hurt when her mother didn't turn up to see her perform. She had no intention of letting Nikki down. And if Greg didn't like it, then as far as she was concerned, he could bloody well lump it.

That night, for the first time, she turned her back on him and pretended to be asleep when he got into bed. From then on she noticed a subtle change in their relationship. He didn't ask her to accompany him again; in fact, he pointedly avoided mentioning it, and Claire felt guilty. She knew he enjoyed showing her off to his colleagues as if she were some sort of prize. To Greg, she guessed that's just what she was. She'd never been under any illusion as regards to Greg's feelings towards her, and suspected that, had she been more free with her favours before they were married, he would probably have tired of her long before the wedding. Knowing men as she did, that didn't surprise her. Greg had a huge opinion of himself and an ego to match. It suited him to have a young attractive wife. She doubted that he would remain loyal, but the thought didn't trouble her. He had married an image, just as she had married an image of respectability in him. As far as she was concerned, they met a need in each other. What did surprise her, however, was Greg's relationship with Nikki.

She had supposed that the child's mother's death would make Nikki cling all the more to her father, but it was quite the opposite. Nikki seemed to almost avoid him, even preferring to eat her meals in the kitchen with Mrs Pope. Claire didn't feel that this was right, and in the early weeks of their marriage she asked Greg on numerous occasions if the child could join them in the dining room. But he always insisted that Nikki was happier eating where she was, and as Claire came to realise that he was right, she eventually gave up asking.

Her own relationship with Nikki was improving daily. The little girl was still fairly secretive with her and had never, as yet, confided her feelings about her mother. Claire hoped that with time that would come, and had endless patience with her.

During their daily outings on the beach, Nikki became a different child. With Cassidy she would romp and giggle as she never did with adults, and this was something that Claire could understand and relate to.

Nikki, for different reasons to herself, had lost most of her childhood too, and Claire was determined that from now on she would make it up to her. But as her friendship with the little girl grew, so did Greg's jealousy. It was almost as if, although he didn't have time for the child, he didn't want Claire to have time for her either. Claire couldn't understand it. She had thought he'd be pleased that she was befriending his daughter, but instead it seemed to annoy him.

The following week, Greg went off to his business dinner alone and Claire drove to the school as promised. She sat completely spellbound through the nativity play. Nikki looked enchanting as an angel with her little tinsel halo, and when she caught sight of Claire amongst the mums, dads, nannies and grandads, her face lit up. It was a magical night for Claire, one that she would never forget. The children looked so innocent as they acted their roles, and by the time the play was over, she was crying unashamedly. It was all she could do to stop herself from rushing onto the stage there and then and hugging the child. But instead she applauded loudly and smiled at her stepdaughter with pride.

By the time they reached home, Nikki was falling asleep. Claire made them both a cup of hot chocolate before tucking her into bed. She began to read her a bedtime story, but only got as far as page four before Nikki was snoring gently. She smiled down on the sleeping child. She looked just as much of an angel now with her fair curls fanned across the pillow as she had in the nativity play. After kissing her gently, Claire quietly tiptoed from the room.

It was almost midnight when Greg arrived home, and to her relief he was in good spirits. 'The dinner went well,' he informed her, shrugging off his dinner-jacket. 'Though of course I would have preferred it if you'd been there.'

'Was it someone important?' she asked.

He nodded. 'It certainly was – Edward Taylor, a business colleague of mine up here from London. He puts quite a lot of business my way; he and his wife were most disappointed that you weren't there. They remembered you from the wedding.'

Claire felt herself go pale, but luckily Greg didn't notice. 'I've invited them here for dinner tomorrow night – that's all right, isn't it, darling?' he asked. 'Does it give you enough notice?'

Claire nodded. 'Of course it does,' she assured him, and nodding with satisfaction Greg entered the en-suite.

Claire sank onto her dressing-table stool and stared at her reflection in the mirror. There was a sick feeling in the pit of her stomach, and her hands were trembling. Suddenly, all the joy of the night was gone. Over the last months, she'd managed to lull herself into a false sense of security, but now some deep foreboding told her that her shameful past was about to come back to haunt her.

Chapter Twenty-Nine

The following evening, when Greg introduced Mr Taylor and his wife, Claire felt like a rabbit caught in a trap, although outwardly she played the part of hostess to perfection,

Mrs Taylor was plump, overly dressed, overly made-up, and wearing more jewellery than Claire had ever seen on one woman all at the same time in her whole life. She gushingly declared that the house was a credit to Claire, and sighed over the beautifully laid table. Mr Taylor had very little to say but eyed Claire with a look that made Claire flush furiously. Every time she glanced up, his eyes were on her, seeming to devour her, and she cursed herself. How could she ever have thought that her past wouldn't catch up with her? She could have cried there and then at the injustice of it all. Luckily, Mrs Taylor chatted on and on about nothing in particular and Claire was grateful for it.

After dinner, to Claire's relief, Greg and Mr Taylor retired to the study to enjoy a glass of port and to discuss some business matters. Claire was left to serve coffee to the chatty Mrs Taylor in the lounge, and by the time the couple left, Claire's nerves were almost at breaking-point.

She and Greg escorted them outside to their car. The business side had obviously gone well and Greg was in high spirits as he shook Mr Taylor's hand heartily.

Mrs Taylor hugged Claire as if she'd known her for years and kissed her soundly on each cheek. 'You take care of that handsome husband of yours now, my dear,' she laughed.

Claire nodded. 'Oh, I will.'

Now it was Mr Taylor's turn. He planted a wet kiss on her cheek, which made Claire feel like retching, and squeezed her hand. 'I think it's *you* who should look after this lovely little wife of yours, Greg,' he said, looking her straight in the eye. 'She's a rare find and no mistake. You wouldn't want anyone running away with her now, would you?'

Greg put his arm about Claire's waist possessively. 'No, I wouldn't,' he agreed. Claire was grateful that it was dark so that he couldn't see her flushed face.

At last the Taylors were in their car, and as it headed down the drive Claire and Greg waved until it was out of sight, Claire praying that she would never see it or Mr Taylor again.

That night, as Greg lay fast asleep at the side of her, her mind was in turmoil. If Edward Taylor told Greg of her past, she would lose not only him, but her lifestyle and Nikki too, and she knew that she wouldn't be able to bear it. Once again she must battle for survival and she intended to do just that. She had suffered too much and worked far too hard to let someone like that insufferable little hypocrite spoil it for her now.

By morning her eyes were red from lack of sleep and Greg looked at her with concern. 'Are you feeling unwell, darling?' he asked.

Claire pushed her breakfast around the plate. 'Oh, it's just a headache.' She smiled sweetly and waited impatiently for him to leave for the office.

As soon as he was a safe distance down the drive, she did something she had never done before. She hurried into his study and began to rifle through the piles of papers on his desk. At last she found what she was looking for, business accounts with Mr Taylor's London address on them, and also a phone number for the hotel he was staying in at Blackpool. Frantically now, she wrote both addresses down on a scrap of paper and then carefully put everything back as she had found it and removed herself from the room.

She dressed carefully that morning. Some inner voice warned her that she might have a visit from Mr Taylor today, and her intuition was right. When she heard a car pull up outside the front door at eleven o'clock she guessed it would be him without even looking. She steeled herself for the doorbell's ring, and when it came she strode with a confidence she didn't feel to open it. Edward Taylor eyed her hungrily, almost licking his lips with anticipation. Claire stared back at him coolly, glad that Mrs Pope had gone out shopping.

'Yes?' Her voice was as cool as her look, but grinning, he chose to ignore it.

'Now then, Claire, that's no way to greet an old friend, is it?'

Claire didn't budge. 'I would hardly class you as a friend,' she spat.

He merely laughed and walked past her into the hallway, eyeing the huge crystal chandelier and plush furnishings with appreciation.

'Not bad for a hooker's home, is it?' A nasty note had crept into his voice and now Claire flushed.

'I'm *not* a hooker.' Her eyes were flashing fire, but he threw back his head and laughed.

'You know what they say – once a hooker, always a hooker.' They were face to face, and Claire was conscious that she was about to fight a battle. 'It would be just terrible if Greg were to find out about your past, wouldn't it?'

A cold finger ran down her spine but she stood her ground.

'Mind you, if you were to be nice to me, like you used to be, I wouldn't need to tell him, would I?' He was inching towards her, and Claire was suddenly afraid that she was going to vomit. Sensing her fear, he seemed to grow in stature as he told her huskily, 'That's better. Now, how about a nice cup of coffee?'

Turning on her heel, Claire strode towards the kitchen, conscious of the fact that he was right behind her. She lifted the coffee percolator with trembling fingers as he settled himself in a chair.

Not a word passed between them until she placed a cup in front of him and stepped away to lean heavily against the sink. He was obviously enjoying every single moment of her discomfort and sipped at his coffee as if he had all the time in the world. When he had drained his cup he rose from his seat and looked at her pointedly. 'I think it's time we went upstairs now then, don't you? I seem to remember you owe me quite a large sum of money, and there's more than one way to pay it off.'

'B . . . but I can get the money.' Her voice was quivering. 'Just give me time to get to the bank and I'll have every penny for you.'

'I'm sure you could, my dear. But the thing is – I've quite missed our little rendezvous. I think I would rather it be repaid in *another way*. Or are you going to be difficult? If so, I could always have a word in Greg's—'

'That won't be necessary,' she interrupted him as panic set in. Then, seeing no other way out of the predicament she found herself in, she told him resignedly, 'Follow me.'

As she led him up the stairs her heart was pounding so loudly that she felt sure he must be able to hear it. On the landing, she hesitated. It seemed wrong to take him into the room she shared with Greg, so instead she walked on to the door of one of the guestrooms.

He followed her inside, already removing his jacket. Not so very long ago, Claire had sold her body for a living but now she cringed at the thought of the ordeal ahead.

'Get undressed.' The words were an order and seeing no alternative, Claire did as she was told. When Edward Taylor rolled off the bed almost an hour later there was a broad, satisfied grin on his face. Claire lay beneath the sheet, hating him more than she had ever hated anyone in her whole life.

'That was most enjoyable,' Edward rattled as he pulled his trousers up his hairy fat legs. 'When I'm next in Blackpool we'll have to meet up again.'

'B . . . but I thought that today was . . .'

'A one off?' he finished for her. 'Oh no, my dear. Not even *you* are worth one paltry session. I think that you are going to be in my debt for quite some time to come.'

He had her completely where he wanted her, and Claire knew it. Now as he slid into his jacket and straightened his tie he looked at her for one last time.

'Right, I'd better be going. Expect a phone call in the next few weeks.' He swaggered from the room and as Claire heard the front door slam behind him and the sound of his car engine starting up, the tears began to slide down her cheeks. Once again, just as she had so many times before, she hurried to the bathroom and filled the bath with water as hot as she could bear it before climbing in and methodically scrubbing every single inch of herself. For the very first time she wondered if she would ever be able to be the person she had dreamed of becoming, for it seemed that no matter how hard she tried, Claire McMullen was always there, just beneath the surface, to haunt her.

Deeply unsettled by her confrontation with this ghost from her past, Claire could only pray that it would be some time before she was forced to see Edward Taylor again. For several days she held her breath every time the doorbell rang. She felt as if she was walking on eggshells, and each day when Greg came home from work she expected him to confront her. But he didn't. After a whole week of feeling totally vulnerable and depressed, Claire was thrilled when he mentioned one evening that he'd concluded his business with Mr Taylor, and that Edward and his wife had returned to London. That night, for the first time in a week, she sank into an exhausted sleep. It was terrifying to think of what might have happened. The prospect of losing the lifestyle she had grown accustomed to was frightening enough, but worse than that was the fear of losing Nikki. She realised now just how much she'd come to love the little girl and she would have done anything to keep her. Strangely, the thought of losing Greg was nowhere near as daunting. She had never pretended that she loved him, although she tried to be a good wife, and underneath she didn't believe that Greg really loved her. She was more of a possession, like his expensive car and luxurious home, and so she felt no guilt. They rarely argued and Greg was more than generous with her monthly allowance, although they no longer went out together so much any more.

The Seabourne Hotel had still not been sold, but the temporary manager that Greg had appointed was still there and doing a remarkably good job. Each month Claire visited him to go over the accounts, and even after paying him his wages, she was still in profit. And so, for the first time in her life she was a lady of leisure and once again in possession of a very healthy bank balance. And yet, she still felt empty inside and sometimes, unbidden, her mind would fly to Seagull's Flight and remind her of the peace she had found there. She supposed that Christian would have married Lianne by now, and the thought was painful, but as she hadn't seen him, she had no way of knowing for sure. She missed Mrs M and their cosy chats, but more than anything, though she tried to deny it to herself, she missed Christian.

Nikki and Cassidy were now the focus of her life. Greg had never taken to Cassidy, nor even tried to, so whenever he was home, Cassidy was confined to the kitchen to save arguments. But when he was out, Cassidy had the run of the house.

Claire began to visit Mary and Betty fairly regularly. They were the nearest things to friends that she had, and when Nikki came with her, the older women spoiled her shamelessly.

'Eeh, love,' Mary sighed one evening as she and Claire sat in her modest sitting room. They were laughing at Nikki who was trying to train Cassidy to offer a paw in return for crisps and failing dismally. 'That little girl could be yours, you both look so alike.'

Mary wasn't the first person to make that comment and it made Claire feel wistful. The bond between them was steadily growing but Claire knew that she still had a long way to go before the child would trust her completely. Even now after all this time, Nikki had never mentioned her mother to Claire even once. Claire guessed that the scars, much like her own, must go very deep, so she never pressed her. The time might come when Nikki would need her to talk to, and when that time came, Claire was determined to be there for her. She just hoped that the child wouldn't keep her feelings bottled up for ever as she herself had. But then, she better than anyone knew that some secrets ran just too deep to ever disclose to anyone. She had considered herself to be hard and streetwise, but recently, since the distasteful encounter with Edward Taylor, she'd had to come to terms with the fact that underneath her assumed exterior, she really wasn't hard at all.

Her one perfect night with Christian, which was all she would ever have of him, and her feelings for Nikki, had shown her this, but it wouldn't do to let her guard down too much. She had too much to hide.

After spending another pleasant hour with Mary and Tom, Nikki began to get tired and so, after exchanging hugs and kisses all round, Claire shepherded the sleepy little girl and Cassidy into her stylish new car. It was a present from Greg, who was adamant that his wife should not ride around in a dilapidated old van. Cassidy's dog hairs did show up terribly on the dark seats and she seemed to be constantly having to clean it to avoid Greg's sarcastic comments, but she loved it all the same.

Mary and Tom waved them away and by the time they arrived home, Nikki and Cassidy were both fast asleep, snuggled up close together on the back seat.

Greg had gone to what he'd told her was a business meeting, though Claire wondered if he was telling the truth. He had lately acquired a new, very attractive secretary, and she had seen him flirting outrageously with her on more than one occasion. Not that it gave Claire any cause for concern.

However, tonight after settling Nikki into bed and reading her a couple of chapters from her favourite book, Claire wandered restlessly about the house. Eventually she threw open the French doors and stepped into the garden.

It was a wonderful mild evening. The stars overhead winked like diamonds and the sea was as calm as a millpond. In the distance, a ship's lights stood out on the horizon. The beach appeared to have been painted in silver moonlight and the night was so still that even the grass on the sand dunes seemed to be standing to attention. She had a sudden longing to be on the beach with the sand between her toes, but she didn't give into it. It was Mrs Pope's evening off and she didn't want to leave Nikki alone in the house. Instead, she stood enjoying the tranquillity of the scene.

After a time, a couple came into view on the beach. They were totally oblivious of anyone else as they strolled along hand in hand in the moonlight, hardly taking their eyes from each other. Even from this distance, Claire could sense that they were deeply in love, and a little pang of envy rippled through her. No one would ever look at her like that again, she thought as a vision of Christian's face came to mind. Again she felt the warmth of his lips on hers, and she realised with a little shock that he was the only man she had ever allowed to kiss her on the lips. Her thoughts turned to Cindy and Billy. Were they happy? She hoped so, because Cindy deserved it. For the first time in a very long while she then allowed herself to think of Tracey and her foster parents. As she wondered what they would be doing now, a sense of loneliness filled her. Wherever they were, and whatever they were doing, she knew that they were far better off without her. Just then, she felt something warm brush against her leg, and looking down, she saw Cassidy gazing up at her.

Dropping down beside him, she hugged him to her. 'I'm a silly bugger, ain't I?' she whispered through her tears. With him she could be herself, there was no need to put on airs and graces. 'You and me have got each other, haven't we, and now we've got Nikki to look after too. That's all we need, ain't it?' But the empty feeling inside remained as the memory of Christian's face came back to haunt her.

Three weeks later, she received another phone call from Edward Taylor. His silence had made her lapse into a false sense of security.

'I'll be round to see you on Wednesday morning. Make sure you are alone,' he said. Claire knew that she had no choice but to agree, and so the nightmare continued.

*   *   *

As the end of the financial year approached in April 1994, Greg was very busy, and Claire found herself alone most evenings. She was bored and started to go swimming twice a week. If Greg wasn't home to babysit, Mrs Pope stayed on. Nikki didn't seem to mind if Mrs Pope babysat, but fretted when she had to stay with Greg. Claire found this amusing and quickly guessed the reason why. She and Mrs Pope always spoiled the child shamelessly, but her dad was much stricter and Nikki couldn't get away with so much with him.

Greg had been even less attentive to Claire of late, but because it was his busiest time of the year Claire forgave him. She was quite happy for his secretary to attend his business dinners instead of her. Nowadays she found most of his acquaintances thoroughly boring and felt more at home in the company of Mary and Betty.

In the second week of June she received an offer on the hotel. It had felt comforting somehow to know that it was still hers, and now she was reluctant to let it go. But Greg was firm. It was a very good offer indeed, he said. Better than they had hoped for, and as he pointed out, the money from the sale would be hers to do with as she saw fit; he certainly didn't need it. Eventually she reluctantly agreed on the sale, and in August the new owners moved in. It was a sad day for Claire. The hotel had been the first thing of worth she had ever owned. But still, she had another life now and was determined to make the best of it.

She had practised no form of birth control at all since her marriage and longed for a baby, but as yet nothing had happened. Now as the months passed by she began to worry. When she and Greg had talked of having children he had said that he didn't mind either way. She began to fret, fearful that having Yasmin when she was so young might have done some damage. Or perhaps the abuse she had suffered at such a tender age had harmed her internally? She flatly refused to visit a doctor, however, even when Greg offered to pay for her to see a top gynaecologist. She was too afraid of what they would discover or what they might tell Greg, and so she bore her worry alone. By the time they celebrated their second anniversary in June 1995, Claire was beginning to think that by giving up Yasmin, she had given up all her rights to ever becoming a mother again.

Greg had been staying out until all hours, and although he insisted that it was business, Claire was fairly sure by now that he was seeing someone else. She could accept this. She'd always known that Greg was a lady's man, and as she didn't love him, the thought caused her no pain. The novelty of being a lady of leisure had long since worn off, and now during the day when Nikki was at school, she was becoming very bored. Greg did make sure that he was home at least one evening a week so that she could go swimming, and she looked forward to that.

Nikki was now a lanky, lovely, almost nine year old. But lately, Claire had noticed a change in her. She'd become sullen and moody and hardly had a kind word for anyone except Cassidy, who she kept possessively at her side whenever she could.

When Claire mentioned her concerns to her, Mrs Pope did her best to reassure her. 'Take no notice of her, love. It's just her age. She'll come out of it, you'll see.'

Claire worried anyway. Nikki had started to push her away pettishly whenever she tried to get close, and this hurt Claire far more than she could say.

'What's wrong, Nikki? Talk to me,' she pleaded, but the girl just folded her arms and looked away with a deep scowl on her face. The one thing that they still enjoyed together was their afternoon rambles on the beach, yet even that gave Claire cause for concern, but this time on Cassidy's part. He was slowing down a little now. He still followed Nikki in and out of the surf and still enjoyed rolling in the sand on his three stubby little legs. But these days, he tended to tire much more easily and Claire had to accept the fact that he was getting old. She dreaded the thought of how she and Nikki would cope when anything happened to him.

Despite all Claire's efforts, Greg continued to seem oblivious to his daughter for most of the time, and now Claire had given up hope of it ever being any other way. Instead, she showed Nikki as much love as she could. Deep down, she felt that Greg's attitude towards the child could partly be the reason for Nikki's mood swings. The child had suffered a double blow – firstly by losing her mother, and secondly by having a father to whom she could not turn for comfort. It was very sad, but Claire had long since given up any hope of a fairytale ending. Instead, they must all make the most of what they had.

Chapter Thirty

In November, Claire again entertained Nikki's friends at her birthday party, and for once the house rang with laughter. They hired a magician and played games indoors.

Before the guests arrived, Claire brushed Nikki's hair until it shone and remarked on how pretty she looked in her new party dress. To Claire's delight, Nikki's eyes shone almost as much as her hair and she thoroughly enjoyed herself. They played Pass the Parcel, amongst shrieks and giggles, and more than a little cheating, and Hide and Seek — and the house seemed to be crawling with children from top to bottom. Claire was grateful that Greg wasn't there to see it. He would have had a fit, for sure. One little boy even slid down the whole length of Greg's beautifully carved banister. By the time the magician ushered the unruly crowd into the huge sitting room to begin his act, Claire was more than ready to slip away to the kitchen to enjoy a well-earned cup of tea with Mrs Pope. She spotted Cassidy hiding under the kitchen table, more than a little disgruntled at the invasion of so many children. Mrs Pope was sitting with her slippers kicked off and her feet resting on a chair. She grinned as Claire entered and pointed at the teapot. 'Grab yourself a brew, love, while it's quiet.'

Claire obeyed willingly.

'Ooh, me poor feet are killin' me,' grumbled Mrs Pope.

Claire chuckled. 'It's worth it though, isn't it, to see Nikki so happy?'

Mrs Pope nodded in agreement. She had always adored Nikki, and now she was more than fond of Claire too, especially at times like this, as she sat there with her hair escaping from its pins, and with jelly stains all over her skirt. Without even knowing why, Mrs Pope felt sorry for her. Of course, there were many women who would gladly have stepped into Claire's shoes, for she appeared to have everything – and yet, Mrs Pope had noticed that the young woman only ever seemed to be truly happy when she was with Nikki or Cassidy. The housekeeper also knew that Claire was longing for a baby, and thought it was a damn shame that as yet, there was no sign of one. To her mind this house was made to ring to the sound of children's laughter but instead it was little more than a showpiece, everything always exactly in its place. She shook her head, momentarily lost in her thoughts, and it was only the sound of children pouring from the sitting room that brought her back to the present with a start.

'Here we go again,' she sighed. 'There's no peace for the wicked!' Pushing her weary feet back into her slippers, she left the kitchen arm-in-arm with Claire.

By the time Nikki's guests had left, the house resembled a bombsite from top to bottom, but Claire was glowing. She had never seen her step-daughter looking so happy, and to her all the mess was worth it. Luckily Greg wouldn't be home until late, so after tucking a contented Nikki into bed, she and Mrs Pope set to with a vengeance. Two hours later, the house was spick and span again.

They were putting the cleaning things away when Claire suddenly noticed that Mrs Pope had slowed down and looked thoroughly exhausted.

'Oh, I shouldn't have kept you so late,' she apologised guiltily, and suddenly without meaning to, she gave the woman a warm hug. 'I don't know what I'd do without you,' she said sincerely. It was the first time she had ever done anything like that and Mrs Pope was deeply touched.

'It's all right, love,' she said, returning the hug. 'I won't say it wasn't hard work but I have to admit I've enjoyed it.'

As Claire helped Mrs Pope on with her coat and walked with her to the door, the older woman eyed her seriously.

'Do you know something, Claire?' she said quietly. 'I reckon you're the best thing that could have happened for that little girl upstairs.' Gently squeezing her hand, she then stepped out of the front door and hurried away down the drive.

Claire stood and watched until she was out of sight before thought-fully making her way up the stairs to run herself a nice hot bath.

In no time at all Christmas was upon them. Greg wanted to go abroad but Nikki and Claire talked him into staying at home. Claire took Nikki to choose a Christmas tree and they had great fun decorating it together. They hung brightly coloured streamers from one end of the sitting room to the other and collected holly and mistletoe and strewed it all about the place.

Greg was horrified and declared it was thoroughly tasteless, but Nikki and Claire just giggled at him.

Claire spent hours trudging round brightly decorated toyshops buying Nikki anything that caught her eye. On Christmas Eve as Mrs Pope helped her to wrap all the presents up, she declared that there were enough toys here to keep at least half a dozen little girls happy. Claire supposed that Mrs Pope was right, but was determined that Nikki should have everything she hadn't.

She, Greg and Nikki spent Christmas quietly at home. After Christmas dinner, Claire took Nikki and Cassidy down onto the beach and they passed a pleasant hour strolling along the wind-whipped sands searching for shells. Greg refused to accompany them, but Claire was past caring. Their marriage now, although they still slept together, was little more than a business arrangement. She was determined that nothing should spoil Christmas for Nikki and nothing did.

On New Year's Eve, she and Greg were invited to a party at the home of one of his business colleagues, and for the first time in months, Greg asked her to accompany him. Claire took especial pains getting ready, and looked stunning. Heads turned as she entered the room and no one seeing them together would ever have guessed that she and Greg were anything less than the perfect couple.

January brought heavy snowfalls and Greg complained bitterly. Claire bought Nikki a sleigh and they had endless fun sledding down the sand dunes with Cassidy chasing after them. In February Claire resumed her swimming twice a week and again Nikki became sullen. Claire suggested to Greg that perhaps she ought to stop going. He was horrified at the idea.

'You can't let her rule you,' he pointed out and Claire admitted grudgingly that perhaps he was right. All the same, she found that she didn't enjoy it quite so much now. The snow was still heavy on the ground one evening as she set out after a particularly tearful tantrum from Nikki. The roads were treacherous, and she'd barely guided the car out of the drive when she began to wish she hadn't bothered. As the car slid all over the icy road, Claire pulled it into the kerb fearfully when she was barely halfway to her destination. It was snowing so hard now that the windscreen wipers could barely cope with it.

'I must be mad, venturing out on a night like this,' she said to herself, and suddenly making up her mind, she started up the engine again and turned the car around. 'I'm going home,' she muttered, and set off at a crawl. By the time she pulled up outside the front door, she was shaking with cold. She didn't even dare go on to the garage, but instead locked the car up and headed for the front door, keeping her head down. As she stepped into the warm hallway, she heaved a sigh of relief. She considered she'd done well to get home unscathed and was glad to be out of the storm. Greg wasn't in the study, the sitting room or the kitchen, so she made her way upstairs quietly, thinking that he must have decided to have an early night.

It was as she reached the top of the stairs that she heard Nikki crying. She paused for a moment, then hurried towards her bedroom door. Without bothering to knock she threw it open. Greg's startled eyes flew to her. Nikki was clutching her duvet to her chin and crying softly.

'She was having a bad dream – I came in to settle her,' Greg explained hastily.

'Are you all right now, sweetheart?' Claire was deeply concerned. Sinking down onto the side of the bed, she wrapped the child's trembling body in her arms. 'It's all right, love, I'm here now,' she soothed as Greg quietly left the room. Claire didn't leave her until she was fast asleep, and when she finally entered their bedroom she found Greg waiting for her.

'Is she all right now?' he asked.

When Claire nodded he went on, 'I'm glad you were back early, you're better with her than I am.'

'I'm glad I was too, the roads were terrible,' she told him as she began to get undressed. 'I shouldn't have gone in the first place with the weather as it is.'

He patted the bed. 'Well, seeing as you *are* home, we may as well make the most of it.' It was the first time in weeks that he'd shown any interest in her, so Claire smiled resignedly and joined him.

In the middle of March the thaw set in and life returned to normal, but the snow was replaced by bitingly cold winds and driving rain. Claire developed a heavy cold that quickly turned to flu. For two weeks she hardly left her bed and couldn't remember a time when she had ever felt so ill. Mrs Pope fussed over her and ensured that Nikki was cared for. Once again Claire couldn't imagine what she would have done without her and told her so.

Eventually, she began to improve and at last ventured from her bedroom to the sitting room, where she sat on the couch wrapped in blankets feeling more than a little sorry for herself. She was bored, but Mary and Betty visited regularly and she was always glad to see them. Lately she'd been feeling incredibly lonely and sometimes yearned for someone to confide in. And yet she knew that she never could. She must keep up this façade for ever. With so much time on her hands, she decided to bring her secret diary up to date. She had ignored it for a long, long time. It was hard at the beginning, and the words came slowly, but as the memories flooded back, it became easier and the story flowed. She held back nothing. This was a book that must never be read by anyone, and so she could be completely honest in it.

But before she did any writing, Claire reread the whole thing. She read of the very first night one of her mother's boyfriends had abused her and of the horror, guilt and pain she had felt, even at such a tender age. She read of how it had felt to be constantly hungry. She read of the abuse that had become an accepted part of her life, of the love she had felt for Tinker, the little mongrel who had died at her mother's hands. And as the story unfolded, her tears constantly smudged the ink on the pages. She relived the horror she had felt when Tracey became a victim like herself and the terrible feelings of uselessness she had experienced because she had been unable to keep her little sister safe. That was something she would never forget for as long as she lived, and as she read what she had written so long ago, her sister's terrified cries rang in her ears as loudly now as they had done then. She wept when she remembered the way Tracey had stared at her the morning after she had been abused, her eyes haunted and empty. It was when she came to the part where she and Tracey had gone to live with her foster parents that she finally realised just what she had lost.

At the time, she had been too confused to realise that Molly and Tom had only ever wanted what was best for her. Back then, she had been too bitter to see it, and had thrown their love back in their faces. She recalled the terrible rejection she had felt when her mother abandoned her. Then reaching her teens and becoming aware of the power she could wield over boys – and the way she had used it. And then she remembered her unwanted pregnancy and the beautiful baby girl that had resulted from it. The lovely child to whom she could offer nothing, only to her away. Hardly a day passed when she didn't think of her ...

At this point, Claire stopped reading for some days, unable to go on. But eventually she went back to it and the story continued. The time in London had been particularly hard to write about, but she had been determined to leave out nothing. She wrote truthfully of the cold street corner where she had sold her young body to anyone who would pay for it, and of her rise to becoming a high-class escort. Of her need to find so-called respectability.

The diary took two weeks to bring up to date, to cover the period since she had moved to Blackpool and everything that she had done and felt here. She only ever added to it when she was completely alone, and it was kept hidden deep in a locked drawer of her dressing-table, for her eyes only.

By this time it was almost the end of March but she couldn't finish now until the book was completed. The words flowed, following her move to Blackpool and her determination to own her own hotel. Then she wrote of finding Cassidy and of her meeting with Christian and the time they had spent together at Seagull's Flight. Writing about it made her realise that this had been the only truly peaceful time she had ever known. But once again, happiness had eluded her. She wrote of her meeting with Greg and how she had cold-heartedly married him, knowing deep down that she didn't love him. Of her love for his daughter, who was one of the best things that had ever happened in her life next to Tracey and Yasmin. It was a book full of heartbreak and pain. And if anyone had read it, they couldn't help but be moved to tears.

It helped her to write her feelings down on paper. She had achieved what she had set out to achieve, but now, too late, she realised that luxury and respectability without love were worthless. Her marriage to Greg was a farce. But even so, now she at least had Nikki and the child made her life worthwhile.

Once the book was up to date, she locked it securely away: never to be seen by anyone, ever.

Its writing, like her life, had been painful and for days she was unwell, unable to eat and restless.

Mrs Pope was deeply concerned about her. 'Why don't you go and see the doctor?' she pleaded. 'You're as white as a sheet. Happen he could give you a tonic or something. You've never got over the flu properly.'

For days, Claire adamantly refused, but then as she grew tired of Mrs Pope's constant nagging, she finally agreed to make an appointment and one rainy April day, she set off for his surgery.

The doctor was an elderly man, much respected by his patients. He'd met Claire on more than one occasion when she'd taken Nikki to him with coughs and colds. He could easily see the love the young woman had for her stepdaughter and liked her.

'What's the problem then?' He peered at her over the top of his glasses.

'I'm sure it's nothing,' she mumbled, wishing she hadn't come.

'I'll be the judge of that,' he said kindly. 'Now hop up onto the couch and let's have a look at you, eh?'

He examined her thoroughly, and when he was finished and Claire was sitting in front of his desk again, he began to write on her files.

'Right,' he said eventually, 'I'm sending you into the nurse for her to take a specimen of urine and a blood test. I'm sure it's nothing to worry about, but better safe than sorry. Phone the surgery in three days' time for the results.'

Claire left the surgery feeling worse than she had when she arrived. Mrs Pope was waiting for her when she got home.

'Well?' she demanded, the second Claire stepped through the door. 'What did he say?'

'He said exactly what I expected,' Claire replied. 'I'm a bit run down, that's all.'

Mrs Pope bit her lip. 'We'll see,' she said, unconvinced. 'But I'll tell you now, if you ain't got a bit of colour in your cheeks by this time next week, I'll waltz you back there again myself.'

Claire tutted in exasperation, but all the same was forced to admit that it was nice to have someone to care.

Four days later, the phone rang and when Claire answered it, the doctor's receptionist asked to speak to Mrs Nightingale.

'Speaking,' replied Claire. She should have rung the surgery yesterday, but as she was feeling slightly better she'd forgotten all about it.

'Ah, Mrs Nightingale, the doctor would like to see you this evening, if possible. We have the results of your blood test.'

'Is something wrong?' Claire asked, with a note of panic in her voice.

'I'm afraid I'm not allowed to divulge any information on the phone,' the receptionist explained apologetically. 'But call in this evening and the doctor will see you.'

Claire thanked her and put down the receiver, feeling sick and afraid. All sorts of thoughts swarmed in her mind. It was only ten o'clock in the morning, Mrs Pope hadn't even arrived as yet, and suddenly the hours stretched endlessly ahead of her. After pacing up and down the hallway for a few moments, Claire glanced at her wristwatch and made a hasty decision. The surgery was open until ten-thirty and if she hurried she could catch the doctor this morning instead of having to wait until tonight. If something was wrong, she wanted to know now. Not even stopping to change, she snatched up her car keys and made for the garage.

It was eleven-thirty by the time she pulled back onto the drive. Mrs Pope was there by then, polishing the windowsill in the lounge and waving to her through the window, but Claire didn't even see her. She was in a state of shock.

Mrs Pope hurried into the hall to meet her but stopped in her tracks when she saw Claire's face. 'Why, whatever's the matter, love?' she asked. 'You look like you've seen a ghost.' Grabbing her by the elbow, Mrs Pope propelled her into the kitchen and pushed her down onto the nearest chair. 'You sit there,' she commanded. 'By the look of you, a good strong cup of tea wouldn't go amiss.'

Hurrying over to the kettle she switched it on, and when she turned back to Claire, her mouth dropped open in amazement. The young woman was laughing and crying all at the same time.

'Are you going to tell me what's going on or what?' Mrs Pope demanded, placing her hands on her hips.

'Yes, I'll tell you, Mrs Pope.' Suddenly hopping off the chair, Claire started to dance the startled woman around the kitchen. 'I've just been back to see the doctor and he's told me that I'm going to have a baby!' Her face was alight and suddenly Mrs Pope was crying too, and hugging her.

'Oh, love, that's wonderful,' she cried. 'Though I have to admit it ain't really a surprise. I've been having me thoughts in that direction for the last couple of weeks.'

Claire returned her hug. She could hardly believe it. She'd almost given up hope and felt as if she was being given a second chance. This time she was determined that she would get it right. This baby would have all the love in the world and never know a single sad moment. It would be a brother or sister for Nikki, and for the first time in her whole life she would have a proper family of her very own, which would go a long way to compensate for the fact that she was trapped in a loveless marriage.

Chapter Thirty-One

Once Mrs Pope had left, Claire began to wonder how best to break the news to Greg. Should she phone him at the office? Or perhaps she could cook a romantic candlelit dinner for two and tell him about it then? She suddenly came back down to earth with a bump as she thought of Mr Taylor. There was no way she could ever sleep with him again now, not with a child growing inside her. She decided that first she would tell Greg about the baby, and then she'd worry about how she was going to get rid of Mr Taylor once and for all.

Despite all of her plans to inform Greg of the news in a sensible way, the second he walked in the door that night she blabbed it out to him.

Truthfully, she hadn't expected him to be as thrilled about the baby as she was because in all fairness, he'd never made a secret of the fact that he wasn't really bothered if they had any more children or not. However, she was pleasantly surprised when once over the initial shock he told her, 'I dare say it would be quite nice to have a son to carry on the family business.'

'Then I'll have to see what I can do. Now will you tell Nikki or shall I?'

'Oh, you can tell her,' he said, happy to leave everything up to her.

Unlike her father, Nikki was ecstatic at the idea of a new baby brother or sister.

'Will I be able to help you bath it and feed it?' she asked.

Claire hugged her. 'Of course you will,' she promised, and once again the future looked bright. Or at least it would do if she could escape from Mr Taylor's clutches.

'When will the baby be born?' Nikki asked and when Claire said that it would be sometime in November she was even more thrilled.

'It might even be born on my birthday,' Nikki said dreamily, and at school the next day, she told all her friends and they were envious. From then on she could speak of little else.

'We could turn the bedroom next to mine into a nursery,' she suggested to Claire.

'But what if the baby cries in the night? It would wake you up,' Claire pointed out.

Nikki shrugged. 'I wouldn't mind,' she said, and so together they went to view the room. Claire had to admit that it would make a wonderful nursery. It was airy and bright with a clear view of the sea and the sand dunes.

'But we won't start it just yet,' Claire warned her. 'There's plenty of time.' And so it was decided.

It was the following week as they were having dinner together that Greg informed her, 'Edward Taylor will be coming to Blackpool again next week. I thought perhaps we might invite him over for a meal?'

Normally, Claire was only too happy to oblige when it came to entertaining Greg's business acquintances, but this time she surprised him when she told him bluntly, 'I don't think so, Greg. I'm not feeling so good at the moment, and certainly not up to playing hostess to that little creep.' The words had slipped out before she could stop them and she saw his eyebrows rise into his hairline. Thankfully, her statement seemed to amuse him.

'I take it you're not too keen on Edward then?' he chuckled. 'But I can't say the same about his feelings for you. Don't think I haven't noticed how he almost slobbers every time he looks at you. I think you've got yourself an admirer there.'

Claire flushed and lowered her eyes.

'Anyway, don't worry about it,' Greg continued. 'I'll take him out for a meal in a restaurant somewhere. It's more his wife I need to impress and luckily she isn't coming with him this time.'

'What difference does that make?' Claire asked as she raised a forkful of minted lamb chop to her mouth.

'Well, Edward is simply the puppet. It's his wife's business – he just runs it for her. I hear she leads him a merry dance for the privilege too.'

Could Greg have known it, he had just unwittingly given Claire the solution to her problem. Very soon now I'll turn the tables on that little pervert and he'll dance to my tune again, she promised herself, and the opportunity to do just that came the very next week.

She was enjoying a mid-morning coffee break on her own as she pored over wallpaper samples for the nursery when the doorbell rang. Opening it, she found Edward Taylor standing on the doorstep with a licentious grin on his face.

'Good morning, my dear.' Without waiting for an invite, he stepped past her into the hallway and Claire's blood began to boil. I'll soon wipe that filthy smile off his face, she thought.

He eyed her up and down with a smirk on his lips. 'So, aren't you going to tell your Teddy how pleased you are to see him?'

'Actually, I'm not pleased to see you at all,' Claire told him scathingly. 'So, if you wouldn't mind, I'd like you to leave now.'

'Now, now, my dear,' he remonstrated, 'you wouldn't want to upset me, would you? I have a little meeting with your husband this afternoon – speaking of which, Greg tells me that congratulations are in order. Seems a shame to spoil a figure like yours with childbirth. But still, we should be able to have a little fun for some months to come yet.'

'Your *fun* as you call it, is well and truly over,' Claire informed him as she backed away from his groping hands.

'Just what is that supposed to mean?' he demanded.

It was her turn to smirk now. 'Exactly what I said. It's finished, Edward, so I think you ought to leave. And take this with you. You'll find three thousand pounds in there.'

Shock flickered briefly across his face as he looked down into the envelope she had pressed into his hand, but then he tried to take control of the situation again. 'I should think very carefully about what you're saying,' he ground out. 'Don't forget, one word from me to your husband and all of this could come crashing about your ears.'

'Mm.' She cocked her head to one side and stroked her chin as if she was pondering on what he had just threatened. Inside she was shaking like a leaf but outwardly she was as cool as a cucumber. It wouldn't do to let him know just how terrified she was feeling.

'Do you know, Edward, you're quite right. Still, if it would give you pleasure, why don't you phone him right now and have done with it? There's a phone right there – look.'

'What game are you playing, eh?' he asked, and Claire knew that it was now or never. For the whole of her life she'd had to fight to survive and she would fight again now.

'I'm not playing any game, Edward. But the thing is, I've recently found out that I could ruin your life just as easily as you could ruin mine.'

'Just what do you mean by that?' he asked as sweat broke out on his forehead.

'I mean that I just happen to know that your wife owns the business you make out is yours. In fact, from what I can gather, she owns everything – lock, stock and barrel. So, go ahead and phone Greg if you feel you must. But I assure you, I shall be following your call up with one to your wife – and do you know what, I think she might be just as shocked to hear what we've been up to as my husband will be, don't you?'

'You . . . you wouldn't know how to get hold of her,' he spluttered.

'Oh, but I would, I assure you. Not only do I have your business address in London, but I also have your home address.'

Somehow he knew that she wasn't bluffing and now his fear turned to white-hot rage.

'Why, you . . . you *little whore!*' Knowing that she had him over a barrel, he stormed towards the door, his hands clenched into tight fists. 'You'll get your comeuppance,' he snarled. 'Dirty little guttersnipes like you always do. I hope you rot in hell and that bastard you're carrying inside you with you.'

Claire's hand fell subconsciously onto her stomach and now her anger swelled to match his. He could curse her as much as he liked, it was like water off a duck's back. But to curse her unborn child was unforgivable.

'Get out *now*,' she breathed at him, 'or as God's my witness I swear I won't be responsible for my actions.'

He flung himself out of the door, slamming it resoundingly behind him.

Claire leaned heavily against the hall table as she began to shake. It was over and she could hardly believe it. But already another fear was growing along with the child inside her. Edward Taylor was only one of many men she had slept with. What if another one were to put in an appearance? Staggering towards the kitchen she forced the terrifying thought from her mind and wondered when she would ever find peace.

*   *   *

The following week, Claire allowed Nikki to choose the wallpaper for the nursery. It was covered in nursery-rhyme characters and Claire praised her choice. 'It won't matter if it's a boy or a girl with this pattern.' She smiled. 'What colour would you like the paintwork to be?'

'Yellow,' Nikki replied without hesitation, and so a decorator was called in to begin.

Claire didn't really mind if the baby turned out to be a boy or a girl so long as it was healthy, but Nikki, like her father, was longing for a little boy.

'It would be lovely to have a little brother,' she would sigh dreamily, and so Claire began to hope for their sakes that it would be a boy.

Everywhere she went with Greg, as news of the baby spread they were congratulated. There was a bloom about her; her eyes twinkled, her hair shone and her slim figure slowly began to blossom. She and Nikki spent countless hours shopping for everything that a baby could possibly need. As money was no object, Claire was determined that everything would be just right for this baby. She and Nikki chose a cot and a tiny Broderie-Anglaise-trimmed Moses basket for when the baby first came home. They bought a small wardrobe with drawers to match, which was soon bulging with nappies, vests and more Babygros than one baby could ever possibly wear.

When Claire was four months' pregnant, her flat stomach turned overnight into a tiny bulge, which Nikki would stroke lovingly.

'How big is it now?' she asked daily and Claire would smile at her impatience as they looked through baby books together. They still went on their afternoon strolls along the beach but Claire took her time now, content to let Nikki and Cassidy dash on ahead of her.

That year, July was swelteringly hot and Claire began to put her feet up for an hour in the afternoons. She refused all offers of alcohol and made sure that she ate only healthy food as she daydreamed of what the baby would look like. Would it be fair like her, or dark like Greg? Would the birth bring Nikki and Greg closer together? She could only hope so.

The pregnancy progressed without a hitch and when she was six months' along, her waistline suddenly shot out of control, much to Nikki's amusement, and she had to buy tent-shaped maternity dresses.

'You waddle like a duck,' Nikki teased and Claire swiped her ear playfully.

Claire was content to stay at home for most of the time now and Greg didn't seem to mind. She gave up swimming too for the time being, and now just drove into Blackpool once a week to visit Mary or Betty instead. Nikki still hated her going out without her, but thankfully, she had stopped having tantrums and would just be sullen with her the morning after instead.

Claire felt incredibly guilty about leaving her and told Greg so.

'Don't be silly. You have to have some time to yourself,' he said, and Claire supposed that he was right.

Mary and Betty were delighted about the new baby and were both knitting furiously as if trying to outdo each other. Almost every week when Claire visited one or the other of them, she would be presented with another little hand-knitted garment until the drawers in the nursery were brimming over with matinée coats, bootees, mittens and bonnets all the colours of the rainbow.

At one stage, Mrs Pope got her knitting needles out as well, determined not to be outdone, and the resulting matinée coat caused much hilarity. One sleeve was longer than the other, and there were so many dropped stitches that they almost formed a pattern. Even Mrs Pope laughed at it, but keen to save her feelings, Nikki claimed it for her doll. One thing Mrs Pope was good at, however, was crocheting and eventually she presented Claire with a shawl so fine that it took her breath away.

'It's absolutely lovely,' Claire gasped as she fingered it admiringly. 'I'll put it away for the christening. It's far too nice for everyday use.'

Claire hadn't been so happy in a long time and would sit outside with Cassidy at her feet watching the ships out at sea. This baby could never take the place of Yasmin, but she hoped that its birth would go a long way towards easing her sense of loss.

It was one night in September that Greg came in and suggested she should go and see Mary. He had a huge pile of paperwork to get through, he said, and there was no sense in them both staying in. Claire was almost seven months' pregnant and had barely ventured from the house for the last couple of weeks as she was now uncomfortably large. Deciding that a break might do her good she began to get ready as Nikki flew off to her room in a sulk.

'Perhaps I shouldn't bother going after all?' she said to Greg indecisively as she listened to the child thumping away up the stairs.

He waved aside her concerns. 'Don't be so silly. She'll be perfectly all right here with me. Now go on, get off with you and have a good time.'

Claire walked out to her car. It was only seven-thirty in the evening, but already it was very dark and there was a bitterly cold wind blowing in from the sea. She drove through the back streets of Blackpool to reach Mary's house to avoid the crowds who would be cruising the front to view the illuminations. Once there, she parked and hoisted herself up the path to Mary's modest little terraced house. Tom answered when she knocked on the door and smiled at her, genuinely pleased to see her.

'Why, hello, love. Mary was only on about you today, saying she hadn't seen you for a while. But I'm afraid she's not in. It's hers and Betty's night for Bingo.'

'Oh, of course it is,' said Claire, remembering.

Tom pulled the door wide. 'Well, seeing as you're here, come in anyway. You must have smelled the tea. I've just brewed a pot so you can help me to drink it.'

Claire followed him inside. She had a cup of tea with him and then half an hour later set off for home. Usually she stayed at Mary's for at least a couple of hours, but she suddenly felt tired and the thought of a nice long soak in the bath and an early night with a good book was more than welcoming.

After parking her car in the garage she let herself into the house, noting that Greg's study light wasn't on. Normally when he brought paperwork home he was closeted in there until the early hours of the morning. She wandered into the lounge. He wasn't there either, but the brandy decanter she had filled earlier in the day was now on the coffee-table, only two-thirds full. She grinned to herself. If he had drunk all that it was highly unlikely that he would be in any fit state to do any paperwork at all tonight. Clicking off the light she headed for the stairs, but once she had climbed them and found that he wasn't in their bedroom either, she frowned.

I bet he's in Nikki's room, she suddenly thought, and waddled along the landing. She had just reached for the door handle when a voice from within the room made her hand freeze in mid-air. It was Nikki's and she sounded terrified.

'No, *please*. Please *don't*,' she heard the child beg. Claire's heart began to hammer in her chest. Someone was in there with her stepdaughter, and whoever it was, they clearly intended to hurt her. But where was Greg? Peering over her shoulder she prayed that he would come to her aid, but the landing was empty. Taking a deep breath, she threw the door open.

The sight that met her eyes made her knees buckle with shock. It would be carved into her memory for the rest of her life as she saw history repeating itself. Nikki was huddled naked at the far side of her bed, sobbing and trying to cover herself with her nightdress, and standing at the end of the bed was Greg. He too was naked, and there was lust shining in his eyes. When he saw Claire, a look of panic swept across his face.

'It's not what you think,' he said, holding one hand over himself and the other out to her beseechingly, but Claire had no need to think. This was a scene she had witnessed too many times before. Nikki slipped past him and threw herself into Claire's protective arms as Claire gazed at him with hatred blazing in her eyes.

'You bastard! How could you?' she spat.

'It wash her fault,' he slurred, obviously the worse for drink as he stabbed a finger towards Nikki. 'She kept asking me to come in.'

Claire could never remember hating anyone as much as she hated him at that moment. She screwed her eyes up tight at the pain in her heart as angry tears spurted from her eyes and poured down her pale cheeks. How could *she*, of all people, have missed the signs? They had been there, staring her in the face, yet she hadn't seen them. Now, too late, she realised why Nikki had hated to be left alone with her father. The child was trembling uncontrollably and Claire hugged her to her as if she would never let her go.

'I'll ruin you for this, you just see if I don't,' she whispered. 'When I've finished with you, *you bastard*, you'll never be able to hold your head high again.'

The words were said with such menace that he shuddered and took a step back. Her eyes were as cold as ice and suddenly he saw his reputation in tatters.

'You wouldn't do that,' he bluffed. 'Think of all this.' He spread his hands to encompass the room. 'If you take me down, then you'll lose everything too.'

'Huh! That won't stop me. I'll do anything it takes to make sure that you never lay a finger on Nikki again.'

To her horror he began to cry, great wracking sobs that tore through him as he saw everything he had worked all his life for, slipping away. 'Claire, *please*,' he begged. 'One word of this and you'll destroy me. I . . . I'm sorry. It was a mistake. It will never happen again.'

Unmoved, she stared back at him, as cold as marble. '*Get out*,' she spat contemptuously. 'Or I won't be responsible for what I might do.'

Weeping he snatched up his boxer shorts and struggled into them as she averted her eyes, unable to bear the sight of him.

As he began to move towards her she stepped to one side and now he became angry too. 'You bitch!' he cried. 'She's *my* daughter anyway. It's none of your bloody business what we get up to. She enjoys it really.'

Claire couldn't believe what she was hearing. He was sick. He had to be.

'First thing in the morning I shall be calling the police,' she warned him.

Suddenly bringing his hand back, he slapped her hard across the face. Her neck snapped back on her shoulders, but she just clung on to Nikki all the more tightly.

Instantly, he was contrite as he saw the hatred burning in her eyes. 'I'm sorry.' He was desperate now. 'I didn't mean to do that.' He could see his whole life, his future, in ashes and was terrified. 'Please, Claire, just give me one more chance. I'll never touch her again, I swear it.'

Even as he begged and pleaded he could see that she meant every word she said and his shoulders sagged. Without another word he turned and walked slowly to the door. As soon as he was through it, Claire ran to lock it firmly from the inside.

'Are you all right, Nikki?' she asked anxiously. As the girl stared up at her from haunted, tear-stained eyes, Claire's heart went out to her. Dear God, *why* hadn't she realised what was going on right under her nose? She was shaking too now, even more so than Nikki as they clung together. Eventually, they sat down on the edge of the bed, each lost in the horror of it all.

'Why didn't you tell me what was happening?' Claire asked despairingly.

'I couldn't,' Nikki whispered. 'Daddy said that he'd send me away if I told anyone. I told Mummy once a long time ago, and they had a terrible row. Then she picked me up and put me in the back of the car and drove away very fast. And then we crashed and Mummy died and went away. Daddy said that if I told you, you would leave me too.'

'Oh, Nikki.' Everything was dropping into place. This then, was the explanation for Greg's first wife running out to her car in her nightdress. But Claire had had no idea that the poor woman had taken Nikki with her. She had obviously been trying to get her daughter to a place of safety. Claire was totally devastated. Nothing could have prepared her for this. She had considered Greg to be a decent man, a gentleman – that was why she had married him. Yet all the time he was no better than the sick perverts who had abused her as a child. She shuddered, deep in shock, hardly able to take it all in. It was too terrible to believe; yet she had seen it with her own eyes. However, her main concern at the moment was for Nikki. How she must have suffered. Claire knew only too well the terrible burden of guilt the child must have been bearing on her slight shoulders, and white-hot rage surged through her. But now was not the time to dwell on her feelings. Nikki needed her and so she rocked her comfortingly in her arms until the child's sobs subsided to whimpers. Eventually she helped her back into her nightdress and tucked her into bed.

'Don't leave me, Claire, *please*.'

'I won't leave you, darling. Not ever,' Claire soothed, and climbing onto the bed she lay down beside her and placed her arm protectively around her. 'Don't worry,' she whispered. 'I'll stay with you all night, and I promise this will never, *ever* happen to you again. You're safe now.' She meant every single word she said. If it was the last thing she ever did, she was determined to get Nikki away from here.

Chapter Thirty-Two

When Nikki finally slipped into a deep but troubled sleep, Claire inched her way off the bed and crossed to stare from the window, rubbing her aching back as she went. The scene was breathtakingly lovely but tonight it was lost on Claire. Nightingale Lodge now was no more than a loveless, luxurious prison and soon she would be gone from it for good. Once again her dreams had crumbled about her. She fingered her lip where Greg had slapped her and found that it was swollen and tender, not that it concerned her. She had suffered far worse than that and at the moment it was the least of her worries.

Crossing to the bedroom door, she pressed her ear against it and listened for sounds of Greg. All was silent, so turning the key she peeped up and down the landing. There was no sign of him. Slipping off her shoes, she quickly descended the stairs. The lights were ablaze all through the house and as she passed the sitting-room door, which was slightly ajar, she noticed that the brandy decanter had gone from the coffee-table. Her lip curled in contempt. Greg must have taken it and she hoped that he would drink himself into oblivion. As she entered the kitchen, Cassidy rubbed himself against her legs. Sliding to the floor, she hugged him as her warm tears dampened his coat.

'Oh Cassidy,' she sobbed, 'how could I have been such a blind fool? Why didn't I see him for what he really is?'

The dog licked her face with his moist tongue. He always seemed to understand her moods and tonight was no different. After a while she rose and made herself a strong cup of coffee. She didn't usually drink it this late at night as it tended to keep her awake, but tonight she wanted to be on the alert. She wouldn't feel safe again now until she, Nikki and Cassidy were far away from here. First thing in the morning that's just what she intended them to be, once she had told the police what a pervert her husband was. If it hadn't been for the fact that Nikki had fallen into a fretful sleep she would have dialled them there and then. But the child was obviously exhausted and Claire knew that she wouldn't be up to questioning tonight. Far better to wait until the morning when Nikki was a little calmer and more rested.

When she eventually crept back up the stairs she took Cassidy with her, but this time she heard Greg pacing up and down their room as she hurried by it. Flying back to the safety of Nikki's room she again securely locked the door and now she waited.

The night was spent in Nikki's bedside chair as she forced herself to stay awake. A watery sun finally rose up from the sea to herald the dawn, and slowly the grounds of Greg's beautiful home came to life with the sound of early-morning birdsong. Inside, Claire felt dead. Nikki started awake at seven o'clock and her eyes were instantly fearful.

'It's all right, sweetheart, I'm here,' Claire reassured her, and as the child caught sight of Claire and Cassidy she relaxed a little. Claire's eyes were bloodshot from lack of sleep and she felt tired and ill. The sounds from her own room had ceased long ago, so Claire brushed the child's hair and waited while she tugged some clothes on.

They were about to leave the room when Nikki suddenly clutched at her hand and implored, 'Don't call the police, Claire. Let's get away from here first. They'll ask questions like they did when Mummy died, and . . .' Her eyes filled with tears.

Claire caught her in a fierce embrace as she told her, 'All right, sweetheart, don't get yourself all upset again. It'll be all right, you'll see.' She unlocked the door and after checking that there was no sign of Greg, she led her stepdaughter downstairs.

Soon she would have to confront Greg, and once she'd placed Nikki's breakfast in front of her, she decided to get it over with. Now that it was light she felt a little braver. 'I'm going to speak to your dad,' she told the child. 'I want you to stay here.'

Nikki's eyes were frightened but Claire reminded her, 'Cassidy's here. You're quite safe.' She felt quite frightened herself as she left the room, knowing that if she didn't face her husband now, she would never find the courage to do so. The baby inside her suddenly ceased kicking, as if he too was nervous.

Pausing outside their bedroom door, she listened for sounds of Greg getting ready for work. Only silence greeted her, so turning the handle, she threw the door open. The room was in darkness, the curtains drawn tight, but she could see Greg's silhouette lying on the bed. Crossing to the window, she pulled the curtains aside, allowing the early-morning light to flood the room. Greg didn't even blink as she cautiously approached the bed. The empty brandy decanter was on the bedside cabinet and she saw that he was clutching one of the cut-glass tumblers that they had received from one of his business acquaintances as a wedding present. Some of the amber liquid had spilled onto the white lace bedspread and formed a dark stain. He was still in his boxer shorts, and as she stared down at him, a wave of anger now replaced her fear. In that moment she hated him so much that she could willingly have killed him.

Marching across the room, she shook him roughly. His head lolled to one side and she saw something roll from his other hand onto the bed. It was an empty paracetamol bottle. Her heart lurched and she shook him again, even more roughly this time, but again there was no response – and now she began to panic. What should she do? Shaking uncontrollably, she snatched up the phone and dialled 999.

'I need an ambulance!' she screamed incoherently. Then as the operator tried to calm her down, she managed to babble out their address. Next she phoned Mrs Pope's number, although it took two attempts because her fingers were trembling so badly. At last the older woman's welcome voice came on the line.

'Mrs Pope, I need you,' she sobbed.

'I'm on my way.' The phone went dead in her hand.

After that, everything became a blur. Mrs Pope arrived within seconds of the ambulance. The paramedics pushed Claire out of the way as they hurried to Greg's still form and within minutes he was on a stretcher being loaded into the ambulance. Mrs Pope helped Claire in after him, a worried frown on her brow. She had no idea what had happened, but now was not the time for questions.

'You go with him, love,' she urged. 'And don't worry. I'll take care of Nikki.' The ambulance doors slammed shut and suddenly they were driving at break-neck speed towards the hospital. Claire was sobbing but the paramedics were too busy concentrating on Greg to even notice. As soon as they pulled up at the emergency entrance they whisked him away and someone led Claire to a small waiting room, assuring her that they would keep her informed. And so there she sat for what seemed like an eternity, all alone and trembling. Eventually the door opened, and a young doctor in a white coat entered. He took in her heavily pregnant condition at a glance and frowned with concern.

'Mrs Nightingale, I'm afraid I have some very bad news for you.'

When Claire's bleak eyes stared back at him he gulped, hating what he had to tell her. 'I'm afraid your husband didn't make it.' He lowered his head. 'We did everything we could, I assure you, but he was dead when he arrived at the hospital.'

Unable to comprehend what she was hearing, Claire visibly shuddered. The doctor was telling her that Greg was dead. Unable to face the consequences of what he had done, he had taken the coward's way out, and she was glad. He could never hurt Nikki again now, and with that realisation came a great wave of relief. She supposed that she should feel guilty for the way she felt, but she couldn't help it.

The young doctor was stunned when she suddenly broke into hysterical laughter. Tears he would have expected, but he didn't quite know how to handle this reaction. As he watched, the laughter soon turned into sobs, and then into silence as she slipped from the seat to the floor in a dead faint.

It was lunchtime before she was allowed to take a taxi home. They had wanted to keep her in for observation, but Claire insisted that she must be with Nikki.

As she climbed the steps to the house, Mrs Pope ran out to meet her and wrapped her in a warm embrace.

'Oh love, what a terrible thing to happen. I can hardly take it in.'

Claire was totally exhausted both mentally and physically, but Mrs Pope had everything in hand. 'Come along,' the kindly woman told her. 'It's bed for you, my girl. You look fit to drop.'

The woman fussed over Claire as she struggled into her nightdress. In no time at all she had her tucked into bed and then she bustled away to put the kettle on. When she carried the tray back into the bedroom minutes later, Claire had already sunk into a deep slumber. Reluctant to disturb her, Mrs Pope tiptoed away.

Claire slept straight through to the early hours of the following morning. When she awoke she looked around in confusion, then as the events of the last twenty-four hours flooded into her mind, she sat bolt upright.

Mrs Pope was in the chair at the side of the bed and seeing how distraught Claire was, she gripped her hand reassuringly.

'It's all right, love. I'm here,' she soothed.

'Where's Nikki?'

'She's tucked up in bed and she's fine.'

Claire sank slowly back onto her pillows. Surely this whole thing must be a nightmare? She would wake up in a minute and everything would be as it had been. But no – it was all true. Scalding tears splashed down her cheeks.

'Oh, Mrs Pope. Everything's such a mess.'

The older woman's heart went out to her. 'Don't despair, love,' she said softly. 'Things will come right in the end, you'll see.'

The way Claire was feeling at that moment, she doubted if things would ever be right again. But then, she asked herself, when had her life ever run smoothly?

In years to come, when Claire looked back on the dark days that followed, she wondered if she would ever have got through them if it hadn't been for Mrs Pope. The woman moved in without even being asked, and soon proved to be a tower of strength to both Claire and Nikki.

Mrs Pope took it upon herself to call Mr Smythe, one of Greg's business partners, and he kindly agreed to see to all the funeral arrangements. It was just as well, for Claire was in no fit state to organise anything. Because of the circumstances of his death, a post-mortem was performed on Greg, and a verdict of Accidental Death was duly recorded. They chose to assume that he had accidentally taken too many paracetamol tablets whilst intoxicated. After all, they said, what other verdict could there be? He was a successful businessman with a beautiful young wife and daughter and a baby on the way; highly regarded, with everything to live for.

Claire knew otherwise but it seemed pointless to expose him now. It would only have caused yet more grief for Nikki, and Claire was determined to protect her at all costs.

Unable to sleep in the room she had shared with Greg, she moved into a room across the landing and as the day of the funeral approached she began to dread it. The police had been to interview her on the day following his death as a matter of routine. Claire told them that Greg had been overworking a great deal lately and that he had gone to bed on the night of his death complaining of a headache.

'Didn't you see him take the tablets?' a grim-faced Inspector had asked.

'No. You see, because he wasn't feeling well, and as I'm finding it hard to settle at the moment, I decided to sleep in the spare room.' She had lied for so long now that she was adept at it, and she played the part of the grieving, heavily pregnant widow to perfection.

By the time the interview was concluded, the Inspector was completely convinced that Greg's death had been nothing more than a tragic accident.

'It's a bloody shame, if you ask me,' he was heard to say to a younger officer as they were leaving. 'A nice young wife like that and a new baby due any day. And that poor kid losing both her parents . . . It doesn't bear thinking about, does it?'

When the police had gone, Claire spoke to Nikki at great length about what had happened.

'But what if they find out what he did to me?' the child asked fearfully.

'They won't, if we don't tell them,' Claire said, and all the time her heart was aching, for she knew only too well about the shame and guilt the child must be feeling. Nikki had taken the news of her father's death remarkably calmly for one so young, and Claire knew why: Nikki was relieved that he could never abuse her again.

'Why don't we get you back to school, eh?' Mrs Pope suggested a few days after Greg's death. 'There's nothing to be gained by you moping about the house, love. You'll feel better once you get back into some sort of routine.'

Nikki grudgingly agreed and so the very next morning, Mrs Pope took her to school. Claire was up and about but feeling unbelievably ill. She supposed that she was suffering from delayed shock. So much had happened in such a short time and once again her life had been turned upside down. She hadn't ventured out of the house since Greg's death but after lunch she left Mrs Pope tidying the kitchen and took Cassidy for a gentle stroll along the beach.

'Good idea,' Mrs Pope smiled when she suggested it. 'Happen the fresh air will clear your head a bit and put some colour back in your cheeks. Just don't get overdoing it, that's all.'

'I won't,' Claire promised as she set off. She hadn't gone very far when she realised that she must be more tired than she had thought. The baby inside her felt incredibly heavy and she had developed a dull backache.

'Come on, Cassidy.' She rubbed the small of her back. 'I don't think this was such a good idea after all. Let's go home, eh?' He wagged his tail and fell into step beside her as she turned and started back towards the house, his three paws leaving an amusing pattern of prints in the sand. The pains in her back were becoming worse and her steps began to drag. They had just reached the sand dunes that would lead them to the back entrance to the house when the first contraction ripped through her. It was so totally unexpected that Claire bent double. Thankfully, it was over almost before it had begun, but the shock of it had made sweat stand out on her forehead.

'Oh, please God no,' she groaned. 'It's too soon. Don't take this baby away from me too.' Her prayers went unanswered and she had barely straightened when the second pain hit her. Something warm and sticky gushed from between her legs and dripped onto the sand. Her waters had broken and she began to cry. Her labour had started and she knew that somehow she must get home. Her baby's life depended on it.

Gritting her teeth, she staggered on. The contractions were coming frequently now but she tried to ignore them as she concentrated on putting one foot in front of the other. At last the back of the house came into sight and she gasped a sigh of relief. Luckily, Mrs Pope spotted her from the kitchen window and realising that something was wrong, she flew down the lawn to meet her.

'What's the matter, love?' she asked breathlessly, but at that moment another contraction wracked Claire's body, and the housekeeper guessed immediately what was happening. It was far too early for the baby to be coming and Mrs Pope knew that she must act quickly if yet another tragedy was to be diverted. Manhandling Claire to a bench positioned beneath an old oak tree, she unceremoniously dumped her onto it.

'Stay there and don't move,' she ordered, and then with a speed that would have done credit to a woman half her age, she sprinted back up the lawn. Ten minutes later, for the second time in only a matter of days, an ambulance sped up the drive.

Claire gripped Mrs Pope's hand tightly as the older woman tried to comfort her.

'She's not quite seven months yet,' she informed the ambulancemen with fear in her eyes.

They patted her shoulder. 'Don't worry. We'll have her in the labour ward in no time,' one of them said kindly. Mrs Pope had briefly informed them of the recent tragic death of Claire's husband, explaining that there would be no proud father at her bedside as she gave birth to this child.

Almost before she knew it, Claire was being lifted onto a stretcher and into the back of the ambulance. Her painfilled eyes never left Mrs Pope's face as she clung onto her hand until the very last minute.

'I'll come to the hospital as soon as I've collected Nikki from school,' Mrs Pope promised her as the doors of the ambulance closed. 'I'll drop her off at Mary's and then I'll be there.'

Claire nodded numbly then the lights were flashing and the siren was screaming as the ambulance sped back down the drive.

Mrs Pope watched until it was out of sight, then, turning about, she looked up at Nightingale Lodge. It had lost all its charm now and she began to wonder if it was cursed. The Nightingale family had suffered one catastrophe after another, and she found herself praying as she had never prayed before that Claire's baby would not be its next victim.

Claire was haemorrhaging heavily now, and at the hospital they wheeled her straight into the delivery room. Within minutes she was on a delivery table with a drip hooked into the back of her hand. Voices seemed to be coming from a long, long way away as she floated on a sea of pain. Wires fixed to her bulging stomach were transmitting the baby's heartbeats and the doctor was watching the monitor with growing concern.

'The baby is in distress,' Claire heard him say and her heart began to hammer in terror. She wouldn't be able to bear it if she lost this baby now. She knew she wouldn't.

'We'll have to deliver it now and quickly.' Learning over to Claire, the doctor looked her in the eye. 'Mrs Nightingale, we're going to help you get this baby out. Can you understand me?'

Claire nodded numbly.

He patted her hand. 'Good, good. Now I'm going to use forceps but you *must* do exactly as I tell you. Will you try to do that?'

Again she nodded, but then another contraction gripped her and she writhed in agony as she felt another warm flush of blood flood from her.

Within seconds she felt the cold steel enter her and the pain was unbearable as she fought to stay conscious. Her baby's life depended on it and
she knew it. As another contraction tore through her, the doctor ordered
firmly, 'PUSH!'

Sweat streamed down her face as she did as she was told but nothing
happened, and as the contraction passed she dropped exhausted and battered
back onto the pillow.

'AGAIN!' he snapped, but still nothing happened, and now as Claire's
eyes moved to the monitor she began to panic. She was no doctor but
even she could see how erratic her baby's heartbeat was. After all that had
happened over the last few days she knew that she didn't have the strength
to obey the doctor's orders for very much longer. By now, he was sweating
too and seeing that she was almost at the end of her endurance he made
a quick decision.

'Pass me the scalpel,' he ordered the midwife and he bent to Claire
again. She vaguely felt the knife cut her and then the doctor reinserted
the forceps. 'Now, the next time you feel a contraction coming, I want
you to push with all your might.'

Seconds later, the pain came again. Gritting her teeth, Claire pushed
with the very last of her energy and suddenly the doctor shouted excitedly, '*That's it!* I can see the head. One more good push and it will all be
over.'

Claire bore down for one last time and suddenly she felt the child
slither out of her. She watched a nurse snatch it up from the bed. No
newborn wail filled the room but she had a brief glimpse of a tiny little
face as the nurse ran from the room with the child wrapped in a towel.

'Well done, Mrs Nightingale.' The doctor was working furiously to
deliver the placenta and stem the bleeding. 'You have a lovely little son.'

A warm feeling crept over her. William Christopher Nightingale was
born, and nothing else mattered as she slipped into unconsciousness.

Chapter Thirty-Three

Hours later, she came to. She ached all over and there seemed to be wires and drips attached to every inch of her. Mrs Pope was sitting at the side of the bed and as Claire stirred she bent and kissed her lightly on the forehead.

'You've got a lovely little boy, Claire.' Her eyes were full of tears.

Claire's heart filled with joy. 'Where is he?' she asked faintly.

'He's in Intensive Care, but I'm sure they'll let you see him soon.'

Claire had lost a tremendous amount of blood, and was very weak but happy. They remained in silence for some time, Claire drawing comfort from the older woman's presence. It came to her that in all the time she had known her, she had never discovered what her first name was. It didn't really matter. She would always be simply Mrs Pope to Claire now. Eventually the doctor who had delivered the baby entered the ward and approached the bed.

'Ah, so you're back with us then, are you?' He smiled. 'How are you feeling now, Mrs Nightingale? I don't mind telling you, you had us worried for a time back there.'

His eyes as he looked down at her were kindly and Claire managed to smile back. 'I want to see my son,' she told him.

The doctor drew up a chair to the side of the bed and sat down. 'We'll take you to see him in a while,' he promised. 'But I ought to warn you . . . he's very tiny and the way we had to deliver him so quickly was a great shock to him.'

Claire's worried eyes were fast on his face. 'He will be all right though, won't he?'

The doctor patted her hand. 'We're doing all we can.'

Claire began to cry and Mrs Pope looked as if she would too at any minute.

'Please let me see him,' begged Claire, and after hesitating for an instant, the doctor made a decision.

'All right then,' he conceded. 'But you'll have to go in a wheelchair, and it's only for a minute, mind.'

He didn't want her to get too distressed in her present state, and would much rather she had stayed in bed. But then, he could understand her need to see her baby. He hurried away to speak to the ward sister, and within minutes a nurse pushed a wheelchair to the side of Claire's bed. It took all of the nurse's and Mrs Pope's efforts to get Claire into it, as she had so little strength. But she was determined to see her baby, and soon Mrs Pope was pushing her along the corridors with the nurse beside them, wheeling the stand that held all the drips. At last they came to the Intensive Care Unit and were admitted inside. A number of clear glass incubators stood along one wall and Claire noticed that most of them were empty. The nurse pointed to one at the far end. Another nurse was standing beside it, writing notes, and as they approached she smiled at Claire encouragingly.

'Mrs Nightingale?'

Claire nodded, her face ashen. As the nurse stood aside, Claire had her first proper look at her son. He was incredibly tiny, and so perfect that a rush of love for him swept through her. He looked nothing like Greg at all, but took after her, with blond hair and blue eyes. Claire would have given anything she owned at that moment to hold him, but knew that was impossible. There were tubes and drips all over him, and she noticed immediately that he was on a ventilator. The sight of it made her heart lurch but the nurse quickly assured her, 'It's all right, Mrs Nightingale. Your baby was very early, which is why the ventilator is there, to help him breathe until he gets a little stronger. But look, you can put your hand in and touch him if you like.'

There was a hole in one side of the incubator and Claire now tentatively put her hand inside and touched him. The nurse and Mrs Pope then tactfully retreated to the far end of the room to give Claire a few moments alone with her baby.

She stroked his arm, and gazed at him with all the love she felt for him shining in her eyes. His skin was incredibly soft, and he looked so sweet and innocent.

'Hello, William.' Tears slid down her cheeks. 'I'm your mummy and I love you so much,' she told him. 'You are the best thing that has ever happened to me. You just hurry and get stronger now, do you hear me?'

The baby stirred slightly as if he understood what she was saying, and as she tenderly stroked him, his tiny hand curled around her little finger. She was totally wrapped in wonder at how beautiful he was, and would gladly have sat beside him all night. But soon the nurse came and gently ushered her away.

'He needs complete rest for now,' she advised gently. 'And so do you.' Claire nodded, devastated at the thought of leaving him. It was so cold and clinical here, but she knew that for now at least he was in the best place. By the time she was wheeled back into her own ward, she was completely exhausted but feeling easier.

As they helped her back into bed she smiled at Mrs Pope sleepily. 'He's a lovely baby, isn't he?'

Mrs Pope nodded, choked. 'He's the most beautiful baby I've ever seen,' she agreed.

Sighing contentedly, Claire's head slipped to one side of the pillow and within seconds she was fast asleep.

The sound of a gentle voice woke her in the early hours of the next morning. Claire struggled to open her eyes, to find a nurse bending over her.

'Mrs Nightingale, the Intensive Care Unit has just phoned the ward to ask if you would like to go and be with your baby?'

Every instinct she had screamed at Claire that something was wrong. The ward was in semi-darkness and so quiet that she could have heard a pin drop as she asked fearfully, 'Is something wrong? Is he ill?'

The nurse nervously straightened the bedclothes. 'I can't answer that question, Mrs Nightingale. The doctor on duty will explain everything when we get you down there. Now, would you like me to take you to him? I have a wheelchair all ready.'

Claire swallowed as panic engulfed her. This couldn't be happening – not after what had already gone before. William was perfect – she had seen it for herself. But why then would they be sending for her at this ungodly hour unless something was wrong? There had to be some mistake. Perhaps it was someone else's baby who was ill?

As she swung her legs to the edge of the bed everything started to swim around her, but she gritted her teeth and with the help of the young nurse, managed to shrug her arms into her dressing-gown before clambering awkwardly into the waiting wheelchair.

The journey to the ICU seemed to take for ever but at last they arrived, to be met by a solemn-faced doctor, who wheeled Claire straight into a small office at the side of the ward.

'Mrs Nightingale,' he began without preamble. He had faced this situation too many times before and as there was no easy way of saying what had to be said, he came straight to the point. 'I'm afraid William is very ill indeed.'

'But . . . but why? I thought he was just in here for observation until he got stronger?'

The man sighed as he took his glasses from the end of his nose and studiously began to polish them on the edge of his crisp white coat.

'Your baby is suffering from hypoxia, Claire. We have had the results of the blood-gas tests we took and they were not promising.'

When Claire looked totally bewildered he told her, 'Hypoxia leads to respiratory failure. Many premature babies suffer from it because their lungs are not completely developed. I'm afraid William has slowly deteriorated throughout the last few hours and as I said, the blood-gas tests showed that his lung function is severely compromised. It means he can't and won't ever be able to breathe for himself. So now . . .'

'Now *what?*'

'I think the kindest thing to do would be for you to permit us to turn off the ventilator and allow him to have whatever time he has left in comfort.'

'You mean . . . he's going to *die?*'

'Yes, Mrs Nightingale, I'm afraid he is. I assure you we have done all we can but there is nothing more we can do. I'm so very, very sorry.'

Claire tried to absorb what the doctor was telling her. This couldn't be happening. *It couldn't be.*

'So, would you like us to get him out of his incubator so that you can hold him?'

The doctor's voice pulled her sharply back to the present. She wanted to scream and cry, but somehow the noises seemed to be locked somewhere deep inside her.

'Are you *quite* sure that there's nothing more you can do?' Her voice was strangely calm.

'I'm afraid so.'

She nodded numbly and the doctor strode from the room as she sat there with her life falling apart around her, staring blankly off into space.

Some minutes later, he returned and wheeled her to the side of William's little incubator. A nurse was standing there with William in her arms, and for the first time Claire saw him properly without all the wires and drips attached to him. The nurse placed him gently into her waiting arms and then she and the doctor slipped away as Claire held her baby son to her and crooned a lullaby.

William Nightingale died peacefully in his mother's arms at 3.05 that morning, and a little piece of Claire died with him.

'Ah, you're awake, Mrs Nightingale.' The nurse seemed nervous. Claire had just lain there with the curtains drawn tight about her bed and without making a sound since they had brought her back to the ward in the early hours of the morning. 'I'll just go and get you a cup of tea, shall I?'

Before Claire could answer her, she was gone.

Through the curtains she could hear the sounds of the other women on the ward tending to their babies, and it hit her afresh that she would never tend to William now. Yet still the tears stayed trapped inside, like a great choking lump in her throat that refused to budge.

Claire lay waiting for the nurse to come back, but when the curtains eventually parted, it was a doctor who stepped through them. He came and perched on the edge of the bed at the side of her, and Claire stared at him dully. It was the same doctor who had tended to William.

'I just thought I'd pop in and see how you are doing,' he said.

When she remained silent he looked at her gravely. There was a closed look in her eyes as if she had shut herself away from the world and he felt powerless to help her.

There was not a single tear. The terrible pain she was feeling went too deep for tears. Even the pain she had endured in labour was as nothing compared to this, and now she just wanted him to leave so that she could be alone with her loss.

'Is there anyone I can call for you?' he enquired tentatively.

Claire shook her head. She was as white as the sheets she lay upon and the doctor's heart went out to her. Word of her husband's death only days before had swept through the hospital like wildfire and he wondered how she would cope with yet another loss so soon. He stood up, his shoulders stooped, and after awkwardly patting her hand he wearily disappeared through the curtains.

Claire just lay there, her eyes fixed on the ceiling above. Strangely, she felt nothing. It was as if all sensation had been drained from her. She had longed and yearned for this baby; all her hopes and dreams had been pinned upon him and now he was gone too, the way everything else that was good in her life had gone before. But she wouldn't fight this time; she was tired of fighting. It felt suddenly as if her whole life had been one long struggle to survive, and now she didn't want to fight any more. She just wanted to close her eyes, go to sleep and be with her baby, never to wake up again.

Mrs Pope was totally devastated when she arrived at the hospital. She sat for hours at the side of Claire's bed, chattering, nagging, crying and doing anything she could think of to bring the girl back from the silent world she had entered. But it was all to no avail. They asked Claire if she wanted to see her baby again, before his funeral, but she just shook her head. The day following the baby's death, Greg was buried but Claire still lay in hospital, seemingly oblivious to all that went on around her.

Mrs Pope was almost at her wits' end. Nikki and Cassidy were staying with Mary, and Nikki begged Mrs Pope to let her go and see Claire. Mrs Pope refused. She didn't want the girl to see her stepmother that way, and didn't think that Claire would want her to.

'I don't know what to do,' she confessed to Mary tearfully. 'It's as if she's lost the will to live.'

Mary nodded sadly. 'Well, we've got to pull her out of it. Nikki really needs her right now.'

Mrs Pope nodded thoughtfully. Mary had just given her an idea, and the very same afternoon when she visited the hospital, she put it into practice.

Claire still lay as if she hadn't moved since Mrs Pope last left her as the older woman sat down and took her hand.

'I know this is hard, love,' she whispered. 'We all wanted this baby, but you know, there's someone else who really needs you right now.' Claire's eyes didn't even blink and a single desperate tear slipped down Mrs Pope's cheek.

'It's Nikki,' she went on desperately. 'She misses you so much; you're all she's got left now and she's so very lonely.' For a second she thought that Claire hadn't heard her. But then, to her joy, Claire's head slowly turned and when she looked at her, there was recognition in her eyes.

Mrs Pope pulled Claire's thin body into her warm, motherly arms. If she was not very much mistaken, Claire had just taken her first step back towards them. She was right; the mention of Nikki's name had touched something deep within Claire's frozen heart. For a time she had switched off her feelings; they were too painful for her to endure. But now she knew that she must go on, for Nikki's sake if nothing else. The staff were as pleased as Mrs Pope to see Claire responding to them; they all felt sorry for this young woman who had suffered two such terrible tragedies in a short time.

For the first time in days Claire ate and drank a little, and at teatime the doctor came to see her. He was vastly relieved to see that she had come out of her trance-like state. They had moved her into a private room, where the cries of the other babies couldn't distress her. And although she was pale and weak, he felt that she was finally on her slow journey to recovery.

'I want to go home,' she told him. He nodded. In his opinion that would be wise as there was nothing else that they could do for her now. He had done all he could to repair her body, but only time could heal her mind.

'I don't see why you shouldn't,' he said. 'How about going home in the morning? Can someone come to collect you?'

Claire nodded. She was longing to see Nikki now, but there was something that had to be done first.

'I want to see my baby one last time,' she said.

He nodded understandingly. As yet she hadn't shed a single tear at her loss, and the doctor knew only too well from past experience that this was deeply unhealthy. Tears to his mind were a great healer, and he had no desire to stand in the way of her request.

'I'll arrange it.' Turning about, he quietly left the room, heading for the mortuary.

Almost an hour later, a nurse entered, carrying a Moses basket. She said not a word, but placed it gently on the end of the bed, then silently slipped from the room.

Claire stared at the basket for some minutes before cautiously reaching out and lifting it towards her. They had dressed William in a tiny blue romper suit and he looked so peaceful that Claire could almost have believed he was fast asleep. His long eyelashes curled on his cheeks and he looked even tinier than she remembered him, almost like a little doll. Tentatively, Claire lifted him into her arms and unwrapped the shawl that he was swathed in. A picture of the beautiful shawl that Mrs Pope had crocheted for his christening appeared before her eyes, and it hit her then that now he would never be christened in it. A great lump swelled in her throat as she cuddled him to her. He felt so right in her arms. But this would be the only time she would ever hold him and suddenly, the huge lump erupted into great soul-shaking sobs. As tears splashed onto his perfect little face Claire kissed them away, trying to memorise every tiny part of him. She felt as if her heart was breaking and the pain that ripped through her was worse than any she had ever felt before. He had been hers for such a short time, but her love was so deep, that she would never forget him for as long as she lived. When they finally took him away, they handed her a photograph of him. It would be placed with Yasmin's, his sister's, and treasured as hers was. Now she must go on for Nikki.

The next morning, Mrs Pope took her home.

Three days later, William Christopher Nightingale was laid to rest in a churchyard in Bispham. It was a simple service with few mourners. Only Claire, Nikki, Mrs Pope, Betty, Mary and their husbands attended.

A watery sun shone down on the little crowd assembled at the graveside as his tiny white coffin was lowered into the earth. William was wrapped in the beautiful shawl that Mrs Pope had so lovingly made for him, and at his side was a teddy bear that Nikki had bought for her little brother. As for Claire, she put in a part of her heart.

Chapter Thirty-Four

'Why Betty, you're a sight for sore eyes. Come on in out of the cold an' I'll make us a nice cup o' tea.' Mrs Pope held the door wide as Betty stepped past her into the hallway.

'Where are they then?' she enquired as she followed Mrs Pope into the kitchen.

'They've taken Cassidy down onto the beach.'

'Oh, I would have thought the weather would have put them off.' Betty shrugged off her coat and dropped gratefully onto a kitchen chair.

'No, it would take worse weather than this to do that. They're down there morning noon an' night. At least, that's how it seems. Still, if they can find some comfort there I suppose it's not a bad thing.'

Betty nodded. 'How are they?'

'Not good, but then I don't suppose we could expect them to be, could we? They reckon as the good Lord never places more on your shoulders than you're able to bear, but between you and me, I reckon Claire has had more heartbreak these last few weeks than most souls have to bear in an entire lifetime. It just doesn't seem fair, does it?'

Betty shook her head as Mrs Pope joined her at the table with two mugs of tea. 'So how long will you be staying?' she asked.

'For as long as they need me,' Mrs Pope replied quietly, producing the biscuit tin, and the two women lapsed into silence.

Six weeks after William's funeral Nikki returned to school. Claire was relieved. There were a lot of things that needed attending to, but up until now she hadn't felt ready to do anything. Mrs Pope finally returned to her own home, and Claire wondered how she could ever repay her for what she had done. Cards of condolence still arrived daily, but she tore them up and threw them into the bin unread. She was glad that Greg was dead and couldn't pretend otherwise.

She made an appointment to see Mr Temple, Greg's solicitor, and on a blustery day in November, she set off to keep it. When she entered the office he shook her hand firmly. He was a distinguished-looking man in his mid-fifties; he was also highly efficient and on his desk was a huge pile of papers ready to go through with her. Her heart sank when she saw them, but his manner gave her confidence. He eyed her admiringly. She was dressed in a plain Chanel suit and looked sophisticated and elegant, her figure back to normal. She held herself proudly, only the raw pain in her eyes giving any hint to the tragedies she had recently endured.

'Don't worry, Mrs Nightingale, it isn't as bad as it looks.'

Claire inclined her head. 'I'm pleased to hear it.'

She took a seat, and soon Mr Temple was explaining her financial position to her. He had taken it upon himself to approach Greg's two business partners, regarding Greg's share of the partnership, and they were willing to buy it from Claire. The price that they had offered was more than fair, and seemed to her to be a ridiculously large sum of money. Luckily, he had also drawn up a new will for Greg shortly after the marriage, and Nightingale Lodge and the cars belonged to her too, together with various insurance policies and pensions which added up to a huge amount.

Claire signed numerous documents and forms without a qualm. She didn't even bother to read most of them as she trusted Mr Temple implicitly. Soon the daunting pile of papers in front of them began to shrink. She then requested him to set up a trust fund for Nikki, to be available to her on her twenty-first birthday.

Mr Temple looked at her with respect, since the amount that she was asking him to transfer totalled half of her inheritance. In truth, Claire would have loved nothing more than to sign away every penny; she had learned the hard way that money didn't buy contentment. However, commonsense told her that she and Nikki needed something to live on. Even after setting up the fund, the money that she already had in the bank from the sale of the Seabourne Hotel, plus the money that Greg had left her, made her a very wealthy young widow. It had all been far more straightforward than she had dared to hope, and she was more than happy to leave everything in Mr Temple's capable hands.

Once the financial details had been sorted, he said there was one more matter that he needed to discuss with her. He asked his secretary to make them some coffee, and then broached the subject on his mind.

'May I ask,' he said tentatively, 'what is going to happen to Nikki now? Do you intend to keep her with you?'

Claire gazed at him, amazed that he would even ask. 'Of course she'll stay with me!' she declared indignantly.

He smiled with relief, then strummed his fingers on the edge of the table and went on: 'Mrs Nightingale . . . did your husband ever tell you that Nicole was his *adopted* daughter?'

Claire's mouth dropped open and she sat in stunned silence for some minutes, trying to absorb his words. When his secretary entered the office and placed a tray of coffee on the desk, Claire was so lost in thought that she barely noticed her. *Nikki was adopted.*

'Are you quite sure?' she stammered eventually.

He nodded. 'Oh yes, I'm quite sure. I actually have her adoption papers in my safe, along with the deeds to your house. I hate to raise the matter so soon after your loss, but you see, legally, you have no claim on her. However, if you intend to keep her, then I'm sure that I will be able to help you.'

Claire was completely lost for words.

'I'm surprised Greg didn't tell you,' Mr Temple admitted. 'I believe that he and the first Mrs Nightingale adopted Nikki when she was just a baby. Apparently the first Mrs Nightingale couldn't have children of her own for medical reasons, and I believe that they adopted Nicole shortly before they moved to Bispham.'

It was too much to take in and Claire's mind reeled.

'Look, I could show you the adoption papers, if you like,' he offered. 'In the circumstances I see no reason why you shouldn't look at them.' The solicitor was deeply sorry to give her yet another shock, so soon after her husband and baby's deaths, and in that moment he felt angry towards Greg for not being honest with her.

'I'll go and get them from my safe.' He excused himself, and Claire's confused eyes followed him from the room. Minutes later, he returned. Claire was sitting exactly where he had left her and he eyed her ashen face with concern. Sitting back down at his desk, he began to draw documents from a large brown envelope.

'Ah, here we are then.' He passed her an official-looking document and

Claire's eyes scanned it. He was telling the truth. It bore an official court stamp and the date on which the adoption had taken place. Nikki really was Greg's adopted child. The words suddenly blurred one into the other, and Claire had to grip the edge of the desk, as the floor rushed up to meet her. The colour had completely drained from her face and Mr Temple stared at her in alarm.

'Are you all right, my dear?' His voice seemed to come from a long, long way away.

With an effort, Claire managed to nod. 'Yes, yes, I'm all right,' she assured him, as her eyes flew back to the paper trembling in her hands. She was remembering the baby that she had given up what seemed like a lifetime ago. It was unbelievable to discover that Nikki had been adopted too, and yet the evidence was here in her hands in black and white. She was vaguely aware that Mr Temple was staring at her, a deep frown on his forehead. With a great effort she pulled herself together and handed back the paper.

'Please excuse me,' she apologised shakily. 'It's just that this has come as a bit of a shock after everything else that's happened.'

He nodded understandingly. 'Of course it must have,' he agreed. 'But if you'd like me to set the wheels in motion so that she's legally yours, we could apply for either a Residence Order or you could adopt. I really don't envisage any problems at all. You obviously care for the child and I assume your feelings are returned. I doubt there's a court in the land that would consider separating you under the circumstances. However, if you need a little time to consider which course of action you'd prefer to take, I'd quite understand.'

'I want to adopt,' Claire said immediately, and for the first time in weeks, she felt a sense of joy. She was going to adopt Nikki!

Mr Temple went on to conclude their business. His words passed over Claire's head and finally, after a firm handshake, she left his office on legs that had suddenly turned to jelly. She sat outside his office in her car for a long time, unable to trust herself to drive just yet, whilst the news she had just learned sank in.

Mr Temple had told her that she could adopt Nikki, and once she had, no one would ever be able to separate them. Finally she managed to calm down a little, and after starting up the engine she headed for home.

★   ★   ★

Claire felt that if she didn't share her news with someone, she would burst. Mrs Pope was the first person who sprang to mind. The woman was waiting for her in the hall when she arrived; she still came every day, as much in the role of a friend now as a housekeeper. When Claire saw her kindly face, she did something that she had never done before. To Mrs Pope's amazement, she fell into her arms and sobbed as if her heart would break.

'Oh, dear me, what's happened now?' Mrs Pope fussed. She sat the young woman down in the kitchen and made her a strong cup of tea.

When Claire had finally composed herself, she stared across the table at Mrs Pope. She had always found it hard to trust anyone, but she felt that she could trust this kindly women. Choosing her words carefully, she began to tell her of Nikki's adoption. Like herself, Mrs Pope had been totally unaware of it, and assured Claire that neither Greg nor the first Mrs Nightingale had ever breathed a word of it. Mrs Pope was almost as stunned as she had been. But now Claire was faced with a dilemma.

'What should I do?' she asked. 'Should I tell her the truth, or should I just leave things as they are?'

Mrs Pope could see the predicament that Claire was in, but to her mind, this matter needed a lot of thought before a decision was made.

'I'd sleep on it,' she advised. 'It's easy to let your heart rule your head and go in like a bull in a china shop, but you have to decide what's best for Nikki. She's been through a lot lately, and we don't want to set her back again, do we?'

Claire shook her head. She longed to tell Nikki the truth, but could see the wisdom of Mrs Pope's words and respected her opinion.

'I think you're right,' she agreed. 'I'll sleep on it and then decide what to do.' That proved to be much easier said than done, for the minute Nikki walked through the door that afternoon, Claire had an overwhelming urge to hug her and tell her that she was about to be adopted for the second time. Only Mrs Pope's eyes on her made her stop herself as a warm smile passed between them.

That night, Claire couldn't sleep; she paced the bedroom restlessly as she tried to decide what to do for the best. By the next morning, after she had seen Nikki off to school and Mrs Pope had arrived, she still hadn't decided.

It was Mrs Pope who made her mind up for her. 'I'd tell her,' she said calmly. 'I've been up half the night thinking about it, and I think she has a right to know.' And so the decision was made.

That evening, when she and Nikki were curled up on the sofa together with Cassidy at their feet, Claire plucked up courage and began. 'Nikki, I have something to tell you.' The girl's eyes were instantly fearful, and Claire said immediately, 'It's all right, it isn't something bad. In fact, I hope you'll think it's something wonderful, as I do.'

'You're not going to leave me, are you?' Nikki asked.

Claire hugged her fiercely. '*Never*,' she promised. 'But I'm going to tell you a story about something that happened to me when I was just fourteen. It's something that I've never told to anyone before, not even your dad.'

Intrigued, Nikki nodded. She loved stories and Claire went on, choosing her words carefully. 'Well, you see, when I was a little girl my mum wasn't able to look after me so I went to live with a foster mum and dad.'

Nikki was horrified. 'Were they horrible to you?'

Claire shook her head sadly as memories poured back. 'No, they weren't. It was quite the opposite – *I* was horrible to *them*. You see, I was hurting inside because my real mum had let me down, and I wouldn't allow myself to love them.'

Nikki frowned. This was a sad story, but she wanted to hear it all the same.

'Anyway, when I was fourteen,' Claire went on, 'I got pregnant and I had a beautiful baby girl. But I had no way of looking after her, so I decided it would be better if she went to a mummy and daddy who could love her and give her everything she needed. So I . . . I gave her away.'

Nikki's eyes filled with tears. 'Didn't you love her then?'

Claire nodded quickly. 'Oh yes, I loved her very much indeed. That's why I gave her away, because I wanted her to be happy. But every single day since then I've missed her – and yesterday I found something out, Nikki.'

The girl's eyes were as big as saucers. She was totally intrigued now. 'What did you find out?'

'Well, Mr Temple, your dad's solicitor, told me that you were adopted when you were just a baby too.'

Nikki stared at her in disbelief, trying to take this shocking news in. 'You mean my mum and dad weren't my *real* ones?' she asked, and Claire nodded.

She stared at her, praying that Nikki would understand. '*I'm* going to adopt you now, Nikki, and then I promise that no one will ever hurt you again.' Suddenly they were both crying as Nikki threw herself into Claire's arms.

'You mean you'll be my *real* mum?'

Claire stroked her silken hair, her heart full of love. 'Yes, Nikki, I'll be your real mum.' She meant every single word she said. She had been through so much, but now she had something to live for again. She had lost her son but was to gain a daughter. Now the healing could begin.

A social worker visited first Claire, then Nikki, frequently over the next few weeks. Claire filled in numerous forms and answered endless questions. The woman was content with what she saw. Claire and Nikki were obviously very close and the woman assured them that she could see no problem at all with the adoption going ahead. Of course it would take a little time, but Claire had all the time in the world now. Mr Temple gave Claire a glowing reference, as did Mr Smythe, Greg's former business partner. And now it was just a case of waiting for the proposed adoption to be approved in court.

Claire continued to keep her diary up to date whilst Nikki was at school, and when Mrs Pope had a rare day off. She held back nothing; her life-story was written from the heart. She wrote of the terrible shock she had experienced when she discovered Greg abusing Nikki; of his suicide, and of the utter devastation she had felt at the loss of her much longed-for son. She pressed a tiny lock of his hair between the pages, and her tears smudged the ink. Finally she wrote of the indescribable joy she had felt when she realised that she would be allowed to adopt Nikki. The diary was now up to date, and it was time for Claire to go on, but there was one more thing she had to do first. Something that she had been putting off because she knew that it would be painful.

She made her way along the landing, and for the first time since she had come home from the hospital, she entered the nursery. It was just as she had left it. The winter sunshine shone through the window onto the cot so lovingly chosen by herself and Nikki, and onto the drawers and wardrobes bulging with tiny clothes that would now never be worn. The brightly coloured windchimes, made up of tiny farmyard animals, tinkled merrily in the draught from the door, and Claire stared about her sadly.

Yet despite the pain, the memory of the baby this room had been so lovingly created for was sweet. It was time to let him go. She had lost two babies, but now she had Nikki, and from now on she would live for her. Give her everything that she herself had never had.

Claire looked around for one last time then, closing the door, she locked it securely. She put the key into the back of her drawer with the diary, silently vowing that she would never enter the nursery again. William was in her past. Nikki was her future.

Chapter Thirty-Five

Christmas 1996 and the New Year of 1997 came and went uneventfully. Claire, Nikki and Mrs Pope spent the holiday period quietly at home. It was a surprisingly relaxed and happy time. There were no formal dinners, no reason to wear cocktail dresses; the three of them just ate when and what they wanted, and dressed in comfy clothes. On Christmas morning, they woke to find the world hidden beneath a blanket of crisp white snow. After eating the huge turkey dinner that Mrs Pope had cooked, Nikki, Claire and Cassidy spent an hour out in the garden playing snowballs and building a snowman as Mrs Pope watched from the kitchen window with an amused smile on her face.

Claire was now twenty-five years old. She was very attractive and very wealthy, and soon the dinner invitations from hopeful admirers began to arrive. Claire had no interest in any of them. She'd had enough of men to last her a lifetime, and had no intention of ever becoming entangled with anyone again. Nikki was her reason for being now, and that was how she wanted it to stay. She still went to see Mary and Betty occasionally, and was also now a regular visitor to Nikki's primary school, although the girl was due to start at a secondary school come September. She would go in for hours at a time helping children who were struggling with their maths or their reading. The teachers were more than grateful for her help.

The house was no longer the showplace it had resembled when Greg had been alive. Balls and roller-skates and various toys were often left lying about; Nikki regularly had friends to stay for sleepovers, and the sound of giggling was often heard coming from her room late at night as she and her visitors tucked into midnight feasts. Claire would smile at the sound. It was wonderful to hear Nikki laughing again after all she had been through.

*　　*　　*

In early April, when the spring flowers were turning the garden into a rainbow of colours, Claire received a phone call from Social Services. The date for the adoption hearing had been set for mid-June. When she put the phone down, she danced Mrs Pope around the spacious kitchen in her excitement. She could hardly believe it; she felt as if she was being given a second chance. It was a dream come true. Mrs Pope was delighted for her. To her mind, Claire had had a raw deal and deserved some happiness, and so did Nikki.

A few days later, as Claire and Mrs Pope were arranging some daffodils in vases, Nikki burst into the kitchen with a small friend in tow. 'Come on, Cassidy!' she cried. 'We're going to take you down on the beach.' Cassidy rose stiffly. He wasn't as young now as he had used to be, but he still loved the beach.

'Don't be too long,' Claire shouted as the boisterous little crowd disappeared through the back door. 'Your tea's nearly ready.'

'I won't, Mum.' The door banged shut behind her.

Claire stood rooted to the spot with shock. 'She called me Mum,' she said incredulously as tears slipped down her cheeks.

Mrs Pope grinned. 'Well, that's just as it should be,' she said softly. 'You *are* her mum.' And she knew even as the words left her lips that from now on, she wouldn't be needed. Nikki and Claire had found each other, just as it had been meant to be.

Claire sat back on her heels and wiped the sweat from her eyes. Even with the bedroom window wide open, and the curtains blowing in the sea breeze, the room was still stiflingly hot. Still, she was on the last lot now, thank goodness. She folded another jumper and loaded it into the box with the others. Then, turning to the bed, she lifted the last pile of perfectly folded shirts and put them in too. She sighed, glad that the job was done. She knew she should have tackled it long ago. Greg had been dead for almost a year now, but she had kept putting it off. Today, Nikki was staying overnight at a friend's, and as Claire had had nothing better to do, she had decided to get it over and done with, and out of the way. It had been easier than she had thought it would be. She had never loved Greg, and any feelings that she *had* felt for him had died on the night she had caught him abusing Nikki. She had phoned the local charity shop less than an hour ago and soon their van would come and take all of the boxes away. She could imagine their surprise and delight when they opened them. Greg had had very expensive tastes in clothes, and now she hoped that someone else would benefit from them.

She looked down to where Cassidy lay, as usual, not an arm's length from her. He had fallen fast asleep and was snoring softly. He slept a lot lately, and Claire wished that she could turn the clock back. She dreaded anything happening to him. Not just for her sake, but Nikki's too. Usually once the child got home from school they were inseparable and Nikki totally worshipped him. Nikki had come through her ordeal remarkably well, although she had become very clingy with Claire.

A young male teacher at her school had developed a crush on Claire not long ago, and Nikki had become remarkably possessive. But she needn't have worried because Claire had absolutely no interest in him.

Nikki was beginning to feel more secure now and tonight would be the second night she had spent at her friend's house in as many weeks. Claire took this as a good sign and encouraged it. She wanted what was left of Nikki's childhood to be as normal as possible. That didn't stop Claire missing her when she was away, and now that she had finished packing up Greg's clothes, the rest of the day seemed to stretch endlessly before her.

Mrs Pope now only came twice a week and then only as a visitor, although she was still happy to babysit for Claire if ever she needed her, which was seldom. Usually, Claire took Nikki with her if she went out. Mrs Pope, like Cassidy, was beginning to feel her age, and now that Claire and Nikki were settled, was glad to be able to retire and spend more time in her own home. Claire would never forget how good she had been to her when she needed her, and there was nothing she wouldn't have done for her, had the woman asked.

She carried the heavy boxes downstairs one by one and stacked them all neatly by the front door, and had just heaved the last one into position when the charity shop's van pulled up. She watched Greg's clothes being loaded into it and driven away without a qualm. Thank goodness they were gone.

After making herself a cool drink, she pottered about in the garden for a time. After tea, she was just about to take Cassidy on his usual stroll along the beach when the phone rang. Hurrying into the hall, she answered it.

'Hello, Mum. It's me, Nikki.'

Claire smiled. 'Hello, sweetheart. Are you having a good time?'

'Oh yes. Laura's mum wants to know if it's all right if she takes us to the pictures?'

'Of course it is,' Claire assured her. 'You just have a good time and I'll see you tomorrow. And Nikki . . . I love you.'

'I love you too, Mum. Bye.'

The phone went dead in her hand and Claire slowly replaced it in its cradle, suddenly feeling incredibly lonely. As she glanced down she saw Cassidy sitting at her feet looking up at her expectantly and she grinned.

'Aw well. At least I've still got you to keep me company, haven't I, my old faithful? Come on. Let's see if we can't walk ourselves into a happier frame of mind, eh?'

Once on the beach she wandered along with Cassidy pottering contentedly at her side. At one time he would have raced excitedly ahead. But his days of chasing seagulls were long gone, and now he was happy to keep to Claire's pace.

For some reason, Claire had felt strangely restless lately, and thought that perhaps the house had something to do with it. It was a beautiful house, she couldn't deny it, but it was far too big for just her and Nikki. At one time she had dreamed of filling it with children, but that dream had died with Greg and now she and Nikki rattled about in it like two peas in a pod. The deeds to it had been changed into her name and were locked securely into Mr Temple's safe. She would have sold it in a minute and moved to something smaller and more manageable. It held very few happy memories for her now, but she worried about how Nikki might react to the thought of moving, and as yet, hadn't dared to broach the subject. Some day she would; she just had to wait for the right time.

The right time didn't come until a particularly bitterly cold day in October. Claire had picked Nikki up from school in her car because it was raining heavily, and on the way home Nikki was full of her friend Laura's news.

'Guess what?' she said. 'Laura and her mum and dad are selling their house and moving to a new one.'

'Are they?' Claire peeped at her out of the corner of her eye. 'It sounds like Laura's pretty pleased about it.'

'Oh, she is! When they get their new house, Laura is being allowed to choose everything for her new bedroom.'

'Mm, sounds exciting.'

Nikki nodded in agreement.

Claire didn't think there would ever be a more opportune moment to voice her idea. 'Have you ever thought about us moving house?' she asked, and to her amazement Nikki nodded.

'Lots of times,' she said. 'Sometimes I feel that we're a little out of the way where we are. It would be nice to live nearer to town.' 'I'd like to be able to walk to my new school next year.'

'Yes, I've thought the same,' Claire admitted. 'Plus our house is a little large just for us two, isn't it?'

Nikki nodded in complete agreement and for the rest of the journey home they weighed up the pros and cons of moving house. They continued their discussion over tea, and right up until Nikki's bedtime, and by then they had made their decision. They were going to move house. Claire couldn't believe how easy it had been and wished now that she had suggested it before, but there was no rush. They had all the time in the world.

The next day Claire rang a local estate agent and the day after that he came out to give her a valuation. Almost before she knew it, Nightingale Lodge was up for sale and all she had to do now was to wait for a buyer. She and Nikki could then begin to look around for something more suitable.

In late October they suffered two weeks of gale-force winds. The sand blew from the beach almost up to the front door. It was so bad that Claire wouldn't allow Nikki to take Cassidy for his walks on the beach. Mrs Pope dared not venture out, and so now it was Claire and Nikki who visited her. She was always delighted to see them, though she continuously scolded Claire. 'You ought to get out more. It's not natural for a young woman your age to stay in all the while. You know I'm always happy to have Nikki.'

'I know you are,' said Claire gratefully. 'But I'm fine, really. There's nowhere I want to go.'

Mrs Pope sniffed. 'Well, I still say it's not natural,' she said huffily.

Claire grinned. She was sure that Mrs Pope had a heart made of pure gold.

Thankfully the gales ended, but they were replaced with bitterly cold frosts that turned everything white and made it treacherously slippery underfoot. Claire and Nikki began to feel housebound.

'Cassidy misses his walks on the beach,' Nikki moaned.

Claire grinned. 'You mean *you* do.'

Nikki grinned back.

'I'll tell you what,' Claire promised. 'The first half-decent day we have, we'll take him.'

Nikki nodded, and three days later, after school one afternoon, they set off, huddled up in gloves, hats and scarves. The wind had dropped slightly but the sky was heavy and overcast.

'We hadn't better be long.' Claire cast a worried glance at the dark skies. 'I've got a feeling we're in for a downpour.'

Nikki laughed and ran on ahead as Cassidy did his best to keep up with her. The waves pounded onto the beach but they hadn't gone far when, just as Claire had predicted, the first heavy drops of rain began to fall.

'Come on, Nikki.' She had to shout to make herself heard above the roaring waves. 'We'd better get back or else we're going to get soaked to the skin.'

Nikki turned reluctantly and once she was at Claire's side they joined hands and began to hurry, heads bent against the wind that had suddenly blown up again. They had just reached the sand dunes when there was a loud clap of thunder and the heavens seemed to open. The rain literally poured down and within seconds they were drenched to the skin. By the time they reached the shelter of the imposing porch, they resembled three drowned rats. Water was dripping from them and Nikki, catching sight of Cassidy, began to giggle. His shaggy coat was plastered to him and he looked very sorry for himself. As if he realised that she was laughing at him, he shook himself furiously and Nikki was covered in wet sand. Claire grinned at the comical picture they presented.

'Come on, you pair,' she ordered. 'Let's get inside before we all catch our death of cold.'

She sent Nikki straight off to the shower. Then she took Cassidy into the kitchen and began to rub him down with a towel. Once he was dry she tucked him into his basket with a warm blanket and made herself and Nikki a hot drink. The weather worsened and by the time they went to bed, the wind was howling about the house and the rain was coming down in torrents. Claire tucked Nikki in; Cassidy was already fast asleep in the basket at the side of her bed.

'Look at him, you've worn him out,' she told Nikki, and after giving her a kiss and a hug, she made her way to bed.

It was the early hours of the morning when the sound of her bedroom door being flung open made her start awake. Nikki was standing in the doorway, agitated and close to tears. 'Mum, it's Cassidy. He's not well.'

Claire instantly swung her legs out of the warm bed. 'What's wrong with him?' She struggled into her dressing-gown.

Nikki's lip trembled. 'I don't know, but he's breathing sort of funny like. Will you come and see him?'

Claire gave her a comforting hug. 'Of course I will.' Hand-in-hand, they hurried back to Nikki's room. Cassidy still lay in his basket and Claire saw at a glance that Nikki was right. His chest was rising and falling alarmingly with each breath and instead of wagging his tail at the sight of her as he usually did, he looked at her appealingly with his soulful brown eyes.

Dropping to her knees beside him, Claire stroked him. He was shivering spasmodically, yet he was hot to the touch, and his nose was dry and burning.

'Oh you poor thing,' she said softly. She was worried, but kept herself calm for Nikki's sake. 'Go and fetch him a bowl of cold water,' she ordered, and without question Nikki flew from the room to do as she was told.

Minutes later she ran back in, with Cassidy's water bowl held before her. She had spilled most of it on her way up the stairs, and it was now less than half-full. It didn't matter because Cassidy turned his head away from it.

'Look, you've got to get up for school in the morning,' Claire said. 'I'll take him into my room for the rest of the night and you try and get some sleep.'

Nikki shook her head but Claire was firm. 'Come on,' she urged. 'Into bed, young lady, do as you're told. Cassidy will be fine, he's probably just caught a chill, that's all.' She spoke with a confidence that she didn't feel and reluctantly Nikki climbed back into bed. Claire tucked the covers around her and gave her a gentle kiss.

'Are you sure it's just a chill?' Nikki asked her fearfully.

Claire nodded. 'I'm sure it is. He'll be as right as rain in the morning.'

Crossing to Cassidy again, Claire bent and lifted the basket into her arms and carried him into her room. She laid him down and stroked the wheezing animal lovingly as tears sprang to her eyes. The little dog had been a part of her life for so long. Somehow she couldn't envisage being without him and didn't know what to do. She was no vet, but she knew someone who was – Christian. She would have given anything for him to be here right now; he would have known what to do.

The rain lashed at the window as she sat there stroking the mongrel and talking to him soothingly. After another half an hour had passed his breathing became even more laboured and she knew that she must act. Making her way down to the hall she dialled the number of Seagull's Flight. There was no need to look in the phone book; she could remember it off by heart. It was almost three o'clock in the morning, but somehow she knew that Christian wouldn't mind. There was no thought of ringing anyone else. He was the only one she could trust with Cassidy's life. On the fourth ring his voice answered. 'Hello,' he said sleepily.

Claire's heart leaped into her throat. 'Hello, Christian, it's me . . . Claire.' Silence answered her. They hadn't spoken since before her marriage to Greg, and she guessed that her phone call must have come as a shock to him, particularly at three o'clock in the morning. 'I'm sorry to ring you at this hour,' she plunged on before she had a chance to lose her confidence, 'but it's Cassidy. He got drenched in that downpour we had yesterday afternoon and now he's having trouble breathing.'

This time he answered her. 'I'll be right there. Give me your address?'

Claire gave him directions and he hung up. Replacing the receiver, she mentally shook herself. Hearing his voice had brought back vivid memories. She clamped down on the feelings they awakened. What she had shared with him so briefly was well and truly in the past and must remain that way. Positioning herself by the front door, she looked down the drive for a sight of his headlights. At last they appeared, and minutes later he screeched to a halt and jumped out of the same old van clutching his bag. His hair was tousled and his eyes looked tired. She experienced a weird sense of déjà vu. He looked just as he had all those years ago on the night she had found Cassidy – and now, just as then, his mind was completely on his patient.

'Where is he?' he asked as he bounded up the steps. Without a word Claire led him upstairs.

She could have sworn that Cassidy recognised him even after all this time, for as Christian rushed into the bedroom, Cassidy's tail gave a feeble wag.

'Hello, old friend,' Christian said fondly, dropping onto his knees beside him. 'In the wars are we then, eh?' As he spoke gently to the little dog, his hands were expertly examining him. He listened to his heart, he looked into his mouth, his ears and eyes, and finally he sat back on his heels. 'Well, our old fellow's caught a nasty chill and no mistake,' he said sadly.

'Will you be able to help him?'

He smiled at her. 'I'll certainly do my best,' he promised as he snapped open his bag. He drew out a syringe and after filling it from a clear bottle he expertly injected Cassidy. It was done so gently that Cassidy didn't even flinch. 'That should make him feel more comfortable and ease any pain he has,' he told Claire. 'Now, where's the warmest room in the house?'

'The kitchen.' Claire didn't even have to think about it. The central-heating boiler was in there and that room was sheltered from the cold wind that blew in from the North Sea.

'Right then.' He lifted the little three-legged mongrel as if he were no heavier than a feather. 'Let's get him in there. He needs to be kept warm.'

Claire led the way, feeling easier in her mind now that Christian was there. She knew now that Cassidy would be all right, for she trusted Christian implicitly. He laid him down in his comfortable basket and as he sat back on his heels, Claire noticed that Christian looked worn out.

'Still working hard then?' she asked shyly.

'You could say that,' he replied. An awkward silence stretched between them as they avoided each other's eyes, until Claire broke it.

'Have you got time for a cup of tea? You look like you could use one.'

He nodded gratefully and soon they were sitting at the kitchen table whilst Christian kept one eye on his patient. 'I want you to try and get him to drink,' he told her and she nodded.

'How's Lianne?' she asked finally, for want of something to say, and when he ignored her question, she felt desperately embarrassed.

'I was sorry to hear about your husband,' he said instead.

Claire shrugged. This was awful. It was as if they were strangers, and she was relieved when he eventually stood up to leave.

'I'll be back to have a look at him first thing in the morning,' he promised.

Once he had gone she hurried back to the kitchen and sank down beside her faithful old friend. She was still there when Nikki came down for breakfast the next morning. Claire's eyes were red and sore from lack of sleep but thankfully Christian's injection seemed to have worked.

Nikki ran to him and cuddled him. 'He looks a bit better,' she cried delightedly.

Claire rose stiffly and made her some breakfast. It was a battle to get her to school that day; she didn't want to leave her pet but Claire promised that she would stay with him all day, and so reluctantly Nikki finally got into her uniform.

'*Promise* you won't leave him alone, Mum,' she begged again.

Claire nodded. 'I won't. Cross my heart and hope to die.' Laughing, she patted Nikki's bottom and pushed her out of the door. She felt absolutely exhausted but relieved. Cassidy's breathing seemed a little easier and so she sank down onto a chair at the table, rested her head on her crossed arms and before she knew it, had fallen fast asleep.

The ringing of the doorbell woke her almost an hour later. She jumped up startled, then hurried to answer it. As she caught sight of herself in the large mirror that hung in the hallway, she sighed with dismay. Her sweatshirt was creased and her hair looked like it hadn't been brushed for a month. But it was too late to worry about that now. Opening the door she found Christian standing on the doorstep. Her heart leaped at the sight of him. He took in her dishevelled appearance at a glance and his blue eyes twinkled.

'How's the patient today then?'

'Looking much better, thanks to you.' She led him to the kitchen and put the kettle on whilst Christian examined Cassidy.

'He does seem a little better today,' he agreed cautiously, but then, not wishing to build up her hopes. 'I'm really pleased with him, but he's not out of the woods yet. Not by a long shot.'

'What do you mean?' Claire was dismayed.

'Well, he's getting on a bit,' he said softly. 'Last night I wouldn't have given you tuppence for his chances, but he's a tough old chap.'

'He *will* make it.' But for all her brave words, Claire's lips trembled and her eyes filled with tears.

Christian hoped she would be right. He knew how much the little mongrel meant to her, but there was only so much he himself could do.

Claire turned abruptly to mash the tea. She was tired and weepy, and the last thing she wanted to do was burst into tears in front of Christian. Fortunately, he drank his tea quickly and left, explaining that he had a lot of other house calls to make, and Claire was almost relieved to see him go. Despite all the promises she had made to herself, seeing him again had thrown Claire into confusion, but it was madness. She had Nikki to think of now, and once the house was sold, they would move away and she would never see him again. Besides . . . there was Lianne. She sighed as his van disappeared down the drive then slowly made her way back to the kitchen and Cassidy, wondering as she went why it was that, every time she managed to get her life into some sort of pattern, something always happened to spoil it.

By the time Nikki arrived home from school, Cassidy did seem to have improved, and the girl was thrilled. She loved him almost as much as Claire did, and flatly refused to leave his side for a moment. He was still terribly weak, and when he attempted to rise from his basket, he fell back. He did take a drink, although he still refused any food.

'Don't worry, it's early days yet,' Claire said, as Nikki tried to tempt him with titbits.

It took Claire all her time to prise her daughter away from the little dog long enough to take a bath, and at bedtime she had to threaten the girl to get her to go to bed, but eventually she managed it.

By then, Claire had decided that she would take him into her own room to sleep, and she struggled up the stairs with his basket, placing it at the side of her bed within arm's reach. She then stepped into the shower and stood underneath the hot water, letting it wash away some of her cares. After putting on a clean nightdress, she climbed wearily into bed. Trailing her hand into Cassidy's basket, she gently stroked his furry head. His hot tongue softly licked her hand and he stared up at her. Her eyelids were drooping as she smiled at him sleepily.

'Right now, I want you all better in the morning, my old friend, do you hear me?' she ordered him, then still fondling his silky ears she sank into an exhausted sleep.

It was Nikki who woke her the next morning. Claire had intended to just have a nap, but had been so tired that she had slept straight through the night.

'His temperature's gone down, Mum!' Nikki cried happily. Only half-awake, Claire blinked at her. Yawning, she pulled herself up on to one elbow and gazed into Cassidy's basket. Just as Nikki had said, he did feel cooler. In fact, he felt cold – and as this thought registered, Claire was instantly wide awake. The little mongrel appeared to be fast asleep and looked incredibly peaceful.

Nikki's eyes were huge. 'Why won't he wake up, Mum?' she whispered.

Claire didn't answer. 'I'm going to call Christian, the vet friend of mine I told you about,' she threw over her shoulder as she ran to the phone. Christian answered immediately. He was in the middle of his breakfast and recognised her voice instantly.

'Please come,' she begged, in a deep panic now. 'I can't get Cassidy to wake up.'

'I'm on my way.'

When he arrived, he took the stairs two at a time with Claire close behind him, but the second he entered the bedroom, he knew that he was too late. Nikki was on her knees at the side of the basket, stroking Cassidy lovingly and she raised tear-stained eyes to him.

'Er . . . this is my daughter, Nikki,' Claire told him.

When Christian raised an eyebrow she quickly explained, 'Greg was her father but I've adopted her now.'

He smiled at the child kindly and then dropping to his knees, felt around the old dog's chest for a heartbeat. Just as he had feared, there was nothing. Nikki and Claire stood close together with their arms wrapped tight about each other. They stared at him hopefully but he slowly shook his head.

'I'm so sorry,' he told them. 'I'm afraid his old heart just packed up.'

Nikki began to sob brokenheartedly, and Claire's eyes were so full of pain that he felt his own eyes moisten.

'Would he have suffered?' she asked brokenly.

Christian shook his head. 'No, he wouldn't have felt a thing,' he promised. 'He would have just gone to sleep and peacefully slipped away.'

Claire was grateful for that at least. She couldn't have borne it if he had suffered. She remembered how he had stared up at her the night before and realised now that he had been saying goodbye. Then the tears came in a great gushing torrent, and suddenly Christian had her and Nikki wrapped in his great powerful arms and she clung to him unashamedly.

Some minutes later he led them from the room and down the stairs. After seating them both at the kitchen table, he then made them a strong pot of tea, but it sat in front of them untouched. Nikki was totally inconsolable as Claire tried to calm her. There was no way that Christian could bring himself to leave them in that state, so he sat back and waited patiently for their sobs to subside. After a time he slipped from the room and fetched Cassidy, still in his basket, down the stairs. He then covered him with his old blanket and placed him by the front door.

'What would you like me to do with his body?' he asked Claire. 'I could bury him in the garden for you, if you like?'

She shook her head. 'The house is up for sale, and once it's sold, I'd have to leave him here.'

He chewed on his lip. 'You could let me bury him at Seagull's Flight,' he suggested. 'He always loved it there, and me and Gran have opened a little pet cemetery now. It's very peaceful there; I think you'd like it.'

Claire thought about it. She remembered how Cassidy had loved to go there. A picture of herself, Christian and Cassidy walking the strays along the beach sprang to mind, and she smiled though her tears at the memory. She could think of no better place for Cassidy to rest in peace.

'He would have liked that.'

'Good. That's settled, then.' Christian went to load Claire's beloved pet into the back of his van. When he re-entered the kitchen, Claire had pulled herself together a little but Nikki was still sobbing.

'Would you like to see him buried?' he asked.

'Yes, please,' Claire and Nikki said in unison.

'Then come to Seagull's Flight at, say, two o'clock this afternoon after morning surgery and I'll have everything ready,' he promised.

Claire nodded numbly as Christian turned and walked away.

Chapter Thirty-Six

It was ten to two when, in a heavy downpour, Claire turned into the well-remembered drive that led to Seagull's Flight. The moment she pulled into the yard, Mrs M hurried out to meet her, sheltering under a big umbrella. The old lady wrapped her in her arms, and Claire felt as if she had never been away. She had missed this woman so very much, over the past four years, and her time spent helping with the dogs.

'I'm so sorry, love,' whispered Mrs M, then she smiled at Nikki. 'You must be Nikki,' she said, bustling her into the porch. 'And you're every bit as pretty as Christian said you were.' The child offered her a half-hearted smile, but Mrs M wasn't offended. She could understand how she must be feeling and only wished that they could have met under happier circumstances.

'Come away in, loves, Christian will call you when everything's ready.' So saying, she ushered them into the kitchen. They had barely sat down when Christian's large frame filled the kitchen doorway. His Barbour jacket was dripping with rain.

'Shall we start?' he asked, and the three of them rose from their seats. They followed him across the yard, and past the dog pens. Eventually they reached an enclosed area with a white picket fence around it, nestling in the sand dunes. It was partially sheltered here from the wind, and as the seagulls wheeled high in the sky overhead, Claire thought of how Cassidy would have loved it. They picked their way past tiny graves marked with neat little wooden crosses bearing the names of much-loved departed pets, until eventually Christian stopped at a small grave he had dug in the most sheltered corner of the pet cemetery. At the side of the grave was a simple wooden box and Claire guessed that this was Cassidy's coffin.

The rain was still pouring down from leaden skies as if the heavens were crying too, and Claire was glad. She couldn't have borne to bury Cassidy in the sunshine. He had loved it so much. Christian had no wish to prolong their agony, and so without a word he lowered the little box into the grave. Claire threw in a much-chewed, bedraggled cloth monkey that Cassidy had favoured above all his other toys and it landed with a dull thud on his coffin.

Nikki sobbed uncontrollably, her hair plastered flat to her head with the driving rain. Claire remained dry-eyed. Cassidy had been a loyal and devoted friend. He had loved her unconditionally, regardless of her moods, as she had loved him. But now their time together was at an end. She felt strangely peaceful, for she knew that he would never be more than a thought away. She would only have to close her eyes and an image of his face would be there.

'Is there anything you'd like to say?' Christian asked respectfully and for a second Claire screwed her eyes up tight.

'God bless, old friend, sleep tight,' she murmured. Then Mrs M led her and Nikki away, leaving Christian to fill in the grave with the sandy earth.

Mrs M marched them straight back to the comforting warmth of her homely kitchen. A huge fire burned in the grate, and although the room was modest in comparison to Claire's and lacked labour-saving devices, Claire had a strange sense of coming home.

While Mrs M bustled away to put the kettle on, Claire and Nikki huddled miserably in front of the roaring flames. Their clothes began to steam in the heat and Mrs M fetched them some towels. She handed one to Claire, then without asking she began to dry Nikki's wet curls with the other. She took their wet coats from them and hung them over a large wooden clothes-horse. Then she handed them both a cup of tea, served in delicate rose-patterned china cups and saucers. Gradually Nikki's sobs subsided to dull whimpers and by the time Christian came in, muddy and frozen with cold, they were sitting in subdued silence, their hands clasped together.

His entrance pulled Claire's thoughts back to the present, and rising quickly she offered him a smile that didn't quite reach her eyes.

'I'm sorry,' she apologised. 'We ought to be going.'

He shook his head. 'There's no hurry,' he assured her. 'They can stay for dinner, can't they, Gran?'

'Course they can.' Mrs M beamed at them. 'There's enough beef stew cooking to feed a dozen. You're more than welcome.'

Claire wasn't sure, but Nikki looked at her pleadingly. She had taken a shine to Mrs M and Christian, which was quite surprising, as she was usually nervous with strangers.

'All right then, if you're sure,' Claire said, and Mrs M nodded with satisfaction. She had missed Claire, and it was nice to have a child about the place.

She served a delicious meal, but Claire couldn't eat it. The food somehow wouldn't pass the lump that was lodged in her throat. Nikki, however, cleared her plate and then tucked into a portion of home-made apple crumble served with Mrs M's creamy custard. Once or twice Claire's eyes met Christian's across the table and she flushed and looked away in confusion. She was glad when the meal was over, and insisted on helping with the washing up.

'Would you like to come and help me feed the dogs?' Christian asked Nikki, and much to Claire's surprise, her daughter eagerly agreed. Once again she was amazed at how resilient children could be. Once the pots were washed and dried, Mrs M then made yet another pot of tea, and she and Claire carried their cups to the fireside chairs.

Claire kept glancing at the clock, anxious to be gone now, as Mrs M eyed her curiously.

'Sit back and drink your tea, love,' she encouraged. 'There's no rush, is there? Christian will be another good half an hour yet at least.'

Claire sighed. 'I just thought we ought to be on our way before Lianne gets home.' She had assumed that Lianne was at work.

Mrs M's eyebrows rose almost into her hairline. 'There's no chance of that,' she told Claire. 'Christian and Lianne called off their engagement at about the same time as you stopped visiting us.'

Claire almost dropped her cup. 'Why?' she gasped.

Mrs M shrugged. 'Well, to tell you the truth, I think his affections were elsewhere.' She was amused to see that Claire had blushed a deep brick red. Claire was hardly able to believe it. She had always assumed that Christian and Lianne would be married by now.

'I wasn't sorry, to tell you the truth,' Mrs M continued. 'Lianne was a nice enough girl, admittedly, but she and Christian weren't right for each other. Lianne was very career-conscious and Christian . . . Well, you know what he's like; he just lives for this place and the animals.'

Claire nodded slowly. She had never known anyone who loved animals as much as he did, except herself. That was what had drawn them together in the first place. But even without Lianne, things could never have worked between them. She was living a lie, every single day. She had dreamed of wealth and respectability, and once she had attained them, what had they brought her? Heartache. But then it was no more than she deserved, she supposed. Christian thought of her as Claire Louise Hamilton, but underneath she was still Claire McMullen, nothing more than a former common prostitute. Christian deserved better and she knew it. Even so, she had to admit that she still loved him; she always had, though she had spent years trying to deny it to herself. Perhaps if they could have met in another time and another place, things could have been different? But in this life it could never be, and she would only be fooling herself to pretend otherwise.

The full impact of their loss hit Nikki and Claire when they returned home late that afternoon. There was no hairy little mongrel with his tail wagging furiously waiting to greet them and they glanced at each other, both missing him already.

Tea was a subdued meal. Nikki was restless, she couldn't settle to watch television or read, and went to bed early, which was a rare occurrence, pleading a headache. On top of losing Cassidy, she had been greatly saddened at the sight of all the homeless dogs at Seagull's Flight, just as Claire had been so long ago.

Claire tucked her in then set about the unenviable task of collecting Cassidy's toys and dishes from around the house. She loaded them all into his dog basket, which Christian had returned, then with heavy heart, she carried them all out to the garage. It was too upsetting to come across them dotted all about the place. She then drew herself a hot bath and sank back into the water. Totally drained, both mentally and physically, she lay there as the tears that up to now had only come in dribs and drabs gushed from her in a great torrent. She cried for Cassidy, for Nikki, and finally as she thought of Christian and Mrs M at Seagull's Flight, she cried for what might have been.

Nikki had just set off for school and Claire was washing up the breakfast pots when it suddenly struck her that she hadn't asked Christian for her bill. She flushed at her negligence. What must he think of her? He had been so good. She bit her lip. She had promised herself that she wouldn't get in touch with him again, but this was a matter of pride. Still in her dressing-gown, she made up her mind that once she had tidied up and dressed she would phone him. But she didn't have to, for she was just putting the clean things away when the doorbell rang. She frowned, wondering who could be calling so early, and answered the door to find Christian standing on the step. Thinking that he had come to deliver his bill she blushed, and as she led him into the kitchen she began to apologise.

'I'm so sorry I didn't pay you for all you've done, I was going to ring you this morning.'

Christian looked insulted. 'You don't have to pay me,' he told her shortly. 'I didn't do it for payment. I thought a lot of Cassidy too, you know.' Then, more gently, he said, 'I just called in to see if you were both all right, that's all.'

Claire's eyes filled with tears that threatened to fall at any minute. 'We're fine.'

He could see that she was lying. She was pale and her eyes were sore from crying. As he stood there awkwardly, he tried to think of something to say that might ease her heartache a little.

'You know, Claire, you were wonderful to him, he had a good life,' he said eventually.

She smiled tremulously. 'He was wonderful to me too. He was one of the best friends I ever had.'

Understanding exactly what she meant he nodded. 'How's Nikki taking it?' he asked.

'She's missing him too.'

He stroked his chin thoughtfully. 'Actually that's one reason I called round. I know it's very early days and of course you could never replace Cassidy, but have you thought of getting her another dog? Sometimes it helps if you're used to having a dog about the place. And unfortunately we have more than enough to choose from at Seagull's Flight.'

Claire considered his suggestion and had to admit that it made sense. 'I'll ask her when she gets in from school,' she promised.

He turned and made for the door, not wishing to outstay his welcome. 'Right, I'd best get on then. I'm just off to do my house calls.'

Claire followed him into the hallway and broached the subject of the bill for one last time. 'I wish you'd let me pay you for all you've done,' she told him.

He shook his head adamantly. Claire sighed; he was as stubborn as she was, which was another thing they had in common.

'Well, thanks again then,' she said gratefully. 'I don't know how we would have coped without you.'

'Think nothing of it.' With a final wave he sprinted down the steps towards his van. 'Let me know if Nikki decides she'd like another dog.'

Claire watched him leave.

As his van trundled away down the drive he passed Mrs Pope, and the minute she entered the house she asked, 'Who was that I just passed in an old van? Nice bit of stuff, he was.'

Claire began to relate the events of the last few days and by the time she had finished, Mrs Pope was sniffling loudly into a large white handkerchief. 'Oh, God bless him,' she wept. 'He were a lovely little dog.'

Claire couldn't have agreed more, and sadly made her way upstairs to change.

The estate agent rang early that afternoon to tell her that he had a couple who wished to view the property. She made an appointment for the following afternoon, and then Mrs Pope set to and helped her clean the house from top to bottom. Claire was glad of the diversion, and by the time Nikki arrived home from school, was feeling a little better. Mrs Pope baked them a homemade steak and kidney pie and they all sat down together at teatime to eat it. Nikki was still very quiet, but much to Claire's relief her appetite was as hearty as ever.

During the meal, Claire cautiously asked her how she would feel about having another dog. The girl shook her head sadly. 'I don't think it would be fair to have another one,' she said. 'There could never be another Cassidy, could there?'

'Just as you like,' Claire said softly and for now the subject was dropped.

The following afternoon the people who were to view the house turned into the drive. Claire was watching for them from the window. A smart estate car pulled up. A tall dark-haired man climbed out of the driver's seat and hurried round to the other side of the car, to open the door for his wife. Claire noticed with a little shock that she was heavily pregnant. Then he opened the back door and three young children of various ages spilled out onto the drive. Claire grinned, they were all pointing down the garden towards the sand dunes and the sea, and their parents were obviously having a job to persuade them to enter the house. They hopped from foot to foot with excitement and when Claire opened the door, she was met with three cheeky grins. The man quickly climbed the steps and shook her hand firmly.

'Mrs Nightingale, I'm John Birch and this is my wife Olwen and my children.'

Claire gave them a welcoming smile. She knew that they had travelled from Manchester and must be longing for a drink.

'Would you like a drink before I show you around?' she offered thoughtfully.

Mrs Birch flashed her a grateful smile. 'That would be lovely,' she said as Claire led them into the kitchen. As she made the tea and supplied the children with glasses of lemonade and biscuits, Mrs Birch stared about the kitchen admiringly. 'What a very nice room,' she commented. Claire smiled at her. She liked this family. She showed them around the whole of the ground floor and in every room, Mrs Birch beamed with delight, particularly at the spectacular sea view from the lounge window.

'Oh, it's gorgeous,' she sighed, and Claire noticed her husband smile at her fondly. They were obviously a very close family and Claire liked the idea of them living here. Over the last few years Nightingale Lodge had witnessed so much sorrow and so many tears that it was comforting to think that soon it might ring with laughter again.

Just before they left the study, she took a brass key from the desk drawer. They all oohed and aahed over the bedrooms and the children began to argue over who would have which one, which made the adults smile. Once they had seen every other upstairs room, Claire stopped outside the nursery and, steeling herself, she slowly unlocked the door. Mrs Birch entered and gasped at the sight of the cheerfully decorated room.

'Oh, Mrs Nightingale,' she breathed. 'This is *absolutely* beautiful.' Her hands stroked her swollen abdomen and in her mind's eye she pictured her new baby in here, just as once, Claire had pictured hers. She turned to her husband. 'Oh darling, this is just perfect,' she said, and as if he had forgotten that Claire was there, he hugged her lovingly.

'Is this your baby's room?' Mrs Birch enquired innocently.

Claire nodded, but said no more. It was painful enough just being in there, without going into explanations.

By the time the Birch family had all piled back into the car after Claire had shown them around the gardens, she felt fairly certain that the house was sold, and less than an hour later the estate agent phoned her to confirm it. Claire was glad. She felt that the Birch family would be happy here, and now she and Nikki could move on.

Nikki was excited at the thought of moving to a new home. She and Claire began to pick up property details from various estate agents and go through them together. Claire wasn't quite sure exactly what she was looking for, but fortunately it was going to be three months before the Birches could move from Manchester, so she had time to be choosy.

The following weekend, after endless nagging from Nikki, Claire agreed to take her to visit Seagull's Flight. Nikki was missing Cassidy dreadfully and had decided that she might like to choose another dog, after all. Claire was quite pleased at an excuse to visit. She felt guilty for all that Christian had done for them, and even if he wouldn't let her pay him, then he couldn't stop her putting a sizeable donation in the charity box. She also wanted a chance to thank Mrs M for her kindness.

When they set off, she was fairly certain that they would return with a new pet. Although she couldn't imagine ever loving another dog as she had loved Cassidy, if it made Nikki happy then she didn't mind. By the time they pulled into the yard, Nikki was in fine spirits, and Claire grinned at her. But the grin was wiped from her face when Mrs M opened the door to them. Her right arm was heavily plastered and supported in a sling, and she looked terribly pale.

'Oh, Mrs M! Whatever's happened?'

The old lady smiled sheepishly, 'Oh, it were me own fault. I weren't looking where I were going and I tripped over a bucket in the dog pen.' With her good arm she hugged Nikki and the child returned her hug. They were both obviously delighted to see each other.

'How are you managing?' Claire asked.

Mrs M frowned. 'Oh, it's not me I'm worried about, it's Christian. He's running himself ragged trying to keep this place going on his own, and at the minute I'm about as much use to him as an umbrella in a snow-storm.'

'Don't worry, Nikki and I can help, can't we?' The girl nodded eagerly.

'Well, I ain't in no position to refuse an offer like that, am I?' chuckled the invalid.

Claire took Nikki's hand. 'Right,' she said firmly. 'We'll go and clean out the dog pens first. And you needn't worry, I can remember where everything is, so you just go and sit down and put your feet up.'

Mrs M watched them walking away with a little smile on her face. She was a good girl, was Claire. Mrs M was a great believer that everything happened for a reason, and right now she was thinking that perhaps this accident wouldn't turn out to be such a bad thing, after all! Sighing happily to herself, she scuttled back into the warmth of the kitchen.

As Nikki and Claire entered the long dog enclosure, Claire said to the girl, 'Don't worry, it's not as bad as it looks. A bit of elbow grease and we'll have this lot shipshape and Bristol fashion in no time. What's more, it'll give us a chance to have a good look at every dog – and who knows, there might be one that you take a fancy to.'

Nikki's face brightened. The two of them set to with a will, but it took a couple of hours to clean out every pen, and when they were finished they sank down side-by-side on a bale of hay, tired but contented.

'Well?' asked Claire. 'Have you found one you like?'

Nikki looked down the row of pens. 'I like them all,' she admitted. 'But perhaps it is still a bit soon after Cassidy. I think I'll wait a while longer.'

Claire nodded, understanding exactly how she felt. As they left the enclosure they saw Christian's van pulling into the yard. His face registered surprise, then pleasure, as Nikki scampered ahead to greet him.

'We've been cleaning out the pens for Mrs M,' she told him excitedly. It amazed Claire how Nikki had taken to him. Usually she was extremely wary of men, yet with Christian she was completely at ease.

After a while, Claire called Nikki to her side. 'We ought to be going now,' she said.

'Couldn't you stay for a bite to eat?' Disappointment clouded Christian's features but Claire shook her head, her face solemn. She hated to leave poor Mrs M with her broken arm, but something told her it wasn't a good idea to stay any longer.

'Well, thanks for helping out then.'

'It's quite all right.' She loaded Nikki into the car and started the engine, all fingers and thumbs as he stood there watching them.

By the time she and Nikki arrived home, darkness was closing in. Nikki sat down in the kitchen and yawned. 'I like it at Seagull's Flight,' she

333

declared. 'And I like Christian and Mrs M too. Can we go back and help again tomorrow?'

Claire glanced at her. 'We'll see.'

Contentedly, the girl began to peel some potatoes while Claire took the sausages out of the fridge and laid the table for their supper.

Chapter Thirty-Seven

The following morning, after breakfast and much nagging from Nikki, they again set off for Seagull's Flight. Claire felt apprehensive about visiting again so soon, and yet at the same time she was reluctant to let Mrs M down.

Just as she had anticipated, they found Christian in his surgery. Every Sunday morning without fail he ran this free surgery for people who could not afford vets' bills. There were budgies, dogs, cats, mice, rabbits and more animals than Nikki had ever seen all together in one room before. With Claire's help, Christian tended to every single one, while Nikki scampered away to keep Mrs M company in the kitchen.

There was a tin on the table by the door for people who could afford to make a small donation if they wished, and when the last patient had been tended to, and Claire was helping Christian to tidy up, he emptied the tin and exclaimed as a wad of banknotes fell out amongst the small change.

'Good God!' he cried, delighted. 'Look at *this*! There's enough money here to feed all the dogs for weeks.'

Claire tried to look as surprised as he did, but then as a thought occurred to him, he stared at her suspiciously. 'You didn't put this in here, did you?'

Crossing her fingers behind her back she shook her head before slipping past him into the yard and hurrying to take refuge in the dog enclosure.

'We could come and help out at night after school,' Nikki suggested to Claire on the way home later that day. 'Just till Mrs M is better – couldn't we?'

Claire sighed resignedly. There was really no way she could refuse without looking incredibly mean. 'I suppose so,' she agreed. 'But only till Mrs M is better.'

For the next week, Claire picked Nikki up from school and they went straight to Seagull's Flight. Claire had never seen her daughter so happy. Mrs M doted on the girl, as did Christian. Nikki would change into jeans and Wellington boots and take the dogs along the beach every evening with Christian while Claire did jobs about the house for Mrs M.

Sometimes, when there was a quiet moment, Claire would make her way to the grave where Cassidy rested in the shelter of the sand dunes. The wind had already drifted a deep layer of sand across it, and only a simple wooden cross bearing his name marked the spot now. She always felt peaceful there and smiled sadly at the memories of their time together. It was Cassidy who had inadvertently brought her to Seagull's Flight, and it seemed fitting somehow that now it should be his final resting-place.

The sale of her house was going ahead with no hitches, and two weeks after their visit, the Birches rang Claire to inform her that they now had a new baby son. The news was bittersweet. A baby boy would use William's nursery, after all. She negotiated a deal with them and agreed to leave practically all of the furniture too, which was a relief. The less she took from that house, the better. She intended to give Nikki a completely new start. But there were still all of their clothes and personal things to pack and as yet she hadn't even started. Still, she consoled herself, there was plenty of time.

At the moment, she and Nikki were still spending every spare moment at Seagull's Flight. Her daughter had never looked so well; her eyes shone and her skin glowed from all the time spent in the fresh air, and she followed Christian about like a shadow. Sometimes he would even take her out on the odd home visit and when they got back she would be full of it.

It was following one such visit one evening when they had just arrived back at Seagull's Flight that the Dog Warden's van pulled into the yard. The driver, a great bear of a man, jumped down from the cab, and Christian hurried to meet him with Nikki close in tow. Despite his enormous size, Ted Elliot, the Dog Warden, had what Mrs M described as 'a heart as big as a bucket', and was an all-too familiar sight to them. He often dropped off strays and had a great respect for both Christian and Mrs M.

'There's just the one tonight,' he told Christian. 'Though to tell you the truth, I don't think you'll need to worry about finding a home for her. Between you and me, I doubt she'll last the night.' He threw open the rear van doors, and Claire and Nikki gasped with horror at the state of the poor bedraggled little dog inside. 'I caught some louts poking her about with sticks in a back street in Blackpool,' he told them angrily. 'I reckon they'd have finished her off if I hadn't come along.'

Christian lifted the barely conscious creature into his arms. 'Leave her with me, Ted,' he said. 'I'll see what I can do.'

'I know you will.' Ted shook his head sadly then, with a final nod to them all, the Warden jumped back into the cab and drove away.

Christian strode purposefully towards his surgery, and after sending Nikki away with Mrs M, Claire ran after him. She had studiously avoided being alone with him for weeks, but tonight she guessed rightly that he might need some help.

Once inside, he laid the poor creature on the examination table and expertly ran his hands across her frail body. The poor little thing was slipping in and out of consciousness and her coat was so matted and filthy it was impossible to even see what colour it was. 'I'm going to have to shave her,' Christian said. 'She's covered in fleas and I can't assess her injuries properly until we've got rid of this matted mess.'

Claire nodded and without being asked, hurried away to get the clippers. Christian gently shaved the filthy coat from the little dog's body, but once it was gone she looked even more pathetic: every rib protruded from her chest and with each breath her chest rose and fell alarmingly.

'It's a little Shiht-zu,' Christian informed her, and Claire gazed at him in amazement.

'Are you sure?'

He nodded. 'She's badly dehydrated, dangerously underweight and she's taken a right beating,' he said sadly. 'I reckon the most humane thing I could do for her is to put her to sleep.'

Tears sprang to Claire's eyes. 'Oh no, Christian, *please* don't,' she implored him. 'There must be something you can do for her.' Her tears touched him deeply and he thought back to the night she had taken Cassidy in.

'Well, I'll need to get some fluid into her, for a start,' he said, and at that moment Nikki rushed in and stood at Claire's side.

'Oh, the poor little thing,' she sobbed, and just then the dog briefly

337

came to and looked at her with liquid brown eyes. Nikki's heart was lost. 'Oh Christian, *please* make her better,' she begged tearfully, and his mind was made up.

Within half an hour he had the tiny dog hooked up to a drip, she had had two injections, and he had washed her in warm water. She was now resting peacefully on a blanket in the corner of the surgery.

'That's all I can do for tonight,' he told them. 'We'll just have to wait and see if she pulls through.'

Nikki stroked her gently. 'She will,' she said confidently, and Claire and Christian exchanged a smile.

Nikki could talk of nothing else on the way home. 'Do you think she'll be all right, Mum?'

Claire didn't know how to answer her. 'We'll just have to wait and see,' she said, and with that Nikki had to be content.

The next afternoon, when they arrived at Seagull's Flight, Christian informed them that not only had the dog pulled through the night, but she was now conscious too. She was still terribly weak and as yet hadn't managed to eat or drink anything, but Christian still had her on a drip to stop her from dehydrating further. He was now fairly hopeful that she might survive, after all.

Nikki smothered him with kisses. Then she scampered off to see the unfortunate patient. She was so taken with the little dog that from then on, she spent every moment of her free time at Seagull's Flight at its side. It was Nikki who encouraged the little dog to take her first sip of liquid. It was Nikki who tempted her with titbits until she got her to eat and it was Nikki who snatched her up into her arms the minute Christian disconnected her from the drip. She progressed from the surgery to a basket at the side of the fire in Mrs M's kitchen, and to Nikki's delight she slowly started to regain her strength and her hair began to grow back. It was gold and cream, and as she gained weight she began to look quite pretty.

'I think we should call her Gemma,' Nikki declared one evening.

They all laughed.

'Isn't that a bit of a strange name for a dog?' Christian questioned but Nikki's mind was made up, and so Gemma it was.

Almost a week later, Christian pronounced Gemma fit enough to join the other strays in the enclosure and Nikki's lip trembled at the thought.

Gemma was scampering about the kitchen getting under everyone's feet, almost unrecognisable now from the poor little waif that she had been. With her covering of short gold and cream fur, she resembled a fluffy teddy bear.

'Couldn't *we* keep her, Mum?' Nikki pleaded.

Claire grinned. She had seen this coming. 'I'd love to,' she told Nikki. 'But it's up to Christian.'

He threw back his head and laughed, his deep blue eyes twinkling. He too had seen this coming and couldn't have been more pleased.

'I think that's one lucky little dog there,' he chuckled. 'I know she'll have a good home with you two, and she's yours if you want her.'

Nikki cuddled her new pet. They were all pleased at the outcome of this situation and as Claire loaded the child and the little dog into the car she smiled properly for the first time in weeks.

On their way home, they called into a pet shop and Claire spent a small fortune on everything that Gemma could possibly need. She planned to give all of Cassidy's things to Christian, to be used by the other dogs. For Gemma, they would get everything new. She bought her a basket, a collar and lead, toys, dog dishes, food, biscuits and anything that took Nikki's fancy. By the time they arrived home, the car was loaded almost to the roof. Once they let Gemma out of the car she scampered about the garden, her tail wagging furiously as she sniffed everything in sight. Nikki giggled and followed in hot pursuit, and Claire's heart warmed at the sight of them. It was wonderful to see Nikki looking so happy again.

Two days later, Claire drove Mrs M to the local hospital and the plaster was removed from her arm. Claire was relieved. The house move was looming dangerously close, and as yet she had found nowhere for her and Nikki to live. With being so busy at Seagull's Flight she hadn't had much time for househunting, but now that Mrs M was recovered she threw herself into studying various house details. She would be glad to leave now. She loved Christian with every ounce of her being – she always had – but things were no different now to when she had married Greg. Christian stood for everything that was good. He was kind and gentle and decent. She shuddered to think of how he would react if he ever learned of her sordid past. She was tainted and he deserved better, but it was becoming increasingly difficult for her to be in his company without betraying her feelings, and she knew that it was a good thing that soon she and Nikki would be gone. She had no intention of even staying in this area. That would have been pointless, for if they were within distance of Seagull's Flight, Nikki would have insisted that they visit.

So now she began to look at properties further afield. She intended to make a clean break once and for all with Seagull's Flight and all it stood for. That was the only way it could be, but the thought of it made her heart ache.

At one stage she ever considered moving back to Warwickshire. Sometimes the longing to see her foster parents and Tracey was so strong that she had to stop herself from picking up the phone and ringing them. But she never did. To go back to her past would just be swapping one heartache for another, and anyway she doubted whether any of them would even give her a second thought now. It had all been so very long ago.

Amongst the literature that the estate agents sent her, Claire found the details of a house in Liverpool that interested her. It was a modest house compared to the one that she lived in now, but it appeared to have every-thing that she and Nikki would need. It was detached with three bedrooms and a small garden.

On the next visit to Seagull's Flight, she showed the pictures of it to Mrs M. The old lady's face fell.

'Liverpool!' she gasped in dismay. 'Do you *have* to move so far away?' In actual fact, it wasn't that far. But it was far enough to stop Nikki being able to visit Seagull's Flight easily.

Claire gazed out of the kitchen window to where Christian and Nikki, with Gemma close on their heels, were entering the dog enclosure. 'I think Nikki deserves a completely fresh start,' she said quietly. 'She's had enough heartache in the past few years to last her a lifetime.'

'Well, I won't argue with that,' agreed Mrs M. 'But even so, there are people here that care about you both, and if you drag her off to Liverpool she'll know no one. You could do her more harm than good.'

But Claire wouldn't be swayed from her decision. When she and Nikki finally set off for home, Mrs M watched them go with her heart full of misgivings. She felt that Claire was making a grave mistake, but was power-less to stop her. She dreaded to think how Christian would take their leaving. Mrs M knew that he loved her and had a feeling that Claire loved him too. So why couldn't they both face it and have a happy ending? The old lady sighed wearily. Up until now she had been content to sit back and let nature take its course, but if interfering was the only way to bring them together, then interfere she would. Deep down she felt that if they lost each other again now, after being given this second chance, they would regret it for the rest of their lives. Loving them both as she did, she had no intention of letting that happen if she could prevent it.

It was ten o'clock that evening and Claire had just had a relaxing soak in the bath. She peeped in on Nikki and smiled at the sight of her and Gemma cuddled close together fast asleep. She intended to make herself a cup of cocoa and curl up in front of the fire with a good book, but just as she reached the bottom of the stairs, the doorbell rang and her heart lurched. The house was very secluded and she had no idea who would be visiting this late at night. She approached the door cautiously and called out: 'Who's there?' When Christian's voice answered her she sighed with relief. Quickly drawing back the bolt, she unlocked the door, and without a word he strode past her and into the kitchen. There was no smile, no greeting, nothing. She silently followed him.

He rounded on her and to her astonishment she saw that he was angry. He began to pace agitatedly up and down the length of the room.

'What's this I'm hearing then?' he demanded. 'About you and Nikki going to live in Liverpool? It's not true, is it?' When he stopped directly in front of her, Claire slowly nodded.

'Why, Claire? Why must you go so far away?' His eyes were full of pain.

'You wouldn't understand,' she said in a low voice. 'It's best this way.'

He shook his head in vehement denial. 'Best for whom?' he asked. 'It's not best for me and I don't think it will be best for Nikki either, so what are you running away from?'

'From myself,' she whispered brokenly, and now he gaped at her.

'I don't understand.' Suddenly his anger left him and his shoulders sagged. 'Look, Claire, I don't want you to go.'

Claire flinched. 'I have to,' she told him.

'You *don't* have to, Claire – you could stay here and marry me instead. I love you. Do you hear me? I want you to stay and be my wife.'

Her eyes almost started from her head and for a second she could only gape at him open-mouthed. 'You don't know what you're saying,' she murmured.

'Oh yes I do, and I should have said it long ago. I left it too late then and you married Greg but I've no intention of ever losing you again so I'm asking now. *Will you marry me?*'

Scalding tears gushed from her eyes and poured down her cheeks as he gathered her into his strong arms and rocked her gently. 'There,' he soothed. 'Can I take that as a yes?'

Claire pushed him away. 'I can't marry you, Christian,' she said bitterly. 'I can't marry anyone.' She couldn't face the thought of living a lie with him. He was in love with the image she had created, not the real person she was underneath.

'Don't you love me?' he asked hoarsely.

Claire looked away, unwilling to answer. 'I'm not what you think I am,' was all she said. 'If you knew what I *really* was, you wouldn't want to marry me.'

'I would,' he insisted urgently. 'There's nothing you could ever do that would stop me loving you.'

Claire laughed grimly. She wanted him to leave yet the urge was on her to throw herself into his arms and never let him go. But she knew for his sake that she must, and now there was only one option left open to her.

'Wait there a minute,' she told him, and with heavy tread she made her way upstairs to her dressing-table. With shaking fingers she withdrew her diary and the key that would unlock it and then went back down to the kitchen. Christian was standing exactly where she had left him with a look of bewilderment on his face as without a word she handed him the diary. 'I want you to take this away and read it. Once you have, you'll see why I can't marry you. But you won't want me then anyway.'

He shook his head, not understanding any of this. But somehow he knew it would be pointless to stay any longer tonight. At the front door he said, 'Just answer me one question, please. *Do* you love me, Claire?'

She found that she couldn't lie. 'Yes,' she replied. 'With all of my heart.'

He slipped out of the door and into the night. She stood there for a long time shaking from head to foot. Then slowly she dropped to her knees and sobbed.

Throughout the long sleepless night that followed she tortured herself with thoughts of how Christian would despise her as her story unfolded itself to him through the pages of her diary. By morning her eyes were bloodshot and swollen, but her shoulders were straighter. She was relieved when she had seen Nikki off to school. With Gemma curled up at her feet she sat at the kitchen table staring out of the window. There were no tears now; she felt as if there were no tears left to cry and yet she felt strangely at peace with herself. For the first time in her whole life she had shared her dreadful past with someone, and sharing had lifted a great weight from her shoulders. She had now come to some new decisions, and felt all the better for it.

The doorbell ringing pulled her thoughts back to the present, and she rose automatically to answer it, thinking it must be Mrs Pope, having forgotten her key again.

She had barely opened the door when two great arms lifted her into a fierce embrace.

'Oh, Claire.' There was a catch in Christian's voice. 'My God.' He held her at arm's length. 'Why didn't you tell me before about what you'd been through? I could have helped you – supported you – loved you.'

She stared at him incredulously. She had the strange feeling that she was dreaming, and any minute she would wake up and she would be alone.

'How could you think that I wouldn't love you, after reading all that you've had to endure? None of it was your fault, can't you see that?'

She held her breath, hardly daring to believe that this was really happening. 'Do you mean . . . you forgive me?'

'*Forgive you?* There's nothing to forgive! You've been a victim since you were a child, my darling, but you can put it all behind you now. From now on, life will be good, I promise. I can't take away what's happened – nobody can. But now you can start to come to terms with it. I'll help you, and if you'll do me the honour of being my wife, I'll never let anyone hurt you again.'

She was laughing and crying all at the same time. This was a dream come true. Things like this didn't happen to her. But it *was* happening. Christian was here. It was real.

As she stared at him, tears of joy shining in her ravaged eyes, he fumbled in his coat pocket and produced a faded little velvet box. 'This was my gran's,' he told her tenderly. 'My grandad bought it for her when they got engaged, and she wants you to have it. Of course, if you don't like it, I'll get you a new one.'

He sprang back the lid and Claire was confronted with a gold band set with a heart-shaped sapphire. It was nowhere near as glamorous as the sparkling diamond that Greg had bought her, but to Claire it was the most beautiful ring in the world. She gazed at him, all the love she felt for him mirrored in her eyes, as he dropped comically onto one knee.

'Claire McMullen, Hamilton, Nightingale or whatever you want to call yourself, I ask you again from the heart: will you please, *please* marry me?'

Claire drew herself up to her full height. 'There is nothing I would like better than to be your wife,' she told him softly as hope lit his eyes. 'But . . . I can't, Christian. You see, first of all, I have to find myself. For years I've lived a lie; tried to be someone that I'm not. I always felt dirty – that somehow, the things that had happened to me as a child were *my* fault. I've lived with guilt and despair. Hated myself and wished myself dead. It wasn't until I discovered that Greg was abusing Nikki that it occurred to me for the first time that the things that happened might *not* have been my fault after all.' She paused and took a shuddering breath. Hoping he would understand, she went on: 'Nikki will go through all these feelings and I have to be there for her. Please, try to understand. It's not because I don't love you – *I do,* with all my heart – but before I can come to you I have to learn who I really am and come to terms with what happened. Last night, I decided that I have to go back to my roots and see my sister and my foster parents, and lay the ghosts to rest, make my peace with them.'

He rose and looked deep into her eyes. 'If you find who you really are, will you come back to me?'

Tears slid slowly down her pale cheeks as she made the solemn promise. 'Yes . . . I will.'

He walked towards the door, his shoulders stooped. Then, pausing, he looked back at her. 'I'll be waiting, Claire. For ever, if that's what it takes.'

The door closed softly behind him.